Ageless Love

ABOUT THE AUTHORS

JEAN CONRAD is a writer, English teacher, and part owner of a bookstore. She is a descendant of a circuit-riding preacher and a family of pioneers. She grew up in the woods and fields that are portrayed in *Applegate Landing*. In Jean's spare time she cultivates exotic flowers in her prize-winning garden, raises canaries in a rainbow of colors, and plays gospel music on her Betsy Ross piano, an ancient instrument that has followed her throughout her travels.

MARY HARWELL SAYLER has long been interested in Native Americans — even before she realized her great, great, great, great-grandmother was a member of the Cherokee nation. Historical romances have long been favorites, too, and Mary hopes this is one of many she is to write. She also writes children's books and poetry and instructs beginning writers through correspondence study with the Christian Writers Fellowship. It's only natural then, that after developing a series on poetry writing for CWF, Mary wrote two study units on writing the romance novel.

MARYN LANGER is so full of fancy and tall tales that one would never suspect she spends her days teaching math to classrooms of children, nor that she has written textbooks in her chosen field. She confesses, however, that her mind, whether asleep or awake, cannot help creating wonderful characters from the past whose lives reflect her own strong Christian faith and fortitude.

Historical Romance COLLECTION

Ageless Love

VOLUME 3

Applegate Landing
Jean Conrad

Beyond the Smoky Curtain
Mary Harwell Sayler

Moon for a Candle
Maryn Langer

ZondervanPublishingHouse
Grand Rapids, Michigan

A Division of HarperCollinsPublishers

Applegate Landing

Jean Conrad

CHAPTER 1

GRAY WISPS OF OCEAN FOG curled around massive redwood trunks, deepening the quiet gloom of the primeval forest. From her rough seat on a mule-drawn freight wagon, lurching slowly along a rutted path through the trees, Gloriana Windemere peered into the shadows, trying not to imagine savage, dark faces peering back at her. Overhead in the treetops, sunlight filtered through the branches in shimmering shafts, but none reached the wet, green twilight of the forest floor. Giant ferns seemed to float in the mist. Rose-red azaleas, twelve feet high and covered with clusters of spiked blossoms, crowded the trail.

"The West has its own cathedrals," her uncle Ralph Windemere, a medical missionary in Oregon Territory, had written, and Gloriana had imagined giant stone walls rising in the wilderness. Now she understood and rejoiced anew that she had answered his call for help at the Klamath Lake Mission; yet she could not suppress a small shiver of apprehension. The way had not been easy. In 1851 the country had not forgotten the massacre of the Whitmans at their

5

Waiilatpu mission four years earlier. Moreover, the Mission Board had objected strenuously to sending an unmarried young lady—a "spinster," they had called her, although Gloriana was barely twenty-three—into the frontier. But she had persevered through appeal after appeal to the Foreign Missions Commissioners and through protest after protest from family and friends.

"If you hear the call of God, you must answer on the outside as well as the inside," she had told them all, and finally they had listened—perhaps as much because they could find no one else qualified to assist Dr. Windemere and willing to face the hostile native tribes as because they believed God had called Gloriana to be a missionary nurse.

Now, after months spent sailing around the Horn to San Francisco; days, plowing up the coast line on a small freighter to Crescent City in northern California, she was in the last stage of the journey, and her heart sang while her knees shook.

"These trees were here when Jesus was born in Bethlehem." She remembered with awe what her uncle had written about the great age of the redwoods. The fact made them seem closer to her and, somehow, less alien.

The grove they were passing through dwarfed the freight train. Mammoth trunks tapered to distant, sky-fringed tops. Where trees had been felled for the Crescent City-Jacksonville Trail, massive stumps, uprooted and dragged from the path, towered above the wagons. The tangle of moss-hung, black roots looked almost, but not quite, like the writhing tentacles of some prehistoric beast in the lingering mist.

"What a magnificent forest!" Gloriana voiced her impression, drawing a sardonic glance from the hulking driver.

"Good place for an ambush of hostiles," was his discouraging answer, and Gloriana thought she detect-

6

ed a malicious gleam in the corner of the driver's eye as she darted a startled look into the dark covert made by a particularly menacing fallen giant.

She had not liked Graham Norton from the first moment she had seen him, leaning against the rough redwood counter in the Siskiyou Freight Company office at Crescent City. That the antipathy had been both instantaneous and mutual was small consolation. He had at first refused to take her on his freight run to the gold fields at Jacksonville.

"No room," he had growled, looking Gloriana over from the top of her neatly bonneted head to her tightly buttoned boots—as though she, rather than the supplies sitting on the dock where the sailors had unloaded them would personally crowd him. He had relented only after much urging from the company agent and her own avowed purpose to hire other wagons and drivers.

But the battle lines had been drawn early on, and the hostilities had escalated throughout the afternoon as Gloriana supervised the loading of a small pump organ sent to the mission by her home church in Philadelphia and innumerable boxes and trunks—all and sundry of which the recalcitrant freighter had declared unsuitable for travel or unnecessary to existence on the frontier.

While seething with indignation, Gloriana had been unable to subdue a slight twinge of disappointment. Strange! She had never allowed herself much interest in men, thinking it would be futile folly. Handsome rather than beautiful, she was—in spite of her radiant name—the plain Jane of the family. Masses of dark hair, although silky and curling, were no match for her sister Juliana's corn-colored crown; and giant hazel eyes, although heavily fringed with black lashes, could not compete with her sister Marianna's china-blue orbs. If her complexion was creamy and her figure, tall and well-formed, they went unnoticed, flanked by one sister's fairylike grace and the other's charming plumpness.

She had imagined, if only unconsciously, that in the West she might receive her share of admiration. In fact, her father, who cherished the delusion she was a general favorite, secretly admired by but forbidding to the young men of the church he pastored, had given his hopes that she would "find a man more to your taste" as a major reason for permitting the journey into Oregon Territory.

If Graham Norton were any indication, they had both been mistaken. He had taken one look at her fresh face, bare of cosmetics, and the trim, erect figure clad in the dove-colored garments Gloriana considered suitable for a traveling missionary and obviously pronounced her unfit. Well, she would show him—not that Graham Norton was at all the kind of man Gloriana Windemere would care to impress. Much larger than allowable for any degree of elegance, he reminded her of the surly grizzlies— called *ursus horribilis* or "devils in bears' clothing" by the settlers. Or a tawny cougar, as fierce and unscrupulous an animal as any in the Western woods, her Uncle Ralph said.

Nearly six feet, four inches in his stocking feet, Graham Norton conveyed a sense of the savage and untamed, less by his appearance and speech than by an aura of tense, leashed energy that surrounded him. His dress blended the fantastic and picturesque with the serviceable. A buckskin coat decorated with beading, dyed porcupine quills, and fringe opened over corduroy pants and a soft doeskin shirt. Instead of a tie, he wore a loosely knotted bandanna in a red paisley print. A flat-brimmed felt hat tilted back to reveal a mop of carelessly brushed, carrot-colored curls—much too long and garish for Gloriana's suddenly fastidious taste. Completing the barbaric picture, a black-handled gun with a menacingly long

8

barrel protruded from a smooth leather holster beneath his coat, and a long-nosed rifle leaned against the wagon seat, suggestively close and ready.

"I'm sure the natives have learned their lesson," Gloriana commented with a careful air of unconcern. "The *Philadelphia Enquirer* carried a full account of the trial and hanging of the Indians who murdered the Whitmans." Her tone implied that he had probably never heard of the highly touted Eastern paper, or, if he had, was undoubtedly incapable of reading it.

His look was one of mingled impatience and contempt, and Gloriana noticed inconsequentially that his dark blue eyes had little golden flecks that made them seem to spark dangerously. His bronzed face was clean shaven and handsome, although the square cut of his jaw was in keeping with the obstinacy she had already experienced from the man.

"Yes, ma'am," was all he said, but he managed to infuse the two words with a host of negative comments on her ignorance of the West, her inability to understand the dangers of the situation, her unfitness for the life.

"Well, don't you agree that it's a mark of civilization's advance when a massacre is settled, not with more killings but by legal means?" Gloriana prodded him unwisely.

"Chief Telokite and his henchmen were hanged after the trial," Graham returned. "That's more killing. Besides, Cayuse law allows for the killing of bad medicine men. They considered Dr. Whitman bad. He let too many of their people die."

Gloriana lapsed into an offended silence, made all the more unbearable by the feeling that behind his sardonic mask this uncouth Westerner was laughing at her. The very idea of calling Dr. Whitman, one of the greatest medical missionaries of the age, a medicine man! And a bad one to boot! She refused to stoop to reply to such a ridiculous charge.

She wondered what Graham Norton would say if he knew she had come West to be her uncle's nurse. Somehow she doubted he would see her as an angel of mercy sacrificing a comfortable life in the East to minister to the Klamath Indians. He would probably imply that she was a goody-two-shoes, bent on bringing Saturday night baths and box socials to the West, or worse, an old maid come husband-hunting. Gloriana's cheeks burned at her own imaginings, and as though he could read her mind, Graham Norton chuckled, a deep, rich chuckle, totally out of keeping with the nature of the man.

The freight train in which they were traveling was a large one—twenty wagons in all, each drawn by teams of long-eared mules. Fifteen of the wagons were loaded with the supplies for Jacksonville, the new gold-boom town in the Rogue River Valley. The rest carried her trunks and the gifts from her father's church for the Klamath Lake Mission.

Glancing over her shoulder, Gloriana tried to catch sight of the wagon that carried the organ, but too many trees and giant ferns obscured the winding trail. She tried not to imagine that the frequent thumps and crashes she heard were branches, knocking against the precious instrument, or her trunks, bouncing from the wagon bed to be forgotten in the dense undergrowth.

Gloriana was not the only passenger on the train. There were several prospectors, conspicuous for the pickaxes and shovels that figured prominently in their gear and the almost universal feature of bushy, uncut beards. Nor was she the only female. Three hard-featured women in bright-colored dresses, cut much too low for a wilderness trek, were traveling to the gold camps. No one had introduced them to Gloriana, but the men of the train, including Graham Norton, had clustered around them before the wagons had left Crescent City that morning, each driver apparently

10

vying for the pleasure of their company. Somewhere behind Gloriana and Norton, the brittle laughter of one of the women mingled with the loud guffaws of a freighter, and Gloriana wondered why she had ended up traveling with the unpleasant train boss. Probably he had lost a bet, or perhaps it was his practice to take the most odious chores upon himself.

"What do you call these woods?" Gloriana turned to her companion with the determination to behave with civility and perhaps also with the half-formed hope that she could make him as uncomfortable as she.

Surprisingly, Norton responded with a running travelogue that required only her occasional word as the strong mule teams pulled their heavy loads along mile after mile of forest trail. True, he seemed to dwell unnecessarily long on accounts of massacres and scalpings. Once when they rumbled past a burned-out cabin, he gave her a detailed account of the warring customs of the Shasta tribe, including their throwing their victims into the burning throat of a volcano. And Gloriana listened in fascinated horror, although she remembered well her Uncle Ralph's assurance that the magnificent volcanos that towered over the region were extinct.

Gradually, as the morning wore on, the chilly mists dissolved, and a muggy warmth settled heavily around them. To Gloriana's shocked dismay, Norton removed his coat and, with a grin that acknowledged and relished her discomfort, drove on in his shirt sleeves. Back East a gentleman would not have appeared before a lady in his shirt sleeves. Many times Gloriana had seen her own father slip hastily into a coat when she or one of her sisters entered a room. But she was not back East now and Graham Norton was certainly not a gentleman. Gloriana sighed, sending a quick prayer toward heaven for the civilizing as well as the conversion of the West.

Heat in the rain forest was almost tangible. It penetrated the shade, rising in steamy waves from marshy puddles at the side of the trail and pricking the lungs on needle-spiced breaths. Perspiration beaded the skin and stayed there, wet and sticky, refusing to evaporate in the humid air.

Although she debated how ladylike it would be to ride uncovered, Gloriana at last removed her poke bonnet and set it neatly in her lap. She had never been a prude, but she could not bring herself to unfasten her cuffs and collar; the very freedom of her surroundings seemed to have afflicted her with inhibitions she had never dreamed of before. Or perhaps it was her companion. Surprised to see an appreciative look at the glossy braids wound in a crown around her head, she hid the mounting color in her cheeks by dabbing at the perspiration on her forehead with a lace-edged handkerchief.

It was a relief to stop for the noon break. The redwoods were gradually giving way to firs and pines as the wagons climbed steadily away from the coast, and with the smaller trees more of the sun's hot rays found their way to the forest floor. Pebbles, instead of sand, lined the white-water creek where the mules splashed and drank, thankful, it seemed, to be out of harness and less eager for their feedbags than for the soothing touch of the water.

The creek was cold in spite of the day's heat, and Gloriana wondered how quickly it must have come from some snow-capped peak not to share the torpor and sluggishness that humans and animals alike felt. She ate as much as she could swallow of what the camp cook offered her. A short, stocky teamster, with midcalf boots and a floppy hat that nearly covered his eyebrows—he had piled her plate with enough stew and biscuits to feed a family. She had looked from his cheerful face to his grimy hands and accepted the whole along with his admonition to "eat up." But her quick blessing included a reminder of the Lord's promise: "If ye eat any deadly thing, it shall not hurt you."

Wandering away from the other travelers, Gloriana found a quiet place, just out of sight of the camp. She leaned back against a tree trunk at the edge of the stream, luxuriating in the feel of the deliciously cool air on her face and neck. She had closed her eyes and was drinking in the musical sounds of the water, thrumming along its pebble bed, when a rough hand closed over her shoulder and jerked her to her feet. Then an arm, corded with muscles, fastened around her waist, and she looked up into the gleaming blue eyes of wagon boss Graham Norton.

He was stripped to the waist and wet, as though he had been washing in the stream. For a moment Gloriana felt a shiver, either of fear or of excitement, travel down her spine before a surge of fury reminded her of her dignity and her rights.

"How—" she started, but had barely gotten the first word out when he crushed her against him and kissed her—a quick, hard pressure of his lips.

"How dare you!" she choked it out this time.

"Shut up and look over my shoulder." His muttered response startled her nearly as much as his actions.

Standing just within the shadow of the forest, barely ten yards away on the other side of the shallow stream, was a band of Indian braves. Whether there were a dozen or fifty Gloriana was too frightened to tell. But she could clearly see the bands of war paint slanting down their cheeks. The feather-decked spears in their hands looked no less menacing because they pointed skyward instead of in her direction.

"Turn around slowly and walk back toward camp. Don't look back. I'll be right behind you." Norton released her with a little shove that sent her stumbling backward. She imagined she heard muffled laughter

13

from the braves as she retreated in a less-than-dignified manner. She knew that she felt their eyes and Graham Norton's burrowing into her back, noting the red flush creeping up the back of her neck, and enjoying her discomfiture.

The teamsters and other passengers looked at them curiously as Gloriana and Graham Norton appeared. Gloriana thought she caught the exchange of a knowing look between two of the women, but the incident was quickly forgotten as Norton explained the presence of the Indians—"renegades," he said, which seemed to carry some special significance for the men. The order to harness the mules was scarcely necessary; the drivers had already begun pulling the reluctant animals toward the wagons.

The party was large and well-armed. Most had fought in more than one Indian war, but the experiences had taught them to be cautious rather than overconfident. They broke camp quickly, leaving the remains of a generous meal to tempt the war party. No one knew how many more braves might be hiding along the trail, waiting for them or following invisibly through the forest. The men drove with their reins in their left hands and their rifles cradled across their knees, but the intelligent mules had caught a sense of urgency tinged with fear from their drivers and found their own way along the trail, staying as close to the wagon before them as the great, lumbering loads of freight would allow.

Graham Norton's wagon had taken the lead. No one had thought to direct Gloriana to another seat, so she had scrambled up beside him and tried to supplement the keen looks he shot into the forest with an intense scrutiny of her own. She thought about offering to drive the mules, for she had often driven a team of horses, once taking an ambulance wagon from the scene of a factory fire to the hospital. But she doubted her ability to drive four-in-hand, and the

14

mules seemed less obliging than the more-familiar horses.

The trail broke unexpectedly into a mountain meadow, and the momentary relief at escaping the confines of the forest with its myriad hiding places gave way to panic at being exposed to invisible eyes, watching from a thousand trees at the forest edge or on the hillsides overlooking the clearing. Once Gloriana thought she saw a dark head dart back around a tree trunk; she grasped Norton's arm and nodded in the direction of a massive escarpment, not knowing whether she should continue the fiction of being oblivious to the savages' presence. He said nothing but quickened the pace of the team.

Late in the afternoon a teamster misjudged a sharp turn and a load of mission supplies, although fortunately not the organ, tumbled down the hillside. Gloriana heard the sharp scream of the woman passenger and was out of the wagon before Norton could stop his mules and set the hand brake.

The woman had been thrown clear, but she was stunned, and her arm had bent under her as she fell. The driver was pinned under the wagon and from the angle of his pelvis, wedged under the heavy wheel rim, Gloriana thought broken bones would be the least of his trouble.

"You there, help me move this woman." Gloriana took charge as she would have at home in the Philadelphia hospital, calling on the amiable cook who rushed forward to help. "Don't right that wagon until you have pulled the driver out," she cautioned the teamsters. "We'll have to make camp now," she informed Graham Norton as he hurried up with his rifle still in the crook of his arm.

He looked at her intensely a moment, then nodded. "There's a place not far ahead. We'll get this wagon right side up and put them in it. We'll come back for your boxes."

15

"I'll have to find some of the medical supplies," she told him.

He sent a man with her to find a box marked with red crosses, containing, she hoped, the bandages, splints, and antiseptics she would need.

The box had rolled nearly to the foot of the brush-covered hill. As Gloriana bent over it, she spotted the soft gray-brown toe of a moccasin protruding slightly from a covert of grasses and manzanita. She glanced quickly at her companion to see if he had noticed, but the teamster was busy hoisting the heavy box. Breathing a quick prayer for help, Gloriana grabbed hold of another, smaller package that looked like the medical bag her father had sent his brother and scrambled up the hill without a backward glance.

CHAPTER 2

PRACTICING MEDICINE under the open sky by star and firelight would have seemed impossible to Gloriana if she had had time to think about it. Two dozen men lounged nearby as she prepared her instruments. Ordinarily their obvious expressions of distrust would have angered her, but the situation was too bizarre for ordinary reactions.

The woman's injury would be easiest to deal with. The fall had broken her arm, but the fracture was clean, with no bone perforating the skin. The teamster's injuries, as she had feared, were more serious. A rib had torn its way through the skin, the pelvic bone was bruised but thankfully not shattered, and there were signs of some internal bleeding.

Lord, I'm not a doctor; I'm just a nurse, Gloriana sent her protests heavenward, knowing full well that however inadequate she might be, she was all the help these people had.

She worked slowly, feeling her way. One of the men who had once served as a hospital orderly came forward to help, and she directed him to hold the injured driver as she manipulated and taped the broken rib, then sewed up the gash in his side and applied a pressure bandage to stop the bleeding.

The woman provided more resistance since she was conscious and feeling the pain. "Don't hurt me," she whimpered. Then more belligerently, she demanded Gloriana leave the break for the doctor in Jacksonville to set. "I can't chance it not being done correct-like," she explained. Gloriana realized she did not mean to offend but was attempting to reason with her. "I ain't got no one else to take care of me and I havta play the piany at the Golden Horse Saloon."

She was just past youth. A fine etching of crow's feet radiated from eyes that burned in pale skin. The thin arms and hollow chest suggested a consumptive tendency and an intolerance to the alcohol such women usually depended upon. Gloriana had seen it often in the street women of Philadelphia, and she supposed their end was likely to be the same whether they were in the city or on the frontier.

"Perhaps you could sing for a while," she began talking soothingly while her fingers probed the swollen arm.

The woman—Rita was her name, she said, "just plain Rita with no fancy handle after it"—seemed to consider the suggestion but rejected it for one of her own. "I maybe could deal blackjack. I'm good at that and the gents always like to see a purty gal at the table."

The former orderly, who had worked quietly during most of the evening, spoke up in a voice that was surprisingly gentle. He assured Rita that he would be happy to play at her table, and, if her boss at the Golden Horse didn't like it, he would buy her her own saloon with the gold he planned to find. Gloriana glanced at her helper with a new respect and decided a woman like Rita might be better off on the frontier after all.

The bone was easy enough to set. Rita's frail arm provided little resistance as they pulled the edges into place. But the operation took all the strength Gloriana had left, and she was trembling with fatigue when she bound some of the mission's splints tightly around the broken arm and asked the orderly/miner to give Rita some of the herb tea Gloriana used to fight fever.

By midnight most of the company had fallen asleep, but the campfire burned brightly, casting eerie flame-shaped shadows over the wagons and tents. Gloriana sank down on a wooden box that someone had placed close to the fire. She noticed for the first time that the wagons had been turned in a circle, warding off but not quite excluding the darkness outside. They were in a cleared area, not a meadow, for manzanita and scrub juniper bunched thickly around the wagons. A few ragged widow-makers, as they called burned timber in the logging camps, made darker gashes against the gray night sky.

Night sounds were magnified in the darkness. Somewhere close by, another creek, or perhaps the same one they had followed for much of the afternoon, rilled its way through the wilderness. Crickets seemed to have moved into the camp, and their creaky fiddling sounded from the rocks that bounded the fire. And around the camp the bushes and dead leaves rustled with nameless scurryings.

"Would you like some coffee?" Graham Norton asked the question a second time before Gloriana could stir herself to answer. She accepted the hot tin cup he offered, conscious of his curious gaze on her face, and wondered rather remotely if her hair had come undone or her rolled-up sleeves showed too much of her round, capable arms.

"I want to apologize," he started after a moment. "I did not know you were a doctor."

Gloriana looked at him, bewildered for a moment, then remembered his remarks earlier in the day about bad medicine men. "I'm not," she told him with a tired smile and sipped the scalding coffee. The tin cup burned her fingers, and she held it carefully around the rim.

"You can't tell me you learned how to do what you did this evening in your fancy ladies' seminary."

"I'm a nurse," she told him finally, recalling her determination earlier in the day not to expose herself to this man's ridicule. Now it didn't seem to matter. "I've never had to do so much alone before, but I think they'll be all right." After a moment she added with a little laugh, "And I've never been to a fancy ladies' seminary."

He grinned rather sheepishly, and the expression lightened his face, dropping years from the hard, if handsome, features. Since the day before Gloriana had watched mask after mask cover that face—unreachable obstinacy when he was refusing her request for transportation, sardonic humor as he needled her on the ride through the redwoods, grim determination when they fled from the renegade Indians. Now she imagined she was seeing the real Graham Norton behind the facades of the invincible Westerner, and she could not help admitting his was a good face—strong but not quite invulnerable; serious, without being humorless.

"We lost most of your supplies," he told her, seemingly not a little embarrassed by the fact. "We found the places where they had been dragged into the forest, but the boxes had been broken open and were empty. It would have taken fifty braves at least to carry that much stuff away."

Gloriana told him then about the moccasined foot she had spotted in the brush.

"They must have been shadowing the trail, waiting for a chance. Lucky for us it came before they attacked. Too bad about those supplies, though." He came back to the sore spot with a persistence that told

20

Gloriana more than any words could how much
responsibility and accomplishment meant to this man.
He had not wanted to take her load on the freight train
he was bossing, but having accepted the extra duty,
he hated to admit failure. Besides, he was probably in
the best position right then to judge the true worth of
Eastern-made goods in the wilderness, and he realized
better than Gloriana how difficult they would be to
replace.

"Most of those things were intended for the Indians
anyway," she told him with a little shrug. "They just
got there in a different way than we planned."

Norton showed her the lean-to that had been built
for her comfort just outside the circle of firelight. She
hoped she would have a chance to use it, but the
teamster was in danger and would require nursing
through the night. This was the work Gloriana did
best, and she settled to it, thankful to be back on
familiar ground after the unaccustomed demands on
her skills earlier in the evening.

Gloriana liked best to keep watch in the night.
Whether there were stars overhead or a soft lamp at
her elbow, she felt most in charge in the dim light.
Usually she would pray softly through the hours
between midnight and dawn, stopping only to change
the cold compresses with which she sought to temper
a fever or to administer a dose of medicine at the
prescribed hour. Most often she had watched with
children—and looking thoughtfully at the injured
man's face for the first time, she was struck by how
near a child he was.

The valiant attempt at a manly beard on his chin
showed more fuzz than bush. The dark lashes curling
against his cheeks looked absurdly boyish, and several times during the long hours of watching and
praying, Gloriana heard a whispered appeal for
"Ma."

The crisis passed just before dawn. Noting the even

rhythm of her patient's breathing and the reassuring dampness of his skin, Gloriana thanked God. Her other patient, though not in danger, seemed to be suffering more, but a careful sponging with water from the cold stream and more of the special herb tea eased her discomfort.

Her patient's needs cared for, Gloriana allowed herself the luxury of a stretch and went looking for the traveling bag she had packed for the trip. She found it just inside the lean-to of evergreen boughs on her unused bedroll. Taking a fresh blouse and her toilet things, she headed for the stream.

With the experience of the previous noon still fresh in her mind, she chose a little backwater, well screened from the opposite bank as well as from the camp, and removed only part of her clothing. She was dismayed at the grime that had accumulated in just one day on the dusty woodland trail and hoped her supply of soap had not been among the items pilfered the day before. The dirt responded to her ministrations, but her hair proved recalcitrant. The humid mountain air had kinked the masses into showers of curls that refused the discipline of braids. Finally she settled for tying it back from her face with a ribbon, and with a clean blouse and sponged skirt, she felt refreshed.

She had hardly finished when she was startled by the massive frame of Graham Norton, stepping through the bushes. Her first thought—that he had been spying on her—was not altogether dismissed by the look of surprise on his face.

The circumstances reminded her uncomfortably of the incident of the day before, and after answering his questions about the injured members of his company, she determined to make her dissatisfaction with his methods, if not, she hoped, his motives, clear.

"I want to thank you for . . . coming to my rescue yesterday," Gloriana began with dignity but could not bring herself to look directly into those piercing, gold-flecked eyes. I had no chance to mention it before." She thought of the night before, when she *could* have mentioned it and started again. "That is, it didn't occur to me before. I mean, I know I should not have wandered away from the group like that, and I appreciate your sparing me from any unpleasant consequences of my actions. However, I must say that does not excuse such behavior. I want you to know that I do not condone liberties . . . ."

A grin had been growing on Norton's face throughout the latter part of this speech—a grin so mocking and mischievous that it would have fully unnerved Gloriana if she had happened to glance up and see it. Now Norton cut her short with an explosive laugh.

"You don't have to thank me any more, lady," he managed between chuckles. "It wasn't half bad. You can take liberties with my person any time you feel like it. Besides, I figured if those braves thought you already belonged to someone, they wouldn't be so ready to start a fight over you. But as it turned out, it wasn't you, after all, but our supplies they wanted."

Speechless with rage, Gloriana glared up into Graham Norton's mocking face, and before she knew what she was doing, her hand had come up in a resounding slap across his cheek. The blow sobered him instantly, and she shrank from the menace in his eyes.

"You had no call to do that, Glory," he told her quietly.

"Don't you dare call me Glory!" she burst out, and then, on the verge of tears, turned and ran toward the camp.

The scene that greeted her was so unexpected it wiped the humiliation of her encounter with Graham Norton from her mind. The teamsters were breaking camp. Already the main tent had been felled and the mules were being hitched to the wagon. The cook

23

spotted Gloriana and motioned her cheerfully toward a plate of food he had saved for her by the fire. But he too was moving swiftly, packing utensils and carving fist-sized sandwiches to be eaten on the trail.

"They can't just go," she appealed in bewilderment to Graham Norton, who had followed her from the creek.

"Don't worry, Miss Windemere. We won't leave you behind," he assured her coldly, his stern Western mask now firmly in place.

"I'm not worried about myself," she turned on him fiercely. "We have sick people here. They cannot be moved. I won't allow it."

"You have nothing to say about it. We can't stay here, and neither can they."

"You don't understand," she tried again, imagining that his ignorance kept him from grasping the situation. "That young man may die if we move him."

"No, ma'am, you're the one who doesn't understand," he said, brushing her hand away from his arm where she had laid it in her earnestness. "Those Indians trailing us are renegades and killers. They are at war with all white men, and their war code does not permit any prisoners but women.

"If we go, one man may die. If we stay, we may all die, and you and the other women can look forward to a life spent in a wickiup if you catch some brave's eye, or, if you don't, a few days of hell on earth, then a tomahawk in the back of your skull . . . . We're pulling out."

CHAPTER 3

THE FREIGHT TRAIN MOVED FORWARD that second day with a watchful grimness that underscored the seriousness of their plight. Already the hostile braves could have hidden their stolen goods, to return on swift, unburdened feet. They would have no trouble finding the trail, of course. The freight company had slashed a way through the forest that none could miss, and in spite of wagon boss Norton's caution to move quietly with a minimum of talk, twenty heavily loaded wagons drawn by forty stomping, braying mules could undoubtedly be heard for miles.

Gloriana rode with her patients in the nearly empty bed of the same wagon that had overturned the day before. There was little she could do to cushion the bumps and jostling. The freight wagon had no springs and, minus its heavy load of the ill-fated mission supplies, the wagon bed bounced with each rut, rock, and ridge in the trail.

The injured but now-conscious teamster rode better than Gloriana would have believed possible. During the day she learned that he was eighteen years old, that his name was George Mulligan, and that he considered it unmanly to lie in a wagon bed while the company ran for its life through the woods. When Gloriana refused to allow him to return to the driver's seat, he capitulated at the price of being allowed to have his rifle ready beside him. He would not have been able to sit up if she had agreed, but somehow his insistence and her refusal made his incapacity more acceptable.

Rita had a fever, but the color of the bruised skin of her arm around the splinted and bandaged break looked all right. Still, Gloriana could not be sure, and she wished hopelessly for a doctor to consult and prayed hopefully for the end of the trek to come soon.

She had no way of knowing how far away from a settlement of any kind they were—which was, perhaps, fortunate, for if she could have foreseen the hard days of travel, the mountain range to be climbed, and the rivers to be forded, her courage might have failed long before it did.

But if her courage and strength failed, her faith grew. Days passed, the Indians did not attack, and she thanked the Lord. After a few hard nights of watching beside their beds, she saw her patients' bouts with fever break, and their injuries show signs of proper healing. "There is much to be thankful for," Gloriana reminded herself when her backside ached from long hours of riding on rough board seats; her skin burned and peeled, leaving her with a shockingly unfeminine tan; and her feet blistered from walking beside the wagon as the mules pulled and strained their way up steep hillsides.

To occupy her hands and her mind, Gloriana dug out the journal she had begun on shipboard and started to recount the days since they had left Crescent City.

Oregon Territory   August 17, 1851

It is now eight days since we started our journey. So far we have been chased by Indians, suffered a wagon accident, and endured a variety of hardships, nonetheless trying because they were foreseen. Everything is somehow bearable except for the dirt. It rises in clouds from the trail, sifting through tightly laced boots to be ground into the heels and toes of stockings and burrowing through the clothes to smear the skin with a scratchy layer. I would give anything for a hot, soapy bath and the chance to wash my hair properly.

The people of the freight train are a motley assortment of adventurers, pioneers, and lost souls who have wandered to the edges of civilization searching for identity and acceptance.

The more I see of them, the more I become convinced of the need for missions in Oregon Territory. On Sunday I was permitted to read a verse of Scripture and pray over the company before the day's journey, but even George Mulligan and the cook laughed when I reminded them that the Lord would have us rest on His day. I shudder to think what a wasteland these pioneers will make of their glorious land if women do not come to make the family the center of Western life and ministers do not come to remind them that this land, like all others, is God's.

On the fourteenth day of their journey, the trail broke from the forest, and the train rolled into a lush, green valley dotted with log cabins and presided over by an impressive timbered blockhouse and fort.

The coming of a freight train was apparently a great event in this frontier community. Women in gingham gowns hurried from the cabins, wiping their hands on their checkered aprons. Men in straw hats and overalls looked up from their work in barns or fields. Barefoot children ran after the wagons, ignoring the teamsters' gruff reminders to stay away from the mules' hooves.

Called Applegate Landing for its founders, the settlement boasted, in addition to the fort, a general store, a combination flour and sawmill, and a brand-new, whitewashed church with a steeple and a small bell. Most of the structures were made of logs, stacked and chinked and capped by a heavy roof of shake shingles, but a few of the leading citizens had built salt-box houses of planed boards from the mill and whitewashed them in imitation of the new church. Minute yards, filled with every variety of eastern flower that could be coaxed to grow in the acidic valley soil, held out the wilderness with prim picket fences.

To her surprise Gloriana found herself something of a celebrity to the inhabitants.

"We know your uncle well," a jovial older man told her as he commandeered her and a trunk that she pointed out as absolutely essential to her comfort, and shepherded both toward a large white house on the edge of the settlement. His status in the community was suggested by the string tie and black suit he wore in spite of the informality of his surroundings, and she soon learned that he was Jesse Applegate, frontiersman, man of letters, and pioneer, who had figured largely in Uncle Ralph's letters as the Sage of the Yoncalla, the location of his land claim.

His wife, Cynthia Ann, made Gloriana welcome in a two-story home that denied its presence in the wilderness. Frilled curtains framed glass windows, and figured carpets softened the hardwood floors.

"I never really wanted to leave Missouri," she told Gloriana, "so Jesse promised me that here in the house it would seem as though I were back home." And indeed, if it had not been for the tangled forest and the rather ominous blockhouse of the fort, visible from the windows, the Applegate house would have seemed like any of the farm houses Gloriana had visited in the Pennsylvania countryside.

Oddly enough, she felt a little let down. Her uncle had built a legend of the Applegates as one of the first families of the Oregon Territory, and her own active imagination had added a semi-barbaric picture of Daniel-Boone-type figures and primitive surroundings liberally decorated with bear skins, buffalo robes, and Indian rugs.

But it was heaven to enjoy the luxury of a tub bath and clean clothes from the skin out. Unexpectedly, Gloriana's hostess urged her to hurry rather than to relax and pamper herself. It seemed that a company of soldiers had arrived in the settlement, dispatched by Army Headquarters at Fort Winnemucca to protect the settlers from the same renegades who had stolen Gloriana's supplies. So many visitors at one time had inspired the hospitable Applegates to sponsor a banquet on the town square, to be followed by a country dance. Gloriana was urged to put on her prettiest dress and offered rice powder to disguise the rosy tan which her pioneer-style poke bonnet had not kept from her face and neck.

She agreed to the former and politely rejected the latter, rather liking the look of unaccustomed color in her usually pale face. She was rather startled to notice that the prospect of an evening of dancing in this remote frontier community, under the shadow of danger and the threat of Indian raids, had nonetheless left her excited and eager to look her best. She wondered absently who would ask her to dance. Would Graham Norton be there? If so, would he expect her to dance with him? If he did, what would she say? Or not say? What would he say or not say? They had barely spoken for days after she had slapped him (she winced at that memory); yet he had been friendly enough before they reached Applegate Landing. Did that mean he had forgiven and forgotten? Hadn't he begun to show an interest in her that went beyond her status as a passenger on his wagon train?

Thus the time before the festivities were to begin passed quickly and pleasantly, the anxieties of preparation balanced by the anticipation of minor triumphs.

When she left the Applegates' house at dusk, walking confidently between the effusively friendly couple, Gloriana knew she looked her best—and in fact, for the first time in her life came close to living up to her rather intimidating name.

Her dress was a simple muslin, sprigged in cherry on a lighter background with its chief ornament a deep, gathered flounce at the hem that would look nice, Gloriana knew, as she twirled in dancing. But if the dress was simpler than Mrs. Applegate, hungering for Eastern fashion, had hoped for, the cut was elegant and set off Gloriana's tall figure. The sleeves were puffed; the neckline, square and modest, but exposing an expanse of creamy skin. Gloriana added a pink coral necklace of carved roses, given her long ago by her grandmother, and tucked matching rosette stickpins in the curls which she had piled on top of her head.

"Gloriana Windemere is a remarkably pretty girl," she heard Jesse Applegate tell his wife, and for possibly the first time in her life, Gloriana felt "remarkably" pretty. She had, of course, been to many parties in Philadelphia, but always she had been cast in the shadow by her entrancing sisters. Still, this evening she felt she could have competed with Juliana and Marianna at their best. Moreover, she had a wonderful consciousness of being like these Westerners—strong, intelligent, resourceful, able to contribute something to the new world and to build and defend a home in the wilderness.

Tables had been laid beneath a stand of pines. The fallen needles made a pleasantly cushioned carpet, and nearby pitchy trunks filled the air with a spicy scent. Bonfires to be lit later had been laid in cleared circles, and someone had thoughtfully placed round sections of sawed tree trunks for seating around the grassy area that would serve as a dance floor.

Gloriana saw Graham Norton lounging beside a

barbecue pit where great strips of beef and pork and whole chickens turning on spits were roasting. His immediate, if offhand, wave said that he had seen her first, and Gloriana imagined there was an interest in the gaze he fixed on her that had not been there before.

The woodland banquet hall and ballroom would have been attractive at any time of the day, but at dusk an enchantment settled over the place. Far down the river valley to the west, a watercolor sunset brightened the soft twilight sky with glorious smears of orange, rose, and red. In the soft shadows of the trees, lamps beckoned and voices seemed unnaturally magnified, causing speakers to lower their voices to a soft murmur.

"How perfectly magnificent!" Gloriana breathed softly, then flushed in embarrassment as hearty male laughter greeted her words. She realized belatedly that Mrs. Applegate was trying to present a young uniformed officer to her distracted guest.

"I have been given cordial welcomes before, but I don't believe anyone has ever called me 'magnificent,' " he laughed down into Gloriana's upturned face. " 'Dashing' perhaps or even 'charming' but never 'magnificent.' "

Gloriana joined the laughter at her expense, all the while wondering why Lieutenant John Tilton seemed so instantly familiar, as though they had met a day or a week before. He was as handsome as only a uniform seems to make some men. Straight black hair covered his forehead and just touched the top of his collar. His face was a ruddy tan that made his flashing smile literally dazzling. And there was something in his eyes—a spark, a glint, a gleam of deviltry—that stirred a sense of adventure and danger in Gloriana.

"Haven't we met somewhere before?" she finally asked him.

"Here now, that's supposed to be my line," he told

her and, somehow securing hold of her arm, Lieutenant Tilton drew Gloriana away from their beaming hostess. "You're supposed to say, 'Pleased to meet you,' and I say, 'You have been in my dreams from the first moment we met at the garden party or the symphony or the box social.'"

Gloriana laughed again and was not totally displeased to notice that Graham Norton was watching them intently from across the grassy dance floor.

"More probably if we did meet at all, it was during one of the West Point balls," she told the lieutenant, looking over her shoulder in what she hoped was a fair imitation of her sister Juliana's best flirtatious manner. "My youngest brother entered the Point three years ago, and he often invited us for the balls."

"How extraordinary to meet a lady of social distinction in this God-forsaken place! Tell me why you are here, and promise me you will not leave, no matter how dreary the days and the company."

"But God has not forsaken this place," Gloriana countered quickly, not noticing the officer's skirting the question of whether or not they might have met at West Point. "That is why I am here. I'm to join my Uncle Ralph Windemere in his mission at Klamath Lake."

Lieutenant Tilton, it turned out, knew her uncle and was full of news about the general locale of the mission. If his account lacked details about the mission work or praise for Dr. Windemere's accomplishments, Gloriana could excuse him, for what young man was as enthusiastic about church work and good deeds as about military life, battles, and guns?

The evening wore on and Gloriana met the residents of the settlement; ate roast beef, Oregon cheddar cheese, fresh bread, and huckleberry pie; listened to reminiscences about homes left long ago in Pennsylvania, Ohio, or Missouri; and shared what news she could remember—all, it seemed, with Lieutenant

Tilton at her elbow, acting the part of old and privileged friend, even though he did not claim it.

When the music of fiddles and guitars began, he demanded the first and then the second dance and would have insisted upon a third, but Gloriana turned him aside with a laughing reminder about the impropriety, well understood in the East, of a young lady's dancing more than twice with the same gentleman.

Although the lieutenant protested that the West was less restrictive—the one characteristic of the region that he seemed to approve—he surrendered her to her host who danced with her once himself, then introduced a string of eager partners, mostly fresh-faced young farmers.

It was late and the bonfires were burning low before Graham Norton approached her. He had been on the edge of the festivities all evening. When she had not seen him, Gloriana had felt him there, watching her with his inscrutable eyes. He didn't wait to ask but grasped her around the waist and swung her out onto the grass. Numerous couples continued to dance, although a late-rising moon had already begun its descent, and Gloriana's feet ached with the unaccustomed activity.

"You seem to be having a good time for yourself," was his opening conversational gambit, so unlike the teasing flattery she had been listening to all evening that Gloriana was too taken aback to reply.

"Like the pretty-faced lieutenant a lot, don't you?" he continued in the same vein.

"I don't see that it is any of your affair," Gloriana told him haughtily and drew back slightly from his clasp, which threatened to become more of an embrace than the light touch demanded by decorum. She tilted her head back to look up into the marble-smooth face and was surprised to see an open earnestness there instead of the mocking indifference she had expected.

Suddenly he swung her behind the shelter of a broad tree trunk. She thought for a moment he was going to kiss her. Their faces were close, almost touching; her heart pounded with abandon and she imagined she could hear his beating rapidly, too.

Instead, he moved back a foot, letting his arm drop from her waist but keeping her hand tightly in his, as though he were afraid she would try to run away.

"Glory, I shouldn't say anything. You're a female and likely to blab what you know. But I can't see you make a fool of yourself. Stay away from John Tilton! He's not what he seems."

Whatever reaction he expected, it was certainly not the wild fury that Gloriana unleashed upon him. That he should presume to dictate to her was past tolerating. That he should criticize her behavior, suggest that she was making a fool of herself, was beyond belief.

She told him in terms no less certain because they were ladylike that he had no right to speak to her about such things, that he should mind his own business, that a gentleman always faces one he accuses, and, for good measure, that she hoped she would never see him again.

"And don't call me Glory!"

34

CHAPTER 4

WATERY SUNLIGHT. DAMPENED BY EARLY VALLEY MISTS. flowed through the thick windowpanes of the Applegate guest room. Feeling its soft touch on her face and the crisp roughness of muslin sheets, Gloriana awoke, half expecting to hear her sisters, chattering in the room across the hall. Somewhere outside, a rooster greeted the morning. Bird choruses twittered and chirruped in the nearby treetops. From somewhere in the distance came the sharp rhythmic cracking of an ax splitting wood. It was almost like a summer morning in Philadelphia—but not quite.

Gloriana opened her eyes wide, remembering where she was and savoring the differences as the physical evidence of her adventure. She was lying in a pink-and-gold nest, like her bedroom back home. A flowered carpet on the floor waited to receive her bare feet. A gilt mirror hung over the white porcelain washbasin, and sprigs of pink flowers adorned the white water pitcher—cracked ever so slightly around the rim. But no Philadelphia bedroom had furniture of the rosy, streaked wood Gloriana was coming to recognize as the rich, heavy heart of the redwood; nor had she ever awakened back home with the strong infuriating face of Graham Norton vividly in her mind.

"How dare he?" she fumed, once again, not quite willing to examine whether she was angry because the freighter had presumed to lecture her or because she had imagined he was thinking about romance when he only wanted to deliver his unwelcome advice.

The incidents of the night before seemed intensified rather than subdued by the daylight. Gloriana's face grew hot as she tried to remember her actions, wondering if she had perhaps forgotten herself in the excitement of these Westerners' admiration and behaved with too much abandon. What had she said? What had she done? Had she laughed too much? Danced too much? Her eyes closed, and she tried to call up a picture of herself, dancing with her usual gracious reserve. Instead, her relentless morning-after conscience replied with the image of a romping hoyden. "Gloriana Windemere, you had better get hold of yourself," she scolded, bouncing out of bed to face her image in the gilt-framed mirror.

The reflection that looked back hardly seemed that of a sedate missionary nurse. Her hair, which persisted in curling in the damp Oregon air, had pulled itself out of her bedtime braids to riot in dark profusion around her face. Her suntanned cheeks were rosy and her lips a bright red. Even the usually modest flannel nightdress had come open at the top in a daring décolletage.

Gloriana sighed, hoping her behavior had not damaged her Christian witness. "We have to be sure you can present the proper picture of Christ and the church," the Missionary Board had said when they had first rejected her application. At the time she had considered their caution an expression of narrow minds and a narrow religion. Now she wondered if perhaps they had had some experience with the effect of the frontier on young, unmarried women—"spinsters"—she recalled with a little grimace.

In any case, she was one spinster who was going to take herself in hand before it was too late. And not without a sense of the humor of the situation, Gloriana set about transforming the belle of last night's ball into once again the proper young missionary. She tamed her wayward curls into a sedate crown of braids, donned one of the dove-colored dresses that made her look like her Pilgrim forebears, and even applied some of Mrs. Applegate's rice powder to tone down the color in her complexion.

"That should be enough to discourage anyone," she told the thoroughly proper and, she had to admit, thoroughly dull-looking reflection in the mirror when the transformation was complete. She had no doubt that, put in her place, her sisters Juliana and Marianna would have made the most of their position as single women on a frontier teeming with men, but she was equally certain that becoming a Western belle was not what the Mission Board would want—although perhaps they expected it. For the sake of the other young women who might apply for mission posts, she would have to be doubly careful to "abstain from all appearance of evil."

"This is one Cinderella who won't become a princess," Gloriana told herself with a little laugh, but she could not resist wondering: if she had been Cinderella last night, who had been the prince—Graham Norton or John Tilton? She made a face at her prim reflection before turning away from the mirror.

She noticed again the beauty of the little room. It seemed to be bathed in a special light, which Gloriana soon discovered was from the thick glass in the latticework windows. The heavy panes, instead of transmitting the light, refracted it slightly to send glimmering rainbows dancing across the walls and floors. The effect was lovely but made her realize how difficult it must be to get something as ordinary as window glass in a frontier settlement like Applegate Landing.

In one corner, wreathed with rainbows, someone had made an old-fashioned prayer altar. A little picture of Christ hung on the wall, and beside that, a beautiful cross carved from a gold-colored wood Gloriana had never seen before. A rocking chair and footstool of the same glowing wood sat beside a night stand that held a well-worn Bible.

Sitting in the chair, she rocked for a few minutes and let the peace of the little haven flow through her. How often in the last few weeks and months had she forgotten the reason for her coming to the Oregon Territory? First, there had been the battles with the Mission Board and objections of her own family to overcome, then the packing and traveling and meeting new people. (She would not let herself single out anyone specifically.) But she was not here by accident. In fact, she could remember the first moment she had felt called.

The whole family had been sitting in the parlor one Sunday. They had been pursuing the quiet occupations that Philadelphia and her father's church considered proper for a sabbath. Gloriana's fingers had been quietly occupied in embroidering, but her mind was far from being quiet or sedate. She was thinking about the people and places in the letter from which her father had been reading. It had been from Uncle Ralph, and he had, as always, been effusive in his praise of the people and the land of his beloved Oregon Territory.

"I wish I could transplant every Eastern sapling into this rich land," he had said, "I guarantee that they would grow taller and stronger."

They had laughed at her uncle's favorite image of young people like trees taking root in the West.

"I hear some young ladies are having trouble finding suitable husbands in Philadelphia. If so, it's because all the finest young men have come West."

The girls, including Gloriana, had all blushed at that, and Marianna had looked indignant. She considered her favorite suitor, Morris von Pelter, a very fine man indeed, but it was difficult to imagine him as anything except a primly efficient bank teller in a primly efficient bank.

"You have heard the phrase 'noble redman,'" Uncle Ralph had continued. "Nothing better describes the Klamaths, Modocs, and Shastas—the people whose ancestors have lived in these forests for thousands of years. Although not originally Christians, the hunger for God is so great among them that they begged for the missionaries to come." And then he had described the poverty and illnesses—the epidemics of the white man's diseases, which to the unprepared immune systems of the Indians brought almost certain death.

She had not heard a loud or even a still, small voice call her, but when Uncle Ralph had mentioned his need of a nurse, she had known as surely as anything that here was something she could do, was meant to do, perhaps had even been born to do.

"I will go," she had said very quietly. Her father had looked stunned, her mother had begun to argue, and Juliana had said slyly, "She wants one of Uncle's fine young men; none of those here are good enough for her." But no arguments, mockery, or hardships had stopped her.

"And here I am," Gloriana reminded herself, looking out the window at the thick forests and the rounded cone of a volcano that towered over the valley. Yet honesty demanded that she examine her sister's charge. Was she really here first and foremost to find a husband? "Am I more interested in the Western men than I am in the native people?" she asked half-aloud, thinking back over the days on the trail with Graham Norton, reminding herself uncomfortably of her reactions to his physical presence and touch. She remembered her pleasure the night before, the excitement of being, for the first time in her life, the belle of the party. Then she shifted her focus to her uncle's mission, the people he served. Again she felt that high resolve and quickening in her spirit that had made her determined to become a missionary, but she could not deny that she was looking forward to seeing Graham and John again.

"Perhaps my destiny here holds more than I realize."

Sunday services at Applegate Landing were held in the community church that doubled as a one-room school. A whitewashed building with the tiniest of bells in a miniature bell tower, it was removed from the main cluster of buildings, presumably to supply the worshipers and young scholars with some quiet for their prayers and studies.

Surprisingly to Gloriana, Graham Norton joined her and the Applegates as the small, high-pitched bell in the church steeple called Applegate Landing to worship. He fell into step beside her with a self-conscious grin that suggested he could read her thoughts and was perhaps as surprised as she.

"Sorry if I overstepped last night," he told her after a moment. "I guess I was just jealous. A pretty girl is an event in the life of a community like this one, and a girl like you is bound to cause a sensation."

Gloriana caught her breath and looked up at him to see if he were serious. A teasing smile lit the big man's features, softening the square jaw and transforming the blue eyes that could be so hard and menacing into sparkling messengers of mischief and fun. He had taken off his hat, letting the coppery curls fall boyishly across his forehead. And in place of his savagely picturesque buckskins, he was wearing a simple dark suit. Yet the common attire emphasized, more than the frontier costume, the breadth of his shoulders, straining impressively against the rich broadcloth, and accentuated his towering height. *What a grand man!* Gloriana thought to herself and then remembered too late as Graham laughed pleasantly that her family had always said that she had a transparent face, often articulating her thoughts better than words. To cover up her embarrassment, she began to chatter about why she had come to Oregon Territory, about her problem with the Missions Board, and her hopes for the future.

Again to her surprise, Graham listened sympathetically, and she was highly gratified when he laughed outright at the Mission Board's calling her a spinster.

Sunday services had always been a special time for Gloriana. In the spacious sanctuary of her father's church in Philadelphia, she had felt an inner soaring as the organ intoned the old hymns and the sunlight enhanced the jeweled pictures of the stained-glass windows. She had often wondered if the spiritual experience were intensified by the beauty of the surroundings. Yet in the little frontier school house with its bare board floors and a teacher's desk and a chalkboard where the altar and pulpit should be, God seemed as near, perhaps nearer.

The congregation sang unaccompanied and slightly off-key but with an enthusiasm that underscored their strong belief. The minister's message was as simple as the people themselves and reminded Gloriana of something her Uncle Ralph had written,"God is more real to us on the frontier because of our utter dependence on Him, every moment of the day."

Lord, help me to walk closer to You, she prayed earnestly. *Let me share the here-and-now faith of these people.* And with her head bowed, Gloriana felt a sudden premonition that she might soon need the Lord to strengthen and hide her, but just as surely came the assurance that when she needed Him, He would be there.

She had all but forgotten the freight master in the depths of her worship so that his voice startled her as they left the schoolhouse.

"You really believe in what old Reverend Samuels was talking about, don't you?"

"Why, yes, don't you?" Gloriana countered. She had assumed that because he went to church, she had misjudged Norton and he must be a Christian.

He waited a few minutes before answering, and his face looked more thoughtful, sad, and somehow vulnerable than she had ever seen it. "I don't know," he said finally, as much to himself as to her. "I don't know."

CHAPTER 5

SUNDAY AFTERNOON IN APPLEGATE LANDING WAS a social time. Neighbors dropped by to "sit a spell" on the Applegates' wide porch, and the sociable pioneer couple seemed tireless in their enthusiasm for their neighbors and for the frontier home they shared.

In the course of two hours Gloriana met the Jabbots, teenaged newlyweds whose beaming faces held no hint that their early marriage had come after a massacre left them the only remaining members of their respective families; Grandma Tuttle, who had raised two children and six grandchildren on the frontier, only to lose all but one in a typhoid epidemic the year before; Zack Humbard, the lone, fire-scarred survivor of the burning of the small mill town of Ashland by Rogue Indians. Every inhabitant of the little community, it seemed, came with a story, and Gloriana was astonished at the quiet heroism of these people who had suffered so much.

"Why do they stay?" she posed the question to her journal later that afternoon, and glancing up from her comfortable seat in the shade of a blooming trumpet vine, she thought she could see the answer. Near at hand the Applegate yard was like any she might have been sitting in during a warm summer afternoon back home. But beyond the cultivated yard was an uncultivated paradise. To her right a gentle, sloping path lined with sunflowers, paintbrush, and the bright blue cornflowers that the pioneers called bachelor buttons climbed to a forested mountain. The dark stands of pine and fir seemed more inviting than forbidding, and the air was heavy with the spicy scents of pine, cedar, and juniper.

Just below the house the hillside gave way to a bluff that overhung a magnificent river, and to her left the community of Applegate Landing was a picturesque cluster of log buildings and square white cottages.

Gloriana had started to sketch the little community when a small moth the color of warm butter landed on her pencil. Its round body was covered with a soft, downy coat. Long antennae waved flirtatiously at her, and she had leaned forward to study the attractive little creature more closely when a voice just inches away startled her.

"Watch out! It might bite."

In spite of herself Gloriana jumped, and the harmless little creature took flight.

"Oh, how could you?" She looked up for a second into the disturbingly close face of Graham Norton and then let her eyes return regretfully to the retreating moth.

He laughed and stepped over the low porch rail to join her on the bench. He had changed from the conservative suit of the morning and was once again dressed in the trail buckskins that made him seem a bit savage and uncontrollable.

Graham had spent the early part of the afternoon preparing the freight wagons for the resumption of their journey the next day. He would be taking most of the wagons on south to the gold fields at Jacksonville, he told her, but he had arranged for her own wagons to move east to Klamath Mission under the protection of the cavalry troop.

"I have no choice but to go on with the main part of the wagon train. But you'll be safe. I'm sending you with the soldiers. And I've detailed some of my best teamsters to drive your wagons. Jones, Blackjack, and Smitty will take care of everything," he assured her. The three teamsters, Gloriana noted, were some of those she had known and liked best on the trip from Crescent City.

With the arrangements for the next day's journey made, an uncomfortable silence fell between the two. Gloriana, faced with the realization that she might not be seeing this infuriating but strangely intriguing man again, wanted to ask him if he ever visited her uncle's mission. But Graham, intent on some brooding thought whose secret was hidden somewhere in the valley mists, seemed remote and unapproachable.

She was about to make a lame excuse about needing her rest and escape the silence by retreating inside the house when Graham suddenly grasped her hand and pulled her to her feet.

"Come with me," he said, taking her hand and starting toward the forest pathway.

The pathway was the same one, climbing through tangles of wildflowers to the lush tree forest, that Gloriana had found so appealing earlier. What she had not noticed before was that it was a rather lonely and secluded path, hidden from the community by the bulk of the Applegate house and by a stand of jack pines.

She tried not to dwell on the impropriety of being alone in the forest with a young man, but she pulled her hand away from his grasp, then wished she had not as the trail proved to be rougher than it appeared from a distance.

"Where are we going?" Gloriana asked after a few minutes of scrambling up the hillside.

"Blessing Waters. It's just a ways further," Graham answered imperturbably, taking hold of her arm to steer her toward the trees. Gloriana hesitated, remembering that she did not know this man well and that she was in the West where standards of behavior were decidedly more liberal than what she was accustomed to in the East. But the cool shadows beckoned, and soon she found herself gliding between massive tree trunks on a thick, springy carpet of pine needles.

Graham's earlier dark mood had dissipated, and he was at his best, showing her how to read directions in the forest by looking for the spidery green moss growing on the north sides of the tree trunks or where to find fragrant mountain lilies in the dense sheltering growth around fallen logs.

"How long have you been in the West? How do you know all of these things?" Gloriana asked him.

"I came in '39," he told her, "before there were any trails. And I know most of what I know because of the Klamaths. I lived among them for several years after my parents died." He said no more, and Gloriana did not press him further, but the confidence revealed another side of the man, one more vulnerable and more feeling than the tough wagon boss usually exposed to view.

Blessing Waters proved to be an icy cold spring in a glade so well-hidden and beautiful it seemed a dream. The water bubbled up from the base of a black rock thick with moss and lichens to spill into a little stone basin at its base. Charged with some kind of gas deep beneath the earth, the waters frothed mysteriously, and a white crust of mineral deposits had formed around the edge of the pool.

"Make a cup of your hand like this." Graham showed Gloriana how to squeeze and curve her fingers so that they would hold the water. Then he knelt down in the grass at the edge of the pool and proceeded to scoop up the sparkling liquid.

Feeling self-conscious but determined to be a good sport, Gloriana followed suit. At first the water dribbled quickly between her fingers, but after a few tries she managed to hold enough to take a few sips. "Why, it's delicious! Tangy and kind of salty as though there were minerals in it."

"The Indians say it's blessed by the spirits," Graham told her in the quiet voice, almost a whisper, the hushed glade seemed to call for. An almost perfect circle of blue-green colored firs—silvertips, Graham called them— enclosed them in a magic ring. The usual forest sounds of birds' calling and animals' rustling through the undergrowth were muffled by the music of the spring. The forest-scented air was still and so spiced with cedar and pine that it stung the lungs to breathe deeply.

"Is all of this natural?" Gloriana asked, feeling the softness of the grass carpet they were sitting on. "I mean, did someone plant the trees so they would grow that way? And who keeps the grass so short, almost like a lawn?"

"Probably the deer come here at night to graze. Maybe some enterprising brave planted the trees."

"You mean sort of like a shrine to honor the spirits?"

"More likely to have some privacy with his sweetheart."

Something in Graham's tone as well as his words made Gloriana suddenly aware of how alone they were and how close. She moved her arm, and it brushed against Graham's sleeve, sending something like a lightning bolt through her. Glancing up, she found his face close and a disturbing light in the depths of those sea-blue eyes.

"It's getting late. We had better go," she said hastily and started to rise, but he held her back with a strong arm that enveloped her gently, but firmly.

"Not quite yet," he said, still speaking quietly and

47

moving nearer. His free hand came up to trace the soft outline of her lips and wipe away a stray drop of the blessing water.

"This is outrageous. I insist you release me immediately."

She had no time to protest further before Graham's searching lips found hers, and Gloriana found herself picked up and cradled as though she were no larger than a child. For an awful instant she felt something inside of her, thrilling to Graham's kiss, willing her to return it, to let the growing force of his passion carry both of them along to some unknown realm. Pressed against him, she felt her own body yielding, molding against the hardness and strength of his. Then the realization of what was happening shot through her, numbing her senses and lending her the power to wrench herself free of his embrace.

"Glory, wait! You don't understand." Graham started after her, but the speechless fury he read in Gloriana's face said she would not, could not listen.

The Applegate table had an uncharacteristic lack of company that evening. The meal began silently with Gloriana deep in her own thoughts and the Applegates at a loss as to how to entertain their suddenly moody guest.

"I understand you took a walk to the Blessing Waters," Cynthia Ann said at last when several attempts at introducing a suitable topic for conversation had failed. "It's a magic spring, you know. Legend has it that if a man and a woman kneel together to drink at the spring, their love will be blessed and their union eternal, extending even past the grave to the stars. Isn't that a lovely notion?"

She was totally unprepared for Gloriana's stricken expression or for the quick tears that leaped to her eyes, sending her with hasty, choked excuses from the table.

"Why, whatever did I say?" the bewildered lady asked her husband.

"I'm afraid that for once the blessing of the waters didn't take very well," Jesse Applegate, who had witnessed the young couple's abrupt departure for the spring and equally abrupt return, replied enigmatically.

Upstairs in her bed Gloriana shed quick tears of shame, until she lay still as questions shot through her mind. Why had Graham Norton tricked her into the blessing ritual of kneeling together and drinking from the spring? Had he known about the ritual? He must have. He knew all the legends and stories about this place. Why hadn't he said anything? But wait! Hadn't he called her back, wanting to explain? Why hadn't she waited? Would she ever know what he wanted to say?

It was past midnight before she remembered to seek help from the only unfailing Source.

Lord, help me deal with this, she prayed quietly. From deep inside her came the question of a still, small voice: *What would you have done if this young man had declared his love for you? Would you have accepted him, knowing, as he told you this morning, that he does not share your faith?*

A truthful answer was the only possible one. "I would have had to say no," she admitted at last.

Then how much better it was that he did not ask, that whatever may or may not be between you was left for God's will and the future to work out.

Tear stains still on her cheeks, Gloriana slept with renewed peace, assured that once again "all things had worked together for good" and that her future held more excitement and promise than she had dreamed when she left home to be a missionary.

CHAPTER 6

LEAVING APPLEGATE LANDING was like leaving home. Gloriana looked back regretfully as her wagon crept farther and farther down the valley. A light fog, rolling off the river, wrapped the just-waking community in a filmy white haze, giving it a dream-like appearance. The mist obscured the southbound wagon route, but she could imagine the heavily loaded wagons of Graham Norton's train moving slowly up river toward the place they called Jacksonville.

Graham had checked her wagons carefully and watched them start. His expression had been carefully noncommittal as he hurried from place to place, giving orders and testing the loads to see if they had been securely packed, giving special attention and adding an extra rope to hold the organ. But before they had started, he had come to stand beside Gloriana, his hat in his hand, seemingly having something to say but not knowing how to say it.

Finally, he asked her to tell her uncle that he would be at the mission in two months to do some work they had apparently agreed upon. Then warning Gloriana

50

once again to watch her step with Lieutenant Tilton, he had ordered the teamsters to start the wagons.

Graham had also had a few words with John Tilton—not very pleasant words, it seemed, from the scowl on the lieutenant's face. Gloriana imagined she knew the gist of what was said from her own driver's repeated assurances that he would be "lookin' out fer her, extry special."

Her driver was Smitty, her favorite of all the teamsters, for he combined a fine sense of humor with a highly developed love for conversation, something Gloriana had learned to appreciate when she had ridden with one close-mouthed driver on the trip from Crescent City. Yet even Smitty took a while to warm up and, during the early hours at least, Gloriana found herself alone with her thoughts.

They were not unpleasant. She recalled joyfully the new friends she had made—the villagers who had welcomed her so uncritically; the admiring young farmers; the Applegates, who had assured her they would look for her to come for a long visit in the spring. The episode of Blessing Waters and Graham Norton was one thing she studiously avoided; she found an odd gratification in knowing that the matter would be there to consider when she chose. Moreover, the frontiersman himself might be planning to take up where they had left off when he visited the mission in just two short months.

In the meantime she was on the last leg of her journey, and the excitement was mounting at the prospect of seeing her beloved uncle and beginning the work she had come so far to do.

It would take four days to climb the remaining mountain range, Smitty told her when he finally emerged from his own private early morning fog— perhaps the result of a long Sunday night in the village tavern, rather than the dampening effect of the river mist.

"We c'ld make it a mile shorter if we went by the Greensprings," the man confided what appeared to have been a disagreement with his boss, "but all things rightly consider'd, yu bein' a female 'n all, this here root may be the best'un."

The route they were taking was called the Dead Indian Pass, and Gloriana shuddered a bit at the implications of the name. Still the soldiers did not seem unduly concerned, so she supposed they were not in any real danger. Lieutenant Tilton himself found ample opportunity to ride alongside Gloriana's wagon. She had no doubt that if it had not been for Smitty's inhospitable glowering, the lieutenant would have forsaken his horse for a bumpy four-day ride on the hard wagon seat.

"I wouldn't be payin' no mind to that un's jawin'," Smitty told her with a curt nod of his bushy head in the lieutenant's direction. "There's sum thet only means t'alf o' what they say and less'n thet o' what they look."

"Now, Smitty, you are going to have to back that up with something more substantial," Gloriana tried to pump the driver for more information. "What is it you and Mr. Norton have against Lieutenant Tilton? Do you know something about him? If there is something I should know, I want you to tell me. Otherwise, I have no choice but to think you are entertaining some ill-natured grudge against the man."

But for once the talkative Smitty would say nothing, and in fact, his offended silence stretched into several hours and only began to thaw when Gloriana made a sketch in her journal of a grumpy bear driving a freight wagon while a timid girl peeked nervously over the wagon seat behind him.

"Don't draw me unless you make me a dashing knight on a prancing horse," John Tilton said when he saw her handiwork, "or maybe a cavalier in a long, flowing cape, climbing the balcony to woo the beautiful lady."

"I could as easily make you a savage chief in warpaint on a wild Indian pony," Gloriana countered his extravagance with some of her own, but she could tell by the expression on the lieutenant's face that he did not like the idea and she dropped it. *What absurd vanity*, she commented to herself, determined not to draw someone who had such a high opinion of himself that he had to play only the roles he chose even in someone else's fantasies.

The Dead Indian Pass was as rugged as any they had passed through. The wagons crept slowly along a trail at times barely discernible in the hard, rocky canyon floors. Several times they had to unhitch the mules and use block and tackle to get the wagons down a sharp incline or across a deep gully. Once or twice Gloriana was certain her precious organ had reached the end of its eventful journey, but each time Graham Norton's teamsters managed to save it.

The soldiers, Gloriana noticed, including the tirelessly gallant lieutenant, were less helpful. In fact, she had the distinct impression that if it had not been for their leader's interest in her, they might very well have moved on about their business, leaving the slow-moving wagons to make their own way, unescorted. With every mile she appreciated more her sturdy drivers and the careful watch they mounted over her.

The first night's camp was made in a wildly beautiful spot with the unprepossessing name of Lake of the Woods. A perfect gem of blue in the late afternoon, the lake turned to a silvery mirror at evening, reflecting an enormous yellow moon. Sitting by a fire built especially by Smitty for her bedside, Gloriana marveled at the brightness of the moonlight magnified in the mirror of the lake.

She had leaned back against the trunk of a tree, her eyes closed, her thoughts straying again to the two days at Applegate Landing, when a faint cracking sound, like boots' stepping quietly over mats of dry pine needles brought her upright in time to see John Tilton step out of the darkness.

"Did I startle you?" he asked, his speech seeming a bit slurred to Gloriana's heightened senses. "I couldn't sleep and thought you might like to go for a walk down by the lake." His words were casual enough, but in the darkness he seemed to be staring at her with a peculiar intensity.

"I was just getting ready to retire," Gloriana excused herself hastily. "It has been a long ride, and tomorrow will be even longer."

"All right," he seemed to accept her decision easily enough. Still, he did not leave but crouched down on a branch of the fallen tree that screened Gloriana's bed from the others and began talking about the lake and moonlight in a oddly thick voice, struggling, it seemed, over the pronunciation of some words and sliding over others.

"Lieutenant, I would really like to get some sleep," she told him pointedly, assuming her most authoritative tone.

He stood up, but instead of starting back toward the men's camp, he took another step in her direction. What would have happened she was thankfully never to know, for at that moment the underbrush erupted with crackling and snapping and Blackjack stepped out of the bushes with an enormous load of firewood in his arms.

"Enough wood to keep it burning all night," he told her cheerfully, not seeming to see the lieutenant. Then he took an enormous gun out of his belt and handed it to her. "I almost forgot that Graham said to give you this to keep close by to guard against skunks and other varmints."

Gloriana accepted the gun thankfully. She had never liked guns or known what to do with them, but this one gave her at least the look of meaning business.

Blackjack took his time stacking the wood close by her bedroll where she could easily reach it to pile on the fire. Then he added a few sticks to the flames. By the time he had finished, the lieutenant was gone.

The three days that followed were as tense as any Gloriana had experienced. Her three drivers rode on guard, their usually jovial attitudes submerged in a grim watchfulness that included the soldiers as well as the forests in its scope. After the second day, when Gloriana had half-expected to awake to find the cavalry gone, she decided that nothing more unusual had happened than that the lieutenant had had too much to drink and had become unfortunately amorous.

Lieutenant Tilton acted as though nothing had happened, which of course was literally the case. If he felt any embarrassment for the episode, he did not show it. Perhaps he did not even remember. Gloriana had known patients at the hospital where she had worked in Philadelphia who could not remember entire weeks during which they had been drinking heavily.

In any case, she thought it best to go on in the old way, smiling at the young man's constant sallies and seeming to enjoy his flirting. She had an idea that it would not be wise to alienate this mysterious young man. And when she caught him in an unguarded moment looking at the driver Blackjack, something dark and menacing in his expression confirmed her suspicion and caused her to wonder how much was hidden behind the handsome, laughing face of Lieutenant John Tilton.

Dead Indian Pass   August 27, 1851
   We camped today on the cone of a volcano. Mount McLoughlin has a spectacular beauty like no mountain I

have ever seen before. It rises abruptly from the rolling, forested hills and soars upward until its rounded peak is lost in the clouds. The trees seem to grow taller and lusher in the thick gray volcanic ash on its sides and the rounded cone of the mountain is ribboned with enchanting, lacy waterfalls as the edges of a white snow cap, still deep in spite of the August heat, melt.

Yet for all its beauty, I cannot help thinking of the enormous destructive power lying just out of sight, perhaps building unseen beneath the surface of the mountain.

The Indians, I am told, call these ethereally lovely peaks devil mountains. I appreciate the comparison and will be glad when we break camp in the morning.

"Miss Windemere, I think you would enjoy seeing Bridal Veil Falls. Would you care to accompany me?"

Gloriana looked over her shoulder into the smiling face of John Tilton, close enough to have been reading her journal. She felt a moment's relief that she had not been writing anything about him. Something in the man's eyes put her thought of pleading fatigue aside. She and her little wagon train were still dependent on his protection. Forcing a bright smile of assent, Gloriana let the man help her to her feet and was relieved to see that the indefinable something had vanished from his expression, letting the smile on his lips touch his eyes.

"You can hear the falls from here," he told her, showing a marked tendency to hold onto her hand rather than release it. "But nearby the rocks pick up the music, and it sounds like a chorus of water nymphs."

"How is it that something as temporary as a waterfall caused by the melting snow has earned a name?" Gloriana asked brightly, trying not to see the disapproving looks which her drivers—Jones, Blackjack, and Smitty— threw in her direction.

"This one isn't temporary," the lieutenant laughed as she managed to extract her hand; he offered his arm instead with all the aplomb of a ballroom gallant. "It starts in a hot spring near the summit. The warm water melts the snow whatever the time of year, though in the summer the falls sometimes expand to a broad curtain across the face of the rock." Was it her imagination, or did the man send a sly grin in the direction of Graham Norton's teamsters as he tucked the hand that she had placed lightly on his sleeve securely into the crook of his arm?

Gloriana was surprised to find a path leading to the falls. "Could that many people have found this place?" she asked Tilton.

"The path is a deer trail. If we move quietly, we may see a doe or two. The bucks are usually more cautious."

Peering into the shadows made by the sinking sun and the tall trees, Gloriana imagined she could feel the deer close by, their great liquid brown eyes following her curiously.

As they neared the falls, the simple tune of the water expanded to a water fugue as the echoes multiplied the sounds. But nothing had prepared Gloriana for the witchery of the falls. Tumbling from a rocky cliff nearly a thousand feet above, the white, splashing water made a lacy curtain hundreds of feet across, then billowed high in the air at the base. It looked indeed like a bridal veil falling into a long, frothy train.

Spellbound, Gloriana couldn't speak, but after a moment she realized that her companion's eyes were on her face and not the falls. She felt a tension in the air and sensed the volatile depths of this man, held in check just beneath the surface.

They were several yards back down the deer trail before the falls' wild ecstasy of sound subsided enough for voices to be heard. What the lieutenant said surprised Gloriana no less than the careful courtesy of his touch as he helped her across a tiny rivulet of water that appeared suddenly in the trail.

"I beg your pardon for frightening you the other night. I am afraid sometimes it takes a beautiful, cultivated woman to remind us what brutes this wilderness can make of men. I hope you can forgive me and allow us to be friends." He stopped in the trail and held out his hand in the manly gesture of friendship.

"I'm happy . . . that is, of course we can be friends," Gloriana faltered and held out her small hand to be captured in his large one.

"And I hope you will allow me to see you when you are busy spreading salvation among the poor red devils," he continued in the old teasing way. "We white devils could use some saving too."

Gloriana had no idea what she answered, but she had a distinct impression of Graham Norton's scowling at her from somewhere as she smiled tentatively at the handsome cavalry officer and allowed him to take her arm as they followed the lengthening shadows slowly back to camp.

CHAPTER 7

NEVER WOULD GLORIANA FORGET her first glimpse of Klamath Mission. Her wagons and their escort had emerged from the trees at the end of a hazardous morning's travel to find themselves on the edge of a fresh-water lake so large it seemed almost like an inland sea. Then she had seen it—a small cluster of buildings under massive willow trees. And stretching for acres and acres around the buildings were little huts that looked as though they had been made from sticks and animal skins.

"But I don't understand! That looks like an entire Indian village. I thought my uncle had only a few natives staying at the mission."

"Perhaps there's a celebration," Tilton said. "Sometimes the natives gather for a pow wow—a kind of religious get-together with singing and dancing to honor their gods." Why the Indians would be holding a celebration for a native religion at a Christian mission, the lieutenant didn't hazard a guess, and Gloriana received the impression that the man neither knew nor cared much about the Klamath Lake Medical Mission.

Their coming was greeted by a few black-haired children who ran to meet the wagons, but for the most part the faces that watched their progress through the Indian encampment were guarded and expressionless. "Cap'n, these reddies ain't lookin' none too friendly," Gloriana thought she heard one of Tilton's men call to him, but she realized she was mistaken since Tilton's rank was lieutenant, not captain.

Uncle Ralph was standing on the porch of the largest cabin—a long, low building of peeled, whitewashed logs, which Gloriana immediately realized was the hospital. Smiles wreathed the cherubic face with its little fluff of white whiskers and wisps of white hair winging out above round ears. But she read weariness and relief in the welcome as well as gladness to see his niece, and the doctor's attention turned quickly to the wagons of supplies.

She explained their loss quickly but had not finished her inventory of items taken before Smitty stepped forward and said in a low voice, "Ma'am, Graham and old Jesse Applegate made up most of yer losses with supplies at the Landing before we left. They reckoned as how it'd be a mite easier for them to bring up more from San Francisky th'n fer you'all to git more, bein' off the beaten track 'n all."

The boxes of camphorated oil were especially valued, and when he had assured himself of an ample supply, Uncle Ralph explained that there was a measles epidemic, and the oil helped sooth the rash on the children's sensitive skin.

Gloriana paled as she recalled what a measles epidemic meant among the native peoples. She had nursed in several epidemics in Philadelphia, and always the disease had claimed more than its share of victims. For the Indians, whose immune systems were less developed, even the milder strains of the illness could prove fatal. She had heard of entire tribes' being wiped out before the epidemic had run its course.

In the midst of such an emergency there was little time to deliver all the messages from back home or to dwell on the delight of being on the mission field at last or even to say goodbye to the companions of her journey from Applegate Landing. Gloriana had a glimpse of a small whitewashed room with shutters instead of glass windows where Uncle Ralph directed the teamsters to put her trunks and boxes. She met the staff as they worked—a second doctor, Eugene Midfield, a young man just out of medical school and his wife of a year, who during the emergency had taken on the task of cooking for the staff. Matilda (Tildy) Brown, her uncle's housekeeper, Gloriana already knew. Tildy's sturdy hands and loud voice were busily managing the outdoor washroom. From steaming cauldrons she covered a labyrinth of clotheslines with clean sheets, rags, and an assortment of shirts and missionary-barrel garments that were serving as hospital gowns.

"The hospital was filled long ago; now we'll need to set up a children's ward in the schoolhouse," Uncle Ralph told her. He introduced her to Oweena, a Shasta girl who said she had contracted and recovered from the illness years before when she had lived in the white man's settlement of Eureka on the coast. Together the young women set about clearing the long schoolroom of its makeshift desks and scouring the bare wood floor, where for want of beds or pallets they would lay their charges.

It was past midnight when Gloriana found her way to the kitchen of her uncle's cabin for a bite of supper. She was surprised to find the teamsters there and even more surprised to find that Jones, Blackjack, and Smitty were leaving the mission. "We're gittin' while the gittin's good," was all Jones said, but Smitty confided that they would return by the Greensprings, the route he had preferred all along.

"Hsst! Ye needn't tell everythin' ye know," the

usually silent Jones interjected with a quick look around the empty kitchen with its still hot iron range and the split-log table and benches, as though he were looking for some invisible enemy.

Mystified, Gloriana said a silent prayer for the men. Perhaps there were hostile Indians in the mission camp that Uncle Ralph did not know about—although what he could do if he could tell the dangerous from the nondangerous she had no idea. Minutes later, just slipping off to sleep, she heard the wagons roll by her window; the usual clip-clopping of the mules' hooves sounded muffled as though they had been bound with something soft, and someone must have greased the squeaky wheel on the wagon that had carried the organ, for she could no longer hear its agonized, nerve-shattering whine.

She woke a few hours later to a timid knock on her door and a sense of urgency.

"Miss Glory, Dr. Ralph says we should hurry to be ready for the sick ones by chapel time." Having no idea how chapel time and her patients were related, Gloriana nonetheless followed Oweena's advice and hurried. But she took the time to find and don one of her hospital uniforms. The gray-striped gown with its heavy gray wrap-around apron made her feel thoroughly the nurse once again, and her assistant's covertly admiring glance made her determine to cut down one of the uniforms to fit the Shasta girl at the first opportunity.

It was a little past dawn, and the wonderful lake smells of clean water and wet tules filled the air. Overhead, gulls were winging across the blue waves, intent on a breakfast of fish. Their ragged calling reminded Gloriana of the months at sea, and, in spite of the grim atmosphere hanging over the epidemic camp, she felt a deep thankfulness to be at the mission and about the work she had chosen.

"You have come just in time," Uncle Ralph told her over a quick breakfast of some bland cooked grains that she was too tense to want but too experienced to refuse. She forced Oweena to eat a small bowl too and urged some as well on the sweet-faced cook. Mrs. Midfield refused with a wan smile and a movement of her hand to her stomach. Noticing the slight fulness of the woman's gown, Gloriana guessed morning sickness and hoped that it was not a German measles epidemic they were dealing with.

"Isn't it still early to be experiencing an epidemic of this type?" Gloriana asked, remembering that back home the summer months were the time to worry about typhoid but rarely measles.

"I usually expect something like this in the spring," was her uncle's frowning reply. "Coming now could mean we will have a short siege; let's pray it's not the direct opposite." Then he gave Gloriana instructions about the ages of children he wanted her to house in the ward, the treatment he was using, and the arrangements for sanitation. He repeated Oweena's enigmatic statement about finding her patients at chapel, but again she let it pass without questioning. She would find out what was meant soon enough.

Unlike Applegate Landing, the mission could boast a schoolhouse separate from its church. Set away from the other buildings, it was perched atop a grassy hill where the lake mists would be dispelled rather than linger in the mornings. Two outhouses separated by some bushes were hidden behind the hill. "Too far for the sick ones to travel," Gloriana noticed with concern and wondered if she and Oweena would be able to handle everything alone.

During the night someone had spread the clean floors with comfortable looking beds of animal skins.

"My people give their own sleeping rugs," Oweena told her proudly. Gloriana did not have the heart to tell her that the rugs could be infected. Besides, she knew that she would need some kind of bedding in addition to the assortment of makeshift sheets and quilts she had already taken from the main hospital for the sick babies to lie on. Still she would make her ward as safe as she could, and mixing some disinfectant with water in a wooden bucket, Gloriana went about sprinkling the skins, all the while praying that they would dry before she had to put patients on them.

Chapel bells—a miscellaneous but not unmelodious assortment of dinner gongs and cow bells strung on a tripod beside the church door—sounded at nine o'clock. To Gloriana's amazement the entire encampment, sick and well alike, responded to the summons.

"They come for big medicine," Oweena told her, and Gloriana realized that this was the reason she was to choose her patients at chapel. To the Indians the service with its singing and prayers must be a major part of the healing ritual, more akin to the practices of their own medicine men than the unfamiliar hospital regimen of medicines and constant sterilizing.

The short message that morning was presented by Dr. Midfield, standing on the elevated porch and speaking to the Indians gathered in the church yard since the building itself could not hold so many. If she had not been so busy scanning the crowd for the teary eyes and coughs and the painful itching that would signal measles rash, Gloriana would have been fascinated by the manner of the service.

Some of the Indians at least were not new to Christian worship, for they sang what appeared to be simple Sunday-school choruses readily enough. The words were a mixture of English and Klamath, the language most spoken by the various tribes that had assembled. But the half-chanted music, punctuated by drumbeats was entirely native, bearing little resemblance to the melodic lines and careful harmonies intended by the songwriters.

The sermon itself was more visual than oral, although Midfield spoke in what sounded like an Indian language and there were several interpreters posted around him, all, it seemed, talking at the same time. Several mission Indians, their status indicated by their mission-barrel dress rather than native costumes, held up a twenty-foot long sheet, the different segments of which had been carefully stitched together to show a long mural of brightly painted illustrations. Gloriana had heard of the Catholic Ladder; a kind of scale marking important events in religious history from creation to the coming of Christ and the present missionary movements, it had been used by the priests to give the Indians a sense of perspective and the progression of Church history. She had even seen a copy of the Protestant Ladder, a similar scale with an added dimension to show the differences between Catholic and Protestant theology. Whoever had made the Klamath Mission Ladder seemed to be more interested in presenting an illustrated Bible than in either church history or controversies. The success of the little cluster of pictures representing each familiar story could best be gauged by the eagerness with which the Indians pressed forward to get a closer look as Dr. Midfield pointed to the part of the sheet that illustrated his sermon.

His story was Daniel in the Lion's Den—an odd choice, Gloriana thought, for a sick camp. She would have chosen the loaves and fishes or Christ and the lepers, but the crowd seemed impressed. Perhaps the timid-looking Dr. Midfield felt exactly like Daniel in the midst of so many desperate and not fully comprehending natives. She remembered that one reason given in the Eastern papers for the killing of the Whitmans was that they had let too many of the Cayuse people die in epidemics just like this one.

The sad, feverish faces of the children and the anxious, frightened faces of the Indian mothers wrung

Gloriana's heart. They came to her reluctantly but obediently after the service. With some a quick look at the vivid red rash on arms and chests established the presence of the disease. With others she found the first hectic blotches behind the ears or discovered tiny red Koplik's spots in their mouths. After more than an hour of examinations, she had selected thirty, choosing those with the worst rashes or a deep cough that threatened the dreaded complication of pneumonia.

Dozens of others showed various stages of the disease—teary eyes, fever, a rash just starting at the hairline, or the welcome sloughing off of the skin that indicated that the measles had nearly run its course. In these cases she told the mothers through Oweena to keep the children's eyes shaded and give them fluids but no solid foods—all the while unsure whether there was much milk available in the crowded camp or whether the Indians were in the habit of cooking nourishing soups.

The schoolhouse was soon filled to its limit, but unlike the crying, cranky patients of most children's wards Gloriana had worked in, these were quiet. Their suffering showed only in the dark eyes that followed her as she moved from child to child, spooning liquids into their mouths or dabbing angry blotches with camphorated oil.

Oweena soon recruited two more Indian girls to help, and Gloriana was relieved to learn that they also had survived the "red sickness." The Indian girl was a Godsend, never tiring, always moving quickly and, even before she was asked, coming to explain a procedure to a frightened patient or to help pry open the clenched teeth of a stubborn one.

Usually Gloriana eased her way around a children's ward with smiles and teasing, but her overtures here met only with blank expressions. Thinking she must seem too alien and forbidding, she asked Oweena to teach her some expressions in the Klamath language.

Then after rehearsing the words several times, she confidently approached a girl of about six and spoke the words Oweena had said meant, "Open your mouth." The reaction was electrifying as the girl's face broke into a broad grin and the patients close by all joined in the rhythmic, sing-song laugh typical of the Indians.

Glad to see the smiles but mystified as to the reason, Gloriana turned to her assistant only to find the girl laughing silently behind her.

"Oweena, what did I say to this child?"

"Oh, Miss Glory, you say okay; you just say so fun-nee."

Gloriana supposed her pronunciation could be that atrocious, but she still could not help looking suspiciously at the Shasta girl's wide-eyed, innocent face and made up her mind to check out her newly learned phrases with the mission staff before she used them on any other patients.

At least she had broken the ice. Now Oweena and the other girls went around the room teasing in the Indian way, which seemed to consist in part of poking and pinching and pulling braids. Gloriana herself seemed to be a primary source of amusement and little brown-cheeked cherubs giggled behind their hands as she approached them.

Uncle Ralph checked her ward late in the afternoon, and his tired face brightened considerably at the air of good feeling and the willingness with which the sick children were submitting to the nursing.

"I wish we could have you work some of this magic in the main hospital," he told her with a smile that could not altogether erase the worry in his face.

"I'm afraid the magic is Oweena's." And she told him about her attempt at communication.

"Well, my dear, we all have our own methods," he broke into a hearty laugh that set the ward giggling again. "You told the child you were Sky Woman and had come to bite off her nose."

CHAPTER 8

LONG HOURS OF PATIENT NURSING stretched into days and finally into weeks. The makeshift beds in Gloriana's children's hospital yielded up their occupants— some to return to their families, alive and whole again, some to occupy freshly dug graves in the growing cemetary by the lakeside.

And still there were more sufferers to take their places.

In the third week of September the golden Oregon summer changed into wet, misty fall. Rain fell in a slow, steady drizzle that soaked the grasslands around the mission. The waters of the lake rose inch by inch, and a damp cloud seemed to have settled over the mission.

Among the sick the wetness intensified the danger of pneumonia. Day and night the fires burned in the hospital and the schoolhouse, but though the heavy iron stoves repeatedly came close to overheating, they could not keep out the dampness.

"Miss Glory, I think your God must not like Indians very much," Oweena told her late one night.

Gloriana sent a quick prayer for wisdom winging heavenward, then answered earnestly, "He not only likes you; He loves you so much that He sent His Son to die for you."

"Then why do we suffer so much?"

There it was—the age-old question and one that had often bothered Gloriana. "All I know, Oweena, is that our suffering hurts Him very much and that He has promised a time will come when there will be no more suffering. In the meantime we must do all we can to help each other bear whatever comes. That's why we missionaries are here—to help your people through times of sickness like this one."

The Shasta girl said nothing more, but the thoughtfulness of her expression made Gloriana hope she had said something to touch the girl's heart.

The days of the epidemic had taken their toll on the mission's resources as well as on its people. The medical supplies Gloriana had brought were nearly gone. Even food was running low as the Klamath hunters fell victim one after another to the measles. And with the cold and the need for fires, the mission woodpiles, so laboriously stockpiled in anticipation of the harsh Oregon winters, were disappearing quickly.

Knowing that the army had sent Lieutenant Tilton and his company to build a fort somewhere in the south, Gloriana suggested her uncle send a runner to ask for the army's help. "When there was a typhoid epidemic in Philadelphia, the government sent the guards to help," she remembered. She did not say that perhaps the lieutenant might come for *her* sake, if not the mission's.

Ralph Windemere walked to the door of his hospital office and, swinging it open, watched the steady downpour of rain. The moisture seemed to have washed the color from the landscape and left a gray, fluid world in which the division between sky and earth had blurred and finally run together.

"You must understand, my dear," he told her at last. "I have no doubt that in the East the authorities would be most helpful in a situation like this, but here things are different." He took his pipe from his pocket and clenched it between his teeth, but he didn't try to light it—probably, Gloriana guessed, he had shared his tobacco with some of his patients and had none left.

"Still, if you think it is worth a try, I will send someone to talk to this Lieutenant Tilton of yours."

Gloriana felt herself blushing and protested that he was not her lieutenant, but the truth was that she had been counting on his feelings for her being at least deep enough for him to want to please her. Certainly the young man had shown little concern for the missionaries. *If Graham Norton were here, he would help.* The thought came unbidden, and Gloriana suddenly remembered that in all those weeks she had not delivered the man's message.

"Now that is good news!" Ralph Windemere exclaimed as she haltingly told him what Graham Norton had promised. "Norton is a man who gets things done. We will need him badly when this is over." He paused a moment, then glancing curiously at his red-faced niece, added, "I take it you got to know the man rather well."

"We were on the freight train together from Crescent City—that is, I hired him to bring our supplies from the coast." For a moment Gloriana felt oddly transparent as though her perceptive uncle were looking directly inside her. His chuckle increased the feeling, and she noticed that he had reached in his pocket and was beginning again the ritual of the empty pipe.

"If I may ask, what did you think of this Western giant?" her uncle asked with that teasing tone Gloriana found more annoying in direct proportion to the degree of truth in the insinuations.

For a moment she did not answer. What exactly did she think of Graham Norton? Then, eyes flashing, she said, "If you must know, uncle, I found him vain, overbearing, and . . . insufferable!"

Ralph Windemere's beaming face fell a bit before his niece's apparent anger. "Why, child, I have known Graham Norton for nearly two years, and I have always found him to be kind and generous to a fault. Certainly, he takes charge, but this is the West. It takes strong men to survive. Did you know that his folks were missionaries? They were killed, not by Indians, but by white renegades when Norton was about sixteen. A Klamath chief took him in and treated him like a son—like an Indian prince."

Gloriana listened, fascinated, feeling a sudden rush of compassion for the man but also a little thrill of excitement. She could well imagine Graham as an arrogant native prince—daring anyone to defy him. No wonder he was accustomed to having his own way in everything and no wonder he knew the Indian rituals so well, including the romantic ceremonies of the Blessing Waters.

Lost and unconscious in her thoughts, Gloriana did not see the satisfied smile return to her uncle's face.

The first day of October passed, and still no help had come. Dr. Midfield had taken several of the convalescent men and gone to the nearby forests for wood. The unaccustomed work had resulted in a mass of blisters on his sensitive hands. Moreover, the wood had proved to be so damp that it smoked badly when they burned it.

Klamath Mission   October 3, 1851
    We watch the trails daily for signs of help's coming, yet I am the only one who seems to expect any relief from the army. Uncle Ralph talks hopefully of Graham Norton's promised arrival. Dr. Midfield continues to organize convalescents for hunting and wood chopping parties, but his accomplishments are meager.

In the midst of all our anxieties, my friend and helper Oweena seems to have bloomed mysteriously. She confided in me that help is on the way, and at first I thought she shared my faith in the army's willingness to meet our needs, but now I think she has some other, secret hope that she is not ready to reveal.

The army did come. It was a little after nine o'clock and chapel, still attended faithfully in spite of the storm and the crowded conditions in the small church, had just begun. The organ, which Gloriana had guarded so faithfully through the thousands of miles of travel, had been enthroned on a slightly elevated platform at the front of the church. Gloriana, pumping carefully, for the dampness made the organ notes unpredictable, was playing "A Mighty Fortress Is Our God" when a small boy rushed in with the news that soldiers were coming. A ripple of something like fear went through the congregation, and Gloriana thought she saw a few of the younger men slip out the door. But she breathed a deep prayer of thankfulness.

"Well, my dear, it seems you were right after all," Dr. Windemere told Gloriana.

"I just knew they would answer our appeal if only we had the faith," she answered joyfully, not stopping to think that her words were a criticism of her long-suffering uncle.

But her joy was soon tempered. Instead of the full company of men and the train of supply wagons she had expected, there were three soldiers leading two pack mules, neither very heavily laden. The men did not dismount; the expressions on their faces were guarded and strained, and Gloriana remembered the master sergeant's comment about unfriendly "reddies" when the soldiers had escorted her to the mission in September.

The same sergeant was leading this expedition. When he recognized Gloriana, he stepped forward and handed her a thick packet and inquired after Dr. Windemere for whom he had a smaller envelope.

"Lieutenant Tilton sends his compliments, ma'am," the sergeant told Gloriana briefly. Then he asked where to unload the supplies.

Those supplies included barely enough cornmeal and jerked venison to feed the convalescent patients for a day or two. The bulk of the load was made up of coffee, tea, white flour, brown sugar, canned delicacies—the sort of luxuries that an over-reached group of whites might run out of first if an expected supply wagon were long in coming. The soldiers said nothing about helping with the wood supply, and no one asked them. Their watchful, nervous actions made it abundantly clear that they regarded the mission as hostile territory and were anxious to leave.

Gloriana's uncle saw the crushed expression on Gloriana's face and reached out a comforting hand to pat her drooping shoulder. "At least they brought something, my dear. That is considerably more than I expected. It seems you have made a rather profound impression on the young man." He pointed to the heavy envelope she was holding in her hand.

"But, Uncle, I don't understand. I prayed so hard and believed so strongly that help was coming," Gloriana brushed aside his reference to Lieutenant Tilton's letter; her voice was sharply edged with complaint, and from inside she sent a few reproachful why's heavenward.

Dr. Windemere smiled sadly, thought a moment, and then said quietly, "Gloriana, sometimes we have to stop and ask ourselves who we are believing in, ourselves and the people around us or God. If our faith is truly in Him, we will let God work out the way He answers our prayers and even leave it to Him whether the answer be yes or no."

"Miss Glory, your help came but too small," Oweena added somewhat smugly, Gloriana thought. "Now we see about Oweena's help."

CHAPTER 9

THE NEXT MORNING ACTUALLY DAWNED—for the first time in days. A thin ribbon of liquid yellow sunshine peered beneath the storm clouds in the east. By chapel time the ribbon had widened to a broad band of blue sky, and Dr. Windemere offered a prayer of thanks, both for the army's help (it is not our place to criticize anything the Lord sends, he told them) and for the promise of better weather. By noon the sky was clear with only a few clouds resting heavily on the mountains to remind the missionaries of their ordeal.

As if in response to the brightening skies, the sick showed signs of improvement, and for the first time since the start of the epidemic, fewer new cases were diagnosed than on the day before.

"This could be the break we have been praying for, or it could be just the eye of the storm," Dr. Windemere observed cautiously, but he went about sloshing through the great lakes of mud in the mission yard with renewed energy and even a song, off-key but cheerful all the same, on his lips.

Given a morning to herself, Gloriana decided to

wash her hair. She had avoided the task for several days because of the difficulty of drying it and because of a little soreness about her throat and chest. Now it was a relief to unbraid the thick coils of hair and to feel the warm, soapy water touch her scalp.

"When this epidemic is over, I am going to sleep for a week," she promised herself. Looking in her mirror, Gloriana was surprised to see the dark circles under her eyes, but the faint red flush beginning at the roots of her hair drew her incredulous gaze. 'No, it couldn't be!" she told herself, but she tore open the front of her dressing gown all the same. Tiny pink dots were already raised and, she realized suddenly, itching on her pale white skin. Still hoping to be wrong, she went back to the mirror and, opening her mouth, tried to peer inside. The light in the room with the wooden shutters half closed was dim, but she thought she could see the telltale Koplik's spots inside.

How long had it been since she had had measles? Ten years? Certainly it was possible to contract the disease more than once, but why now, and why here? She had worked with measles epidemics many times at home in Philadelphia and never had shown the slightest sign of infection.

Lord, I don't have time for this. You can't let it happen!

Opening the shutters to catch the sun, she began to dry her long hair. She noticed with some exasperation that the long strands were curling into tight little corkscrews in the still-damp air. The mass of dark hair fluffing out around her pale face brought back memories of Applegate Landing, and she found herself thinking about Graham Norton.

There had been little time for daydreaming during the past few weeks, but if there had been, she probably would have refused to think about the Westerner all the same. But now—perhaps it was the weakness brought on by her impending bout with this absurd children's disease—in any case, she could not seem to keep her mind from conjuring up pictures of Norton in a hundred different attitudes and actions— Norton driving a wagon with his hat tipped back and his red hair bobbing across his forehead like a flame; Norton loading freight or chopping wood, the thick corded muscles bulging and rippling beneath his shirt; and Norton holding her hand on the way to Blessing Waters, a tender excitement in his eyes and an almost shy grin on his lips.

"Am I falling in love with that wild, Western man?" she asked herself finally. The quick denial was not altogether convincing, even to Gloriana.

A dreamy half hour had passed when Gloriana was pulled out of her reverie by a commotion in the mission yard below. What she saw made her heart stop. And forgetting about the measles and the danger of infecting anyone, she pulled on a dark, open-necked dress without noticing how it accented her pallor and exposed the hectic flush of the rash on her neck and chest.

Below in the mission yard, Dr. Ralph Windemere was facing a band of three dozen Indians—all young warriors mounted on sturdy-looking mustangs and carrying full quivers of arrows with the bows draped across their backs. A sense of power and savagery surrounded the party like a tangible atmosphere, and Gloriana wondered if at last she were seeing the heartless war party that had committed so many atrocities.

The leader of the band was a chief; his authority was evidenced in his face rather than in any ostentatious ornaments. He sat as tall and straight on his prancing mustang as any of the younger men; only the iron-gray color of his hair and a heavily lined face betrayed his age.

Ralph Windemere held out his hands in the traditional gesture of welcome. For an instant there was no

76

response; then a warrior who rode beside the chief dismounted and came toward the gathered missionaries.

"Keintepoos!" Gloriana heard a little gasp and turned to see that Oweena had joined her. The girl's glowing face told her story, and from the quick look thrown in their direction by the young giant, it seemed that he had not missed Oweena's presence.

Well over six feet tall, the warrior was strikingly handsome, with an air of command not unlike the leader's. His face was a smooth, sculpted mask except for the large dark eyes that seemed to see everything. Long raven hair had been tied with rawhide at the back of his neck, and the buckskin of his shirt stretched tightly across massive shoulders.

"So this is the reason Oweena has left her home," Gloriana thought, and for a moment she felt a little shiver of fear that somehow this lovely girl might have betrayed them. *But for what purpose? There is nothing to be gained by killing us or destroying the mission. No, Oweena is here because she loves this young warrior and he, whatever his feelings, has not yet asked her to be his bride.*

Gloriana remembered the hint of some secret sorrow that she had sensed in the girl. Reaching out to Oweena, Gloriana gave her arm an encouraging pat. The girl was shivering with excitement.

"I am Keintepoos, Chief of the Warricka. I speak for Chief John and the Federation of the Southern Tribes." The warrior's speech was clipped and commanding; his accent was foreign to Gloriana's ears, but the phrases were correct, suggesting a mission-school education. *Surely,* she thought, *if he has gone among us, he understands us, knows that we mean his people no harm.* Yet there was something ominous about the phrase "Federation of Southern Tribes," calling up images of natives united in uprisings, banded together against some common enemy.

77

If her uncle and Dr. Midfield shared her anxiety, they gave no indication. Their faces remained as courteously impassive as those of the chiefs. In fact, the two doctors, both small and fragile beside the magnificient physiques of the natives, seemed incongruously to exude an almost supernatural courage, and Gloriana was reminded of "Daniel in the Lions' Den," the first sermon she had heard Dr. Midfield preach.

Her uncle answered the chief gravely, speaking the formula phrases of welcome she recognized as, "We are honored by your visit. How may we help our brothers?" He spoke in Klamath, and the face of the old chief registered his pleasure at the courtesy.

"We hear of sickness," Chief Keintepoos continued. Then he added with a note of challenge that made Gloriana gasp, "We hear it kills many of our people. We hear it is red sickness made for red man by our white brothers."

Oweena let out a little cry, but the warrior did not glance in her direction.

"Our brothers" was all Gloriana could make out of her uncle's reply, but she supposed he was trying to explain that among whites measles is a children's disease. She supposed that it must seem strange to these people that in all of the weeks of the epidemic, none of the staff had become ill. Possibly they even imagined the staff were somehow responsible for the deaths; as soon as the missionaries diagnosed patients as having the disease, the patients would immediately become sicker. Even Oweena, who understood much of what was happening, had once expressed amazement at Gloriana's amazing ability to "predict" who would become ill.

Gloriana remembered too the persistent arguments of the Cayuse chiefs accused of the Whitman massacre a few years before. They had not denied the murders but had explained over and over again to the

78

tribunal that Cayuse law called for the killing of bad medicine men. Dr. Whitman had cured the white settlers but not the natives; therefore, he was a bad medicine man and had to be killed. The argument had seemed ridiculous at the time, and even later when Graham Norton had mentioned the chief's charges, Gloriana had found them so absurd that she imagined the man was purposely trying to provoke her. But now after living through the horrors of an epidemic with the Indians, feeling as they did the injustice of the disease that caused so much suffering among their ranks, she could understand the young chief's question and even sympathize with it.

Thank You, Lord, for having a right time for everything—even for catching measles, Gloriana breathed a prayer, and, adding a postscript to send her a quick dose of courage, she pulled away from Oweena's hand, which was clutching hers, and spoke softly in her uncle's ear.

A broad smile crossed the old man's face. "My dear, you are indeed manna from heaven—a fresh blessing with each day's new needs." He had to do no more than glance at the blotches clearly visible on her light skin to confirm the diagnosis. Then, putting his arm around her shoulders, he drew her toward the waiting Chief Keintepoos and began to explain her condition in a detached tone that she recognized as his best clinical manner, though she did not understand the words.

Gloriana's ready blush stained her neck and cheeks, accenting the rash further, as the warrior stepped forward to observe the symptoms her uncle was pointing out one by one. Keintepoos was apparently familiar with the signs, perhaps having suffered from the disease at sometime himself, for he insisted upon seeing the Koplik's spots in her mouth. But she began to suspect his motives when, after a lengthy examination of her tongue, she met his dark eyes for a moment and recognized the amusement lurking there.

Convinced, Keintepoos turned to speak to the waiting Chief John and his warriors. At last Gloriana breathed a sigh of relief; then she felt the pressure of her uncle's hand encouragingly on her shoulder, and she realized that instead of simply reporting her condition, the young chief had invited members of his band to examine her themselves.

For fully twenty minutes the imposing warriors pressed around Gloriana, eager, it seemed, to witness this phenomenon of a white woman with the red sickness. Remembering how amusing her young patients had found her, Gloriana strongly suspected that the warriors were also thoroughly enjoying her embarrassment. When they had finished their inspection, some of the Indians who had already been at the mission crowded forward for a look. All seemed especially interested in the Koplik's spots in her mouth, and again and again Gloriana stuck out her tongue and waited while the tiny red dots were pointed to and exclaimed over.

Even Oweena had to look, and her comment made Gloriana wonder once again how the beautiful girl viewed sickness and the role of the medical staff in treating it. "Miss Glory, why did you let this happen?" She also continued to see God as directly involved in the dispensing of illnesses. "Maybe Lord God is angry with you. Miss Glory must repent." The concern in the girl's face was so genuine that Gloriana felt touched in spite of the implications of her words. When the usually undemonstrative Oweena gave her a quick hug, Gloriana felt as though she truly belonged at Klamath Mission.

She longed to sit down. Her knees had begun to shake, and her stomach was beginning to roll ominously. Still the people came as though none was willing to be left out or to miss the chance of examining the mission nurse. In fact, a few, in imitation of Dr. Windemere's notorious poking finger, even gave her a few jabs and asked tentatively, "Hurt?"

The two chiefs had remained standing nearby throughout the ordeal, though after their first inspection, they did not seem to be watching her. Finally, when the last Indian had stepped off the porch, Chief John turned to Keintepoos with a rush of what sounded like orders in the Indian tongue.

Keintepoos stepped toward them then. He spoke to Gloriana's uncle, this time in Klamath, but she had the uncomfortable feeling that the warrior's eyes strayed laughingly to her face.

Dr. Windemere looked startled for a moment; then he turned to Gloriana and explained carefully, "My dear, it seems Chief John is very impressed with you. He feels you would be the mother of many brave warriors. Therefore, he would like you to become his fourth wife, provided of course you survive the red sickness. He is offering fifty horses for you —an impressive bride gift."

Gloriana had no idea what kind of reply was expected, but she had no need to make any. With an astonished glance at the two chiefs—both looking at her in a kind and almost gentle way—Gloriana, for perhaps the first time in her life, fainted.

She learned later about the remaining events of the day and felt she had learned more than one lesson in trusting God. With the good faith of the missionaries established, the chiefs had announced their intention to help. Orders had been given, and a long string of ponies had come into the mission yard—some laden with the carcasses of deer and elk, some carrying ears of unshucked corn in huge baskets balanced on each side of the animals like oversized saddlebags.

"I think they always intended to help us," her uncle told her late that afternoon. "They just had to test us a bit first." Through the closed shutters of her room, Gloriana could hear the steady ring of an ax, witness to the warriors' helping with more than the food. The appetizing aromas of roasting venison and baking cornbread found their way from the cooking fires.

"I overheard some of the braves talking," her uncle continued with a chuckle. "They were saying how happy they would be to eat Indian food again; they do not seem to have enjoyed our oatmeal and chicken soups very much." He did not comment on God's wisdom in choosing His own deliverers for the mission, but Gloriana was sure her uncle felt it as much as she did.

Klamath Mission   October, 1851
    I am in quarantine. Uncle Ralph feels that if I, with all my years of exposure, can contract measles again, the disease must have mutated, creating a new strain that could easily infect the entire mission staff.

Somehow I doubt there is much danger. The sickness has served its purpose. We have food and fuel again for the winter. Dr. Midfield is no longer blistering his hands trying to add to the wood stacks, and poor Catherine, who is having a harder pregnancy than she would admit, can take to her bed. The Klamath women, encouraged by the chiefs, have taken over supplying meals for the patients. Their corn mush—almost a corn chowder—is more appetizing than our hospital oatmeal, and the soups they prepare are flavored with some delicious herbs. I suspect the cooks are adding healing potions of their own to the recipes.

I have not talked with my good friend Oweena, yet I hear much that disturbs me. Uncle Ralph reports that his housekeeper Tildy complains constantly of Oweena's being absent late into the night. The girls who work at the mission live with Tildy in their own cabin, and Tildy sees herself as their substitute mother. I suppose they find her harsh and restrictive, yet she wishes only the best for them.

Oweena is so passionate and single-hearted; I fear for her if this young chief disappoints her or is killed or injured. I still cannot dismiss the suspicion that these

82

warriors are somehow connected with the renegades who pursued our freight train. It does not seem possible that these fierce-looking braves have banded together for no other purpose than hunting or rescuing beleaguered Christian missionaries.

Still I'm sure I have never seen Chief Keintepoos or Chief John before, and there is something different about their native dress. Their hunting shirts are soft deerskin, stitched together with braided strips of hide, but I seem to remember the Indians who attacked us wore white tunics heavily embroidered across the chest and bound at the hips with sashes of brightly colored fringed material in red, purple, and green.

To try to focus the images in her mind, Gloriana began to sketch. She tried picturing Chief Keintepoos and his men, as she had seen the renegades—over Graham Norton's muscled shoulder, spears in their hands. As she sketched, the memories came more clearly. She remembered broad bands of red warpaint on cheeks and foreheads, bright pieces of cloth tied like sashes at the sides of their heads, long flowing hair that hung past their shoulders in ragged elf locks.

The more she sketched, the less any of the renegades looked like the friendly chiefs and their men. *The renegades are picturesque and oddly barbaric looking like I always imagined Indians to be* , she thought. *Keintepoos and his warriors are less exotic, but more manly.*

She put down her pencil for a moment and tried to go back in her mind to the wagon camp beside the stream to recapture every detail of the renegades' appearance. She could not escape the feeling that there was something she was missing, and it suddenly occurred to her that she would like to discuss the matter with Graham Norton. He knew these people; he would be able to figure out the reason for this faint suspicion hovering at the back of her mind like a cloud, that all was not as it seemed. For Oweena's sake as well as that of all the settlers, she had to find out whether Chief Keintepoos was a brutal murderer.

But when Gloriana picked up her pencil again a few minutes later, it was not the strong, high cheekbones of Keintepoos or the wildly glaring expressions of the renegades that her pencil drew but the square firm jaw and arrogantly handsome face of Graham Norton.

CHAPTER 10

Two weeks had passed before Gloriana was permitted to leave her room; another week before she could again take an active part in mission life. In the meantime the number of new cases of measles had diminished daily until Dr. Windemere declared the epidemic was over. Gradually the encampment, which had grown almost to a small city, was dispersing back into the hills and grasslands. Only a few convalescents remained, and they occupied themselves with repairing tents and making arrows in preparation for their journey to sheltered winter camps.

The weather continued fair, the puddles dried, and a luxurious Indian summer settled over the wilderness. It was weather to dream rather than to work in and, finding her dreams returning uncomfortably often to Applegate Landing and an arrogant Westerner with eyes like blue flames, Gloriana recruited her energy and Oweena for a huckleberrying expedition.

Donning heavy, long-sleeved dresses to protect them against thorns in the berry patch, the girls set out for a promising tangle of vines that nearly filled a marshy hollow where a small stream emptied into the lake.

"I like your Keintepoos," Gloriana told Oweena as they picked their way at a leisurely pace among the rocks along the lakeshore.

"He's not mine," the girl protested quickly.

"But it's easy to see he's in love with you. His eyes when they follow you fairly smolder, and I know you care about him."

Oweena said nothing but picked up a rock and sent it skipping out into the lake. The action drew a protest and a shake of a fist from a small Klamath boy. Fishing from the edge of the lake with his willow pole, he had been sitting so still that neither girl had noticed him. Now he moved out on a rock to recast his line into the deep water below, as if Oweena had permanently disturbed the fishing at his earlier spot.

"Oweena, I hope you don't think I am meddling, but I am concerned about your happiness. Do you— that is, do the two of you have plans to marry?" Gloriana knew she was touching on delicate ground, but she sensed a softening in her close-mouthed friend and pressed further. "Were you perhaps once very close? Did something come between you?"

Giant tears squeezed from beneath lowered lashes before Oweena brushed them away with an angry hand.

"Keintepoos is too busy to marry. He follows warpath with Chief John, forgets Oweena."

"Who are they fighting?"

The girl did not reply, but after a moment she said, "Miss Glory, do you love the bluecoat who bring you here?"

"Why, no!" Gloriana was less surprised at the question than at the vehemence of her own answer.

"Oweena is very glad," was all her friend said, but it left Gloriana with the distinct impression that the bluecoats, as the Indians called the cavalry, were somewhere on that path of war Keintepoos and his braves had taken. Whether settlers and wagon trains were also on it, she would have to wait for another time to find out.

The afternoon passed quickly. All along the lakeshore the huckleberries grew in thick patches. The heavy rains, followed by warm sun, had made the berries grow fat and juicy, and the lush stocks, weighted down with fruit, trailed in the water. The girls filled their pails in spite of the inroads each made on the stores—smudging their lips and making purple rings around their mouths. Then Gloriana took off the bleached flour-sack towel she had wrapped around her waist for an apron, and they began to fill that.

"Tildy has to be impressed with this," Gloriana told the laughing Oweena, "Maybe she'll make us a huckleberry pie." And they took off their shoes to wade into the marshy water after clusters of berries that looked as large as their little fingers. They quickly stripped the fruit from the thorny bushes; ripe and heavy, it seemed to fall into their hands with no more than a touch. They had tucked their long skirts up between their legs and waded in deeper when they heard a sudden splash and a little yelp which was cut off abruptly by a gurgling sound.

A hundred feet behind them, the lake was churning frantically beneath a rocky overhang. In an instant Gloriana knew what had happened. The Indian boy, who had been fishing from the edge, had leaned over too far and fallen in. The dark blue color of the water below attested to the depth of the fishing hole, a sharp contrast to the surrounding blue-green lake. She watched for a second, expecting to see his head break the surface, for even the smallest Klamath boys were adept swimmers. When it did not, she realized he must have struck his head going down or perhaps become entangled in the roots of a nearby willow.

"Oweena, we've got to do something. Find a long

stick. Hurry!" Gloriana shouted. Splashing out of the berry patch, Gloriana was already running toward the rolling water. She tried not to take her eye off the exact spot where the boy had gone in.

"Dear God, help me get there in time!" Knowing that they would only hamper her movements and drag her down in the water, she pulled off her heavy dress and petticoat. She was glad she had already removed her shoes; their awkward buttons would have delayed her by minutes.

She had taken swimming lessons when she was a young girl. Her father had insisted, saying one never knew when an emergency might occur, but she had been an awkward pupil and had not practiced in years. "God, make me remember how," she had just time to breathe before she was at the lake's edge and plunging in.

The cold of the water hit her with a shock. In the shallow marshes where the berries grew, the autumn sun had been strong enough to penetrate and warm the waters; but in the deeper parts of the lake, the chill was more in keeping with the time of the year.

Her arm stroked the water awkwardly at first, then more smoothly as she found the lake waters buoying her up, helping her over the surface. It was only a few yards to the pool where the child had disappeared. Taking a big breath, she dove, kicking to get beneath the surface. The pool was in a shadow and so dark she could see nothing. She felt something slick and cold move against her arm and jerked away before she realized it must have been a fish.

Gloriana's lungs felt as though they would burst, and moving her arms and legs was becoming more and more difficult as the cold numbed them. She knew she would have to go up for air soon. Then her groping hand found a round head, and her arms circled a small limp body.

The few feet to the surface seemed like a hundred.

The boy was a dead weight in her arms, lighter in the water than out, she knew, but still a burden she was barely able to propel upward. Breaking through into the air, she took a deep breath, but the strength she hoped for did not flow into her body. A terrible weakness had invaded her limbs. For an instant she thought the child would slip from her grasp; then she remembered how to float and, turning on her back, held on desperately to the limp form while she fought for her breath.

Somewhere at the edge of consciousness Gloriana thought she heard a sound like hoofs pounding on the grassy lakeshore. She remembered Oweena and hoped the girl had found a long stick, for she knew she would not be able to climb the slight incline of the shore without something to hold onto.

"The Lord is the strength of my life," the words came back to her. And holding the child securely in one arm, she turned and began to crawl slowly, pushing with her legs and pulling with her one free arm toward the shore.

She was in a daze as she approached the lake side. She reached down and felt her feet touch the bottom, but she seemed powerless to climb the last few feet out of the water.

"Oweena," she almost whispered her friend's name and began looking around frantically for something to grasp.

Suddenly she was aware of someone running toward her, calling her name. The water around her rose and buffeted against her as someone leaped splashing and stumbling to her side. Then strong arms closed around her, lifting Gloriana and her burden.

On the shore a crying Oweena was reaching for them; the stick she had had no chance to use lay discarded nearby. She took the boy hastily from Gloriana and laid him on the grass.

Gloriana heard a sharp intake of breath and opened

her eyes to discover herself held tightly against a broad chest, and, lifting her gaze further, looked straight into the intent blue eyes of Graham Norton. Immediately she realized that his hands were grasping her bare legs and arm. The thin material of her wet chemise clung to her form, outlining and emphasizing every detail.

At any other time the modest Gloriana would have blushed furiously to be discovered in such a predicament, but now she had no time for embarrassment. Breathlessly she told Norton to put her down; then she rushed to the still, limp form of the child.

He had swallowed seemingly gallons of lake water. She pumped furiously, trying to get it all out of him, then showed Norton how and he pumped some more. Then pushing on his lungs in a rhythmic motion, she tried to revive the child, to coax his lungs to take a breath and his heart to start pumping again. For ten minutes she worked, the weakness of a moment before seemingly forgotten.

Oweena was sobbing softly and a grim Graham Norton was getting up the courage to persuade her to stop when the child coughed suddenly and began to take in great raspy breaths.

"We've got to get him back to Uncle and the hospital," Gloriana told a jubilant Norton. "Is your horse nearby? Can you take him?"

"He is, but in case you haven't noticed, it's nearly dark, and you're more than three miles from the mission. This is no place for women alone at night."

"But the child must have a doctor immediately!" she told him, exasperated. How could she have forgotten what an unyielding man Graham Norton was?

However, Norton had an alternative in mind. Turning to Oweena, he asked her quietly, "Can you ride bareback?"

She nodded briefly.

Then he was on his feet, stripping the saddle and blanket from his horse and mounting Oweena on the animal's back with the child cradled carefully in front of her.

"Now ride!" he told her and pointed the horse in the direction of the mission. Oweena needed no further instruction. She grasped the reins expertly in one hand while holding the Indian boy tightly against her with the other and with a quick jab of her heels propelled the swift horse into the long swinging stride of his running gait.

"Smart girl," Graham told Gloriana as they watched the pair quickly spring out of sight. "She'll keep him at a run and avoid jarring the boy with a gallop, and with her light weight they could make it all the way to the mission before he breaks gait.'

"Why did you take off the saddle?" Gloriana asked curiously. She was shivering now and feeling at last the embarrassment of her condition, but she was determined to keep up a polite conversation.

"So you could have this," he told her and, picking up the saddle blanket, shook it out and quickly wrapped it around her. The wool had a strong horsy smell and it made her itch, but the warmth from the big animal's body still clung to the blanket and felt delightful against Gloriana's icy skin.

Norton seemed to avoid looking in her direction while he flung himself into gathering wood and making a fire. Finally, he went in search of her clothes. Fortunately, she had not thrown anything into the water, and he soon returned with petticoat and dress. She had to send him back again for her shoes and stockings. They had not fared as well and somehow had been knocked into the water during their berry-picking. He had set them carefully by the fire when Gloriana remembered the huckleberries and sent him to find both the pails and the apron filled with fruit.

"Now Tildy can make her pies," she told him appreciatively when those too had been retrieved.

Behind the mountains to the west the sun was setting. The orange-gold rays struck the lake, setting it ablaze with dancing lights. In the enchantment of the moment Gloriana discovered Graham had somehow found his way to her side. His fingers reached out to wander playfully through her curling tangles of hair, then turned her face gently toward him.

Gloriana supposed she should push him away, but her hands were busy clutching the blanket around her. She was fascinated at how soft Graham's usually hard mouth could become as his lips moved gently on hers. The feather-light kisses teased and excited, tempting her to press her own lips tightly against his. Whether she gave in to the temptation or not, Gloriana was in too much of a daze to be sure, but suddenly Graham drew back. His breath was ragged and his voice, husky.

"Glory, you are such an innocent!" he tried to laugh. "Don't you know how enticing you are, how tempting being with you like this is to a man?"

Gloriana looked at him, wide-eyed and uncomprehending. The blanket had slipped slightly around her shoulders, exposing her white skin to the rosy glow of the firelight. What was he saying? She tried to think. Did he mean he had kissed her because it was what any man would do? Did he mean he did not care about her as a person but had found the situation and her vulnerability irresistible?

She was not aware of the mirror which her expressive face made for those thoughts, nor of the valiant struggle of the man who held her to control his baser instincts and protect her innocence. She did recognize the note of passion in his groan and the urgency with which his arms tightened around her. She tried to pull away but was helpless against the iron muscles pressing her against him.

What might have happened neither would know. Through the darkness came the creaking sound of wagon wheels, and both realized that help was on its way from the mission.

"Here! Put these on quickly now," Graham handed Gloriana her clothes. He turned his back and seemed to be glowering into the darkness.

Gloriana had the rumpled garments securely in place by the time the wagon emerged from around a forested bend and pulled into the firelight. Dr. Windemere was sitting on the front seat with Gloriana's old friend Smitty. Her uncle was on the ground and taking her pulse with an experienced hand before Gloriana had a chance to say she was all right or to ask about the little boy. To her embarrassment, he insisted upon looking inside her throat, though he could see little in the firelight, and listening at her chest with the stethoscope that still hung conveniently about his neck. She thought she caught a glimpse of Graham Norton looking on and laughing but supposed she was wrong; his sudden, inexplicable anger could not have dissipated so quickly.

Finally her anxious uncle was reassured enough to answer her questions.

"The boy will be fine. Midfield was still watching him when I left, but his breathing is regular. You did a fine job, my dear. The child has you to thank for saving his life." He then turned toward Graham Norton. "And if what I gather from Oweena's nearly hysterical story is accurate, we have you to thank for saving both of them. How can we repay you?"

Norton apparently interpreted the question as a rhetorical one, for he did not answer, but the two men clasped hands in a firm gesture that showed clearer than words a mutual respect. However, a moment later as they turned away to climb into the wagon, Gloriana thought she heard a short laugh and the words, "I'll think of something."

The wagon was a two-seated buckboard, its back seat piled high with blankets—probably sent by the quick-thinking Tildy when she heard about Gloriana's swim in the lake. Graham helped Gloriana up, then climbed up beside her, while Dr. Windemere scrambled in beside Smitty who handled the team.

"Wrap her in those blankets, Graham, or Tildy will have my head," the doctor confirmed Gloriana's guess, then turned back to speak to Smitty.

There was a little smile on Graham Norton's face as he carefully followed orders, perhaps tucking a bit more here and reaching around her a bit more there than was strictly necessary for Gloriana's comfort.

"That's quite enough," she told him after a moment. "Any more, and I won't be able to breathe."

The trip back to the mission went much more slowly than the trip out, but in spite of Smitty's care the jarring of the wagon made every bone in Gloriana's body ache. Graham noticing her discomfort, put a protecting arm around her and told her quietly to lean against him.

"You probably have strained every muscle and maybe picked up some bruises," he told her and threatened to call on her uncle for support if she would not do as he said. Blushingly aware of the two men in the front of the wagon, Gloriana tried resting ever so slightly against the strong arm that encircled her. She was soon forced to admit that Graham took much of the shock of bumps and dips for her and gradually found herself nestling more snugly in his arm. Although her uncle glanced back at them from time to time, he gave no sign of noticing that his niece was in the embrace of a man. However, after a glance or two, he did seem to become excessively cheerful, even beginning to whistle the Doxology in his off-tune way and to a totally inappropriate, lilting rhythm.

It took more than half an hour to reach the mission. To Gloriana's surprise they found the cozy living room of the main cabin occupied not only by the mission staff and two or three of Norton's men but also by a family of settlers.

"They came up from San Francisco on the same packet you took," Graham explained hastily to Gloriana. She filled in the rest, imagining the trip overland through the redwoods and then a delightful stop at Applegate Landing.

Roger Welsh was the man's name and he proudly introduced his large family. There was his wife Eugenia, a pale, washed-out woman whose drooping shoulders and listless face showed the effects of too much work and too much childbearing. Five sons ranged in age from about twenty-six to three, and for a moment, Gloriana looked at the fairy-like daughter Bridgette. She felt a rush of intense pleasure as she realized how much the girl looked like her own sister Juliana.

"I am sure we will be great friends," she said impulsively, then immediately regretted the words as she realized the pale blue eyes in the china doll face were cold and calculating.

But it was too late to retract. Bridgette rose to offer her hand, all the while casting sly glances at Graham from under eyelashes that fluttered provocatively. "Thank you, Miss Windemere," she said in a voice that oozed with sweetness and trembled slightly, as though to show how timid and overwhelmed she actually was. "I can't tell you how much it will mean to me to have an older friend like you—someone I can rely on for advice and spiritual guidance."

Gloriana barely suppressed a little gasp, and behind her she thought she heard Graham Norton swallow a laugh.

CHAPTER 11

IN THE DAYS THAT FOLLOWED, the briefly placid mission became once again a hub of frenzied activity. Graham Norton's project for Dr. Windemere was a quadrangle of buildings including a large steeple-topped church to replace the original chapel. The men soon added an orphanage to their plans, for the epidemic had left the mission with nearly twenty homeless children to care for.

"We'll get the walls up and the roofs on before snow flies," Norton said confidently. "Then we can spend the winter putting in floors and finishing up the insides."

It seemed incredible that so much could be done in such a short time. But as the nearby forest rang with the sound of axes and the heavy mule teams churned up dust pulling the straight, sweet-smelling logs to the mission, it began to seem possible.

The site of the building activity was set back from the lake in a sheltered saddle of land. Framed by the log cabins was a beautiful artesian spring, bubbling up from deep inside the ground with such force that

Graham said it would neither freeze in the winter nor dry up in the summer. Giant willows bent possessively over the water; their great girth and luxuriously sweeping branches attested to both the faithfulness of the spring and the richness of the land.

Gloriana had little time to savor the enlargement of her community, for the hospital was busy once again. Colds and pneumonia, aggravated by the deceptive weather—mild during the day but dropping lower each night—afflicted the resident Klamaths, while three of the women who had had measles had given birth to babies with congestion already in their lungs.

Equally distressing were the attacks on miners and settlers by the renegade war party. One man, surprised panning gold only a few miles from the mission had been robbed, scalped, and left for dead. A family of Swedish dairy farmers—too unfamiliar with the language to do more than identify their attackers as Indians—had seen their home on the Lost River burned and looted as they brought their cows in for the evening milking. They had escaped, but others had not. Word came by travelers and scouts of burned cabins and missing wagon trains, and almost daily the wilderness hid more unmarked graves.

For Gloriana the attacks brought the added burden of doubt. She could not help wondering if their Indian friends were responsible for those atrocities. There had been no problem with the renegades during the measles epidemic, but now reports were increasing daily. Moreover, it seemed the war party had shifted its activities from the coast and Applegate Landing to the area immediately surrounding Klamath Lake. That this shift had almost coincided with the arrival of Chief John and Keintepoos deepened her suspicions, though she kept reminding herself of the different costumes of the renegades she had seen.

"But how do I know they don't dress differently when they're on the warpath?" Gloriana asked herself. She was on her knees scrubbing the floor of the small alcove of the hospital that served as a baby ward. Some of the Klamaths who resided at the mission would have helped her, she knew, but she also was well aware that they found her passion for soap and water astonishing, to say the least. Although they would use hot water and soap every crack and corner if she kept after them, the Klamaths found her demands unreasonable, and to avoid offending them by barking like a drill sergeant, Gloriana preferred to do the job herself.

Moreover, working physically would usually take her mind off her problems. Today, however, was an exception, and her mind chewed trouble like a dog a dry bone—distastefully but relentlessly.

"Need some help?"

She looked up in exasperation to see one of her major troubles, Graham Norton, grinning at her from the open doorway. He had what appeared to be a picnic basket over one arm and looked rather boyishly handsome with his head uncovered and his flame-red hair curling damply as though he had washed away the grime of his morning's toil by ducking his entire head and face in a bucket.

"You didn't come to lunch, so Tildy sent me with this," he said cheerfully, holding up the basket. He seemed oblivious to the indignity of her condition, but Gloriana was acutely aware of the wet strands of hair straying across her cheeks and forehead, her soapy arms with the sleeves rolled up above her elbow, and her wet and grimy uniform.

"I can't imagine what possessed her to send you," Gloriana faltered. Then realizing how ungracious she sounded, she added, "That is, Tildy should know how busy you are." She continued kneeling on the floor, not knowing which would be more awkward—remaining in that position or struggling to her feet. Graham settled the matter by grasping her arm with his free hand and pulling her up beside him. "I volunteered," he told her, still grinning, and before she knew what was happening, Gloriana found herself outside beneath a willow tree, ready for a picnic lunch.

Tildy's food was, as usual, delicious, but the quantity as well as the extra treats showed clearly that this lunch had been made as much for Graham, who was a great favorite with Dr. Windemere's housekeeper, as for Gloriana. There was chicken pie—a delicious filling of egg and chicken meat in a tart of flaky pie crust—thick wedges of goat cheese to be eaten with slices of freshly baked bread, a potato salad dressed with Tildy's special mayonnaise, and enormous slices of huckleberry pie for dessert.

"I can see you have gotten on Tildy's good side," Gloriana laughed as she surveyed the contents of the basket.

"Amazing woman, that Tildy," Graham admitted readily. "Good source of information, too. For instance, how else would I have found out about my archrival?"

Gloriana paled slightly, and he seemed to notice, for he added wryly, "I am talking about Chief John, of course."

"Of course," Gloriana repeated quickly, then went on to tell him about the momentous day when she had attracted the chief's attention. "I'll have you know the chief considered me such a prize that he offered Uncle fifty horses for me," she concluded.

"I'll give him a hundred," Graham shot back softly with another of the dangerous smiles that seemed to turn Gloriana's insides upside down, sending her heart up into her throat and making her breath come in little gasps.

The tension of the moment was relieved by their determined attack on Tildy's food. By the time most of it was gone, Gloriana's embarrassment had passed, and she was ready to talk to Graham about what had been bothering her all morning. She told him about her own early suspicions and then her doubt that the renegades and the war party that had helped the mission could be the same. "Still Oweena admits that they are on the warpath," Gloriana finished, feeling at once relieved to have voiced her fears and disloyal for repeating her friend's words.

Graham seemed puzzled but skeptical. "I understand your wish for their innocence. I feel the same. Still, if we look at it from the Klamaths' point of view, they have every right to wage war on the people who have invaded their lands. Besides, if it is not Keintepoos and Chief John, who could it be? What other tribes are on the warpath?"

Gloriana had no answer for that, but she still did not feel satisfied, and some of her earlier exasperation with Graham Norton returned.

"I'll keep my eyes open," he said—rather offhandedly, Gloriana thought. "For now I had better get back to my crew, or they will think it's a holiday." He rose and, after stretching lazily, headed for the doctor's cabin with the remains of their picnic lunch. Just before the path ducked around the corner of the hospital, he turned and winked teasingly at Gloriana. "Remember to tell your uncle about my offer." He was gone before she could think of what he meant; then she remembered the hundred horses and blushed hotly.

"If Graham Norton thinks that will serve for a proposal, he is sadly mistaken," she said so loudly that she woke several patients inside the hospital from their afternoon naps. She ignored, for the moment, the fact that she had somehow made the tacit assumption that the man would propose and that he was, indeed, thinking of marriage.

She had found her way back to her cleaning and had

100

just fetched a fresh supply of hot water when the squeaking board just inside the entrance to her small ward signaled yet another visitor. Glancing over her shoulder, Gloriana was not surprised to see Bridgette Welsh. The Welshes had decided to make their winter home in one of the new cabins at the mission and then move on to their own land in the spring. In the meantime Bridgette had attached herself firmly to Gloriana, relying, as she said frequently, upon the "older woman's advice."

"What can I do for you, Bridgette? I'm busy getting ready for some new arrivals," was Gloriana's discouraging greeting. She feared she would have sunk to absolute rudeness before spring came.

"I'm sorry to be such a bother," the girl began hesitantly, taking a short step backward and faltering in the timid way men seemed to consider so endearing. Gloriana found it unbearably irritating.

"Did you want something?" she prodded, letting the impatience creep into her voice.

"Well, if it isn't too much trouble, I just wanted your advice. You seem to know Graham Norton so well—that is, you seem to be such good friends; I thought you would be able to tell me whether you thought this dress would be appropriate for a moonlight walk by the lake." She twirled around to give Gloriana the full effect of a tight-waisted gauze and lace creation in a shade of blue that enhanced the blond beauty's fragility and air of innocence.

"Don't you think you should ask the man to take you before you plan what to wear?" Gloriana's tone held only a little of the exasperation she felt with this simpering miss.

"Why, Miss Windemere, whatever must you think of me? A lady never asks a gentleman, and I hope I have not forgotten that. Mr. Norton has already requested my company, of course."

To the repeated inquiry about the obviously summer dress, Gloriana managed some comment about the evening chill along the lake. She did not miss the little gleam of triumph in Bridgette Welsh's eyes and for the thousandth time wished her own face were not quite so revealing of her thoughts.

She did not think for a minute that the girl's insinuations were true. Graham Norton had shown much more than a friendly interest in Gloriana herself. Hadn't she been certain just today that his intentions toward her were serious, that he was beginning to think about marriage? Still she remembered wondering that night by the lake whether Graham's ardor was the product of too much moonlight and a romantic campfire.

Moreover, men did seem enchanted with Bridgette Welsh. She had the qualities that Gloriana had always found most deficient in herself. Where Gloriana was strong and self-reliant, Bridgette was like the society dolls back home in Philadelphia, waiting to lean on a man's strong arm and cling helplessly while he faced life's trials alone. Gloriana tended to speak her mind and never worried about deferring to men's opinions; Bridgette seemed to have no thoughts in her own head and waited only to hear some man's ideas before adopting them for her own. And where Gloriana had her share of beauty in flawless skin, glorious hair, and a full womanly figure, she felt like a Juno—huge and awkward—beside petite, graceful Bridgette.

Even Uncle calls her a "delightful girl," Gloriana thought with just a trace of resentment at the blindness of men.

Norton usually took his evening meal with the Windemeres, and tonight was no exception. They sat at a round, carved dining table which, unlike most of their furniture, had been carefully finished. A white tablecloth, silver, and china made the meal seem almost like dining back home, and Gloriana continually appreciated this ritual of civilization that reminded her each evening of their roots and their ambitions for the wilderness.

Dr. Windemere, who preferred to give his thanks for a meal after, rather than before, it had been eaten, began on his roast venison with a gusto that promised to add more pounds to his already ample girth.

"My Klamath weatherman tells me that it will snow soon," the doctor told Graham. "I have never known him to fail. Do you think the cabins will be roofed in time?"

The progress on the new buildings had been little short of miraculous. In just a matter of days walls had risen and stone fireplaces had been built and tested. Loads of an attractive red clay had been hauled in which would later on make a kind of plaster for the inside walls, and the men had split stacks of heavy shake shingles that would be laid in overlapping rows for a watertight roof.

"We need two more days of clear weather, so remember that in your prayers," Graham answered with a humorous glance in Gloriana's direction.

"I will do so," Dr. Windemere returned seriously, before changing the subject to a German philosopher named Kant, whose works he and Norton had been reading.

At first Gloriana had been startled to hear that Graham Norton, the gun-packing Westerner, was interested in philosophy, but the man, as she was learning, was full of surprises. Moreover, she was beginning to suspect that philosophy was a way to escape something he could not bring himself to face in his own spirit.

Tonight, as on many other nights, the subject was goodness and moral behavior. Graham advocated a universal moral law which he said was a law of nature.

"The only good possible in this life," he was saying, "is a good will. Otherwise, what is my good

103

may not be your good. What's good for the white man is rarely good for the Indians. We bring them civilization, which for us is good but for them means loss of dignity, sickness, and degradation."

"There is a higher good," Dr. Windemere responded, "and that goodness is God Himself. His good will extends beyond this short life into the next one and even goes so far as to blend the up-and-down patterns of individual existence to 'work together for our good'."

Usually Gloriana joined in their spirited discussions, but tonight she only listened. She had no doubt that Graham Norton was a good man according to his own standards. She knew that he would not intentionally do anything to hurt anyone. Yet she knew just as surely that his own moral code allowed him much more latitude than her Christian principles allowed her. If he felt that no one would be hurt by his actions, he would have no remorse, he said, about violating any of Christianity's laws. Did that include the laws of marriage, the special bonds and sacraments that Christ had established for the family and for the love of men and women? Could a woman ever fully trust a man who did not share her beliefs and values?

"Gloriana, my dear, I have spoken twice," Dr. Windemere broke through her musings to request a fresh cup of coffee and more of Tildy's buttery popovers.

Gloriana felt Graham's eyes follow her curiously as she hurried from the room.

You might as well come right out and tell him something's bothering you, Gloriana scolded herself angrily.

After dinner the men enjoyed a quiet pipe by the fireplace—a luxury which Graham's thoughtfulness in bringing an ample supply of tobacco had enabled the doctor to enjoy once again.

He is a good man—in many ways, Gloriana

104

reminded herself; then the vague suspicion planted in her mind by Bridgette's visit to the hospital returned, and she remembered for the first time in days that Graham Norton would not be good for her unless he shared her faith. Making an excuse about being tired, Gloriana tried to escape to her room, only to have Graham follow her.

"We'll find out the truth soon enough, Glory," he told her softly, and glancing over his shoulder to see if her uncle were watching, he touched her gently and looked longingly at her lips.

He thinks I'm really worried about the renegades, Gloriana thought. She knew she should move but it seemed she was rooted in place, held by the masculine appeal and fascination of this complex man.

"Graham, how about a game of chess?" her uncle's call broke the spell, and Gloriana retreated thankfully to her room where she alternately wrote in her journal and dreamed away the next hour.

Klamath Mission   November 7, 1851

Life at the mission has grown more complicated with the new arrivals. Graham Norton and his men follow their own schedule of dawn-to-dusk work. Rarely is there a moment when the air is not filled with the sounds of axes chopping or men shouting.

They treat the religious life of the mission with respect, and I suspect that several of the younger men remember Christian homes, but they do not join us. Once Smitty stepped into chapel for a few minutes, but he left after the song service was over.

The Welshes are of another faith, and so they do not attend our services either. I know our Indian flock wonders why the white people do not worship together. I do not know how to tell them that all our people do not follow the Jesus way; I don't think they would understand that it is possible for people to know about Christ, yet not follow Him—or follow Him in such different ways that we must have many different churches to express our belief in Him.

Sometimes I find myself looking back almost longingly to the days of the epidemic when all at the mission seemed united in a common cause. I cannot help thinking how much easier the Klamaths are to reach than are our own people. With them there are no elaborate philosophical or doctrinal differences to overcome; they simply hear and believe.

Uncle told me that when the fur traders first came to this country, they brought Bibles for use at funerals and weddings. They told the Indians only that it was the White Man's Book of Heaven and that teachers would come later to tell them the way. Yet no teachers came, and finally four Nez Perce chiefs traveled east to St. Louis to ask the missionaries to come. Two of the chiefs died on the way. The remaining two wrung the hearts of the Christians when they asked what had happened to the teachers. "My people," one of the chiefs said, "will die in darkness and they will go a long path to other hunting grounds. No white man will go with them and no white man's Book will make the way plain."

I think of those words whenever the hardships make me question our being here and whenever I wonder whether God is blessing our efforts. But always the valiant appeal of those chiefs will remind me of how these people hunger for God and how we, who have been blessed with so much knowledge, take Him for granted.

Hardly an hour had passed before Gloriana heard voices below signaling the end of the chess game. At Graham Norton's good-night call, almost involuntarily, she turned down her lamp and, going to the window, opened the shutters slightly so that she could watch the man cross the compound.

A half moon lit the scene with a pale gold light. On the chill air came the sound of Graham's whistling— more tuneful than her uncle's. In the distance a cabin door opened, and Gloriana could hear the faint, high-pitched sound of a woman's laughter.

He walked with a leisurely step, stopping to look toward the lake and once appearing to glance toward her window. His own quarters were in one of the far north cabins, and he seemed to be moving steadily toward it—past the chapel, past the schoolhouse, across the quadrangle. She had nearly closed her shutters when the tall form took a sharp right, and Gloriana realized that he was entering the Welsh cabin. She did not wait to see whether he emerged again with the dainty Bridgette on his arm but fastened her shutters securely and went to bed with a little coldness about her heart which even nighttime prayers could not entirely dispel.

CHAPTER 12

DR. WINDEMERE'S "WEATHERMAN" proved once again his accuracy as the mission woke the next morning to a light dusting of snow. Overnight the temperature had dropped thirty degrees, and the golden sky of Indian summer had changed to the pale gray of winter.

Cold inside as well as out, Gloriana hurried through her day at the hospital, wishing for something to happen that would take her mind off Graham Norton.

"It's none of my business what he does," she reminded herself several times. Perhaps unnecessarily she added, "I am not in the least bit jealous of that little minx."

But she still felt curiously depressed, and she tried not to notice the looks of concern that Oweena sent cautiously in her direction or mind Dr. Windemere's heavy-handed teasing about her "red-haired beau."

The diversion she had hoped for came late that afternoon from a totally unexpected direction. Gloriana had finished her work and drifted to the window of the tiny children's ward to watch the storm. Snow had been falling for the past hour, but it seemed to come from high in the sky in great feathery flakes that floated leisurely to the ground, decorating the landscape without obscuring their view.

From her special vantage point Gloriana was the first to see them coming—a long straggling line of blue-coated soldiers. The ragged line and drooping riders told her before she could see the makeshift bandages that something was wrong.

Dr. Windemere and Dr. Midfield were both in the hospital, and, alerted by Gloriana's warning, they hurried to check their medical supplies. Gloriana and Oweena began to make up beds for the casualties. Oweena was oddly silent, but when Gloriana tried to draw her out, she responded readily enough.

She's worried about Keintepoos and the Indian braves, Gloriana thought, realizing that she shared that worry. Somehow the brave Indian men who had helped the mission seemed closer to her now than the soldiers who represented the faraway government of her country.

It took nearly half an hour for all the soldiers to ride into the mission. About half were wounded, five or six seriously, but all suffered from loss of blood and exposure. Lieutenant John Tilton was last. A dark stain marked his right trouser leg just above the knee, and he was reeling in the saddle, but he held his rifle ready across the saddle horn and his head turned continuously to check for pursuers.

"The renegades caught us at night," he told them as the mission staff eased the officer from his horse. "Burned the stockade. Wiped out Linkville. It was Keintepoos and Chief John." Then he slipped into unconsciousness.

Treatment for the men's wounds was complicated by the hours they had spent in the saddle. The attack had come, they said, before dawn, two days earlier. They had fought for twelve hours before abandoning the stockade and beginning a fighting retreat north. Blood had flowed and caked or frozen, making it necessary to soak their clothing before removing it. Boots had to be cut off swollen feet, for some had walked to save their horses for the fifty-mile flight. Already, open flesh showed the red edges and whitish pus that signaled infection.

Since the epidemic had left the mission low on cleansing agents, the doctors resorted to cauterizing wounds, and the sickening smell of burning flesh was added to the heavy hospital odors. At first Gloriana had been called on to hold the men through that agony, but her strength had proved unequal to the task, and some of the men in Graham Norton's crew had been applied to for help.

Graham himself had come with the first sign of trouble and had helped with the heavy work of lifting and undressing the men. He had looked sober while the soldiers told of the attack and cursed Keintepoos and his men, but he said nothing.

"What do you think of your Indian friends now?" Gloriana overheard Graham asking Dr. Windemere when their separate duties had brought them momentarily together. The doctor had said nothing but had shaken his head sadly, as though not understanding what was happening and not caring to speculate.

Oweena, who had been going about her work with an increasingly dark expression, also overheard. She turned to Gloriana and whispered angrily, "He did not do it. Keintepoos would not kill the people of Linkville."

Gloriana was more struck by what Oweena had not said than by what she had said, for Oweena did not deny that the warriors might have attacked the soldiers.

"Why is she so angry?" Lieutenant Tilton, whose bandages Gloriana had been checking, opened his eyes to ask.

"She's a good friend of Keintepoos," Gloriana spoke before she thought, then immediately regretted it. The cold speculative gleam in the officer's eye was unmistakable.

More than eight hours passed before all the wounded were treated, and the long watch for fever and complications began. In the mission kitchen the coffeepot once again bubbled day and night on the back of the black iron range, but now the dark brew was a mixture of grains with just a flavoring of their precious store of coffee. Graham and Gloriana sat on opposite sides of the rough, split-log table. Tildy had gone to take Gloriana's place beside the sick soldiers, and Dr. Windemere was resting on a cot in his hospital office. The stillness of the empty cabin was broken only by the ticking of a clock in a room somewhere behind them. Outside, the still-falling snow absorbed the night sounds of the mission, replacing them with an almost oppressive silence.

Gloriana had wriggled out of her shoes and wrapped her throbbing feet in her long skirt. Her back ached, and there was a dull, pulsing pain at her temples. Yet she was not too tired to feel a little glow of triumph as she remembered that Bridgette Welsh had been conspicuously absent all afternoon and evening. *That should show Graham how self-centered she is*, Gloriana thought, although she was honest enough to admit that he might consider Bridgette's helplessness attractively feminine. She glanced at him from beneath lowered lashes, wondering what he was thinking about. His big-boned hands held a brimming tin cup in front of him; his eyes seemed intent on the thin cloud of steam rising from the dark liquid; their expression was dark and brooding.

"I wish you hadn't told the lieutenant about Oweena and Keintepoos," Graham said finally, meeting her gaze seriously.

Gloriana flushed and looked down before she

111

admitted honestly, "So do I! The look on his face as soon as I said it made me want to kick myself." She hesitated a moment. "Graham, there's something I don't understand about this."

A little grin tugged at the edge of the man's mouth, puzzling her, until Gloriana realized that she had unconsciously used his first name. "The lieutenant said Keintepoos and Chief John attacked the fort, and even Oweena doesn't deny that they might have. Yet the lieutenant also calls them the renegades, as though they are the ones responsible for killing settlers and harming women and children, and I don't think that can be."

"Why can't it?" The lazy smile vanished, and Graham was all interest.

"Well, Oweena says Keintepoos would not kill settlers. She says he would not have massacred the people of Linkville."

"But couldn't she be mistaken? I gather she's in love with him."

Gloriana nodded briefly, acknowledging Graham's unspoken assumption that love could cloud a person's judgment. "Perhaps there is more than one band of renegades," she admitted, "but I am convinced that Keintepoos had nothing to do with taking our supplies when we were on the road to Applegate Landing." She told him about her sketches, and he asked to see her journal.

Soon they were occupied in studying her drawings. As Gloriana explained her suspicions and showed him the results of her attempts to remember, she was struck again by the difference between Keintepoos's warriors and the renegades who had shadowed the freight train.

"Oweena has told me that the warriors of each tribe have a characteristic costume, but the renegades don't dress like any of the Indians I have seen."

"Or like any of the tribes from around here,"

112

Graham added. "These shirts and the sashes look almost like the Navajo garb, but I have never heard of Navajos ranging this far north and west. There's some mystery here—something we're not seeing."

Gloriana looked up and found their faces just inches apart.

"I don't like your being involved in this," he told her, his voice softening suddenly, "but it seems you are whether I like it or not." The possessiveness in his manner sent a little thrill through Gloriana. "And I'm going to need your help to find out what's going on."

"What can I do?"

Graham looked for a moment as though he would put his arms around her but settled instead for taking her hand in both of his.

"Watch John Tilton!"

CHAPTER 13

THE ATMOSPHERE OF THE MISSION changed dramatically during the next few days, and with the snowfall—an accumulation of six inches on the ground and more choking the mountain passes—there seemed little likelihood of another change before spring. Instead of blending in a harmonious community, the different groups at the mission withdrew into themselves. The Indians became aloof and somber, while Graham Norton's work crew and the soldiers squared off warily, each watching the other with thinly veiled hostility.

The daily rituals of chapel and hospital rounds continued, but always in the background there were small groups of blue-uniformed men, watching and snickering about "Injuns that get religion" or glowering about Eastern busybodies' trying to "heal savages so they can kill more white men."

"The soldiers are destroying our work," Gloriana complained to Dr. Windemere. They were sitting beside a roaring fire in what Tildy liked to call the parlor. It was a rugged but comfortable room dominated by a massive stone fireplace that nearly covered one wall. Above the polished mantelpiece in the place of honor was an ornately carved peace pipe, a gift to Dr. Windemere from the Klamath chiefs when he had first sought to found a mission on the lake. The head of the pipe was carved from red pipestone, a rare substance in Oregon Territory and, therefore, probably passed from hand to hand over thousands of miles of trading; the smooth bowl ended in a rounded hatchet, symbol of the ill fortunes that would befall anyone who broke the sacred compact. With the pipe the chiefs had also presented the doctor with a sheepskin deed to three hundred acres of lakeshore land. Most importantly to Dr. Windemere, the pipe and the land had been clear gestures not only of friendship but also of welcome, and on that foundation he had built a work to last long after his Heavenly Father called him home.

His eyes were on the peace pipe as he tried to frame an answer for his niece. But even the memories of all that the Lord had done could not quite keep the discouragement from his voice. "Not destroying, my dear, but certainly setting us back."

They spoke in low tones, for both remembered that Lieutenant Tilton was lying in a small room at the back of the house. He had been moved just the day before when his bed in the hospital had been needed for an elderly Klamath who had succumbed to the twin winter maladies of pneumonia and frostbite. The lieutenant was no longer in danger, yet he was far from well enough to take up residence with his men. One of the half-finished log houses in the sheltered quadrangle served the soldiers as a barracks. The fireplaces were working overtime, but even the hottest fires could not keep the cold from the unfloored buildings.

"Can't we send them to Fort Winnemucca or even back to Applegate Landing?" Gloriana persisted, sure there must be some way to rid the mission of the disruptive soldiers.

"If I remember right, it was only recently that you were hoping and praying they would come," her uncle chided Gloriana gently. "We just have to keep believing that God has some plan in all of this."

Gloriana was silenced but not altogether satisfied. She did not see how God's work could be advanced nor Himself glorified by the mission's spending an anxious winter waiting for a fight to break out between the soldiers and Norton's workers, or for someone to run off with an Indian girl and set the peaceful mission Klamaths on the warpath. Moreover, she did not like the idea of having the troublesome lieutenant living in her own home. She supposed she should be thankful to have him close by; after all, Graham Norton had asked her to keep an eye on John Tilton. Where could she better do that than in the Windemere cabin? Yet she had become conscious during his days in the hospital of a warmth in the man's eyes as they followed her, and she felt oddly uncomfortable.

"No, I fear this is a mountain we must climb rather than move," her uncle had gone on, "and only the Lord knows what we will find on the other side."

They sat in silence for a few moments, Gloriana idly filling in the details of a sketch that she had begun earlier in the day.

"Well, if we can't change the make-up of the community, let's change its attitude," she told her uncle finally and launched into a plan that had been stirring in her mind for days. It was nearly the end of November; only three days remained until the twenty-sixth, the day which President Washington had proclaimed a National Day of Thanksgiving in 1789. There had been some talk about making that day a national holiday, but the Windemeres had not waited for any official proclamation. In their home and

116

church, they had regularly celebrated Thanksgiving for many years.

"What better way to bring all Americans together?" she persisted as Dr. Windemere shook his head doubtfully. "We'll recreate the first Thanksgiving feast when the Pilgrims and the Indians joined together in friendship as we at the Klamath Mission should be joined. And it will give you a chance to preach a true Thanksgiving message and remind all the people here of the real purpose of this community."

The good doctor wavered, but Gloriana's last point won him over. He had often said that the only way to end the fighting was to bring all Oregon peoples together in the worship of the one true God; then the senseless massacres would end, and this glorious golden West could become the paradise that Indians and settlers alike dreamed of.

"We'll do it!" he told her enthusiastically.

There was still Tildy to be won over. That conscientious housekeeper's first reaction was to throw up her hands and plop her stout form on the nearest kitchen chair. "Lands, child! Feed more than two hundred people at Thanksgiving dinner in just short of three days? It can't be done!"

Leaving her uncle to deal with his faithful Tildy, Gloriana donned her boots and hooded winter cloak to take the news of their plan to the Midfield cabin. Outside, the late afternoon glow in the west was dimming to twilight. Her eyes intent on stepping in other footprints in the snow, Gloriana did not see Graham until she nearly collided with him. Gloriana told him about the Thanksgiving feast, and she was annoyed when he continued to smile his amused, indulgent smile.

"I guess it takes a party to get a pretty female all worked up," he said finally.

"But it's not just a party. It's a celebration of thanks. Don't you see? We will get everyone to break

117

bread together, just like the Pilgrims and the Indians. Then perhaps we can be friends.''

"It will take more than breaking bread to make some of the people here friends," Graham told her skeptically. But in spite of his skepticism, he soon found he had promised to have his men erect temporary tables in the partially completed chapel, and he had even offered to supply venison and pheasants for the feast. Moreover, he followed along through the twilight toward the Midfield cabin, Gloriana's mittened hand tucked in the crook of his arm while his face wore a bewildered grin.

"Gloriana, Mr. Norton!" Catherine Midfield welcomed them. The summer glow in the cold-nipped faces made her exchange a significant look with her husband as they ushered the beaming couple into their cozy sitting room. Flowered drapes hung at the windows, braided rugs covered the floors, and enough bric-a-brac to warm the heart of any New England matron covered the furniture. Gloriana had made her own contribution to the back-East atmosphere with a pair of Boston watercolors done from memory—one of the Old North Church from whose tower had come the signal for Paul Revere's immortal ride and one of a triple-masted sailing vessel riding majestically amid smaller craft in the bay.

The Midfields too had been regular observers of Thanksgiving and were excited by the idea of resuming the custom in the West.

"If only we had some cranberries!" Catherine exclaimed wistfully. She had borne frontier life cheerfully, but as the time for her baby's arrival drew nearer, the woman's homesickness had become more urgent, evoking the pity and the concern of her friends.

"He seems like a dedicated man, but I don't think they will stay out here for long," Graham commented when he and Gloriana were once more out in the snow.

"Catherine misses home and church socials, and she's worried about raising a child out here." Gloriana would have confided more, but at that moment a treacherous ice slick hidden by the snow pulled her feet from under her. Graham grabbed for her but too late and instead of keeping them both upright landed with Gloriana in a heap of snow.

Anxiously Graham pulled himself up and bent over the still prone girl. The laughing face calmed his fears, and Gloriana began to tell him of winter mornings spent tobogganing and ice skating in Philadelphia.

"I didn't know proper young ladies did those things!" Graham seemed both delighted and amazed as he helped her to her feet, taking full advantage of the opportunity to let his arms encircle her.

"But you see, I was never a very proper young lady."

He grinned and pulled her close. "I never did care much for those delicate, proper creatures."

"Really? I thought that every man adored the pale, fragile type." Gloriana cast a flirtatious look at him from beneath long sweeping eyelashes, but Graham would not rise to the bait.

"Glory, don't flirt with me unless you mean it," he told her with a grin and a little squeeze that suggested what might happen if she ignored his warning.

Although she had planned to go only to visit the Midfields, Gloriana decided now to go on to the Welsh cabin. The pioneer family had been settled in a building that would one day be the mission's administrative offices. Two stories high, it made a spacious winter home, although Gloriana privately wondered if the settlers properly appreciated her uncle's generosity in allowing them to occupy it.

Of all the inhabitants of the mission, the Welshes alone had seemed to enjoy the increased possibility for social life which the coming of the soldiers presented. Each night they played host to several men, and tonight was no exception. As she and Graham entered the cabin, Gloriana noticed two blue-coated soldiers still at the dinner table; the others had apparently just gotten up, for a harrassed-looking Mrs. Welsh was hurriedly clearing stacks of dirty dishes.

Bridgette Welsh was on a comfortable settee by the fireplace. Wearing a charming confection of light blue silk and playing off the attentions of the soldier sitting beside her against those of the soldier leaning over the back of the sofa, she seemed in her element. However, the welcome that had leaped to the girl's face when she saw Graham cooled perceptibly when she noticed who was with him.

But Mr. Welsh came forward with an expansive grin and a warm handshake and ushered them to a bench by the fire. His jollity puzzled Gloriana, for she had thought him an almost grim man; then she noticed the tankard in his hand and in those of the other men in the room. Suddenly she understood the almost unnatural air of hilarity in the cabin. To her amazement, sitting quietly by the fire were two of the younger men from the Klamath settlement. Their eyes seemed slightly glazed, as though they didn't see her, and by each of their sides was one of the large, pewter tankards.

"Miss Windemere, would you care to go upstairs to freshen up?" Bridgette asked sweetly after a moment. "You do look as though you took a tumble in the snow." Then her eyes spotted the traces of white on Graham Norton's broad back and the flakes in his hair.

"They look like they've both been rolling in the snow," one of the soldiers commented with a significant raise of his eyebrows that made the other guffaw coarsely.

Sensing the fury ready to erupt in Graham, Gloriana hurried ahead with her explanation of the Thanksgiv-

120

ing celebration. For once Bridgette seemed genuinely delighted, and she eagerly made promises for her family's contribution to the feast—promises which her father seconded heartily and to which her mother, in between trips to clear the table, assented with a meek smile.

Ordinarily Gloriana would have stayed to help that sad woman with the mountain of dishes that seemed to be her chore alone, but tonight she felt an urgent need to be out of that cabin with its artificial gaiety and undercurrents of domestic problems.

"I should have warned you about that place," Graham told her outside.

Gloriana tried to ignore the implication that he had spent enough evenings there to be well acquainted with the Welshes' social habits. "Does he always give drink to the Indians?"

"This is the first time I have seen it, but I doubt it will be the last. When the snows melt, Welsh plans to set up a trading post on his land claim. As far as I could see on the trip out, the only things he brought to trade were cases of whiskey."

Night had fallen and the sky shone with the cold, winking light of faraway stars. There was no moon, but the starlight reflected from the white snow with a shimmering glow. They crossed the wooded park at the center of the triangle. Even without their leaves the willows looked graceful and shapely, pale gray sentinels for the artesian spring. Amazingly the waters still bubbled and frothed, though ice had formed around the edge of the pond and snow covered the surrounding rocks.

They had paused a moment beside the spring when Gloriana felt Graham's hands on her shoulders turning her toward him. But instead of pulling her to him, Graham lifted her chin with a heavily gloved finger and tried to make her look at him.

"Glory, will you let me kiss you and admit that you

121

want to as much as I do, or do we have to go on pretending that I am stealing kisses from a very proper young miss?"

His words stung but his eyes were tender and compelling. He seemed to read the answer he wanted in her face, for when his cold lips touched and warmed against hers, the kiss was bolder and more demanding—the confident lovemaking of an accepted sweetheart. When after a moment her arms seemed to find their own way about his neck, Graham clasped her so tightly that Gloriana could barely breathe, and she tried to pull herself away with a shy laugh.

He let her go but only a few inches before he caught her back again. With his face pressed into the crown of curls at the top of her head, he breathed huskily, "Glory, darling, now what do you want to do about us?"

Us—Graham's voice lingered over the word, filling it with significance and magic, but warning signals were going off inside Gloriana's head.

"I need time to think," she faltered. He seemed disappointed but not overwhelmingly so.

"I've got to say this for your God," he said at last, smiling down at her. "He's finally done one good thing for me; He brought you here."

The words broke through the raptures of physical sensation to remind Gloriana of the barrier of faith between her and this man.

"Hasn't He ever done anything else for you?" she asked, not quite ready to start a discussion of their spiritual differences, yet curious all the same.

Graham, however, was unresponsive. Instead of answering, he began kissing her again, until he broke away with a shaky laugh and pleaded breathlessly, "Think, Glory, but don't think too long."

He held her carefully with his arm as they crossed the remaining yards to the Windemere cabin. Once he asked her if she was cold, and Gloriana discovered to her amazement that she was not; still she nodded that she was so that he would draw her closer. Another time they stopped to look toward the nearby lake, gleaming with the reflection of the silver starlight.

They had just realized that it was late, and neither had eaten dinner when a slim shadow darted out of the darkness and pulled them both urgently toward the cabin where Tildy and the Indian girls lived.

Even in the dim light, Gloriana could tell Oweena had been crying. "Don't speak. The lieutenant will hear," she whispered desperately. Gloriana and Graham exchanged a look filled with apprehension, then followed her as quietly as the crunching snow would allow.

Inside the cabin the lamps had been turned down, and the girls had pulled the curtains tightly. As Gloriana had half-begun to suspect, there was a still form lying on one of the beds. It took a full half-minute for Gloriana to recognize the proud Chief Keintepoos as the haggard warrior lying as though already dead.

"My land, girl, don't you know what the soldiers will do if they find him here?" Graham exclaimed as he too recognized the man.

"He was wounded in the fight, and there is infection. We must help," Oweena insisted, her agitated face showing the signs of nearing hysteria. The other girls crowded around them, adding their pleas.

"I'll get Uncle," Gloriana said at last.

"No!" He had seemed to be unconscious, but Keintepoos opened his eyes and spoke with surprising firmness. The broken body Gloriana hardly recognized, but the courageous spirit that looked out through those commanding eyes was that of the chief she remembered so well. And in spite of the attack on the soldiers, in spite of the rumors and accusations, she found herself once again trusting this man. He

123

seemed to gather his strength, then went on with quiet dignity. "It is time for Keintepoos to die. I have come because Oweena is Christian. If I die without becoming Christian, we will go to different hunting grounds and our parting will be forever. I will take your Jesus path and go to heaven and wait for her there."

Tears rushed into Gloriana's eyes as she realized what the man was trusting her to do. Oweena had flung herself down beside the bed and, holding the chief's hand in both of hers, was sobbing. He spoke to her softly in their own tongue, then turned to Gloriana. "Keintepoos is ready."

But never had Gloriana felt less ready to lead a soul to Christ. Hadn't she just spent an hour behaving like a lovestruck schoolgirl with a man she knew was forbidden? Didn't she have some things to make right with her Saviour before she came to the Throne of Grace?

Perhaps this is what is meant by being "instant in season and out of season," Gloriana thought. Thanking God that the warrior knew English well and language would be no barrier, she began to tell him the greatest of all stories. When she came at last to the death on the cross, she saw the man's face soften with emotion, and she knew that whatever had been his original motives, Keintepoos had transcended them and believed. She remembered then that she had often questioned the sincerity of Oweena's Christian commitment, so she had her join hands with her sweetheart. Together they prayed a simple sinners' prayer that left Gloriana crying and, if she had but seen it, Graham Norton awed and shaken.

With the soul saved, the battle began to save the man's life. Graham had more experience with gunshot wounds than Gloriana, and he soon pronounced the problem to be a bullet embedded in the muscles of the right shoulder.

"For this we will need Uncle's medical bag at

124

least," Gloriana said and, bundling herself up, she hurried next door. To her dismay she found Lieutenant Tilton comfortably positioned on the sitting room couch, a heavy afghan wrapped around his legs, the only evidence of his invalid state.

"There you are, my dear. I was just telling the lieutenant about your excellent plan," her uncle halted her but, with a little apologetic smile, motioned to his back and did not rise. "A slight twinge of rheumatism," he called it, but Gloriana suspected the onset of arthritis.

"I've been spreading the word," she said with all the cheeriness she could muster. "The Midfields will contribute and also the Welshes. Oh, and Mr. Norton's men will supply venison and pheasants."

"Well, well! It's amazing what a pretty girl can accomplish in the space of a few hours, isn't it, Lieutenant?"

The officer agreed readily and lavished a few compliments on Gloriana's glowing cheeks and red lips. Then he added, "It will be good for the men to have something to occupy them for a day or two. For myself I prefer Christmas—especially since I hear the mistletoe grows abundantly in these forests." He looked meaningfully at Gloriana and laughed when the roses in her cheeks grew rosier.

At that moment Tildy came in and began to scold her for being late for dinner. All the while Gloriana was painfully aware that every second could mean the difference between Keintepoos's living or dying. Finally in desperation she drew her uncle aside and whispered that she needed his medical bag for some task in the next cabin. As she should have expected, the doctor insisted upon going himself, and Tildy demanded to know which of her girls was sick.

Feeling John Tilton's suddenly suspicious eyes on her, Gloriana cast around for a logical explanation. "Is someone injured?" he demanded with a slight edge to his voice that told her he was remembering the stories of Keintepoos and Chief John's kindness to the mission and already was forming a half-guess. "If you must know," she burst out suddenly, "yes, there is something wrong. One of the Klamath girls has been attacked, and I seriously suspect one of your men of being responsible!"

Tilton looked startled, but she could see he believed her, and a fierce tension seemed to drain out of him with his suspicions. Her uncle and Tildy, however, were stunned. Both rushed for the cabin next door with stricken faces that said they somehow felt responsible for this calamity. They had barely gotten through the door before Dr. Windemere's repeated, "Shocking! Shocking!" changed to a businesslike, "Ah, I see." And he set to work.

CHAPTER 14

THE NEXT THREE DAYS, which had promised so much delightful diversion, became a nightmare. The mission bustled with the activities of preparation. The Thanksgiving feast would be held appropriately in the new meeting hall, and temporary tables of long, hand-hewn boards were being hastily erected on homemade sawhorses.

The young Welshes and some of the Klamaths took over decorating the partially finished hall, and soon the dirt floor was covered with sweet-scented wild hay. Shocks of Indian corn, colorful with their mixture of blue, black, yellow, and red kernels, adorned walls and the mantels of the huge open fireplace. Entire sheaves of dried cornstalks were brought in with the round golden pumpkins harvested earlier from Tildy's garden to fill the corners.

Through the bustle, the mission staff—all by now aware of the situation—hurried with bright smiles and troubled eyes. If the prayers at the morning services were a little more fervent than usual, observers put it down to the religious dimensions of the coming celebration or even to the missionaries' concern over the abused Indian girl.

Meant to be a profound secret, Gloriana's fabrication had spread quickly. Tensions had escalated between the workmen and the soldiers, threatening to disrupt the feast, until Lieutenant Tilton promised to find and punish the man. A delegation of wizened old men from the Klamath settlement had visited Dr. Windemere in protest and had to be let in on the secret. And Tildy scolded Gloriana soundly for ruining her credibility as a chaperone and guardian of her girls.

Fortunately, Gloriana had not mentioned a name, although she strongly suspected that none of the girls, including Oweena, would have minded slandering one of the bluecoats. She held firmly to this refusal, in spite of the lieutenant's protest that he needed to question the girl so that he could begin looking for the attacker.

Meanwhile Keintepoos fought for his life in one cabin while a few yards away Lieutenant Tilton regained his strength.

The lieutenant was a problem. Leaning on a cane, he managed to find his way to every room in the Windemere cabin, particularly if Gloriana was there. And she, remembering that he had thirty-nine able men at the mission and a legitimate reason for hating Keintepoos, appeared kinder than she felt.

"What is a lovely thing like you doing in a place like this?"

Gloriana, on her knees in the storeroom, turned and tried to summon a smile. She had been looking for a precious jar of nutmeg that Tildy needed for the pumpkin pies and had not heard John Tilton enter, but still she was not surprised to find him hovering behind her. With a lopsided bandage around his head and leaning heavily on his makeshift cane, he looked vulnerable, and a flashing smile added an almost boyish charm to his features. Yet Gloriana could not escape the feeling of menace whenever she was near him.

"You are a flatterer, Lieutenant," she forced a light, teasing tone. "In this old housedress and with my hair bound in a rag, I can hardly be called lovely."

"But to her most devoted admirer, Cinderella is merely in disguise," Tilton responded gallantly and offered a hand to help her to her feet.

She accepted reluctantly, then wished she had not as his hand grasped hers with surprising energy.

"What a crime it is to bury a glorious creature like you in the wilderness." He still held onto her hand, and the warmth in his eyes was unmistakable.

"How silly! Nobody is burying me here. I chose to come."

But he went on as though he had not heard her, "You should be dressed in silks and satins and spend your days gossiping and drinking tea and your nights dancing and flirting."

Gloriana snatched her hand away impatiently and tried to slip past him to the door. The tiny room was dark and close, and the musty odors of dust and stagnant air mingled with the more pleasant smells of spices and drying fruit. The ceiling-high shelves that lined the walls were stuffed full of jars, tins, and sacks—an effective barrier against sound, and the door, which the lieutenant had nearly closed behind him, admitted only a thin ribbon of light.

"I could make all that happen for you," Tilton said softly, but there was nothing soft or gentle about the hand that grasped her shoulder or the body that pressed her back against the shelf.

Fighting the impulse to struggle, Gloriana summoned a little laugh that she hoped did not sound too nervous. "You could also make me drop this jar of nutmeg, for which neither Tildy nor the pumpkin pies will thank you." She forced herself to smile at him, though the man's closeness chilled her.

His answering smile was tight-lipped, and heavily lidded eyes hid their expression from her in the half-light. "All right," he said finally, "I'll play along for now. But let's hope, my dear Miss Windemere, that your stand-offishness is caused by maidenly modesty, not by some deeper game you're playing." His fingers tightened on Gloriana's arm until she winced, but his smile did not vary, and his voice sank to an even softer, hissing whisper. "Because if you are, the consequences will not be pleasant."

He let her go then, and Gloriana bolted from the room, forgetting to maintain her air of studied nonchalance. The lieutenant's mild threat, delivered in smooth, well-oiled tones, had frightened her more than an angry warning might have. She would have to be more careful. And underlying her terror was the certainty that they were playing a very deep game indeed, and none of the missionaries, she least of all, fully understood all that was involved.

Tildy looked at her oddly as Gloriana delivered the nutmeg, then glanced behind the girl at the limping officer.

"Auntie, will you let me lick the frosting bowl?" John Tilton began teasing, his voice as light and his smile as charming as ever.

"I'm not your aunt, young man," Tildy snapped testily and took a swat at his hand which was reaching for one of the giant round cookies she was frosting. But she made room for him on one of the long benches and gave him a bowl with enough frosting left on its sides to thrill the heart of any youngster.

Gloriana watched them from the corner of her eye as she began to roll out the pie crust. It was difficult to find much menace in the man who was teasing her uncle's housekeeper and scraping every lick of frosting from the bowl as gleefully as a child. Perhaps it was her own guilty conscience that colored his words with so much danger. But once or twice she thought she felt his eyes on her half-turned back and a little tremor ran through her.

"Miss Gloriana, if you keep rolling that crust, it will fill two pie tins," Tildy's sharp tone recalled Gloriana to her work, and she looked down to see that she had absently rolled an oblong instead of a neat circle.

"I'm sorry, Tildy," she murmured hastily and, folding the pastry in half, lifted it gingerly into a plate where it drooped over two sides, leaving bare half moons of pie tin between. She heard Tildy sniff skeptically as she pared off the excess and tried to piece it over the bare spots.

"You young men! Always turning a girl's head and making her useless in the kitchen," Tildy scolded John Tilton.

He did not seem to mind the hint that he had somehow "turned" Gloriana's head but laughed delightedly. "I'll bet Gloriana had a lot of beaus back in Philadelphia," he suggested.

"Gloriana? No, she spent all of her time tagging after her doctor uncle or doctoring birds and sick kittens in her pet hospital. But Miss Juliana and Miss Marianna—now there was honey that attracted the bees!" And with the perfect familiarity of a long-time family member, Tildy began to tell about the romances of Gloriana's more popular sisters. Only half listening, Gloriana missed the point when the conversation turned back to herself.

"Miss Gloriana is a good, serious-minded girl," Tildy was scolding again. "You young jackanapes should leave her be. Do your sparkin' with them that's lookin' for it, like that little Bridgette Welsh. Now there's some honey that goes looking for the bees."

Gloriana smiled. Dear Tildy! She did not miss a thing! And she had come up with the perfect solution if only John Tilton would follow her advice. Bridgette and the volatile lieutenant - would be perfectly matched—he with his insincere charm and she with her insincere sweetness.

But if the lieutenant heard the suggestion, he paid no attention. Instead of questioning Tildy about Bridgette, he asked, "What other young jackanapes are you warning away, Auntie?" His voice sounded pleasant enough, but there was a slight edge to it that made Gloriana hold her breath as she willed Tildy to say nothing.

Tildy, however, seemed to be warming to the subject. "Well, there's that nice Graham Norton and, of course, you heard about Chief John offering for her." Lieutenant Tilton had not heard, and to Gloriana's horror, Tildy told him the entire story, embellishing it in a way that made her pride in Gloriana clear as well as the great friendship that had developed between the warrior and the mission staff.

"Well, well, Norton and Chief John," he said when she had finished. "I can't think of any two rivals that I would more enjoy beating." And catching Gloriana's glance, he gave her a smile that would have been more dazzling if it had reached his eyes.

She wanted to tell him that he had no chance of beating anyone, but she knew she could not. Keintepoos, Oweena, the Klamaths, the Mission—all would remain safe, she knew instinctively, only so long as she and the others played their parts. They were missionaries, and deception did not come naturally to them. How much longer they would be able to play the game, she had no idea, yet she had little doubt of the consequences if they did not play it well.

That they could be in danger from the very men who should be protecting them seemed incredible. Gloriana remembered her brother at West Point, so idealistic and proud in his cadet uniform, and her father's older brother, Colonel Robert Windemere, whose sweeping whiskers and deep laugh always made her think of Santa Claus. In the East the military had been a symbol of all that was secure and grand about her world, but here in Oregon Territory these men in blue uniforms reminded her of nothing so much as Keintepoos and Chief John's band of warriors—wild, powerful, and free, capable of great good but also of great harm. And of the two bands, the soldiers or the Indians, Gloriana felt at this moment that she would more readily trust herself to the Indians.

"Keep your fingers out of those cookies, and I am not your auntie!" Tildy was again scolding the young officer. His laughter as he teased the cranky housekeeper sounded as lighthearted as that of any of her brother's West Point friends, and Gloriana could tell that in spite of her grumbling, Tildy was enjoying his nonsense.

You're making too much of some idle threats, Gloriana told herself, but still she could not shake the feeling of apprehension and enter into the light banter. When Dr. Windemere came to take her on his afternoon rounds, she was eager to escape the house.

"I'm sorry to take away your star pie maker," Gloriana heard Uncle Ralph apologize as she hurried for her cloak. Tildy did not say anything, but her loud "hmmph!" made clear her opinion of Gloriana's pie making for that day at least.

Outside a wet snow was falling. Giant flakes floated lazily on the cold, heavy air, smothering sound. A peaceful hush submerged the distant clamor of hammers and saws as men worked in the new chapel to prepare it for the following day's festivities. On the hillside beneath the schoolhouse some of the children were tobogganing in what looked like giant baskets made of reeds. Excited dogs were chasing the children to the bottom of the slope, but the happy noises of barking and laughing were a faraway murmur.

Picking her way along the half-hidden path beside her uncle, Gloriana relaxed, for what seemed like the first time in hours.

"I think Tildy was getting ready to send me to my room for ruining so many of her pies," she confided to her uncle with a little giggle.

He patted her mittened hand where it rested in the crook of his arm and smiled briefly but did not comment. The rosy old face was nearly buried behind a knitted red cap and muffler, and a thick mask of white beard and bushy eyebrows caught the snowflakes and held them in a wet fringe. Gloriana thought affectionately how like an old elf he looked and realized how much she had missed him since he had left Philadelphia. How glad she was, in spite of the hardships and the dangers, that she had answered his call to Oregon Territory!

"How is our patient?" she prompted gently, trying to prod him out of an abstraction that she feared might look odd to any suspicious viewers.

The old doctor looked startled for a moment, then patting her hand again said reassuringly, "He has a chance, a fighting chance." He would not say any more but, as though his mind were made up about something, steered her determinedly toward the hospital.

On the covered walkway that served as a hospital entrance, they hit their heavy boots against the steps to dislodge the snow, and Gloriana shook the voluminous folds of her cape as well to keep from tracking in any more dampness than necessary.

She never stepped inside this frontier hospital without conflicting emotions. While impressed by what her uncle had accomplished, Gloriana could not help comparing the frontier hospital with the gleaming wards and sparkling operating rooms of the hospitals back home. There the wounds that still held a few of the soldiers to their beds would have been minor afflictions rather than the life-threatening crises they were out here.

"Someday on this spot I will build a three-story

modern hospital," Dr. Windemere said quietly, as though he had read her mind or perhaps seen the same comparisons in his own mind. "Or perhaps your children will have to build it for me." He gave her an odd little half-smile and motioned the way toward his office.

Completely mystified, Gloriana led the way, but once inside the little cubicle, her unpredictable uncle demanded tea. The hot brew had been prepared and was sitting before them in the chipped white shaving mugs that the doctor always kept for that purpose before he would resume.

Ralph Windemere leaned back in his chair and smiled fondly at his niece. "Gloriana, my dear, I think you know how much I have appreciated your being here. I did not think to see any of my own family again, let alone have someone of my own to carry on after I am gone."

"Uncle, what is wrong? Have the soldiers . . .?"

Ralph Windemere held up a hand and shook his head. "Let me finish. I know I am making a mess of this, but you will have to forgive an old man who loves you . . . Gloriana, do you want to stay here? Is your heart with these people and this land of mine?"

Was it? Gloriana dug into herself for a moment, wondering. She had come to Oregon Territory because she wanted to help her uncle and because she believed in the mission—that was true. But it was also true that she had come because life back home in Philadelphia had ceased to have much meaning, because she was tired of the church socials and picnics and tired too of being the older, sensible Windemere sister. Here on the frontier she had found not only meaningful work and excitement, but also a way to make her life count.

"Yes, Uncle, I will stay," she said finally with a calm she was far from feeling.

Dr. Windemere nodded, as though she had said

what he had expected, but Gloriana could tell from the way he reached for his pipe and began absently to fill the bowl that he was nervous.

"Uncle, has something gone wrong? Is there anything I can do?"

Again he held up his hand and motioned impatiently for her to let him continue. "Now, Gloriana, this is hard enough for me without your interrupting. I'm trying to do this the way I think my brother—your father—would want it done." He paused for a moment to try to light the pipe, sucking in through the stem and filling his face with little clouds of smoke while she looked on in increasingly agitated fascination. But she did not try to hurry him again. After a moment he gave up on the pipe and set it down, still unlit.

"I could not discuss this at home because I was afraid our houseguest might make things awkward. Am I right in saying, my dear, that Lieutenant Tilton has more than a passing interest in you?"

"But I have no interest whatsoever in him, Uncle!"

The doctor smiled at the energy of her answer, but he could not resist teasing, "He's a very handsome young man. I should think he would set all of the young ladies' hearts to beating faster."

"Not mine," she said with a little shudder and told him about the threat.

Dr. Windemere looked grim but not surprised. "It's difficult to keep power responsive to the people when it is nearly independent of supervision. The nearest regular army post is at Winnemucca, nearly two hundred miles away.

"Besides, I'm afraid the lieutenant may be doing exactly what his orders say—patrolling and searching for that band of so-called renegades. If he found the chief here, I'm afraid he might be well within his rights to charge us with obstructing justice and retaliate."

"What would they do to Keintepoos if they found him?"

"Hang him—or worse yet, imprison him on some army post chained up like an animal in a box where all could see him."

The mental picture of the proud warrior held up to the mockery and even the pity of his former foes overruled Gloriana's well-trained Eastern conscience; perhaps they were obstructing justice but certainly that was justifiable to avoid an even greater injustice. Still, was Lieutenant Tilton being unjust? He and his men had been brutally attacked; several had been killed; many, injured. And no one, not even Oweena, had claimed that Keintepoos and Chief John were innocent.

"We must face it," mused her uncle, whose thoughts had apparently been following the same course as her own. "It could be better for all of us if our gallant chief does not survive."

"But, Oweena . . .!" Gloriana started to protest.

"I know, I know. The child would be heartbroken, but at least she is assured of being with him in the next life, if not in this."

They sat for a few minutes without speaking, forgetting to drink their tea. Their eyes rested absently on the doctor's desk lamp. It was smoking slightly, and a thin film of carbon on the glass dimmed the light so that in the tightly shuttered office, there seemed to be a perpetual twilight. It would have made an attractive painting—the old doctor and his young nurse, their sad expressions and drooping shoulders suggesting a shared but nonetheless heavy burden. Both realized that by the laws of the civilization they both believed in, they were harboring a fugitive. But just as surely the laws of a higher kingdom and their healing profession required them to care for the injured and provide refuge to those who claimed it in God's name. Moreover, the man was a friend to whom they owed much.

"At least through all this, Keintepoos has been brought to Christ—and Oweena, too," Gloriana said finally. The memory of the glowing wonder in the Indian couple's eyes as they realized the Savior's love for them eased some of the anxiety she was feeling.

Her uncle brightened at that. "What a breakthrough it would give us with these people if we could tell them about Keintepoos! So far our successes have come with the old or the very young or with the women. This would give us a chance to show the men that the Jesus way, as they call it, is for warriors too." He paused a moment and looked speculatively at his niece. "We have already had some success in that direction."

A slight note of excitement in her uncle's voice made Gloriana lean forward expectantly, but she was hardly prepared for what he said next.

"Graham Norton came to me last night. He was deeply moved by Keintepoos's desire to be with Oweena in the next world and by the way you led the chief to Christ. He asked me if it would be just as easy for a prodigal son to get back on the right path.

"It seems he has been a very bitter man where God is concerned. Losing his parents at such a young age when they were working for the Lord appeared to convince him that God was unfair and did not care about him. I think our Indian chief helped him to get a different perspective on Christianity, showed him it is a walk, a pathway leading somewhere and convinced him that he might not have given God a chance in his life."

"He said I was the one good thing God had done for him," Gloriana murmured half to herself.

"Hmmm . . . yes. I understood you were becoming involved, but I had no idea how far things had gone. As your nearest relative out here on the frontier, Graham spoke to me about his feelings for you. Gloriana, I have to stand in the place of your father to you in this, and that means I have a responsibility. I believe Graham cares for you very deeply, and I think he is one of the finest men I have ever known. As a Christian he will be a giant, a man to match this empire-sized country, able to make it everything we pioneers and missionaries dream about.

"But, my dear, he made one thing very clear. If you choose to make your life with him, you will have to do it here in the West. It's possible you will never be able to go back home again."

Dr. Windemere picked up his pipe and began absently to empty and refill it. The strain of balancing his own wishes against what he felt he owed his niece and his absent brother showed in the round, usually jovial face. A few drops of moisture showed on the red cheeks, and he brushed them away hastily with the back of his hand.

"I asked you a few minutes ago whether you plan to stay here and you said yes. Nothing would make me happier than to spend the rest of my years with my dear niece and her family nearby. You know, Gloriana, that you have always been to me the child I never had—from the times you used to pester me to doctor your sick animals until now when you answered my call for a nurse.

"But I want you to be absolutely certain that the West and Graham Norton are what you want. Search your heart, pray about it, and be sure before you make your decision."

It would be several hours before Gloriana would have a chance to follow her uncle's advice.

CHAPTER 15

GLORIANA HURRIED through the rest of her day, feeling something like one of the wind-up toys she had found under the Christmas tree as a child. There was much to do, and she moved quickly from duty to duty. Yet it was as though her spirit were elsewhere. She felt she should be happy. The major barrier between her and Graham Norton was gone. He was now a Christian, and he sought her hand in the accepted way—by declaring his intentions to her nearest male relative and stating what he had to offer.

"My prayers have been answered," she reminded herself, yet she could not escape a little feeling of disappointment that chilled her inside as the wet snow soaking through the shoulders of her cloak and dampening the hem of her skirt chilled her outside. Graham had placed a condition on his love. That it was a condition she would and could meet made little difference. There was an "if" in the man's feelings for her.

"You're a hopeless romantic," she scolded herself and tried to remember that there had been an "if" on

140

her side as well: if he had not accepted Christ, she could not have accepted Graham, no matter how she felt. *I must look at the half of the cup that is full,* Gloriana thought. *We are adults. We can't be expected to "give all for love" like a pair of love-struck youngsters.* Still she could not help envying Oweena whose sweetheart had given up his Happy Hunting Grounds, as he thought, to be with her in heaven. That Oweena stood a good chance of losing Keintepoos either did not occur to her, or at least did not alter her own vague feelings of discontent.

She was truly thankful that Keintepoos's example had moved Graham to return to the faith of his fathers. She was truly thankful that she had found someone in the great West that she could admire and look up to. And she was thankful that her uncle approved of the match.

"So why am I complaining?" She would see Graham, and after the first awkwardness of accepting him was over, then she would feel happy. And perhaps she could even get him to retract that condition, to promise to take her back East if that was what she wanted. *As Lieutenant Tilton offered to do,* the thought came unbidden before she dismissed it angrily. But try as she might she could not dismiss the odd feeling of discontent that made her prayers of thanks perfunctory at best and diluted them with a string of postscripts that seemed more concerned with adding instructions for accomplishing future answers than with expressing appreciation for the answers that had come.

"Glory, wait!" Graham Norton's familiar voice broke into Gloriana's train of thought with a suddenness that left her bewildered for a moment. The snow had stopped falling, and the path she was following across the mission yard had been recently shoveled. Overhead the sun was just visible—a round, muted light through thinning layers of white clouds.

141

Graham's glad smile as he caught up with her was reassuring, while the eager light in his blue eyes made it difficult to meet his gaze. And suddenly Gloriana was aware of being in the center of the mission yard, overlooked by a dozen windows and perhaps watched by half of the mission's population.

Graham reached for the medical bag Gloriana was carrying and then for her mittened hand which he tucked possessively in the crook of his arm.

"Did Dr. Windemere tell you?" he asked with such a tender expression that Gloriana's heart turned over in her chest, even though her mind was crying, *Not here! Not now!*

But for once Graham did not read Gloriana's expression accurately, and he pressed ahead with all the confidence of someone who knows the answer but wants it confirmed. "Well, what did you decide? Will you stay—with me?"

She would have liked to have put off answering him, but there was no denying his air of urgency and eagerness. Still looking at the large, gloved hand that encompassed her small mittened one, Gloriana nodded briefly. She felt his cold lips brush quickly against her cheek; then he laughed with a mixture of embarrassment and jubilation.

"I can't show you here how I really feel," he said huskily, and Gloriana wondered if he had just then noticed their lack of privacy. He pulled off his glove and reached into his pocket. Gloriana felt something cold and hard slip inside her mitten.

"Wear that," the man told her with a grin that made him look rather young and foolish, and her heart began to warm to the happiness that radiated from Graham's face. His red-gold curls fell from under his hat across his still summer-bronzed forehead. The sky-blue eyes that Gloriana had seen spark with anger or harden to mask his feelings, glowed warmly through a thick fringe of gold lashes. His smile

142

softened the hard set of his jaw and completed the thawing of Gloriana's heart.

"It will be a good life," Graham said softly, "and we'll have God in our home."

Gloriana had started to tell him as well as to feel herself how happy his coming to Christ had made her when she was interrupted by a high-pitched call. Tripping through the snow was Bridgette Welsh. Dressed all in light blue wool, her head and hands daintily clad in immaculate white fur, she looked ready for a Sunday skating party. She was carrying a large basket which appeared to grow heavier as she approached Graham and Gloriana.

"Oh, Mr. Norton, I'm so glad I caught you," Bridgette breathed a sigh and gave him her sweetest smile. "Could you help me carry this heavy basket to the chapel? Momma and I have been baking all day, and I find I am just not strong enough to carry everything."

Gloriana glanced at Graham to see how he was responding to Bridgette's clinging-vine act and was pleased to see a look of annoyance on his face. However, he reached for the basket and allowed the girl to take his arm.

"Couldn't you come with us?" he appealed to Gloriana, but she shook her head. "Then come to the chapel later and see our preparations for tomorrow." She promised that she would and, taking back her medical bag, tried not to see the look of triumph in the glance Bridgette flung in her direction.

"Dear Miss Windemere, so dedicated and so competent." Gloriana heard Bridgette gushing as the vision in blue drew Graham away. Gloriana wanted to say that the basket would not have seemed so heavy if Bridgette had not carried it a hundred yards out of her way so that she could waylay Graham. She wanted to suggest that Momma and not Bridgette had probably done all of the cooking. And most of all, she wanted to tell Bridgette that Graham had asked her—the dedicated, competent spinster—to be his wife.

But she did not say any of those things. Instead she stood quietly watching her fiancé of less than five minutes trying to evade the clinging Bridgette Welsh and maintain a respectable distance as he carried her basket toward the large log chapel.

I can't believe this is happening to me, Gloriana told herself, half exasperated and half amused. *I just accepted the proposal of a man who says he will marry me only if I agree to live in the West, a man who forces me to give my answer in a public place with dozens of people watching and then walks away with a blonde on his arm two minutes after I say yes. I must be out of my mind.*

She sighed and resumed her walk along the snow-packed path. She felt the hard circular shape of the ring Graham had slipped inside her mitten. *I even get to put on my own engagement ring. No romantic moonlight or whispered vows or breathless kisses. Just, "Here's a ring and I'll see you later."* By the time she reached Oweena's cabin, Gloriana was thoroughly angry with Graham and just as thoroughly disgusted with herself.

Before I marry that man, he will ask me properly when we're alone and there's no Bridgette Welsh around, and . . . he'll say, "I love you"! she vowed silently, conveniently forgetting that she had already agreed to marry Graham and retracting her promise would be decidedly awkward.

In the meantime there was work to be done. Keintepoos would need his wounds looked to, and to avoid suspicion, Dr. Windemere had sent Gloriana alone to change the dressings and report on the warrior's progress. "No one will think it odd if you visit your friend," the doctor had told her, "but they might become suspicious if I go there too often. I will slip over later tonight after our houseguest has gone to sleep."

Oweena's room was dark and quiet. As Gloriana opened the door, she felt the hush of sickness hanging in the air. Oweena, who had been kneeling beside the bed, ran to hug Gloriana, and the wetness of her friend's cheek told Gloriana better than words the condition of the patient.

Keintepoos lay very still, his massive frame dwarfing the small bed. His pulse was weak and his temperature, high.

"What have you done to bring down the fever?" Gloriana asked. Oweena showed her the wet cloths and basin of water by the bed.

"Dr. Ralph said to change these every ten minutes." There was also chamomile tea, but the man's teeth were clenched and he had taken none in hours.

"We must get his temperature down. Go out the back door where you will not be seen, and fill this basin with snow." And Gloriana set to work with a will, her own problems forgotten in the greater troubles of the Indian chief.

The wounds were many, and most were infected. As she washed them carefully and applied fresh dressings, Gloriana marveled that the man was still alive. It had been weeks since the battle, and many of the soldiers, who had been treated within days of the conflict, were only now beginning to recover. How he had survived so long in the open she had no idea. She wondered briefly what had happened to Chief John and the other warriors. Tilton had insisted that the Indians had wiped out his fort as well as an entire village, yet the presence of Keintepoos alone and near death at the mission suggested defeat rather than victory.

There was some mystery here and the only ones who could explain it were Keintepoos, who could not speak, and the soldiers, who would not. Gloriana remembered her talk a few hours before with her uncle and his regretful comment that perhaps they would all be better off if the chief did not survive.

"Lord, help us," she breathed the prayer, encompassing in three simple words her anxieties about harboring a fugitive and the deeper feeling, an intuition born nearer the heart than the head, that the survival of this Indian chief was somehow essential to the life and safety of all of them.

Ordinarily Gloriana would have watched and prayed with a patient like Keintepoos throughout the night, but she dared not stay long for fear someone would become suspicious. She showed Oweena how to apply the snow packs and thought she felt the first signs of the fever's breaking in the man's burning skin. Then with an encouraging hug and the promise that she would pray, Gloriana left the Indian girls to fight the battle alone.

It was twilight outside, and Gloriana realized with a little feeling of panic that she had stayed with Keintepoos longer than she realized. Soon it would be dinnertime, and if she was too late, she would be missed and questions would be asked.

I could say there is sickness—maybe whooping cough—in the Indian village, she thought and as quickly rejected the idea. What if the lieutenant had his soldiers watching her? They would know that it had been hours since she had visited the Klamath village and there might even be one of those young braves she had seen at the Welsh cabin who would know that she had only lanced a boil and checked on the progress of roasting venison and firepit baked apaws that were being prepared for the following day.

"Whoever said the liar's way is the easy way has never tried it. Deception is hard work."

The half-finished chapel was lit only by fires in the fireplaces and a single lamp on one of the long makeshift tables. It smelled delightfully of hay and wood shavings and burning wood. The young people's decorations looked almost exotic in the half-light, and for a moment Gloriana was reminded of Thanksgivings back home with church suppers and the Pilgrims' play done by the Sunday sshool classes. The memory made her suddenly homesick and she realized how much she longed to hear her father's deep voice singing "We Thank Thee, O God" and her sister Juliana's rippling accompaniment, always a bit too fast with too many trills and arpeggios for a hymn.

To her surprise she saw that someone had moved the organ from the old chapel and set it in the place of honor on a half-completed platform. The pulpit was there, too—all ready with a pitcher of water and a glass at the side for the Thanksgiving sermon Uncle Ralph had been chewing on for days. Very little was left to be done. The tables groaned with baskets of food and stacks of dishes. Kettles and pots waited beside the fireplaces to begin the work of warming food and brewing the mixture of coffee and grains that would be a special treat for the occasion.

There was every evidence of a day's hard work on preparations for the feast but no evidence of the workers. *He didn't even wait,* Gloriana thought and smiled somewhat grimly. She supposed that being stood up was on a par with the rest of the events of her engagement day, but that did not make it any easier to swallow. Perhaps Graham had decided she was not coming. Perhaps he had gone to find her at the cabin and was even now hurrying across the mission yard. In any case, he did not seem to be in the chapel.

Gloriana had just turned to leave when she heard a sound from the direction of the platform. She had forgotten about the small room that was being built there for a church office. Thinking that Graham must have decided to do some work in the little room while he waited for her, Gloriana hurried forward. It did not occur to her to call out.

But what she saw in the shadows on the other side of the door made her heart stop—a man and a woman locked together in an embrace. Even in the dim light the red hair and broad shoulders of Graham Norton and the pale yellow curls of Bridgette Welsh were unmistakable.

Gloriana's gasp startled the pair, and for one breathless moment she looked straight into Graham's horrified face. Then Gloriana ran from the chapel. Behind her she heard Graham's frantic, "Glory, wait!" and the girl's high-pitched laughter.

Dry-eyed, but hardly seeing where she was going, Gloriana ran along the slippery path. Twice she fell, the second time with her arm beneath her. She felt a sharp pain in her left wrist, but she picked herself up and ran on. She could hardly realize what had happened. She felt as though she were caught in a night terror—one of those senseless dreams where one runs blindly, pursued by some indescribable horror. But in her mind she carried with her a vivid picture of two faces pressed tightly together—a picture she could not leave behind nor shut out, not even by closing her eyes.

CHAPTER 16

Oregon Territory   November 26, 1851
Thanksgiving

We celebrated our first Thanksgiving in the wilderness today and I am homesick. I miss my mother's turkey and cranberries and my father's impossibly long blessing over the food. I even miss seeing Juliana's latest gentleman friend—probably another cadet from West Point or perhaps a student from the university this year. She always invites someone to dinner and then introduces him as though he were "the one," only to pick someone different the next year.

Our celebration here was a success, according to Uncle—there were no fights. The soldiers and Graham Norton's men sat at opposite ends of the room with the Klamaths in between. Uncle's sermon was well received, though he looked very tired to me. I doubt he slept at all last night.

I could not play the organ. My left wrist, injured when I fell last night, is swollen and bruised. Catherine Midfield played, and from the feeling she put into the old hymns, I think she must be as homesick as I.

Gloriana would not let her mind go over the events of the day before, but she could not escape the aching

149

emptiness they had left inside her. She had not spoken to Graham since she had seen him with Bridgette in the chapel, though he had called at the cabin several times and sent notes asking to see her. Her pride had willed her to act as though nothing had happened, but her acting ability had not been equal to the task. For once, she was glad that Lieutenant Tilton stuck close to her; still dazed, she had appreciated his help with filling her plate at the Thanksgiving feast and his constant stream of small talk, in spite of her silence. She was not, however, so numb that she missed the puzzled looks the Midfields exchanged or her uncle's sober expression as he watched her. Nor was she completely unaware of Graham Norton's anxious eyes on her and his increasing anger at Tilton's attentions. Finally, Graham had left his place of honor near her uncle to sit farther down the table with a delighted Bridgette Welsh.

"I don't care!" Gloriana said sharply, but not very convincingly.

A few minutes later a soft knock at the bedroom door made Gloriana hastily wipe away a few tears that had somehow found their way down her cheeks.

Her uncle stood at her doorway, spectacles on his nose and medical bag in hand. "Let's take a look at that wrist," he said, after a quick inspection of the bruise on her cheek. If he noticed the rice powder she had used to try to cover it or the little streaks left by her recent tears, he said nothing but went right to work on her wrist, probing and feeling with sure fingers.

"There's nothing broken," he said finally, then added with a keen look into her eyes, "at least nothing in your hand. I'm not so sure about the rest of you." Little by little, he drew from her the story of what had happened the day before. When she had finished and fresh tears were rolling down her cheeks, he was frowning and shaking his head.

"I don't understand it. I have known Graham Norton for several years, and what you tell me does not sound like him at all."

"But I saw him, Uncle! In the chapel behind the platform. And today he was with her again."

"Did he have no explanation? Could she have stumbled and fallen and he caught her? Or might she have thrown herself on him? She seems like a rather forward young woman—not at all above putting a man in a difficult situation."

Gloriana shook her head skeptically, but she had to admit that she had not waited for Graham's explanation.

"Well, he will have to explain to me," her uncle said decidedly.

Gloriana, however, insisted she did not want anything worked out and, when her uncle left, she gave him the beautiful ruby ring Graham had pressed into her mitten—could it only have been the afternoon before? It seemed much longer ago.

"That does not look like the kind of ring a man would give a girl he is two-timing," Dr. Windemere commented, but he put the ring in his waistcoat pocket. Gloriana could still hear him arguing with himself as he went downstairs, and she felt almost as sorry for the trusting old doctor as she did for herself.

If Gloriana's world had turned suddenly gray, it had not been frozen. The work at the mission went on. New babies continued to be born in the Klamath village, sick children had to be nursed, and the conspiracy of silence over the wounded Shasta chief had to be maintained. The attacks by the renegades had begun once again—closer now, it seemed, to the mission. The party of a British lord, wintering a few miles north, had been saved by a band of hunters from the mission, but not before they had been robbed of a considerable quantity of gold and jewels.

There was plenty to occupy Gloriana's time and her

151

mind, and since she had never been given to gloom and self-pity, she soon threw herself into her duties with an energy that could not fail to be rewarded. If her smiles were not quite as ready as before, if she felt a sharp pain in her heart when some chance incident reminded her that that organ existed, it was only to be expected. "Time heals all wounds," she reminded herself, "or at least teaches us to bear them patiently."

She never knew what her uncle said to Graham Norton. The relationship between the old doctor and his young friend seemed as cordial as ever when they met around the mission yard or in his office—a fact that Gloriana tried not to resent too much. Yet Norton no longer came to the Windemere cabin for evenings of talk and pipe smoking.

Surprisingly he was usually in church, sometimes with Bridgette Welsh beside him, sometimes alone. Back at her place at the organ, Gloriana would sense his entry into the chapel before she caught sight of his broad shoulders and uncovered head of red curls. He usually sat in the back row, but he towered nearly head and shoulders above the congregation, mostly made up of Klamaths, with only a few of the other mission inhabitants mixed in. When Bridgette was with him, Gloriana had to steel herself to endure the service. Then the organ seemed possessed of an evil spirit that pressed the wrong keys, made the rhythm of her pumping irregular, and caused the instrument to wheeze awkwardly.

When he was alone, she felt intensely self-conscious, wondering if he was watching her and hoping that he could not feel her awareness of him. Her quick ear even picked out his deep baritone voice in the singing. Her every sense seemed attuned to this man who had hurt her so badly, yet for all the sign he gave, he might not have known she was there.

Meanwhile Keintepoos continued to hang between

life and death. Most of the wounds closed and began to heal, but a deep one near his left lung refused to respond to treatment.

"If I had him back home in a modern hospital, I know I could handle it, but here. . ." Dr. Windemere shook his head. His round, white-fringed face showed as much discouragement as Gloriana had ever seen there.

"Someday you'll have your modern hospital right here," she reminded him, but for once the dream did not bring a light to the doctor's eyes nor start him talking about the better times to come.

"Perhaps," was all he answered.

They had met once again in Gloriana's tiny room— the only place in the cabin where they did not have to worry about John Tilton's walking in or overhearing their conversation. Dr. Windemere was resting in her rocking chair, one hand holding his unlit pipe; the other, absently rubbing the smooth wood of the scrolled arm. Gloriana sat on the edge of the bed, a knitted comforter wrapped tightly around her to keep out the chill of the unheated room.

"I'm afraid the lieutenant is becoming suspicious," she told her uncle after a moment. "He keeps asking me about Oweena and why she isn't helping in the hospital any more."

"What did you tell him?"

"I said she was pining for her Indian sweetheart and gushed a lot about how romantic it was."

"Was he convinced?"

"I don't think so, at least not entirely. I'm not sure how much longer we can keep putting him off. I have a feeling that already he is trying to get a look inside that cabin."

The doctor hesitated and cleared his throat, then spoke. "Graham suggests moving Keintepoos to the Midfields' cabin. Then he would have a doctor with him day and night, and he would be out of Tilton's way.

Gloriana tried to keep the tremor from her voice at the mention of Graham, but she knew she was hiding nothing from her kindly and observant uncle. "When and how could it be done?"

"At night when everyone is asleep."

Two nights later, instead of taking an indirect route around the back of the cabins, Graham and his men carried the wonded chief straight across the mission yard. There was no moon, but stars and snow made the night bright enough that the men and the stretcher were visible. Gloriana watched from the open window of her room, wondering how many other eyes followed them. The scuffling sounds their feet made on the snow-packed path were insignificant in the comparison to the sharp cracking noise of boots' breaking through frozen snow crust that Gloriana had expected to hear.

In the days that followed Gloriana escaped more and more into her work. With the lieutenant seeming to be everywhere in the Windemere cabin, she found the hospital a refuge. The medications she had to prepare kept her mind busy, and the appreciation of the patients made her feel that she was doing something worthwhile.

It was less than a week before Christmas, and the hospital ward looked more cheerful than she felt. A fire crackled merrily in the closed stove—one of the few at the mission. Paper chains and snowflakes decorated the windows, and a large fir tree stood in the coolness near the door. Handmade ornaments of cloth and painted wood covered the green branches, and on top a five-pointed star, cut from tin, shone brightly.

Back home they would be shopping and wrapping presents. Juliana would be practicing Christmas carols on the old upright piano in the living room while Marianna altered Wise Men's robes and angel costumes for another generation of Sunday-school pupils who would be performing in the annual Christmas Eve pageant.

"I wonder if they miss me," Gloriana asked, unconsciously speaking aloud.

"Not half as much as we would if you weren't here." The unexpected answer coming from close by made Gloriana jump, and she looked up with a sinking feeling into John Tilton's face, only a few inches away. He was smiling at her with an odd mixture of tenderness and daring that made her suspect immediately that he had visited the Welsh cabin to enjoy that family's liquid version of Christmas cheer. The bandages were gone from his head, but an ugly new scar across his forehead was a reminder of his wounds. His injured leg was still tender, and a makeshift cane had become a part of his daily costume. But he was in full uniform—army blues and yellow kerchief knotted correctly at his neck inside the regulation overcoat. The clothes made him seem more formidable and threatening, as though he were ready again for action.

"I was thinking about home," she told him, hoping that he would not notice the few tears of homesickness that dampened her eyelashes.

However, if he noticed, it was satisfaction rather than sympathy he felt. "I said you would get tired of this place. Remember that?" He reached out and absently fingered one of the long curls that lay loosely on her shoulder, then let his fingers stray to the soft curve of her cheek. "The offer still stands, you know—bright lights, the city, beautiful gowns, and jewels. I can give you all that. We could go to San Francisco for a while and then maybe to Rio de Janeiro, even Paris, Vienna, Rome. Would you like that?"

Gloriana's fear did not cause her to fail to notice that he mentioned nothing of marriage. "You must be very rich," she faltered and tried to rise from the table where she had been working. But his right hand gripped her shoulder and held her in place while the left reached into his pocket. What he pulled from it at first stunned and then intrigued her—a heavy gold pendant with a large sea-green emerald set in a circle of pearls.

"A Christmas gift," he said and started to fasten it around her neck.

"Oh, but I cannot take it," Gloriana protested. "It's much too expensive!"

"It's nothing. As you said, I am very rich." Then he kissed her—fully on the lips, his mouth lingering on hers with a possessiveness and passion that repelled her as much as the sour smell of liquor on his breath. "We are good together, Gloriana," he breathed after a moment. "Norton is a fool to throw you over for a saloon keeper's daughter."

A few minutes later Gloriana burst into her uncle's office at the far end of the hospital to find him sitting with Graham Norton. It had not occurred to her that her uncle might be occupied, but she steeled herself to face Graham, remembering that he after all had been the one who asked her to watch John Tilton. When she told her story and showed them the emerald pendant, both men looked solemn, but it was Graham who asked the questions.

"He said he was rich and would take you to Paris and Vienna?" The blue eyes were cold and seemed to cut right through her. Otherwise his face was expressionless, the chiseled bronze mask of a stranger.

Gloriana nodded. "That struck me as strange," she explained, "because a soldier might be reassigned to Washington or even New York or New Orleans, but not to those places."

"Did he ask you to marry him?" Graham's voice was indifferent, and he did not look at her when he asked the question, but Gloriana was aware of the embarrassed flush that dyed her cheeks and the shake of her head that answered his question.

"I'm wondering where he got such an expensive jewel out here in the wilderness," Dr. Windemere interposed, fingering the bright pendant Gloriana had given him.

"Could it be a family heirloom?" Gloriana wondered.

"He wouldn't have it here," her uncle dismissed that idea. "If he is really as rich as he says, he would have his heirlooms in a bank back East, not here in his pocket. Besides, I'm not convinced by that story. Rich men are not usually army lieutenants!"

"You warned me about John Tilton months ago." Gloriana turned to Graham with a challenge in her eyes. She half suspected that he was holding something back—some key piece in the puzzle that he did not trust them, especially her, to be able to deal with. Besides, she could not let him think that just being near him made her tongue-tied and shy like a sixteen-year-old. "Now I want to know why."

Then it was Graham's turn for embarrassment. He shifted his position in the straight-backed chair, but he met her eyes when he responded. " I heard about him in Eureka after his troops had been bivouacked there. They said he couldn't be trusted with women and that his men roughed up some of the townspeople."

Outside, the sky was overcast again. Looking at the white denseness of clouds, Gloriana hoped that they were not in for one of the blizzards she had heard so much about. She had left her uncle's office with every intention of going to the Windemere cabin, but she found her feet turning toward the new chapel instead. She had carols to practice for the Christmas service, and somehow the thought of being at home where John Tilton might find her alone again sent a little shiver of dread down her spine.

A few minutes after she had left the hospital, she recognized, as surely as if she could see Graham Norton, the firm stride and the presence behind her.

157

When he caught up with her, they walked along in silence for several strides.

"I don't like the idea of your spending so much time with him," Graham said gruffly, staring straight ahead, his chin drawn into the turned-up collar of his jacket and his gloved hands stuffed into his pockets.

"I thought you wanted me to keep an eye on him," Gloriana retorted. The idea of the man—still wanting to run her life when he had taken himself so thoroughly out of it! Before she had really thought, she blurted out, "Well, it won't be for long now. I'll be going home in the spring, and then you can deal with Lieutenant Tilton on your own!"

"Have you really made up your mind?" He sounded startled, almost unbelieving.

"I have." She had not actually thought about it before, but it seemed like a good idea. Moreover, the statement had so shaken Graham out of his indifference that he looked almost hurt, before becoming suddenly, lividly angry.

"Gloriana Windemere, I knew you were an obstinate, prideful woman, but I never thought you were a coward." And he left her standing on the steps of the chapel. Had she gone too far? Or had she really meant what she had said?

Perhaps the only thing for me to do now is to go back home, Gloriana thought with a little sigh. Life had never been so complicated in Philadelphia. She could go back home and marry one of her father's young assistants—all serious, scholarly men who considered her background and skills qualifications for the perfect minister's wife. Or perhaps she would marry one of the doctors; most were too poor to afford a nurse and a wife both. She would be a bargain for one of them. The possibilities did not exactly thrill her, but that was to be expected.

Inside the chapel a crew of workmen hurried to finish, in time for Christmas services, the benches that would serve as pews. A new floor had been put in since Thanksgiving, and the walls had been plastered and whitewashed. Soldiers were there as well, sent by John Tilton to help with the finishing and decorating. Surprisingly the men were working together. They were not exactly friendly, but at least a truce of sorts seemed to have been called.

The blessed day brings peace, even here in the wilderness, Gloriana thought with a brief prayer for her own peace of mind.

Bridgette, her brothers, and some of the Klamath girls were decking the walls with evergreen garlands. From the girls' angry blushes and the boys' mischievous grins, Gloriana guessed that the Welsh males had been putting the mistletoe, which seemed in abundant supply, to good use.

"Miss Windemere, you are just in time to advise us on decorating the platform," Bridgette called out gaily. Two large fir trees stood in the choir loft already, their wide branches extending at one point to the organ bench.

"Why don't you just trim the trees?" Gloriana suggested without much enthusiasm. She did not relish the thought of playing the organ with an evergreen bough sticking in her back.

"How I wish we had tinsel and glass ornaments!" Bridgette was chattering on. "And wouldn't it be wonderful to have a Christmas ball? I told Graham that we would just have to have a ball when we are married in the spring, and you will be one of the first to receive an invitation, Miss Windemere."

Klamath Mission   New Year's Day, 1852
The new year is only hours old, and already it has brought sorrow. Catherine Midfield's baby was born prematurely last night, a tiny girl with dainty features like her mother and long, slim fingers. She only lived a few hours, and her parents' heartbreak is painful to witness. Dr. Midfield blames himself for trying to stay here when he knew his wife is delicate and likely to have a hard time.

I think she blames him too. There was anger as well as sorrow in her eyes when she was told about little Glorietta. They named her for me, and I too feel like a part of myself is gone with that baby, for I held her when she died, and not all my prayers could hold her here.

Uncle says that this is one of the times when we must simply trust and keep going. In my heart I know he is right, but my head keeps trying to understand how this could happen. Why should missionaries, good people like the Midfields, be called on for such a sacrifice? I know that in a modern hospital in the East Glorietta might have lived; perhaps there too Catherine would not have been under so much strain, and the baby would have gone to full term.

Possibly having Keintepoos in the house contributed to this tragedy, but somehow I think it would have happened anyway. In any case, the chief has been gone for more than a week. All we know is that he slipped away in a snowstorm with supplies from the hospital kitchen and his side half healed. Uncle has hopes that he has gone into hiding somewhere to wait out the winter. But I cannot help feeling that he left so that the mission would not be in danger. He did not expect to live when he came here, but as weeks went by and he realized the possible consequences to us of harboring a fugitive, he became desperate to escape. I could see it in his eyes.

Oweena fears he is dead. I have seen her watching the hills with tears in her eyes. Her anger against the soldiers grows almost daily, and I fear that she will say or do something that will place her life in even greater jeopardy than it already is.

And so the new year began in Oregon Territory. Time seemed suspended as blizzards roared down off the high plains and temperatures dropped to forty below. Several times it was necessary for parties of men to don snowshoes and forage for wood for the fires or food for people and animals. They ran out of coffee and sugar, and Dr. Windemere's pipe was once again empty. Yet the supply of spirits in the Welsh cabin seemed limitless, and during the long winter days with little to do and numbing cold to combat,

160

more and more men—Indian and white alike—found their way to the trader's table.

Dr. Windemere had warned Mr. Welsh several times that a mission was no place for him to sell his wares. Each time the man had vigorously denied he was selling anything, but the traffic continued in and out of his cabin with a regularity that argued something more than social visits.

And not all Welsh's visitors made it home again. A miner whose claim was near Mount McLoughlin missed his way and walked off a bluff into Klamath Lake to resurface near the mission a few days later, his much-boasted pouch of nuggets gone from his pack. A trapper on his way south with a rich load of furs was found frozen to death on the lakeshore, and drifting snow revealed more than one unknown victim on the Umpqua Trail—the only passable route through the mountains.

Accidents? Perhaps. But the missionaries found themselves glancing over their shoulders when they went outside at night and even welcoming the presence of the soldiers as protection against an unknown menace.

"The Klamaths would never hurt us," Gloriana maintained stoutly, but she sensed a new fear in the Midfields, and even her uncle admitted he could not entirely forget the experience of the Whitmans and the Cayuse tribe.

"We lost many in the epidemic, and then gave shelter to the hated bluecoats," he reminded Gloriana.

A brooding danger, as gray and dark as the winter storms, seemed to have descended on the little mission, depressing the spirits of its inhabitants and infusing every wind with a menacing war cry.

If she could not feel safe outside, at least inside the Windemere cabin Gloriana found some relief.

Lieutenant Tilton had moved out at last to bunk

with his men and, Gloriana suspected, to join the nightly festivities at the trader's cabin. Still he did not forget her and holding him at arm's length was becoming more and more difficult. He had nicknamed her his "Puritan Maid" and seemed to accept their relationship as an established fact, but rarely did he mention his plans for them unless the boldness of drink was upon him. Then Gloriana feared him— enough that she carried in her pocket a small knife her brother had given her when she came west; and enough that, when she was alone at night, she watched the shadows for more than the mysterious raiders.

With the lieutenant gone Graham Norton resumed his nightly visits to the Windemere cabin. While the wind howled and the fire roared, he and the doctor would sit and finger their empty pipes and talk. Only now it was the Bible, not philosophy, that they discussed as Graham remembered the teachings of his childhood and sought to expand his understanding of the Christian walk.

Gloriana wondered how, as a Christian, he could plan to marry someone like Bridgette Welsh. She listened for news of their wedding from her uncle or Tildy or Dr. Midfield, with whom Graham had struck up a strong friendship. But with Graham himself she rarely exchanged a word. It was as though an impenetrable wall had been thrown up between them. Gloriana, had she but known it, assumed in his presence an icy hauteur that would have done justice to a Philadelphia matron, while Graham's cold indifference was a match.

Meanwhile the work of the mission crept along. Morning chapel services were better attended than usual—mostly, Dr. Windemere claimed, because there was nothing else to do. However, no new converts joined the fold. Business at the hospital was brisk with frostbite and victims of the mysterious attacks added to the usual list of ailments for treatment. And babies continued to be born, with Gloriana and Oweena as permanent nursemaids.

But overall little else happened. An atmosphere of waiting had descended over the mission. The lieutenant watched Gloriana and Oweena with unspoken plans in his dark eyes, but he could do nothing until spring. The soldiers and the Klamaths watched each other suspiciously, but both knew that any campaigns or battles would also wait until spring. Catherine Midfield's unhappiness was like a heavy weight that she carried with her, waiting for the spring. In the spring too Bridgette had said she would marry Graham Norton, and then Gloriana would have to make her own decision. Should she stay in Oregon Territory, or should she go back home to Philadelphia? Never, perhaps, had a spring been more fervently wished for and so justifiably feared.

CHAPTER 17

THE FIRST SIGNS OF WARMER WEATHER came from the ground rather than from the sky. March's thick, gray clouds still blotted out the sun, and sharp north winds still froze the shallow marshes around the edge of the Upper Klamath while they whipped the waters at lake center into icy, white-topped waves. Snow flurries continued at regular intervals to transform the drab landscape into a dazzling white wonderland. Yet underneath the snow pack the thaw had already begun. Unwary pedestrians, deviating from the shoveled mission pathways, found themselves breaking through a firm-looking crust into slush and cold water beneath. Soon the air was filled with the gurgling and trickling sounds of hundreds of tiny creeks, rushing under the melting snow or breaking through to tumble in icy sheets down the hillsides.

By the first of April most of the snow cover was gone. Wood violets began to appear in sheltered places in the forests, and buds formed on the pussy willows around the lake. The air was filled with the honking of northward bound flocks of geese while vividly colored wood ducks invaded the mission grounds in search of a handout.

The first of the mission's winter inhabitants to leave were Graham Norton and his men. His mule-drawn wagons rolled south toward Lost River country where they would begin blazing the Applegate Trail, a new freighting road that would eventually connect northern California with the Umpqua Valley in Oregon. Behind him Graham left the completed mission buildings—a new chapel with a bell tower, an orphanage with room for seventy children, a recreation hall that could double as a gymnasium, and an office-laboratory building large enough for all Dr. Windemere's records, as well as his lab equipment and experiments.

Graham also left a letter for Gloriana. Written in a clean, bold hand, its character was like that of the man—aggressive, to the point, and as mysterious as the green Oregon forests.

Dear Gloriana,

I can't leave without a final word, but since you and I can't seem to talk without fighting, I will write instead of saying it.

Whatever we might have meant to each other, I will always remember you as the one who showed me the way back to God. I could never talk about my parents' deaths. Suffice it to say that what I held against God then, I have now learned to accept, and I look forward to seeing my parents in heaven.

I hope you change your mind about going back to Philadelphia. We need you here, and if you will be honest with yourself, I think you will find that you need us too.

If you ever decide that you need me—well, we'll leave it in God's hands.

Graham

In her tiny room above the kitchen, Gloriana read the letter, wept over it, and prayed over it. Was it a goodbye? She tried to read an appeal for reconciliation into that final sentence or at least a door left open for the future, but there were too many unanswered questions. Did he still care for her, or was he merely grateful? If she needed him—was he offering help as a friend or as a lover? And what about Bridgette? What about the spring wedding? What about that kiss in the shadow of the organ the day before Thanksgiving?

Memories that had lain dormant during the winter, buried deep in her numbed heart, flooded back again, soft and bittersweet in the pale light of spring. Graham's voice, his touch, the way his red-gold hair curled on the back of his neck, the way his blue eyes warmed with laughter or his lips curved in a half smile—pictures haunted her dreams, waking or sleeping.

That she loved Graham, she could no longer deny. Her dreams betrayed her, overriding the stubborn denials of pride. In the fall when the glamor of romance was fresh and spellbinding, she had been overwhelmed by him and by the sensation of falling in love; her emotions had been close to the surface, rising and falling with the slightest provocation. Now her feelings seemed more deeply rooted—more at the center of her being and less separable from the fabric of her personality. The man had somehow ceased to be an external and had become an internal force in her life.

This must be what they call "true love," Gloriana realized with a mixture of awe and despair. That she could care so deeply for someone who had betrayed her seemed incredible. Yet as surely as she recognized that her feelings could exist independently, regardless of her conscious wishes, Gloriana knew that nothing could or would change them. She could go back home to Philadelphia, Graham could marry Bridgette, she could see him every day or never again, but she knew that she would go on loving this man as long as she lived.

Oddly enough, accepting the fact brought her a kind of peace. There was no longer a need to struggle. The matter was out of her control—in "the Lord's hands," as Graham had said, and if Gloriana could not quite bring herself to believe in the man she loved, she knew she could trust her Heavenly Father.

Klamath Mission   April 15, 1851

Spring in Oregon Territory is a magic time. All the gloom and suffering of the fall and winter are far from forgotten, but it is possible to hope again.

We pray for peace! Yet the spring that promises so much brings also the threat of increased hostilities. A small Mormon community just fifteen miles to the west of us was burned to the ground a few nights ago. Klamath scouts brought us word of the massacre, but they would say nothing about who had done it.

Lieutenant Tilton and his soldiers continue at the mission, but I feel their presence here grows less and less friendly. Daily they scour the country on patrols, but it seems their movements are observed, for no sooner do they ride to the west, than the renegades attack in the east. Oweena is watched constantly while the lieutenant questions us all about Keintepoos. I fear that somehow he has learned the truth, and I remember all too well his threats.

"Gloriana, dear, I am afraid I left my spectacles on the pulpit in the chapel. I wonder if you would mind fetching them for your old uncle." Dr. Windemere appealed to her from his favorite armchair. A book rested in his lap; his feet, on a low footstool. From the way he moved Gloriana guessed that the arthritis she suspected was affecting his knees had intensified with the damp weather. "Just a touch of rheumatism," her uncle added, as though he had read her thoughts.

"It will only take me a minute," she said, and, grabbing up a hand-knitted shawl against the chill that still lingered in the spring breeze, she set out for the chapel.

The afternoon sun had dipped low over the lake,

paving a golden path across the surface. A circus of waterfowl was rising and settling in the tules, and the air echoed with its joyous sounds. Overhead the sky was a pastel blue with white misty clouds as trimmings. Underneath Gloriana's feet the ground felt moist and spongy. A light veil of new green was beginning to color the rolling, hummocky hills and make a bower of the willow grove around the artesian spring in the quadrangle.

Gloriana cut across the quadrangle by the little path that went past the spring. She heard the bubbling waters before she realized the sounds were mixed with angry voices, a man and a woman fighting. Not wanting to overhear something that was not meant for her ears, she started to turn back; then she realized that the voices belonged to Lieutenant Tilton and Bridgette Welsh and she paused, fascinated in spite of herself.

"You said we could leave here in the spring." Bridgette's tone was shrill and accusing. "You promised me San Francisco and beautiful gowns and jewels."

Gloriana suppressed a little gasp. That was exactly what John Tilton had promised *her!* What kind of game was he playing?

"You know, you're beginning to be tiresome," the man's voice responded, managing to sound both annoyed and bored. "I am starting to wonder what I ever saw in you."

"If you think you can just use me and then walk away, you had better think again. I know enough to ruin you. What would precious Gloriana Windemere say if she knew where you got your money? What if I told her who you really are?"

There was a sharp sound that could have been a slap, followed by a woman's crying. Gloriana knew she should run but she was frozen in place, stunned by what she was hearing.

"If you ever say a word to her, I will fix your face so no man will ever look at you again."

"John, please," Bridgette was pleading now, "you don't want her. We're good together. I can give you much more than she ever could."

"You already have," the man sneered. Gloriana could feel the cruelty without seeing his face. "You might take a lesson from Miss Windemere. Never give yourself to a man before the wedding. No man, not even that big oaf Norton, will want to marry a tramp."

Gloriana turned and ran back down the pathway, holding her skirts high to keep them from rustling or tripping her. The soft ground cushioned and absorbed the sound of her footfalls, but she held her breath, almost afraid to exhale for fear she might be heard.

She was astonished at what she had learned. Not the least of her amazement came from the realization that Bridgette Welsh was jealous of her. The beautiful minx, who had so skillfully maneuvered her way between Graham and Gloriana, secretly saw Gloriana as a rival. Gloriana could almost pity the girl. If what Tilton had implied about their relationship was true, Bridgette must have expected to win him with weapons Gloriana could not and would not use. But what about Graham? If Bridgette was planning to elope with Tilton, she must have abandoned her plan to marry Graham Norton. For a moment Gloriana's heart sang at the prospect. Yet what if Graham knew nothing of Bridgette's change of heart? Wouldn't she be all the more likely, now that she had been rejected by Tilton, to go through with her original plans?

Even more puzzling were Bridgette's hints about the lieutenant's money and some hidden identity. If only she could talk to Graham!

Something is wrong here, very wrong, Gloriana told herself as she navigated an alternate route to the chapel. Such an understatement might have made her smile if she had not been trembling so hard.

She found the doctor's spectacles on the pulpit, right where he had said he left them. The wire frames were slightly bent, and they sat at an angle on his nose, giving him a puzzled look as he listened to Gloriana's account of what she had overheard.

"Isn't it amazing how our own insecurities can give power to our enemies?" he commented when she told him about Bridgette's jealousy.

Gloriana did not have to ask what he meant. She knew. Because of her own feelings of insecurity—the sense that she was too old, not pretty enough, not appealing to men—she had let Bridgette Welsh come between her and Graham. She had not fought back but had just accepted her own defeat. Well, if she ever had a second chance, she would have enough faith in herself and in God to make the most of the opportunity.

For the rest, Dr. Windemere had little to say. Like Gloriana, he wished Graham Norton were there, but since Graham was not, he said, they would have to wait and see.

"Back home we would call the police, and they would check out what I heard," Gloriana wrote in her journal that evening. "Here we are alone—far from any official help. The nearest magistrate is at Applegate Landing, and the nearest fort, at Winnemucca, two hundred miles away, across lava flows, canyons, mountains, and desert.

Dear God, help us, Gloriana found herself breathing the prayer unconsciously.

Feeling alone and isolated, she was not prepared for a knock at the door. The firm rapping echoed through the cabin, sending a chill down her spine and making the breath catch in her throat.

"Don't be silly," she scolded herself. "It's probably Dr. Midfield to check on uncle's aching limbs." The young doctor had been especially sympathetic the past few days, taking over most of the older man's duties and urging him to rest. Privately Gloriana suspected that her uncle's colleague was preparing to leave the mission and was feeling guilty about leaving the Windemeres to carry on alone.

But it was not Dr. Midfield at the cabin door. Lieutenant John Tilton leaned against the doorsill, a bouquet of wildflowers in his hand and a dazzling smile on his handsome face.

"If I had come to visit you at your home in Philadelphia," he told Gloriana, "I would have brought roses, but these are the best I can do here."

Gloriana stammered her thanks, but she did not invite him in. "Uncle has gone to bed early." As she started to make the excuse, he pushed past her with a grin that showed his delight at the prospect of being alone with her.

With the familiarity of a long-time house guest, he placed his hat on the rack behind the door and his gloves on the table beneath.

"I have a lot to tell you." Neither his voice nor expression revealed the villainy that had been so apparent in his conversation with Bridgette just a few hours before. It amazed Gloriana that he could look and smile so happily after such a scene, and she searched his face for some sign of remorse or embarrassment.

Instead he appeared eager; in other circumstances, Gloriana might have mistaken the warmth in his eyes for love. He drew her to the sofa with its vivid coverings of Indian blankets and sat so close to her that she could almost hear the stiff material of his uniform creak with the pressure of measured breaths.

"Miss Windemere—Gloriana—I have received a dispatch from Washington; I am being transferred. It means a promotion and new post back in civilization, and I want you to go with me—as my wife."

The proposal, when she had expected a proposition, was completely surprising. But she knew he was lying. Only one letter had come for him in the mail pouch that had arrived from Applegate Landing a few days before. Gloriana had sorted the mail herself, and she remembered the distinctive stationery marked with the return address of a San Francisco hotel.

"This is so sudden," she began lamely.

But instead of being offended, he seemed to expect her conventionality and even to be pleased by it. "You must know I care for you," he said earnestly, and slipping down on one knee, he took her hand and pressed it to his lips.

Gloriana felt distant, as though she were watching such a romantic scene from outside herself. Irrelevantly, she remembered her objections when Graham had made his impulsive proposal in the open mission yard with dozens of eyes watching.

"Have you spoken with my uncle?" Not able to say what she really felt, it seemed safest to continue with the accepted formula.

"Only say the word, and I will speak to him."

Absently Gloriana wondered what this man—this devil in uniform, as she now thought of him—had in mind for her. Surely not an honorable marriage! Or perhaps he did intend to marry her. It was entirely possible, Gloriana realized, that he had interpreted the tinge of coldness she had not been able to keep from her manner to him as a sign of her being a very proper and cultured lady. Gloriana herself had known many society matrons and debutantes who equated coldness with refinement, and she knew enough of human nature to acknowledge the attractiveness a ladylike woman might have for a man as depraved as this one.

Yet when she searched his face for evidence of that depravity, she saw only a smooth, handsome face and dark, appealing eyes that glowed with an apparent affection for her. She could almost doubt that the conversation she had overheard that afternoon had taken place, but in her memory she could still hear the anguish in Bridgette's voice.

How easy it would be for a young woman to be taken in by this man, Gloriana told herself while she met his gaze, marveling in the ability of a foul nature to clothe itself in comeliness. And for the first time she truly felt sorry for Bridgette. Little more than a child and frantic to escape from the frontier, she must have seen Lieutenant Tilton as the answer to her prayers.

"I will need time to think," Gloriana remembered to murmur as she glanced down at the hand he held.

"But there is no time," he answered, pressing closer and moving as though to encircle her waist with his arm. Unable to stand it any longer, Gloriana stood up abruptly and suggested tea. Tilton looked startled but smiled as though she were merely being shy, and he dropped a sly kiss on her cheek as she dodged away.

Out in the kitchen Gloriana rubbed her cheek vigorously with her handkerchief and tried to overcome her intense physical revulsion. Never had she been more repelled, but she knew instinctively that she dared not show it. She wished she could call her uncle, but she also feared for his safety.

"If only Graham Norton were here," she thought for the hundredth time and regretted more than ever her pride—it had kept her from listening to him and had allowed him to believe that she could be interested in the dangerously fascinating John Tilton.

The water had been heated and tea brewed before she remembered that she had left her journal sitting on the table under the lamp. Praying that Tilton had not noticed it, she put the tea things on a tray and hurried back to the living room just in time to see the lieutenant slipping several torn pages into his pocket. If she had had any doubt about where the pages came from, the fury in the dark gaze he turned on her was enough to tell Gloriana he had read the journal.

"I find I cannot stay after all," he said smoothly. His voice still sounded pleasant, almost soothing, but his eyes glared dangerously. Gloriana was reminded of the beautiful Mount McLoughlin—a paradise on the outside but molten lava within.

She followed him, not knowing what to say, to the door.

"I think we can assume that I have your answer to my proposal." He must have read some of her comments about him. Gloriana caught her breath and tried to think of an explanation, some excuse to carry on the deception.

But the game was over. The man turned; his look, traveling insolently up and down her body, made her heart stop with terror.

"You must know that if I can't have you one way, I will have you another." And he smiled, the familiar dazzling smile, but with a touch of malice that made the expression menacing. Before Gloriana knew what was happening, he had seized her wrists and pinned them behind her back. His lips, bruising her cheeks and searing her neck, were harsh, and the embrace was a cruel punishment instead of a caress.

Then he was gone, leaving Gloriana shaking. She bathed her cheeks with cold water and poured herself a cup of the neglected tea with hands that could barely hold the pot steady.

Picking up the journal, she began to leaf through the pages to find what he had taken. All that was missing were the sketches she had made months ago—drawings of the renegade Shastas beside the creek on the Crescent City Trail.

CHAPTER 18

THE NEXT DAY the soldiers rode out. In a column of twos, they crossed the mission yard and headed along the lakeshore. Standing on the steps, Gloriana was too far away to make out the expressions on the men's faces, but she could feel the menace in the lieutenant's attitude and sense the mockery in his salute as he turned to wave at her.

"At least we will have nothing to fear from him for awhile," she told herself with relief. The soldiers had commandeered supplies from the mission stores, and their packs bulged with enough food for a long campaign. Gloriana prayed that wherever the army searched, Chief John and Keintepoos, if he were still alive, would be somewhere else. Her thoughts turned to the young chief and she remembered him as she had first seen him—strong and impassive but with a gleam of humor lurking in his dark, intelligent eyes. Somehow she doubted he were dead, and she believed it would take more than an arrogant lieutenant to capture him.

She felt almost lighthearted as she bathed the two

babies in the infant ward and fed a child whose burned hands were wrapped in bandages. The heavy wooden shutters over the windows had been opened, and the fresh smells of spring wafted through the open casements. Birds were singing ecstatically in the willows on the quadrangle. Sunbeams like liquid gold decorated the bare, scrubbed floor.

Into this happy morning burst Bridgette Welsh with a tear-stained face and fury that bordered on hysteria.

"It's your fault he's gone," Bridgette cried accusingly. She stumbled between the beds of curious patients to corner Gloriana in the dispensary. Pointing a finger at Gloriana and clenching her other hand into a fist, Bridgette looked as though she planned to strike her rival. But no blows came, only more angry words accompanied by such an explosion of fury and abuse that Gloriana felt slightly bewildered.

"I really don't know what you're talking about," she assured the distraught young woman.

"Don't give me your innocent act. He thinks you're pure because you're so cold. But I know better. I saw you kissing Graham Norton in the snow, and those were not the kisses of a shy, innocent girl.

"You think you're so much better than I. 'A lady of taste and intelligence,' John said, but you're not so smart. I took your precious Norton away from you by throwing myself into his arms and kissing him. And you—you are so dumb that you never even knew that he didn't kiss back."

If Bridgette had hoped to hurt Gloriana with her revelation, she could not have been wider of the mark.

"You even believed me when I said I was going to marry him," Bridgette spat out with a scornful little laugh. "Well, maybe I lost John Tilton because of you, but I fixed it so you can't have Graham Norton either. The way you have treated him all these months and the way you threw yourself at my John, you'll be lucky if Norton even speaks to you again."

But he had! When Bridgette had gone, in a flurry of flying skirts and a storm of sobs, Gloriana remembered Graham's farewell letter. Perhaps she had hurt him too badly with her jealousy. Perhaps his love had been killed and all he had left for her was friendship. Nevertheless, there was a chance, and Gloriana was glad that both of them had decided to leave their romance in the Lord's hands.

That's certainly a safer place than in my hands, Gloriana thought ruefully. What a mess she had made of things! Her uncle had suggested her insecurity was at fault; she thought now it was more likely her vanity. She had expected Graham to ignore that girl as though she didn't exist, and then at the first opportunity sent him straight into her arms. She remembered the day of her engagement. *Why didn't I go with him, as he asked me?* Bridgette had been all over him; he must have been trying to get away from her without ceasing to act like a gentleman. Pride had dictated her actions then, and pride would have destroyed her future if it had not been for Bridgette's angry outburst.

"For we know that all things work together for good to them that love the Lord, to them who are called according to His purpose." She recalled the Scripture with a feeling of awe.

The Welsh family left the next day, their still heavily loaded wagons rolling north across the open grasslands to the site of their new trading post. A few of the younger men from the Klamath village went with them, Welsh said, as guides, but Dr. Windemere disagreed. "I fear they are following rather than leading, and the attraction is Welsh's firewater, as the Indians call it."

With the departure of the Welshes, the raids on nearby settlers and lone trappers and miners also seemed to stop. Could Welsh have been the instigator? Could he have used his liquor to make the young

Klamaths kill for him? The missionaries discussed the matter with each other and then with the mission Indians. There was no way to reach a conclusion, but the suspects' being miles away made the little community feel more comfortable, if no less concerned.

"Remind me never to allow a settlement to grow up here," Dr. Windemere told Gloriana as he watched children playing in the mission yard from his cabin porch. The mail carrier from Applegate Landing had brought him a fresh supply of tobacco and, with his pipe in one hand and a book in the other and his swollen knees elevated on a stool, he was content.

Thankfully the spring had so far brought no outbreak of measles, influenza, typhoid, or diphtheria—the special demons of frontier communities and killers of whites as well as Indians. In fact, the warm afternoons had nearly emptied the hospital, and Gloriana and Oweena took long rambles along the lake.

Still, Gloriana did not forget about John Tilton. She feared that they had not seen the last of him, and whenever she picked up her journal, she was puzzled about the missing pages. Why would he want her drawings of those renegades? Perhaps he planned to use them to identify the real killers. Yet why would that make him so angry?

They were questions without answers, and they hung there, in the back of Gloriana's mind, infusing the perfect days with a faint uneasiness, a vague anxiety that made her glance fearfully over her shoulder in the twilight or jump at the sound of a knock on the door.

Nearly two weeks to the day after the soldiers left the mission, Gloriana awoke at dawn. An unnatural quiet, like the hush in the eye of the storm, had jarred her from a nightmarish sleep in which she had been running blindly from some unnamed fear. The eastern

178

sky was dimly lit, but no morning chorus of bird songs came from the willow grove. No meadowlarks greeted the dawn from their grassy hiding places, and on the lake the ducks and geese were strangely silent.

Slipping on a robe, Gloriana opened the wooden shutters of her window and peered out. Nothing moved in the mission yard—no dog, no early-rising child, no hunter, no squaw going for water at the artesian spring. Then below her in the shadow of the cabin, she saw the small yellow flame of a match, and she knew her uncle also had been awakened by the stillness.

"They're all gone," he told her when Gloriana joined him below. "There's no one in the cabins or the hospital. I walked over to the village, and everyone has left." The doctor did not look frightened, merely very old and very tired.

"What does it mean?" Gloriana asked with a little shiver that was less the result of the morning chill than of the eeriness of the moment.

"They were afraid. There's fear in the air. Even the birds feel it and are quiet and hiding." While he was talking, Tildy hurried out of the adjoining cabin to say that her girls were gone. Dr. Midfield and Catherine came running from the hospital to tell them what they already knew: the patients were gone. No horses remained in the mission corral nor any milk cows in the barn. Not so much as a bantam chicken remained in its coop, nor a rabbit in its hutch.

"This awful Oregon!" Catherine cried, burying her face with a little sob in her husband's shoulder.

Looking from one to another, the missionaries knew that they were all thinking about the same thing—a silent morning on the Walla Walla River broken by a shrill cry and the slaughter of the Whitmans and twelve members of their household.

"These people are our friends. They would never harm us!" Gloriana protested against the unspoken terror she saw reflected from face to face.

"This is a risk we took," Dr. Windemere had started to comment resignedly when they heard pounding hoofs across the grasslands. Echoes from the hills multiplied the sound so that the missionaries, steeling themselves for an attack, were startled to see a single Indian pony round the chapel and cut across the mission yard.

At first there appeared to be no rider; then they saw a small figure, that had been nearly covered by the flying mane, leap from the pony's back and run to embrace Gloriana. It was Oweena.

"I saw him. He's coming for you," she cried, the words tumbling over each other. "My people thought they were the ones he wanted; they thought you would be safe. But I've seen him and I know. You must get away; use the tules as cover until you're in the forest. I go for help." She did not seem to hear their questions but leaped back on the pony's back and was gone.

"Gloriana, what was she talking about? Who could be after you?" Catherine Midfield demanded.

"Could it be Chief John?" Tildy suggested.

Gloriana could not answer, though she felt somehow that she should know; her brain was numb with the horror of the situation.

"We must all go," she began confusedly, looking around as though she expected to find some means of escape near at hand. The sun was rising, sending a soft, rosy glow over the mission; it did not look like a scene for violence, yet the emptiness was like an ominous, waiting presence.

Dr. Windemere relit his pipe slowly. "My place is here with my work," he said finally.

To Gloriana's amazement the others agreed. "It makes no sense to just stay here and wait," she protested, but their minds were made up.

"How can we escape?" Dr. Midfield asked. "The horses are gone. We have no idea in which direction to go."

"Oweena said she would bring help," Tildy reminded them all.

They joined hands for a moment of prayer, and Dr. Windemere's steady voice betrayed no anxiety. "Our Heavenly Father, we trust You on this day as on every other to watch over us. Keep us in Your will whatever the storms of life may bring. Give us the strength for each trial we must face and the grace to accept what we cannot change. Give us the courage to do Your work during the night as well as the day, and give us the peace of knowing that You are the Friend who will stay closer than a brother, that when all others forsake us, You will still be there." He finished, and the quiet strength in the old doctor's prayer inspired a confidence in his staff that calmed, if not completely extinguished, their fears. "We may be close to home this morning," he added with a look of genuine affection for each of them. "I for one would not object too greatly to taking my supper with the Master. Now let's all get dressed and see about breakfast."

This attitude of simple acceptance was a revelation to Gloriana. She admired it and recognized it as an integral part of the missionary spirit. They had all known the dangers when they answered the call to the Oregon Territory, and they would face those dangers as uncomplainingly as they faced the hard work and the loneliness of frontier life.

For herself, waiting was not the answer. Oweena had suggested action, and Gloriana was beginning to conceive a plan. Somewhere to the south at a place called Lost River, Graham Norton and his men were building a road. She would find them and bring them back.

In the bottom of her trunk she found a riding habit—wrinkled and unfamiliar, yet sturdy and comfortable enough for travel. She had never been much of a horsewoman, but her sisters had insisted the garments were necessary to a Western wardrobe. Silently blessing them for the forethought, she slipped into the split skirt and heavy blouse and found a jacket that would protect her against thorns and branches as well as against the cold. She had boots and long, knitted socks as well as a knapsack. As an afterthought she added a broad-brimmed hat and long leather gloves and stuffed her journal and Bible and a lighter weight blouse into the knapsack.

Tildy was not yet in the kitchen, so there was no one to question her as she added biscuits and cheese to the knapsack. If they knew what she intended, they would never let her go, no matter how urgent Oweena's warning had been; therefore, Gloriana moved cautiously through the door.

The road to the forest, a two-wheel rut through the turf, was the shorter way; ahead tall timber began abruptly where the lakeshore rose in razor-back hills. The trees were spaced closely together, the gaps between Ponderosas and firs closed by dense growths of manzanita and jack pines. The forest looked safe, and invitingly secret, but after a moment's hesitation Gloriana headed for the thick stands of brush and tules along the lake's edge instead. *It will be slower, but I won't have to cross any open space this way*, she thought, recalling Oweena's warning to move under cover.

Behind her the mission buildings appeared solid and peaceful in the clear morning light. *Oweena said they—whoever "they" are—are after me. Perhaps the others will be safe with me gone*. She had no definite idea where Lost River might be. She only knew that it was somewhere to the south.

The tules and bushes fringing Klamath Lake formed a shoulder-high screen and by bending over, she could make good time without being seen from either the mission or the forest. To her surprise the undergrowth was not deserted; ducks and even some of the mission chickens and rabbits hid in the rushes and under the banks. They darted from one cover to the next as she ran by, but they did not make a sound, and the birds did not fly away.

The ground along the shore was soft and spongy in places, but slippery with sand in others. Several times she stumbled, and the gritty, miry coating that soon covered her gloves made her glad she had remembered to wear them.

Gradually as she neared the forest, a feeling grew that some unseen presence watched and waited there. Almost without realizing she was doing so, Gloriana slowed her pace and ducked down until she was crawling instead of running, and she moved carefully to avoid making a sound.

She wondered if this presence were what the animals felt—a dark, brooding menace on the edge of consciousness, like a sudden movement seen from the corner of the eye or a noise half heard in the night. And she was moving toward it rather than away from it. Every nerve told her to turn and run, but a small inner voice kept urging her toward rather than away from the shadows.

"The Lord is my Shepherd . . . Yea, though I walk through the valley of the shadow of death, I will fear no evil; for thou art with me; thy rod and thy staff, they comfort me." Never had she felt more like a lost sheep and never had she prayed harder for the crook of the Shepherd's staff to close around her and lift her from the precipice where she had wandered.

At the edge of the lake where the grasslands gave way to mountains and trees, two forest giants had fallen. Their branches, now bare of green, were intertwined, and their roots had torn a shallow cave in the brush and turf. Creeping thankfully into the shelter, Gloriana tried to catch her breath. Her side ached and the air entered her lungs with sharp stabs.

A veil of grasses, soap brush, and manzanita

shielded the entrance to the cave, but through that green curtain Gloriana could see past the eaves into the dark aisles of the forest. She had watched, unseeing, for several minutes before she became aware of moving shadows amid the tree trunks. A moment later she recognized the flowing hair and sashed shirts of the renegades.

Like a nightmare her mind flashed back to a cool stream on a hot day, and she heard again Graham Norton's command to look over her shoulder. The menacing faces on the other side of the water came back in vivid detail, and even as she watched him stalk from the cover of a giant fir tree, Gloriana realized that she knew the leader of this war party.

CHAPTER 19

SUDDENLY THE PIECES OF THE PUZZLE began to fit together—the strange lawlessness of himself and his men, the warnings, the feeling they had met before, the sketches torn from her journal, the promises of riches and escape. For the leader of these so-called renegades was none other than John Tilton—savage and fierce looking in his costume and war paint but still clearly recognizable in the morning light.

He thought I recognized him when I made those drawings! Gloriana thought, as stunned by the fact she had not as by the killer's identity.

Her first impulse was to return to the mission and warn the others, but she knew it was too late. "It's me he wants," she whispered, realizing the truth of Oweena's strange warning and, with a shiver, the necessity for her own escape.

It seemed like hours since she had left the cabin, but the sun, still low on the eastern horizon, told her that no more than a few minutes had passed. Leaving this cover would be impossible until Tilton's men had left the forest, and then she would have to move fast

185

before they discovered she was not at the mission and began to hunt for her.

Revolted by the thought of food but knowing she needed strength, Gloriana took some jerked meat from her knapsack and tried to eat, but the food stuck in her throat when she tried to swallow.

The outlaws seemed to be waiting for something. They moved about or crouched under the trees, but mostly they watched. From somewhere back in the trees came the sound of horses' stamping and blowing.

Gloriana wondered how long their Indian friends had known of the identity of the so-called renegades; she suspected at least since Keintepoos's injury. Probably the missionaries' helping the soldiers—undoubtedly the aggressors rather than the victims, as they claimed, of the battle with the Klamath chiefs—had created an atmosphere of distrust. Or perhaps the Indians, including Oweena, felt that the missionaries, being white themselves, would not believe an accusation made against white men.

The cave was warm, but Gloriana did not remove her jacket. She would have to be ready to move at any moment, and she could not risk leaving it behind. Another hour passed. She woke from a light doze to see Tilton pointing toward the grasslands; her eyes followed to see puffs of smoke rising from the opposite shore of the lake.

They don't know the Mission is almost deserted and are attacking from both sides. She breathed a prayer of thanks that the villagers and the children were gone and at the same time saw the wisdom of Oweena's advice. Going toward the forest she had met one band of outlaws, but in the other direction she would soon have run out of cover and been captured.

Dear God, help them, Gloriana breathed a prayer for the mission staff as Tilton gave the signal to advance. Tears filled her eyes, but she hoisted her pack and prepared to move.

186

The outlaws were attacking on foot, leaving their horses behind in the trees. There would be a guard, but perhaps there would be a way to get one of the horses.

Gloriana's heart was pounding, and her knees were shaking again as she slipped from the shelter of the fallen trees and crawled in the direction of the restless animals. A stand of firs screened her movements while thick mats of pine needles cushioned and muffled her steps.

The horses were held in a grassy hollow and, to Gloriana's relief, she saw they had been hobbled rather than tethered. Some of the more adventurous had already drifted from the herd, tempted by greener grass down the next aisle of trees or in the next glade. Tilton was apparently not expecting any trouble, for he had posted only one guard—a sleepy-looking young man whom Gloriana thought she recognized, even in his long-haired wig and paint, as the trooper they called Lazy Harry. He was not watching the horses but was whittling idly with his pocket knife on a piece of wood. He looked bored, and Gloriana wondered with a little shudder how many other times he had watched like this.

Except for the occasional whinny of a horse or the sharp crack of a shod hoof against a tree trunk, the forest was still. The usual scolding of the squirrels and the chattering of the jays were ominously absent, while no scurryings in the underbrush signaled the woodland folk's hurrying about their day's business.

One horse, the boldest of all, had climbed out of the hollow and was hobbling determinedly toward a lush patch of grass in the sun. Gloriana, hidden beneath the drooping branches of a blue spruce, watched the guard for any sign of concern, but he did not so much as glance in the animal's direction. Then, being careful to keep heavy cover between herself and the inquisitive horse, Gloriana followed.

It was John Tilton's own saddle mount, a large, powerful roan with an intelligent eye and a body built for both speed and endurance. He apparently recognized Gloriana, for he did no more than shy away as she tried to approach him.

"Here, Champion," Gloriana called, remembering the great beast's name. His long ears flicked back and forth, listening to the sound of her voice. "Always talk softly to horses," Gloriana recalled Oweena saying. "They are nervous animals, and your voice will soothe them." She tried whispering but Champion jerked away at the sound and she changed to a soft murmur, hoping the sound would not carry to the waiting guard. "Such a pretty horse. Nice Champion. Big, strong Champion."

Her repeated use of his name reassured the intelligent beast. He went on cropping the tender spring grass while she put her fingertips on his velvety nose and rubbed gently between his ears. Then she had her hands on the reins and was leading him to a fallen tree trunk where she could mount.

Fervently wishing she were a better horsewoman, Gloriana struggled to remove the hobbles and then struggled again to get into the saddle. Champion turned and looked at her inquiringly over his shoulder, as though puzzled by her difficulties. But he did not buck and after a few crabsteps, resisting the strange touch on the reins, he began to settle down and accept her directions. "You probably think I am taking you to your master," she resumed talking to the high-strung animal, "but I'm not. You see, we have had a kind of falling out, and I am going to have to take you far away. You'll like it where we are going, though. There will be warm stalls and lots of hay and oats to eat someday in Applegate Landing. But first we have to take a little trip south to a place called Lost River. I'm not exactly sure where it is, but I know we can find it if we just try hard enough."

Champion's ears were turned toward her, and gradually she felt the jumpiness leave his big body and his teeth quit searching for the bit in his mouth. Gloriana had never ridden such a large, powerful horse before. She rarely managed to be completely in charge of any mount, and this one could easily run away with her or rub her off his back on the nearest low-hanging branch. But Champion was well trained and, if not exactly eager to please, he was at least willing.

"I guess the Shepherd's staff found me once again," Gloriana realized with a prayer of thankfulness. On foot it would only have been a matter of time before they found her, but astride this magnificent animal, she had a chance—at least she would have a chance if she figured out which direction to go in.

Although she had lived on the nearby Upper Klamath for eight months or more, she had never been this far into the woods before. The sameness of the trees, the bushy undergrowth, the sudden hills, and equally sudden ravines was bewildering. Overhead, interlocking branches blotted out the sun, creating a green twilight, and it was difficult to tell whether a distant rushing sound was from the soughing of a breeze in the treetops or the tumbling waters of a nearby stream.

Every impulse told Gloriana to bury herself in the forest. Hidden in this maze of trees, she would feel safe from pursuit. Yet she had heard about travelers, lost in the forest, who moved in circles for hours, never going far from their starting point. She thought about giving Champion his head and letting him find his way south. In fact, if left to his devices, he would probably rejoin the other horses, and, unable to tell north from south, she might not even know they had changed direction until it was too late.

"I will instruct thee and teach thee in the way in

189

which thou should go. I will guide thee with mine eyes," she remembered the promises and set out another urgent appeal for guidance.

It was then that she remembered that Klamath Lake ran directly north and south. If she could find the lakeshore, she could follow it south, staying within the protecting shadows of wooded hills the entire way.

Finding the lake turned out to be an easy enough matter. The hills sloped down to the shore all along the west side and by continually following the downward slopes, she soon saw pale blue waves gleaming in the sunshine.

Almost at the same time she became aware of the faint sounds of a battle. Carried across the waters were gunshots and what sounded like distant war cries, but peering almost into the sun, she could see nothing. *Protect them, God,* she prayed again and again. She wondered what was happening. Who was fighting? The missionaries would not be; their way, like that of the martyrs, was a passive acceptance which in itself condemned the violence. Perhaps Oweena had returned with help as she promised. Perhaps the phony warriors of the murderer Tilton were now engaged in battle with real warriors. Gloriana had no way of knowing, and with tears in her eyes, she turned Champion's head south and urged him to a gallop.

Bordering the fresh-water lake, the forest grew taller and lusher. Instead of the scrub pines, thick firs, and rocky, brush-covered soil of the hillsides, giant Ponderosas were separated by wide, cool aisles nearly free of undergrowth. Champion moved tirelessly through this dim, green world. His galloping hooves startled an occasional deer from its cover or sent birds winging through the branches. Yet the farther south they went, the more alive the forest became. Saucy jays or camp robbers mocked them from the treetops, then followed for a short distance on dark blue wings, as though, having given them an ultimatum, they were making sure the intruders left their domain. The bushes rustled with unseen inhabitants as the horse and rider passed, and once a silver fox darted across the trail. How could the wildlife know the awful portent of a war party and go into hiding, yet accept the intrusion of a lone woman as little more than a temporary annoyance? It could be the numbers. At least thirty men had been in John Tilton's party. Or it could be a sixth sense, a built-in warning which made the animals aware of the evil purposes of the men. Gloriana remembered the dark presence that she had felt and guessed the latter.

She sensed no such presence following her now. Often her head turned automatically to look for pursuers, but no one was visible, and she felt no one behind her. Gradually she became aware of a difficulty in breathing and a sharp stitch in her side that increased with each jarring motion of the big roan's haunches. The pain subsided a little if she held him to a walk or increased his pace to a run, but it returned as soon as Champion resumed the gallop.

"You are holding up magnificently," she told him finally, "but I am afraid I am going to have to rest." The bank of a small stream offered green grass for the horse to eat and a soft couch for Gloriana to sit on. She eased herself gingerly from the saddle, trying not to notice the charley horses in each thigh or the soreness of her backside.

Although she had brought food, she had forgotten a canteen, and the clear water of the stream, icy with the continued run-off of melting snow at some high elevation, soothed her face and cooled her parched throat. She noticed how the animal did not drink his fill but took a few mouthfuls and then moved away to graze and wait for his warm flanks to cool before drinking deeply. Remembering that too much ice-cold water when a patient is warm can cause stomach cramps, Gloriana followed suit, and soon she was feeling more comfortable.

The irony of her escaping on John Tilton's horse made her want to laugh, though the ache in her side from the unaccustomed hours on Champion prevented more than a smile. But even the smile disappeared as she looked through the trees to see billowing smoke rising from the direction of the mission on the other side of the lake. *Dear God, they're burning it!* She thought of the beautiful new chapel, the orphanage, the snug cabins. Before she had felt only fear; now a fierce anger began to grow inside her. "He won't get away with this, and this time he will suffer the consequences."

With riding and resting it took nearly seven hours to skirt the giant lake. The sun was halfway to the western horizon when Champion stepped from the protecting forest onto the sands of the Klamath's south shore, and Gloriana realized that from here she would have to find her way by instinct.

"I wish you could talk," she told the horse once again. "I have a feeling your instincts would be more reliable than mine in this situation."

The sun, beginning its western descent, was on her right. Before her was open range—rolling grasslands, wooded shelves, and shadowed valleys, stretching away to deserts in the south and east and more mountains in the west. Crisscrossing that vast gray-green space were meandering bands of dark green, each one of which might be the one they called the Lost River.

Why would they call a river "lost"? How could anyone lose a river? Carefully, she scanned each green stripe, following it from the place it entered the scene until it merged with a larger stripe. One of the green bands stopped abruptly halfway to the horizon; it skirted a plateau and cut through a mesa, then rolled across a wide plain to stop abruptly at the base of a rocky escarpment.

"That looks like as good as possibility as any," she told the now-tiring horse and turned his head in the direction of what she hoped was Lost River.

In the end, it was Champion rather than Gloriana that found the road construction camp. Night had fallen and the rangeland moved and echoed with the yelping of coyotes; the hooting of owls; and the secret, nighttime meanderings of shadowy half-figures that appeared briefly and then vanished in the dim light of a crescent moon. Gloriana drooped in the saddle, hanging onto the saddle horn, all attempts to guide her mount forgotten. Her legs felt numb, but sharp pains continued to pierce her side, and her shoulders ached dully. Champion had slowed to a walk, and his head, usually held high and proud, hung wearily; yet he kept on moving, his quick wits telling him that to stop alone in the open would mean certain death.

It was after midnight when they stumbled into Graham Norton's camp. Trembling, his sides flecked with foam, the horse stood quietly within the circle of firelight while eager hands took the burden from his back and relieved him of his saddle. Soon he was rubbed down and resting contentedly among his fellows, a measure of oats in his nosebag and sleep just minutes away from heavy eyelids.

"Take care of Champion," Gloriana managed to murmur when hot coffee and a warm fire had revived her. She opened her eyes to find Graham's anxious face only inches away. "Graham! Thank God," she whispered and, throwing her arms impulsively around the startled man's neck, she hid her face against his rough flannel shirt.

He held her tightly for a moment, seemingly oblivious to his men's curious looks, then began to question her gently, "What happened, Glory? What are you running from?"

The story of her day's adventure tumbled out then—the silent sunrise, Oweena's warning, the men in the Indian costumes, her recognition of John Tilton, her escape and long ride, and the sounds and smoke of battle. She was crying when she finished, and the men looked grim but not surprised.

"I blame myself," Graham muttered hoarsely, the roughness of his voice betraying his emotion. "I should never have left them unprotected."

"You couldn't have known, boss," reassured one of the men Gloriana recognized as an old friend from her first trail ride.

"I don't think he would have come if he hadn't found my drawings," Gloriana added, and then she had to explain what had happened with the sketches in her journal and her last meeting with Tilton that ended in threats.

"It sounds like it's her he's after," Blackjack commented to Graham, who glared fiercely but said nothing.

"And that there means he'll be a-comin' for her jest as soon as he picks up her trail," Smitty agreed.

The certainty in the Westerners' voices awoke Gloriana to a possibility she had not considered. Somehow she had thought if she could just reach Graham, she would be safe, and he would be able to send back help to the mission. Now she realized that there were only a dozen men around the fire, and a wave of fear dampened her happiness.

"I'm afraid I have put you all in danger," she faltered.

"Don't be silly, Gloriana," Graham told her impatiently. He gave her a little shake but did not take his arm from around her shoulders.

"Whatever we are going to do will have to wait until morning," he said. "Tilton won't travel at night, and there is always the chance that some of the Klamaths will be keeping him busy." He posted a

194

watch and told the others to get some sleep, but he himself continued to sit beside Gloriana, looking gloomily into the night.

Now was the time to resolve their differences, but Gloriana had no idea where to begin. In the firelight Graham's face seemed distant and closed, and though he still held her, he did not appear to be aware of the fact.

She would have preferred for him to make the first move, but it did not look like he was going to do so. With a sigh she let her arm, which had slipped from around his neck, encircle his waist, and she snuggled against him. The action brought an immediate response. He squeezed her closely, but his expression was troubled.

"I'm sorry I allowed you to be exposed to this danger," he told her finally. "I knew Tilton was not to be trusted."

"I should have figured it out myself," Gloriana blamed herself. Then she took a deep breath and added, "I guess I was so busy fighting with you that I couldn't think straight about anything else."

Graham lifted her head from his shoulder with his free hand so that he could look into her eyes. His gaze was searching and his voice serious. "Does that mean that we are through fighting?"

"I don't ever want to fight with you again." She did not wait for his response but lifted her lips to his and kissed him shyly at first and then hungrily. Graham's reaction was everything she could have wished.

After a breathless moment in which she wondered if her ribs were being crushed, he began to explain, "Glory, I want you to know that girl never meant anything to me."

"I know; she told me," Gloriana responded before she thought.

She felt him stiffen, and then he asked somewhat tensely, "Would you have believed me if she hadn't told you?"

But Gloriana would not allow him to move away or be offended. She had had enough of misunderstandings to last a lifetime, so she kissed the hard outline of his jaw and then let her lips travel softly over his neck.

Graham laughed delightedly in spite of himself. "I don't know what happened to my blushing Philadelphia lady, but I like it," he whispered against her hair.

"It's simple. I discovered I couldn't live without you. After that it was easy to see what a fool I had been not to have trusted you all along. I should have known when you accepted Christ as your Saviour, that you were not the kind of man I was accusing you of being, and I think I did know. I was just too proud to admit it."

CHAPTER 20

GLORIANA WOKE THE NEXT MORNING to find herself at the base of the rocky escarpment that she had seen the day before looking out over the rangeland. Nearby was a straggling wood made up primarily of junipers, scrub oaks, and lodgepole pines, and a few yards away a wide, shallow river—its color nearly gray from a bed of slate and pebbles and a border of sage—disappeared into the ground.

"Lost River," she recognized it and looked around for the magnificent animal who had brought her there. She saw him in a rope corral, his nose once again in a feedbag, and hobbled over to tell him good morning. The stitch in her side was gone, but the charley horses in her legs were not, and every muscle in her body felt as though it had been stretched and pummeled.

"You seem to have survived our adventure better than I." Champion responded with a playful nudge that nearly sent her sprawling, then went on eating. He seemed none the worse for wear. His dark red coat had been rubbed free of dust, and a night's rest had made him eager to go again. "I'm afraid I don't have either your stamina or your spirit," she told him with a playful tug on his forelock. How could such a noble beast belong to such an ignoble man?

"Isn't that John Tilton's horse?" Graham asked, joining her with a low whistle as he recognized the animal.

Gloriana nodded and then explained how she had gotten the horse.

"Who would have thought that the little Quaker missionary would become a frontier heroine!" Graham laughed, but his look was genuinely admiring. "You'll have some wonderful stories to tell our children," he added softly, and Gloriana found she was blushing with both embarrassment and pleasure.

She found a secluded place in the wood near the river to make her morning preparations. She was glad she had had the foresight to bring a change of clothing. The heavy shirt she had worn the day before clung to her skin as though she had worn it a week, but washing in the river's cool waters and donning a lighter blouse refreshed her. She combed her hair out of its long braids and tied it back with a ribbon. She could not see her face, but her cheeks and nose stung, and she tried not to imagine how she would look with a red, peeling sunburn.

"Miss Glory, Graham said you were to eat all of this," the cook told her with a grin when she returned to camp. Gloriana looked with dismay at the heaped-up sourdough biscuits, fried meat, and potatoes, but, digging in, she found to her amazement that she was hungry enough to devour nearly all of it. She noticed then that the men were breaking camp. Mules were being hitched to wagons loaded with equipment. The horses that were not saddled were being herded into a tight remuda to be driven along with the wagons.

"I'm going to put you up on Champion again," Graham told her as he hurried past. "He's strong enough to run away from anything if there's trouble, and I doubt Tilton has any other animals with his speed." To Gloriana's unspoken question, he replied. "He should have picked up your trail by now, but we'll have quite a few hours' start by the time he finds this camp."

Such, however, was not the case.

A lookout posted atop the escarpment halloaed the camp and called out, "Riders coming!" He had spotted a moving dust cloud coming fast from the east.

"He didn't bother to track you through the forest," Graham, suddenly understanding, explained to Gloriana. "He guessed where you would be heading and took the easier route along the east side of the lake."

Graham had planned to take the wagons and travel west, hoping to meet the larger part of his workcrew. They should have left Applegate Landing several days before with a party of surveyors and additional wagonloads of equipment. He had gambled on meeting them at Annie Creek, this side of the Greensprings, but that was a chance he could no longer take.

"We could hold them off in one of those caves down in the Lava Beds," one of the men suggested, pointing toward the black, ragged fields of once molten rock on the southern horizon.

"They could keep us there for weeks, starve us out, and no one would ever know what happened," Graham rejected the idea. "No, we'll have to split up. Gloriana and I will make tracks for Fort Winnemucca while the rest of you try to find our work gang and head north to the mission. If anyone's left alive, they'll need help."

The men objected to the plan. Gloriana caught their hint that she would slow their progress, but she could not dispute it. Her journey the day before had been leisurely compared to the pace they would have to set today, and already her aching body felt played out. She dreaded getting into the saddle and she feared the return of the pain in her side that she knew Champion's gallop would bring. But most of all, Graham's words, "if anyone's left alive," echoed through her mind, leaving her with an empty place at the center of her being, where hope had dwelt.

"It looks like about thirty or forty riders," the lookout, who had scrambled down the cliff face, reported to Graham. "They should be here in about an hour, maybe less."

Then everyone was moving. Horses whinnied, mules brayed, and wheels groaned as the wagons got underway. And heading in the opposite direction were Gloriana Windemere and Graham Norton.

"They'll have traveled all night while we've rested," Graham told Gloriana encouragingly, but both knew that it would take a miracle to save them; both were looking for that miracle to the only Source that could grant it. Through Graham's mind raced the outlaw's threats against Gloriana, and he pleaded on her behalf, while Gloriana thought of Tilton's jealous anger and the revenge he would take, as she prayed for Graham's safety.

The horses ran easily, covering ground at a good pace. Graham's buckskin, a solidly built animal with a deep chest and long back legs that evidenced a hint of Arabian blood, was slower than Champion, but his staying power was as great. The ground which looked flat from a distance proved treacherous close at hand. Rain-washed gullies crisscrossed, while prairie-dog towns mined the turf and sandy soil with holes—any of which could break a horse's leg or send a rider sprawling.

To Gloriana's inexperienced eyes, every direction looked the same. There were no landmarks, no trails to go by. Miles and miles of gray-green hills and mesas stretched to dim horizons. Graham worried about the trail they were leaving although Gloriana could see no trace of hoofprints behind them.

"We'll cover our tracks in Tule Lake," he said and pointed toward a misty haze to the south that looked more like a desert waste than a lake.

They had topped a rise when they heard the sounds of gunshots behind them. The long reports of rifles mixed with the shorter reports of pistol fire in a ragged staccato.

"What's happening? Did Tilton follow your crew after all?" Gloriana turned to Graham inquiringly.

The big man shook his head firmly. "My guess is the men set up a rear guard to give us a better chance to escape." He went to his saddlebags and took out a looking glass and used it to scan the horizon.

"John Tilton has one of those," Gloriana remembered.

"Then he's probably using it on us right now," Graham growled, angry with himself for exposing their position. He directed Gloriana to take the horses behind a nearby outcropping of rock and continued to peer through the glass.

What he saw made his tightly set lips press in an even tighter seam. "It didn't work," he told Gloriana briefly. "Tilton left half his men to fight. He and the rest are coming after us."

The chase continued mile after mile. Graham used every trick he knew, starting false trails down gullies and across rocky mesas. For a half hour they walked their horses in the edge of Tule Lake—a vast, shallow plain of water and reeds, more like a dense marsh than a lake. But when they emerged from the screens of cattails and bushes, Tilton and his men were still behind them, closer then before.

"They're running their horses into the ground," Graham commented. Their pursuers were close enough now that they could make out the figures of individual riders in the dust cloud behind them. In the forefront, his anger almost discernible even at that great distance, was John Tilton. "I'm going to hit the

Winnemucca Trail and try to outrun them," Graham told her. "Champion still has a burst of speed in him. When I give the signal, dig your heels into his sides and don't look back."

"I'm not leaving you," Gloriana shot back defiantly, but there was no time to argue.

The Winnemucca Trail was little more than a pair of wagon ruts cutting through the sand, rocks, and grass, but it was free of prairie-dog holes and other obstructions. Given their heads, Champion and Graham's buckskin lengthened their strides drawing upon some inner strength. They had begun to increase their lead, drawing away from the exhausted horses of the pursuers when a single rifle shot rang out.

Graham reeled in his saddle, and the buckskin broke stride. Gloriana pulled frantically on Champion's reins, but Graham shouted "Keep going!" One arm hung limp at his side, but with the other he was pulling his rifle from its sheath by his stirrup.

"I won't leave you!" Gloriana shouted back. Tears were streaming down her face as she tried to turn her plunging mount. The reins cut into her gloved hands, while Champion, frightened by the gunshot and her terror, fought her for the bit.

She heard the pounding of hoofs behind her and the wild shouts of Tilton and his men. Then she became confused as the pounding seemed to be coming from in front of her as well. "Gloriana Windemere, don't you dare lose consciousness!" she yelled at herself, and finally she had Champion turned and running back toward the place where Graham sat, shooting from the back of his trembling horse.

"Wherever thou goest, I will go," she said aloud, though there was no chance of his hearing her in the noise. Still he glanced over his shoulder as she rode up, but his anguished expression soon turned to bewilderment. With twenty outlaws shooting at him, a bullet hole in his shoulder, and the rifle in his hand hot and jammed, Graham Norton broke into a wide grin. For behind Gloriana at full gallop came a troop of soldiers from Fort Winnemucca. They had spread out in attack formation while a bugler sounded the charge. The officer at their head was waving a curved, silver saber that glistened menacingly in the sun and beside him, on a brown and white spotted pony, raced Chief Keintepoos. His shrill war whoop pierced through the din, a sound so savage and fierce as to numb the hearts of his enemies, but it made Gloriana's leap with thankfulness.

"It looks like Someone does care about us," she told Graham, though she doubted he could hear her.

Still he must have read her lips because he answered, "I know He does."

Rounding up the phony renegades did not take long. The men were too bewildered to put up much of a fight, and the horses were too tired to run. Somehow in the confusion John Tilton managed to escape. His horse was found ridden to death near Tule Lake, but though they searched the ground along the shore for miles, looking for his tracks, there was no sign of the outlaw.

"He will probably head south to San Francisco and, if he makes it past the Shasta Indians, he may find a new gang of cut throats on the Barbary Coast." Graham's prediction sounded gloomy, but it was merely a matter of fact. For now with his wound tended and Gloriana close by, he was contented.

The officer in charge of the cavalry troop was Major William F. Creighton, a middle-aged man whose years of service on the frontier were emblazoned in his insignia and evidenced by the calm efficiency of his actions. He dispatched some of his men to relieve Graham's work crew back at Lost River; the rest he set to making camp and treating the wounds of outlaws, soldiers, and animals alike.

"Well, it seems you have had some excitement,

Miss Windemere," Major Creighton began with a kindly smile that seemed to say it was all in a day's work for him. His bearded face and his manner were almost fatherly, and Gloriana found herself telling him about the escape from the mission, the ride south, and their pursuit by Tilton's outlaws. The officer nodded understandingly, but his face betrayed no surprise or astonishment.

"When this West is finally settled, I wonder how many people will realize what it took to tame her," he said musingly after she had finished.

"And I wonder how many will realize that it was often our own white savages, not the Indians, who needed taming," Graham interposed. "But tell us, Major, who is John Tilton and how did you know we needed help?"

Major Creighton looked sad then and his eyes assumed a faraway look. "John Tilton was the son of an old friend of mine—a promising young officer of sterling qualities. He was noted for his bright green eyes and his almost silver-white hair." The Major paused to note their reactions, then continued, "He was dispatched into Klamath territory to make peace with Chief Keintepoos and Chief John. We suspect now that he and all of his troopers were killed— ambushed perhaps by the man who assumed his identity."

"Then who is the man we have been calling John Tilton?" Gloriana asked with a little shudder as she recalled the months she had been in close contact with such a cold-blooded murderer.

"We think he may be a cavalry captain who was drummed out of the service a couple of years ago in Arizona."

"I heard one of his men call him Captain once," Gloriana remembered.

The Major nodded again, but he would say no more about the identity of the outlaw. Instead he turned to their other question. "As for our being here at the right time and place, you can thank God and Keintepoos. The chief showed up at the fort two weeks ago with his story about phony soldiers masquerading as renegades."

"What made you believe him?" Graham asked. "You could have thought of him as an enemy."

"Since I knew the real John Tilton, his description of a dark-haired lieutenant was enough to make me suspicious. But what really turned the trick was he told me he was a Christian. You see, I am also a Christian, which made us brothers, and I had no choice but to believe a brother in Christ."

Late that night the soldiers returned, leading Graham's work crew and more prisoners. The men were sheepish as Graham chewed them out for disobeying his orders. But Smitty grinned slyly at Gloriana and said, "That's just the boss's way of sayin' thanks and he's glad we made it through all right."

Sometime between midnight and daybreak, a Klamath messenger found them in their lakeshore camp. Gloriana, sleeping on an army bedroll just inside the circle of firelight, heard the soft beats of the Indian pony's hooves, echoing through the ground. She sat up quickly, her heart beating faster before she remembered she was safe in an army camp and the man she had known as John Tilton had been defeated. She drifted back into a light sleep only to be awakened a few minutes later by a strong hand on her shoulder.

"It's a runner from the mission," Graham whispered, and in a second she was wide awake.

"Are they all right? Is anyone hurt?" She began asking questions, but he told her to wait. Keintepoos was questioning the messenger while the army major and some of his men looked on. The young brave had no wounds, but his scratched and dusty body showed evidence of a long, hard ride. The rapid speech was difficult to follow, but Gloriana could make out enough to breathe sighs of relief and prayers of thankfulness.

When she had escaped from the mission, she had gone with the feeling that their Klamath friends had deserted them. She understood now what Oweena had been trying to tell them that morning. The Klamaths had thought the attackers were after Indians, not missionaries, and they had withdrawn to a safe place protected by the warriors of Chief Keintepoos and Chief John. But when Oweena had recognized the lieutenant in his war paint and disguise, she had understood who the outlaws were really after and had ridden for help.

"Our people were not in time to save the buildings," Keintepoos told her regretfully, "but the missionaries are safe."

She knew a moment's regret for the picturesque quadrangle around the willow wood, the snug cabins, and the frontier hospital, but regrets were soon swallowed up in the joy of knowing that her uncle, Tildy, and the Midfields had survived.

But the tale had not ended happily for everyone. Before they attacked the mission, the outlaws had massacred a party of pioneers heading north with their loaded wagons.

"The Welshes," Gloriana guessed. "Bridgette knew too much, and she threatened to expose him." She remembered their suspicions that Welsh might be the leader of the renegades and wondered again how they could have been so blind. She could not be sorry that the elder Welsh would not be setting up his trading post to sell firewater to the Indians. But she was sorry for the mousy little mother, who tried so hard to please, and the happy-go-lucky boys who could have grown up to be fine men. And most of all she was sorry about Bridgette. *Perhaps if I had not been so jealous, perhaps if I had tried just a little bit, I could have been a good influence on her,* Gloriana thought with the wisdom of hindsight.

Then she noticed that the messenger was pointing at her and speaking in a low voice to Keintepoos. The warrior's strong face remained impassive, but humor lurked in his eyes as he approached her.

"He brings also a message from Chief John. The Chief has heard of your courage in escaping from the mission. He is raising his offer for you to a hundred ponies and two hundred beaver pelts."

CHAPTER 21

On a golden july morning Gloriana Windemere awoke in a rainbow-tinted bedroom in Applegate Landing. Outside the open window, meadowlarks greeted the dawn while inside sunbeams danced across the flowered carpet. The music and beauty blended with the joy in her heart to make her feel like singing, for today was Gloriana's wedding day.

In the corner of the tiny room beside the prayer altar and rocking chair hung an old-fashioned wedding dress. A creamy confection of lace and silk, it had been Cynthia Applegate's own, and she had lovingly adapted it to Gloriana's taller, fuller figure. A high neck trimmed with lace topped a yoke neckline made demure by a gauze insert that would allow a glimpse without baring the delicate skin beneath. Long, tight sleeves of Brussels lace began in tiny puffs at the shoulders and ended in graceful V's above the fingers to give an appearance of gloves without covering the all-important ring finger. Seed pearls outlined the bodice and waist, dropping the latter slightly to emphasize its smallness. And the skirt was yards and yards of shimmering silk that peeked out from a half skirt of lace. Molded to the bride's form, it fell nearly straight in front, then swept back for an elegant train. A large white bow, fastened above the gathers and ending in wide streamers emphasized the bustle effect while a long veil cascading from a pearl-crusted crown trailed behind.

"I'll look like a living version of Bridal Veil Falls," Gloriana laughed delightedly as she remembered the lacy extravagance of the waterfall. At the same time she remembered the outlaw who had called himself John Tilton, and she breathed a deep prayer of thankfulness to her Heavenly Father who had made this day and her happiness possible.

She and the other missionaries had been at Applegate Landing for nearly a month. The hospitable Applegates had opened their home to Dr. Windemere's household, while the Reverend Samuels and his wife housed the Midfields. The old doctor had at first protested this sabbatical. He had wanted to stay on the Upper Klamath while Graham Norton and his men rebuilt the mission. But the bullet in his leg reduced his walk to a hobble, and the congestion in his lungs from having breathed too much smoke in the fires slowed his pace further. He had had to admit that he might be less than a help.

The Midfields would not be returning with him to work among the Klamaths. Dr. Midfield had been embarrassed and apologetic about their going home, but his wife had remained adamant. "I won't have my babies die in this wilderness," Catherine Midfield had said again and again. No one could assure her that they would not. The hardships and tragedies were as much a fact of frontier life as the glorious scenery.

Moreover, Dr. Windemere was losing Gloriana. After the wedding day her home would be in Applegate Landing where Graham had built a cabin as picturesque as the forest and where he could continue hauling freight from the coast.

"Well, Tildy, it looks like it's just you and me again," the doctor had told his housekeeper with an attempt to be cheerful about it. Then letters had come from the Mission Board at home. They had just heard about the numbers treated at the mission during the epidemic and also the rapport that had been established with the local tribes. They were dispatching a team of three doctors and four nurses and sending funds for the building and stocking of a large new hospital.

With his cup full Dr. Windemere could enjoy his niece's happiness and give her his blessing. There had, however, been one codicil to the Mission Board's decision:

> You have on your staff a single female nurse named Miss Gloriana Windemere. The Executive Committee of the Board has reviewed its policy concerning the employment of spinsters in the frontier settlements and has decided that the Subcommittee on Appointments exceeded its authority in granting her sponsorship. We are, therefore, requesting that her work with the mission be terminated and she be returned home. The board will defray all expenses if she embarks on the return journey by mid-August.

Dr. Windemere had been bemused by the order, but Gloriana had been incensed. She had demanded that her uncle write a letter of protest, and she had herself composed a scathing attack on the Board's reasoning, its competence, and its knowledge of frontier conditions. He had more or less agreed but vaguely enough to suggest that he might put off the task indefinitely. "After all, you are leaving the mmssion anyway," he had reminded her.

And she was. During the past weeks while Graham was back at Klamath Mission, she had been turning his cabin into a home. A large, spacious building of unpeeled logs, it sat on the edge of the settlement on a bluff overlooking the Rogue River. At its back were giant trees, and before it lay the rolling green valley, stretching away to the white-topped peaks of the Cascade Range.

In her room at the Applegate's, Gloriana settled into a rocker and, reaching for her journal, began to thumb through the pages. How glad she was that she had taken it with her when she escaped from the mission. Otherwise, it would have been burned with the rest of her possessions.

She had come far in just one year. Some of her ideas and attitudes had changed, but mostly they had grown, shedding the veneer of sophistication and getting down to the homely truths that gave the pioneers something to hang onto through the trials and hardships of frontier life. She now understood that they were an intelligent, cultured people who needed her God, not her social rules. And no longer was freedom frightening to her, but an opportunity to create a new and better way of life where all of God's people could work together in harmony and kinship.

With a little half-smile on her lips, Gloriana picked up her pencil and began writing her wedding day entry—the last one as Miss Gloriana Windemere of Philadelphia.

Applegate Landing   July 16, 1852
My Wedding Day

Today I stop being a spinster nurse from Philadelphia and become Mrs. Graham Norton of Applegate Landing. Back home the marriage of the elder Miss Windemere, daughter of the Reverend Windemere of Seventh Avenue Church, would have been no more than a minor ripple in the social whirlpool, but here on the frontier it is a major event. For two days now the guests have been coming— pioneers from as far away as the Umpqua Valley, miners from the gold fields at Jacksonville, and Klamath and Shasta friends from their distant summer camps in the Cascade Mountains.

I suppose I should be sad not to have my sisters Juliana and Marianna with me at such an important time, and part

211

of me does miss them. But my matron of honor will be Princess Oweena, wife of Chief Keintepoos. Keintepoos will stand up with Graham. Some people in the village have thought our choice odd and even inappropriate, but we are happy with our decision. These people are among our closest friends. We have gone through fire and water together, and now that we are in a happy place, we want them to share it with us.

I asked Oweena and Keintepoos to wear their own wedding garments for the ceremony. Made of soft white deerskin, fringed, and decorated in intricate designs of beads and dyed porcupine quills—they are as exquisite in their own way as the elegant gown of lace and silk that I am to wear.

Brides are supposed to be nervous, but I feel only a great joy welling up from somewhere deep inside me. Perhaps that is because I have no reservations about my marriage. I know it is what God wants for me, and I know too that the love Graham and I have for each other is rooted in our deeper love for Him.

The years ahead will not all be rosy. I have seen enough now of the Oregon Territory to know that living here will not be like setting up housekeeping on a peaceful boulevard back home. Many of the Indians are our friends, but there are some, I know, who look on us as enemies. Outlaws like the man we knew as John Tilton are still at large. And it will be many years before the quality of medical care will be comparable to that in the East.

Still I would not trade the life I have begun here for a New York mansion or a princess's palace. This is where I belong—in the center of God's will. Here in Applegate Landing I will raise my children, dedicate them to God and teach them to be strong men and women. And here I will do my best to make this wonderful Oregon Territory, the Land of the Golden West, a place where Christian men and women of all races can work together for a better life for everyone.

The sun was setting when Gloriana glided regally down a grassy aisle to meet her groom. In her hand she carried a bouquet of creamy white mountain lilies and delicate maidenhair fern. Her slippered feet trod on the pink and yellow petals of wild roses, and the air was perfumed with wildflowers, pine, and cedar. Around her neck was a tiny mother-of-pearl cross, a gift from the groom and the "something new" demanded by custom. Her beautiful ruby engagement ring was "something old," since it had been a legacy to Graham from his grandmother who had been given it upon her own engagement nearly a century before. The "something borrowed" was her wedding gown, and for "something blue"—Gloriana blushed at the thought of the lacey blue garter that she wore carefully hidden beneath layers of skirt and petticoat. It had been a gift from Rita, the saloon girl turned pioneer wife and church pianist. She had married the compassionate young miner who had sympathized when her arm was broken on the trip from Crescent City.

Graham Norton, watching Gloriana float gracefully toward him, saw the blush and wondered what had embarrassed his beautiful bride. Perhaps it had been the intensity of his expression or the unaccustomed situation of being the cynosure of so many eyes.

The color of Graham's dark suit accentuated his height, while the severe cut emphasized his broad shoulders. His hair had been newly trimmed and vigorously brushed to approximate some order, yet the red-gold curls were beginning to spring above his ears and trail across his wide forehead.

"Chief John would give two, maybe three, hundred horses if he could see her now," Keintepoos, who stood closely beside Graham, told him quietly. The warrior's expression was impassive, but Graham was beginning to understand the man's understated humor.

"Not for a thousand," Graham whispered back.

Gloriana wondered if they were talking about her, but she caught the mischievous glint in the chief's glance and guessed it was some joke. She had to catch her breath when she looked at Graham. Never had he seemed more handsome or more awesomely masculine. Her uncle, who guided her toward the altar, caught the little gasp and patted her hand reassuringly. He had chosen to give her away rather than perform the ceremony himself—"My big chance to play Papa," the old bachelor had said—and it was silver-haired Reverend Samuels of Applegate Landing who waited beside Graham. On each side of the aisle were what seemed like masses of people—a sea of bobbing heads as the guests tried to get a better look at the bride.

The altar had been laid at the base of a magnificent stand of pines. Like green spires the noble trees pointed heavenward. From behind them a setting sun sent golden rays through the branches and lighted the western sky, visible between the green arches, like a cathedral's stained glass windows.

"How glorious!" she murmured as Graham reached for her hand.

His reply was a rapt yes, but he was looking at Gloriana instead of the sunset.

Reverend Samuels smiled benevolently as the bride and groom joined hands. With his nimbus of white hair he looked like some angel sent from heaven, and his voice held an unearthly sweetness when he began speaking the old and precious words.

"Dearly beloved, we are gathered today in the sight of God and man to join this man and this woman in holy matrimony."

Gloriana and Graham turned to each other with the glow of the setting sun on their faces. In their eyes, as in their hearts, was a holy love, and the vows they exchanged were pure and tried, like the gold in the rings that bound them together.

Beyond the

Smoky Curtain

Mary Harwell Sayler

FOREWORD

Dear Reader,

Historical research often means conflicting views, and so it's necessary to find trustworthy sources. For this book, mine were: The Museum of the Cherokee in North Carolina, the Tennessee Historical Society, and the Cherokee Historical Society in Oklahoma.

The resulting story is, of course, fiction, but one "real" person does have a role–Nancy Ward, Nan-ye-hi, best known perhaps as "Cherokee Rose." This woman fascinated me because of her courage, her social concerns, and her unbigoted attitudes during her reign as the Beloved Woman of the nation.

And so, I dedicate this book to the beloved women of *this* nation—the loving women who work to communicate that love to their families, their neighbors, and those people totally unlike themselves.

Special thanks to my uncle and aunt, Vernon and Sara Angel, who pointed me in the right direction for my research, and to my cousin, Martha Henegar, and her friend Claudia Gatewood, who took me in that direction—the Great Smoky Mountains.

God's best to you,
Mary Harwell Sayler
DeLand, Florida

CHAPTER 1

BESIDE HER SOMEONE GROANED, then silence.

"Charles?"

The single word choked out on the little breath she had, and the velvety gray eyes, which she had almost opened, clamped tightly shut from the small exertion. She knew her husband needed help, but she could not lift a leaden finger from the rough log that had carried them both to shore.

Was Charles alive? If only she could turn her head . . . If only . . .

"If only father were home, Priscilla Davis, you wouldn't be talking so foolishly!" her older sister, Lettie, exclaimed. Her long silk skirt swept the room with indignation. "I can't imagine what that frontiersman said to fill you and Charles with such a ridiculous notion."

"You'd understand if you'd been there," Priscilla injected.

"Hmmphf! As if I'd listen to a charlatan! What

7

does this Jones person know of the savage unless he's one himself? And if he is so concerned for the spiritual welfare of the . . . the . . . ."

"Cherokee," Priscilla offered.

"Savages!" Lettie insisted. "Why isn't Mr. Jones among them himself instead of traveling about the Carolinas arousing the sympathies of romantic girls?"

Priscilla's full lips set in a thin line. "I may be nineteen, but I'm hardly a romantic, Lettie. Charles and I are prepared to face whatever hardships are required." Her dimpled chin tilted upward. "God has called us to serve Him among the Cherokee, and that's exactly what we shall do."

"Then Charles Prescott is as foolish as you are, Priscilla! Oh, don't look so stricken! I've known Charles all of his twenty-two years, but apparently I don't know him at all! I've thought of him as a brother, but never as a brother-in-law. Tell me, Priscilla, do you love him?"

"I'm fond of Charles. You know that."

"Fond!" Her sister mocked. "Will fondness sustain you when you bear his children—alone—in some primitive Indian village?"

"Lettie!" Priscilla exclaimed. Her ringless hands flew to her flushed throat.

But her sister continued unmercifully. "Good! I see I've gotten your attention. Perhaps Charles' family can shock some sense into him."

"It's pointless to discuss this, Lettie. I've quite made up my mind." Priscilla struggled to regain her composure. Then assuming a dignity she no longer felt, she rose from the striped, silk loveseat and rang a small, crystal bell.

8

Lettie opened her mouth as if to speak, but the intended words pealed into laughter. "Oh, Priscilla, darling, whatever are you doing?"

"I'm ringing for tea," she said with a haughty lift of her dimple.

"Tea?" Lettie repeated amidst her own giggles. "And who, pray tell, will bring your tea when you're in that unnamed territory with your beloved savages?"

The crystal bell dropped, shattering against the oak-planked floor.

An owl hooted. A twig snapped.

Her dry throat ached, but there was no bell to shatter the deepening quiet. No servants. No tea. No one to call.

"Charles?"

Priscilla's hand unloosed its hold on the log, her palm scraping on the rough bark as her arm fell heavily onto the wet grass. Something supported her other arm, something sodden and unmoving. A whimper, escaped her lips, and a shudder racked her thin body lying face down on the bank of the swollen river. The last time she'd laid her gray eyes on Charles, he'd been unconscious in her grasp as she'd kicked and struggled against the ragging water moving the log closer and closer to the shore.

She couldn't remember reaching her destination, but the grass cushioning her drenched, blond head assured her that she had. Muddied petticoats clung to her tattered stockings, and her linen shawl, still wrapped across her front and tied in the back, molded itself uncomfortably against her soggy bodice. Her water-logged shoes anchored her weary feet to the ground, and her head felt unbearably heavy.

9

She had to move, to stir. She had to find out. With tremendous effort, she arched her neck and scratched her face along the matted grasses until she'd upturned the other cheek. Her long lashes fluttered from weighted lids, and the slitted view confirmed what she had not wished to see. The still, sodden mass beneath her arm was Charles, and his round blue eyes were opened wide as if something had caught him by surprise.

Oh, Charles . . . Oh, Charles . . .

"Oh, Charles! My lovely gown is getting wet!" Priscilla *exclaimed. "Do you suppose that's what Lettie meant when she said it's bad luck to marry on such a dreary day as this." She gave a little laugh, determined not to allow her spirits or her wedding day to be dampened despite the rain.*

Charles extended a gloved hand to help his new bride into the Prescott family's carriage. "That's superstitious talk, Priscilla," Charles rebuked her mildly. "We mustn't concern ourselves with trivial matters."

Trivial? For a moment resentment flared that he should think their marriage insignificant in any way, even regarding omens. It wasn't every day that a girl married, and conventional or not, Priscilla wanted to enjoy it. Her lower lip protruded slightly as she bunched together her white, satin skirt to make room for her new husband. But, seating himself, Charles took no note of her hurt feelings.

Priscilla stole a sidewards glance. Charles eyes glistened with suppressed excitement, and she knew his thoughts lay ahead as hers often did—miles ahead towards the unnamed, reclaimed territory over the Appalachians and beyond the smoky curtain of civilization.

The king forbade settlement west of the mountains a decade ago when the warring French finally gave up their claims, and that was odd, Priscilla thought. Until the French stirred up trouble among the Cherokee, the people generally accepted the British colonists who had settled on the ancestral mountain lands. But the French had wanted the territory for themselves, and so they had armed the Indians with guns and grudges. Then, after a long fight, France relinquished all claims in North America, and in that same year, 1763, the English king said it was too dangerous for colonists to settle beyond the mountains. Strange! Yet Priscilla supposed his highness had lost too many soldiers and too many sleepless nights to concern himself further with the safety of colonial adventurers.

That was ten years ago, and as far as Priscilla knew the king's order was, at first, obeyed. But in recent years, a number of families had drifted into the area, and most had settled near the Watauga River. Last year, 1772, the group banded together to form the Watauga Association, and their elected government was the first organized west of the Alleghenies. Law and order, the Rev. Jones had assured her and Charles.

Priscilla had her doubts. It wasn't that she disbelieved the good reverend but, as much as she hated to admit it, Lettie had a point when she said that, coming from the Carolina territory, the reverend's sense of law and order was probably quite remote from their own.

What did reassure Priscilla, however, was the fact that the people of the Watauga Association leased the land from the Cherokee. Surely that meant the

11

strained relationships had been mended. A promising sign, indeed.

Priscilla sighed. She wished that her relationships with her family were not equally strained. Lettie's sensibilities were in such a state of war that she had refused to come to the wedding altogether. Mama couldn't, of course, being too much the invalid, in and out of her own little world. And Papa, as usual, was off somewhere in England, trying to gain favors from the king. He would probably succeed, increasing their already impressive wealth and landholdings in the process. Poor Papa. He had little else but properties and pleasant titles.

Ironically, Priscilla thought herself the greedy one! She wanted so much more than her parents or her sister had. She wanted to be wanted, to be needed— to serve, to count. And how blessed she felt that Charles, who was from a family not unlike hers, wanted the same. God Himself was calling!

Calling . . .

"Charles? Charles?"

Slowly, steadily, her voice rose from a whisper. "Charles!" she screamed, and the awful sound wailed deep within the forest. Again and again, his name came in a groan from her lips, from her throat, from her heart as she nudged him, shook him, pounded him with impotent fists. At last, she closed his stunned eyes with her small hands and laid her blond head on his unmoving chest.

"Don't, Priscilla!" he had said that first night of *their travels when she, a new bride, had sought his chest for a pillow.*

She had raised her head to look at him, but his pensive eyes stared off into the dark.

12

"Is—is something wrong?" she had asked, suddenly shy.

"No!" The word snapped as he thrust her away from him to sit upright by the fire. "Priscilla, I must think of the consequences of—of lying so close to you."

"But, Charles, we're married!"

"Yes, we are, and I thank God you're my wife. You're lovely, Priscilla, but you must understand . . . ." He turned to her with another passion lighting his eyes. "God has called us! Just think of it! Yet we're going into an untamed land to bring His name to the savages, and our very lives may be endangered for it. I dare not make you more vulnerable, Priscilla," he added gently. "Nor will I risk the precious, innocent life of an unborn child. We must wait until we've made friends of the Indians and the settlers. Then, my dearest, you'll not be able to keep me from your lovely arms."

As a pledge of things to come, Charles had sealed his promise with a searing kiss.

She kissed him now. Lightly, gently, finally.

A virgin widow, Priscilla struggled to her feet, hearing Lettie's "I told you so" in the unearthly quiet. She pushed the comfortless thought away as best she could and surveyed the scene at hand. Her husband was dead. The horses were gone. And she had not a dry stitch to her name.

"Oh, God. Oh, God!" she sobbed. "What do I do now?"

"Good grief, Priscilla! Don't you know how to do anything well?" Charles asked with uncharacteristic exasperation. She'd burned the johnnycake for the third night in a row, and the squirrel, which Charles

13

had used entirely too much ammunition to shoot, wasn't cooked through. He flung his pewter plate down in disgust, and she hurried to scoop the precious meat from the ground. With a little water and a stew pot, tomorrow night's dinner might be intact.

Using conversation to distract him from what she was doing, Priscilla said quietly, "I'm doing the best I can, Charles." Then she pressed her lips together to refrain from saying how much he was beginning to sound like. Lettie.

To her surprise, her husband laid a tender hand on her thin shoulder. "I know you are, Priscilla," he signed. "I suppose we've much to learn, but we've been traveling nigh onto two fortnights. I say! We've done remarkably well."

"Only a month, Charles?" Somehow it seemed much longer since they'd left civilization behind. "And we've passed so few cabins." Without the assistance of those settlers, however, she doubted they'd have gotten this far.

"It's desolate country," Charles agreed, "without even a familiar songbird to cheer us on."

"Why is that?" Priscilla wondered. How she'd come to hate the unnerving quiet.

"Food, I imagine. The forest floor is too thick with oak leaves and pine needles to allow any grass to poke through, and without it, there's no seed for songbirds, or, for that matter, no grass for the deer."

Steathily, Priscilla wrapped the tough squirrel meat in her handkerchief and stuck it in her pocket. "What about us, Charles? Did we bring enough supplies?

"If not, the Lord will provide."

Priscilla gave her pocket a pat. "But, Charles, we

14

can't expect God to provide for our own negligence. He gave us good sense too, and surely, He expects us to use it." Now, she was sounding like Lettie, she realized, to her chagrin.

But Charles' thoughts had wandered dreamily into the green cavern of a forest.

"Soon, Priscilla, we'll cross that shining river we glimpsed from higher peaks. And then . . ."

"Yes, Charles?"

"And then it won't be long until we reach our promised land."

The words now seemed prophetic, for surely Charles had reached his.

Left behind, Priscilla stared at him, willing him to move. He didn't, and she shook her head, trying to waken herself from this haze in which she'd been ever since the flooded waters overtook her. Gradually an apathetic sort of energy restored itself, and her head cleared. Charles was dead, and she must bury him.

How?

Priscilla squinted into the darkening forest that even earlier in the noonday light had seemed oppressive and gloomy. Soon the blackness of evening would extinguish all light, and she had no flint, no fire, no food, no husband. She hoped that Charles would be right—that God would provide. But—frankly, she couldn't see how.

Dragging herself to her husband's body, Priscilla felt a strange detachment from the situation, from what she knew she had to do. With no tools, no supplies, there was no way to dig a proper grave, and she hadn't the strength anyway. She had considered looking for one of the caves they had discovered occasionally in the outcropping of rock, but it would be dark soon. And, she reminded herself, she had no flint with which to start a fire. Animals prowled those caves in which she and Charles had taken shelter, but with a protecting blaze and Charles beside her, she had been unafraid before.

Now her hands trembled as she gathered a mound of stones and placed them in the outspread jacket that she had removed from Charles' still form. She thanked God that he had discarded his gentlemanly attire before leaving home, replacing it with the sturdy leather coat often worn by the frontiersman. The fringed jacket would serve well for her purposes, and so would the river which had taken her husband's life.

When she had gathered enough stones to outweigh Charles' slender frame, Priscilla tied the sleeves of the jacket and belted the loose ends together. Then she secured the apparatus tightly around her husband's middle, and with a mighty heave, she shoved him into the river. She had done her work well. The body sank rapidly out of sight.

Priscilla stared at it until her velvety eyes glazed. How easy it would be to slip into the water. How easy to slide in and out of the tormented, unreal world that only her mother had known. But a wave of nausea spurred her to action, to fight the heavings of her own emotions.

Around her, the forest was a verdant tomb, and she yelled angrily into the silence. "You'll not have me yet!"

Something stirred. She was sure of it. One of the horses perhaps.

On that hopeful note, Priscilla clicked her tongue, but there was no responding whinny, no gentle thud of hooves on the carpeted floor of the woods.

"Hello! Is someone there?" she called into the monstrous quiet.

An owl hooted. Then another. And then the boy appeared.

He stepped soundlessly from behind the massive trunk of a tulip poplar, and stood staring at her with enormous brown eyes.

Priscilla stared back. What lovely skin he had! Perhaps it was the eerie light of the forest, but the boy looked to be made of olives or berries, glistening with oil or dew.

"Don't be afraid," she said, feeling remarkably calm herself. Just knowing that there was indeed another human being alive in these woods had somehow made all the difference.

It occurred to her then that this young man might not speak her language, and if not, she certainly didn't know his. She had to communicate; she had to make him understand that she was harmless and alone. And she had to do so quickly, for he looked as though he might bolt at any moment.

"Please," she said softly, "don't go. I need your help." And whether or not he could comprehend her words, she felt certain that her tone of voice would convey her attitude of peace.

She smiled then and held out both hands, palms up, to show him that she was friendly and empty and alone. His own face remained inquisitive, solemn, but when she continued to stand there, unmoving, his expression cleared, and he gave a single nod.

With a pendulum sweep of his hand, he beckoned her to follow. And, of course, she did without a backward look. Charles was gone – dead without even a glimpse of the Cherokees. And she, Priscilla

Prescott, had no choice but to go ahead into this new territory with a young Indian boy for her guide.

CHAPTER 2

THEY WALKED FOREVER.

Occasionally the boy would pause to select a plant or pluck a leaf or dig a root. Then he'd deposit his find in a leather pouch that swung down from his waist. He never smiled, but Priscilla had the impression that he was pleased with each discovery. Though why a dirty root or broken twig was significant, she didn't know.

Continuously, the boy's large eyes swept the forest floor, the brush, the trees, yet his gaze avoided her watchful stare. Except for her brief inspections of the dwindling soles of her wet walking shoes, Priscilla dared not take her own eyes from him.

This mere child of ten, eleven perhaps, was her only hope of survival. Oh, what would Lettie say to that! Thank-goodness she didn't know, might never know, Priscilla reminded herself. And besides, her real hope was in the Lord. He was the One who had brought here here, and He was the One who would provide.

Except for Charles. What about Charles? Why had God not provided for him?

Perhaps He had, she told herself, as she hurried to keep pace with the tireless strides of the child. God's almighty view was not limited to the material, to the confining matter of a body, and even though her own body grew wearier with each step, Priscilla was not one to question His all-knowing, all-seeing perspective.

She'd thought it would be dark by now, and, indeed, the greens and pinks and browns of the woods had begun to gray. What would she do if the boy strode into the night, intent on his own mysterious purposes, his own destination? How could she keep track of him then? Odd, but her own destination did not trouble her for the moment. She simply did not want to be left alone in the blackening night.

Overhead, a tangle of oak branches charred in the dusk, and Priscilla gave a little shudder. Involuntarily her steps had slowed until her scraps of shoes plowed small furrows in the forest bed. The cooling air penetrated her still damp clothing, so her linen shawl brought no comfort from the chill. Intermittently, her heavy skirts fastened upon briars and twigs until persistent vines snatched and tugged her down. She fell upon the earth, her gloveless hands too limp to catch her, and she lay there, breathless, but struggling to get up.

Apparently the thud of her fall had alerted her young guide, for the boy scrambled back in her direction.

"*A ni si di*," he said when he'd freed her of the clutching vine.

"Thank you." Priscilla managed a wan smile.

20

"Would you help me up, please?" She shifted her weight and held out her hand, hoping the gesture would communicate her need. But the boy stood above her, shaking his head.

" *A ni si di* ," he repeated, and then to show her, he dropped onto the ground, arranging the leaves and himself in a position for sleeping.

A ni si di, a place to lie down, he was telling her, but when he hopped up and started off, panic goaded Priscilla into action.

"Don't leave! Please," she called, and in any language, the fear in her voice was unmistakable.

The boy hesitated in a half-turn while Priscilla tried, unsuccessfully, to rise to her feet.

"I can keep up; I can manage," she said to herself more than to him, but her jellied limbs refused to comply. She sank back wearily while keeping her eyes steadily fastened on the child.

He seemed to be trying to tell her something, but all she could comprehend was that he wanted her to stay put, which was the last thing she herself had in mind.

"Don't go! Don't leave me here!" she begged again. "Yes. Yes. I know I need to rest, but how can I if you leave? You might not come back! You might leave me here to die alone! Charles is gone. Don't you understand? My husband is gone!" But the boy was going, too, and there was nothing Priscilla could do to stop him.

"Oh, God! Oh, God!" she cried. "Don't You leave me! Please," she ended on a groan, and her head bowed in exhaustion and defeat.

She didn't see, then, that the boy retraced his steps until the breath of his presence stirred her.

" *Ha wa* ," the child said, as though letting her

21

know everything was all right. Quickly he unfastened the leather pouch from his waist and pressed it into Priscilla's hand. Then with the bounding grace of a deer, he dashed into the black stillness of the forest.

He would be back, she told herself. Whatever woodsy concoction the pouch contained, it was important to the child, yet he'd placed it in her hands, a pledge. He would be back for the pouch, for her, and with that tender promise held tightly to her bosom, Priscilla slipped into her own black stillness.

Other pledges overtook her rest as she dreamed of lying in Charles' arms, of holding him and being held, but cold fingers of reality shook her pleasant sleep. She shivered against the night air embracing her, and held only the little pouch against her heart for warmth. He would be back. He would be back.

"Charles?"

Someone tugged at the leather pocket clutched against her, and Priscilla rolled over onto it, unable to do more to protect it or herself.

" *Ha wa* ." The child's voice sighed. " *Ga-tli-ha* ."

Relief softened the brittle edges of fatigue, and Priscilla slept as bidden.

A gentle nudge woke Priscilla with the first greening of the morn, and she cried out in joy when she saw the boy standing over her. So, she had not dreamed his return after all! Gingerly, she raised herself on a tattered sleeve and pushed back the blankets which the boy had apparently placed over her during the night. The precious pouch swung once more from his waist, but it was not that movement which startled her.

Beside the dying fire, an old man squatted, staring

at her with sunken, black eyes. His wrinkled skin suggested advanced age, but no sag corresponded in his erect posture, and he looked as though he'd been carved and polished from the straightest oak. He neither smiled nor frowned, and Priscilla, not knowing what to make of him, looked away to the familiar face of the boy.

"*Tsa du li ha tsu ga-du?*" the child asked, gesturing toward the fire.

Not wishing to move her aching body just yet nor place herself closer to the ancient man who guarded the glowing embers, Priscilla shook her head.

"No, thank you. I'm quite warm," she said, giving her blanketed shoulder a rub. "You've been good to me. I wish I could make you understand how grateful I am."

"*Tsa du li ha tsu ga-du?*" the boy repeated. "Ga-du. Ga-du." He offered up something yellow-brown and presumably edible.

"Bread," the old man confirmed it. "He asks if you want bread."

"You speak English!" Priscilla exclaimed, delighted, for she was as hungry for recognizable sounds as she was for food. But the old man did not respond further until she'd nibbled the last tasteless crumb of ga-du, and even then, she realized that any conversation would require her probe.

"Are . . . are you Cherokee?" she asked, hoping it didn't sound rude.

The old man nodded. "*Aniyv-wiya.* Principal People."

Priscilla wasn't certain if she'd received an affirmative or not. Struggling into a position of greater dignity, she sipped the tea, a strange hot concoction which the boy had offered.

"I am Priscilla Prescott, and I'm recently widowed, sir, but my husband and I were, uh, looking for the Cherokee."

"You found."

Priscilla sighed her relief. Not only had she found the people for whom she searched, but she'd been spared the question of why she was looking in the first place. Explaining could be awkward, and she still felt too weak to have her full wits about her. Another night's sleep might help, and perhaps another cup of that unusual tea.

She'd begun to extend the hollowed gourd for replenishment when the old man rose with surprising agility.

"We go now."

"But—but, sir! I don't even know where we're going or who you are or . . ." She stammered to a stop, unsure how to express her curiosity in a manner that would not offend.

A gnarled finger pointed to the boy. "He is Little Spoon. I am Walkingstick, Medicine Man of Chota."

A medicine man! Then the boy must be a helper, an apprentice of sorts, Priscilla realized. No wonder he'd been so fascinated with certain plants and roots. And the tea! Undoubtedly it did have medicinal properties for she felt remarkably better.

Slowly she rose to her feet that seemed ready now to hold her.

"Chota," she repeated, questioning. "Is that the place where you live?"

Again the man nodded. "It is home of the Principal Chiefs. Home of the Beloved Woman."

Beloved Woman. She turned the phrase over in her mind then stored it away for another time.

"And—and you'll take me there? To Chota?" Priscilla asked hopefully.

This time, however, the old man shook his head. "We come to smaller village first. There, Bear Claw will find you."

"I'm sorry. I don't understand."

"You look for Cherokee. Bear Claw looks for new wife. Even Little Spoon knows it is good."

"But—but—" Priscilla's protest went no further for Walkingstick terminated the conversation by setting off down an incline that immediately swallowed him from sight.

Perhaps, she comforted herself, she had misunderstood. But perhaps not. It appeared now that the boy, Little Spoon, had befriended her for a reason—to provide this man named Bear Claw with a wife.

"See! Savages!" she could almost hear Lettie say. But, no. Her treatment thus far had been quite courteous and no more primitive than the conditions under which she and Charles had traveled. She had no desire, of course, for anyone to force her hand in marriage, but had that not been her own father's intent?

Poor Papa, she thought now, remembering with discomfort the harsh words which had passed between them prior to his last trip to England.

"I shall find a suitable young man for you, Priscilla, while I'm away. Lord Chaucey perhaps, or someone equally marriagable."

She'd stomped her slender foot to no avail. "Find someone for Lettie if you will, sir. But not for me."

Even now she could see his handsome face distorted in black fury. "You are my daughter, Priscilla Davis, and you shall do as I say. Let there not be

25

another word on this subject." And there wasn't. Nor would there be now.

Lord Chaucey. Bear Claw. What difference did it make? At the moment, her primary concern was simply to place one ragged shoe in front of another, a feat she found increasingly difficult to do.

The vigor of a night's rest and a morning's refreshment had dissipated all too quickly, and Priscilla feared she couldn't travel much further. Twice Little Spoon had had to retrace his steps when she had stumbled, and both times they had scarcely been out of the night's camp. Now, however, he stopped of his own accord, dropping to his knees on the cool, damp earth.

Gratefully, Priscilla leaned against the smooth trunk of a tulip poplar, watching the boy as she caught her breath. Her keen sight took in every movement with special interest now that she knew what business he was about, but even so, his actions astonished her.

As he searched for a particular species of plant, Little Spoon seemed to count off the first three before taking the fourth. He did not take the plant, however, until he'd spoken to it in a prayer-like way, and Priscilla had the impression that the boy was asking the plant's permission to uproot it. He then carefully dug the tender roots and shoots, and when that task was finished, he dropped a bead in, an offering of thanksgiving, before recovering the hole.

Something told Priscilla that Little Spoon had forgotten her presence and that her watchful stare would be an intrusion. Before he'd noticed her once more, she turned her head away and closed her eyes.

She could have slept, standing there, but the boy's voice beckoned.

"*E gv yi,*" he said, his gesture indicating, "You go first."

Since they had been following a deer path, Priscilla had no trouble obeying, although she walked twice as far, staggering from side to side along the way. Fortunately, however, the downhill slopes had leveled, and with a final descent, she came upon a small creek that was enlarged with the earlier spring rains.

Walkingstick was waiting. Having gone ahead of them, he had packed up the blanket rolls and scant supplies and loaded them into a canoe.

"*U s qua lv hv,*" he said. "It is ready."

Had she possessed the energy, Priscilla would have given a little dance for joy. The grandeur of the Prescott family carriage could not compare with the beautiful sight of this rough dug-out, and with thanks to God, she seated herself on the flat bottom of yellow pine.

Oh, Lord, how good are your provisions! she prayed silently as they slipped without a splash into the water.

With nothing more required of her but rest, Priscilla settled into a semi-reclining position that offered her a brilliant view of the sky. During these many weeks of journey, she'd seldom seen anything but leaf and limb and her own two feet, usually atangle. But now the trees parted at the widest span of the stream, and silky strips of blue peeked through the ever-present green. Her eyes could feast forever, she thought, but a spring breeze whispered and the water gently rocked until the conspiring sound and motion soon lulled her to sleep.

At first her mind drifted as peacefully as the canoe that rested securely upon the water. But Charles' death and the loss of small, but precious items in the river along with all of the supplies, helped contribute to Priscilla's exhaustion and uncertain future. She dreamed she, too, was drowning. Then, rescued at the last minute by the claws of a bear, she awoke with a whimper.

Sometime during her nap, Walkingstick and Little Spoon had changed positions so that the boy now guided the small dugout around large, smooth stones and exposed tree roots. From his vantage point, the old man kept a practiced eye on Priscilla which she found so unnerving that she closed her own heavy lids. She preferred to stay awake, to sort her thoughts until she could ask Walkingstick the most pressing questions that concerned her. Thus far, his short responses had led her to believe that he would not welcome idle chatter or foolish questions, and it was increasingly difficult to separate logic from nonsense.

She supposed she had a fever. If so, she prayed that she could hide it, for she certainly didn't want to be exposed to the strange practices of a medicine man. Charles would not like it. Lettie would not like it. Papa would not like it.

Masks. There would be masks to ward away the evil spirits. And chants. Chants to contact the higher powers, the spirits of good. There would be shakers, hissing and rattling, warning like a snake trapped in a smoke-filled hut.

Fire. Blazing fire, smouldering fire. And the smell of herbs and the taste of bitter brew.

Poultices, heavy and hot. Cool hands on the forehead. Chilling water to sponge away the dirt, the fears, the memories.

Low voices, mumbling yet lyrical. Frowns. And

eyes. Dark eyes, deep cavernous eyes, mystical eyes that drew and tugged one back to life.

Desperately Priscilla fought against it—the shock, the fever, the uncertainties—until finally she relented. She needed these people who had befriended her, and if that meant placing her life in their hands, so be it. Soon Walkingstock would know she were ill if he didn't suspect already. It was foolish to try to hide that fact when she did indeed need his help.

She opened her eyes, prepared to meet his, but the heavily lashed brown ones that stared at her were not the black eyes of Walkingstick. They were, however, familiar, as though she had seen those eyes in a dream, and she realized with a start that she had. But the rugged face attached—the comely face with its straight nose and jagged scar along one cheek—was one she didn't know.

"You're awake," said the well-molded lips, pressed thin. "Don't worry, Little Dove. You're in good hands."

She wasn't worried. Was she? At least she hadn't been until now. She tried to speak, but the questions stuck on a thatched tongue.

Where was she? Where were Walkingstick and Little Spoon? And who was this tall and arrogantly comfortable white man who stood over her as though they were old friends?

Priscilla snapped her eyelids shut. Obviously, she was much sicker than she thought.

CHAPTER 3

"OH, NO, YOU DON'T! Mrs. Prescott! Priscilla Prescott! Wake up!"

That man, that insufferably rude and disquietingly handsome man was shaking her by the shoulders! Priscilla whacked his hands away.

'Sir!" she found her voice at last. "Have you taken leave of your senses?".

"I thought *you* had," he answered. "Sorry, but you have given me a few sleepless nights, you know."

"I know no such thing. I've never seen you before today, so sleepless nights on my account are highly unlikely." She gave him what she hoped was a scathing look to put him in his place. "Now if you'll please get out of my—my . . ." What? Canoe? Not anymore. Hut? It was that, it seemed, but it wasn't hers. "Bedchamber," she finished grandly.

A quick look around had proved her to be on a blanketed shelf that was fastened to the wall as were others around the hut. A thin leather veil separated each sleeping cubicle, but someone—this man, no doubt—had pushed hers aside. And now he stood there, grinning broadly.

"If you please, sir, I'd like to rest." Except for a snort over her use of the word "bedchamber", he'd failed to move one bit. "I'm ill, assuming you hadn't noticed."

"On the contrary, Mourning Dove."

His possessive glance failed to reassure her as she realized that she no longer wore her tattered dress nor linen shawl. Someone had bathed her and redressed her in a loose-fitting garment. Someone had washed and combed her hair that now lay about her shoulders.

The crude implication of his stare brought heat to her cheeks.

"Set your mind at rest, madam. I have not had the pleasure of tending you myself. You'll have to thank Straw Basket for that. At any rate, you look much improved."

Priscilla was inclined to disagree. "I told you, sir, I'm ill. And I don't know where I am or who Straw Basket is, and I especially do not know you, sir."

"That's an improvement. For the last few nights, you didn't know who you were yourself."

"Oh." Actually, it was a comfort to know that she was on the mend instead of the decline. But Priscilla didn't care to give this man the satisfaction of that acknowledgement.

Suddenly he gave a low bow, clicking his heels together as if to show that he'd had proper manners at some time in his life.

"Permit me to introduce myself," he said in such a courtly fashion that Priscilla had no doubts he was mocking her. "My name is Garth Daniels, son of Lord Richard and Lady Elizabeth Daniels from the colony of Virginia."

"Virginia! Then what on earth are you doing *wherever* we are?" she blurted.

Mr. Daniels threw back his dark head, laughing. "I might ask you the same, Madam, but I'll not tax you now. Shortly put, I'm here because I want to be. I trade goods between Indians and whites, and keep the peace as best I can."

"How very noble of you," Priscilla remarked crisply. This man seemed so self-assured, so cocky, that she wanted to set him down a peg. "I should think, sir, that it would be difficult to help keep the peace when you lack simple courtesy and tact."

Instead of being set down, however, Mr. Daniels' temper rose. "You'd better get something straight, little lady, if you want to survive long in this territory. The etiquette you know won't win any ribbons or beaux. Keep it honest; keep it kind, and you might keep that pretty little scalp."

Her blond hair prickled at the suggestion, but Priscilla, at last, had her wish. Without another word, Garth Daniels took his leave.

As soon as he had gone, Priscilla wished he hadn't. Insufferable though the man was, he could be valuable to her. She still had no idea where she was or how she had gotten here except to guess that Walkingstick and Little Spoon had deposited her at the small village near Chota as planned. But now that she was here, what was she to do without an interpreter? She hadn't considered such matters when Charles was alive.

But Charles was dead.

The realization hit her anew, overwhelming her

with grief until she thought her waking was more nightmarish than her sleep. What grotesque dreams she had had. Only now she realized that most of them were real. The eerie chants, the bitter potions, the acrid smells, the not-quite-human masks waving in nose-down designs—all of it had probably occurred right here in this hut.

Was this dismaying world what God had called her to? And if so, what did He expect her to do about it? She had given it no thought until now, having instead some vague notion of immediate acceptance among the Cherokee who would come to her with all sorts of spiritual ills. She had seen herself surrounded by groups of loving children, eager for their Bible lessons while Charles taught the adults, instructing them in the ways of God. *How* she and Charles would accomplish those feats had not been clear.

She wished Charles were here to advise her about the language barrier, the cultural differences, the weakened condition of her own body. But Priscilla supposed it didn't matter what Charles would or wouldn't have done anyway. She, too, had been called, and it was up to God Himself to guide her in what He would have her do.

She tried to place herself in a prayerful state of mind to concentrate on His will, but the dreadful pounding inside her head interfered.

Kaboom. Kaboom. Kaboom.

The constant thudding assaulted her ears until Priscilla realized that the noise came from without rather than from within. Seeking the source, she arose from her bedshelf, but a wave of dizziness thrust her back between the covers.

"U yo i!" A young woman cautioned from the doorway.

Having discovered already that it was not wise for her to get up yet, Priscilla studied the squat figure. The woman, a girl really, had that same beautiful skin as Little Spoon and eyes like shiny black buttons. Her simple dress, woven of hemp, dyed red and black, was similar to the one that Priscilla wore, but the Indian girl's garment was caught about her thick waist with a fringed and beaded sash. Deerskin covered her feet and rose to meet her skirt at the knees so that when she walked, there was no sound. No swishing skirt. No thumping heels on the dirt-packed floor.

"Are you Straw Basket?" Priscilla asked, slowly raising herself on an elbow.

The girl nodded, grinning shyly.

"Then you're the one to thank for taking care of me. Oh." Priscilla stopped, aware of the puzzlement creeping over the girl's face. "You don't understand me, do you? Oh, dear. I did so want to tell you how much I appreciate your help."

"*Wa-do*." Garth Daniels voice came through the entrance of the hut, and Priscilla gave a dizzying start. "*Wa-do* means thank you."

"*Wa-do*," Priscilla mimicked. "*Wa-do*, Straw Basket."

"You're welcome," Daniels injected.

"I thought you had gone!"

"I had." He flashed a smile that Priscilla found annoying. "Gone to fetch your gracious hostess so you two could be *properly* introduced."

"Does she live here alone?"

Daniels shook his head. "This is her parents' house. When she's married, she'll have her own."

Priscilla raised herself a bit higher. "How can she tolerate it?" she whispered, as though Straw Basket might understand.

34

Daniels shot her a harsh glance. "Since you're obviously accustomed to a grand estate, I assume you mean the size, the crudity of this place."

"I mean no such thing, sir. I was refering to that awful noise. How can she bear being so close to it?"

Daniels' frown eased. "That noise is everywhere. It's the sound of the women throughout the village pounding the day's corn. You'll get used to it in time, Mourning Dove, and other unique sounds and sights too, I pray." When he spoke softly like that, he seemed to be another man.

"Why do you call me Mourning Dove?" Priscilla asked.

"It suits you, does it not? I understand you are in mourning. And, your eyes are as gray as the feathers of a mourning dove. Besides," he added, "it's the name Walkingstick gave you, and I don't argue with him."

"Do you only argue with widows confined to their beds, Mr. Daniels?"

"Ah, madam, that is a predicament that time will surely resolve," he said, and Priscilla didn't know to which he referred—her widowed state or her current confinement. Either way, she felt embarrassed.

"Incidentally," he went on, 'there is no need for formality here. You may call me Garth." His dark eyes took on an impish gleam. "And I will call you Priscilla. Or Prissy."

"Certainly not!" Regardless of this man's reasons or preferences, Priscilla did not care to have him call her by her first name. And 'Prissy' had always irritated her—especially when said in the tone of voice Garth Daniels used.

"Then Mourning Dove it is—for now." He gave the bedshelf a thump.

35

"What do you mean, for now?" Priscilla clasped the fluttering heartbeat in her throat. Was she not going to be around much longer?

Daniels snickered. "Names have a way of changing among the Aniyv wiya. Take Straw Basket, for instance." He beckoned to the girl who had been stirring the fire in the middle of the dirt floor. Then he spoke to her in her native tongue.

Straw Basket answered, but her hands provided Priscilla with the only clue. First they rounded about her face, then gestured in a stroking motion, neither of which meant a thing to Priscilla.

Garth nodded, understanding. "She says her name was Little Moon as a child because of her round face. Then she became Painted Rock when she expressed her artistry by dabbing paint on every unturned stone. Now she weaves baskets of straw, and, I might add, they're the sturdiest and most attractive baskets made in the village."

Priscilla gave a little clap. "Then 'Straw Basket' denotes her occupation, like some of our English names—Baker, Carpenter, Smith."

"That's partly right," Garth said, "though every woman in the village fashions her own baskets when she has need. Also, 'Straw Basket' is a given name, showing character or special skill. But, in our culture, her last name would be Wolf. Her mother's family is part of the Wolf clan. There are seven clans in all." Suddenly he stopped. "Forgive me if I've tired you." He swept a low bow. "May I present Straw Basket? And, Straw Basket, Mourning Dove."

The younger girl giggled, and Priscilla couldn't help but smile. Laughter, it seemed, was the same in any language.

36

With Garth functioning as interpreter, Straw Basket expressed her gladness over Priscilla's improved health and welcomed her into the family home. Then, shyly, she added, *"I-gi-do."*

"Sister," Garth explained. "She invites you to become the sister she has lost."

His tone held no emotion, but Priscilla was deeply touched. "Tell her I would be most happy to have her for my sister."

"Perhaps," he replied, "you should tell her yourself."

"Perhaps I should," she answered tartly. Then turning to the girl, Priscilla gave her her warmest smile. *"I-gi-do,"* she said, then added, *"wa-do."*

Straw basket beamed, *"I-gi-do,"* she repeated, but the rest of her conversation was lost until Garth translated.

"She says you must have nourishment to recover your strength, and I quite agree. Would you take some soup?"

Priscilla nodded. *"Wa-do,* Straw Basket."

"Tsa du li ha tsu ga-du?" the girl asked, and when Garth began to interpret, Priscilla waved an impatient hand.

"I know! She asks if I want bread." She nodded in the affirmative, feeling rather pleased with herself. "Yes, Straw Basket. *Wa-do.*"

Garth folded his arms high across his broad chest and gave Priscilla a look of approval.

"I don't suppose I need to tell you to eat lightly for a while?"

"Thank you, no."

"You'll have a varied diet here," Garth went on, unabashed, "wild game, fruits, vegetables, mush-

37

rooms, and nuts in season. But don't expect to sample plum pudding or chocolate bon bons."

"Really, Mr. Daniels . . ."

"Garth."

"Garth, then. You must think me a simpleton."

He shrugged. "Is anyone wise until experience teaches?"

Since she had no real answer, Priscilla changed the subject. "Tell me about Straw Basket's family—especially her sister."

To her surprise, however, Garth shook his head. "Another time. At the moment, you need food and rest more than information, and I have other matters to which I must attend." He gave a light bow. "Rest assured, madam, you've not seen the last of me."

Priscilla didn't know if that reassured her or not. But as soon as Garth was gone, she realized how very tired she was. Odd, how she hadn't noticed until now.

Sinking back wearily on her mattress of corn husks, Priscilla watched Straw Basket busy herself around the fire. Unlike the Davises' home, which had a kitchen set apart for safety's sake, this modest hut centered around the open flame. A hole in the domed roof allowed the smoke to escape, though much of it lingered in the sleeping cubicles and drifted, fog-like, about the room.

A patch of sunny sky covered the vent-hole, allowing Priscilla to glimpse the daylight, but, for the most part, the room was dark with its narrow-cut door and mud-plastered walls. The effect was not dreary, however, since woven baskets and straw mats and colorful clay pots of varying sizes hung about, brightening the interior.

Priscilla judged the one-room hut to be thirty feet

across. Back home, her bedroom was twenty-feet square, as were most of the rooms in the Davises' house.

At this very moment, Lettie would probably be in the music room, Mama on the sun porch, and Papa in his study—assuming that he was yet home. If not, Mama would be abed, wrapped in a dark velvet cocoon.

I have to get up! Priscilla thought, as a thread of panic spun itself around her. One could not serve or count or be needed when stuck away on a bedshelf! But thrashing about only succeeded in gaining Straw Basket's attention.

The girl said something that Priscilla could not understand, yet the soft flow of musical words soothed her, and she ceased her struggle against the heavy blanket. Food. Yes, that was what she needed. That would help.

She watched and waited as Straw Basket dipped a hollowed-out gourd into a clay pot that sat near the fire. Then the girl ladled the pottage into a small wooden bowl and brought it to Priscilla.

"*U-ga-ma.*" Straw Basket pointed to the soup.

"*U-ga-ma.* Soup."

Straw Basket nodded. "Soo-oop," she said, and they both laughed.

For a few moments, the young women took turns identifying objects in their native languages, giggling over the foreign sounds they made. Then, rather sternly, Straw Basket said, "*Hi-ga.*"

Not comprehending, Priscilla frowned. "*Hi-ga?*"

"*Hi-ga,*" Straw Basket insisted. She made movements with her hands and mouth, reminding Priscilla to eat.

Obediently, she complied, making use of the plain wooden spoon that Straw Basket gave her. How light it felt—not at all like the heavy, ornately scrolled silverware to which she was accustomed. But the wooden spoon and bowl stirred a memory, and so did the soup with its beans and corn and chunks of squash, floating in a thick broth.

She couldn't have been more than four or five that day she sat on Mammy Sue's lap in the kitchen house, seeking soup and comfort. Mama and Papa were away, far away in England, and Priscilla wanted so much for them to come home. When they did that evening, however, after weeks abroad, Mama wasn't the same.

Later, Lettie, who was older and knew about such things, told Priscilla that Mama had given birth to a baby boy during those long weeks. But the son, that Papa had wanted so badly, had not lived, and there would be no others.

After that, Priscilla slipped into the kitchen house whenever she could and whenever Mammy Sue's lap was free. A few years later, Mammy Sue died and Mama continued to live. But it was as though they were both away. It was as though Mama had never come home from England.

"Hi-ga!"

"Priscilla jumped. "Yes! Yes, Straw Basket. *Hi-ga.* I'm eating."

She had often been accused of dawdling over her food, even when she was hungry, but Priscilla supposed it was best at the moment since it had been so long since she'd eaten. The bland soup set well, and, enjoying its flavor, she slowly, steadily emptied the bowl.

With her hunger alleviated Priscilla wished that the language lesson could continue, but Straw Basket had other tasks in addition to providing for her guest. No, not a guest, Priscilla reminded herself. *I-gi-do*—sister.

What an unexpected gift that was! She had wanted to adopt a sister once—an orphan girl who helped Mammy Sue in the kitchen house. Papa wasn't impressed, either, even though the little girl could read and write and recite the Lord's Prayer. Priscilla herself had taught her.

Priscilla and little Sally Ann were about the same age, and they had shared their deepest secrets—something that Lettie would never do. Mr. Davis expressed his disapproval of the relationship, but he didn't interfere until, in his mind, it had gone too far. That was the day Priscilla had proudly arrived at the dinner table with her hair painstakingly done up like her friend's. Every square inch of her head was covered with tiny braids in the finest picaninny style. Papa didn't say a word. But the next morning, he sold Sally Ann.

Priscilla sighed. She had no fear of being sold herself, although the thought had crossed her mind. Some Indians, she had heard, did keep slaves, but she had trusted the Lord to keep her from falling into their hands, and He had. Here, she would be a slave to no one; here she felt safe.

But was she? She wondered what it would mean to accept a place in a Cherokee family, a place in the Wolf clan. Straw Basket's invitation delighted her, but being her sister was one thing. It was quite another to be a daughter to some man and woman she had yet to meet! Perhaps they wouldn't welcome her

41

so readily. And, if they did, they might place expectations on her, demands about what she could or could not do. They might even take it upon themselves to decide whom she should marry.

Bear Claw!

Priscilla shivered as she recalled the name. When Walkingstick had first mentioned the man, he had said that it would be good for Bear Claw to take her as his wife. At the time, those were only troublesome words, but since then, Walkingstick had acted upon them by bringing her to this village instead of to Chota. By now, others might have the same idea as the medicine man.

She wondered what ideas Garth Daniels had. Somehow she didn't think a marriage to Bear Claw was what he had in mind. He had mentioned sleepless nights on account of her, and that seemed unlikely if he expected her to become Bear Claw's bride. It could be that his activities as a trader included the bartering of people, but Priscilla didn't think so. Perhaps his interest in her welfare was simply because he was, in fact, a man of peace as he had proclaimed himself to be.

Love, joy, peace—the fruits of the Holy Spirit. But who would expect Garth Daniels to be a man of peace, a man of God? She supposed the Lord could use anyone, though. Even an arrogant man with boorish manners.

She wished she didn't find him so attractive, then wished even more that she knew when she would see him again. She needed his understanding of the language and culture, and she especially needed some advice on the matter of Bear Claw. She really should have done more to gain Garth as an ally, she supposed, but he had a way of antagonizing her that loosed her tongue. In the future, she would keep a watch over it, she vowed.

But now, the soup had appeased her hunger, making her drowsy once again. She snuggled as deeply into the mattress as the corn husks would allow, then closed her eyes.

"Soup 'n rest is best when you's a'mendin'," Mammy Sue used to say.

But Mammy Sue's cherished face wasn't the last Priscilla remembered as she drifted into sleep. Instead, she saw Garth Daniels' heavily lashed brown eyes, and she couldn't help but wonder if the owner was himself in need of a wife.

CHAPTER 4

*K*ABOOM. *K*ABOOM.

Priscilla peered through the doorway of the hut to watch the village women as they raised and dropped their heavy, wooden pounders in a low, echoing refrain. In front of every lodge stood a hollowed-out log that cradled the day's corn, and the pounders plunged against the oak, crushing and grinding the kernels into meal.

Kaboom.

For the last few days, Priscilla had risen little from her bedshelf, complying with the gestured orders of her adoptive parents to rest. But this morning she had awakened, refreshed and ready for adventure. She had bathed herself in the soothing herbal waters that Straw Basket had heated in an earthen pot, then she had donned a clean dress, cinching the loose garment with a leather sash around her slender waist.

How strange it felt to stand here wearing deerskin leggings instead of billowy skirts! But what surprised

44

her more was seeing some of the women in European dress. Unkindly, she wondered what favors those few had granted Garth Daniels in return for the attractive but cumbersome gowns, then immediately, she chided herself for her assumptions. Just because he was a trader didn't mean that he dealt in women's fashions. Or in women.

He certainly had had no dealings with her, and for that, Priscilla was hard pressed to forgive. He had indicated that he would be back, but the better part of a week had passed, and still he hadn't come. She wouldn't care if she ever saw him again, she told herself, except that she had counted on his help in acquainting her with the people and their customs.

Actually, she hadn't done too badly without him. She and Straw Basket had continued with the system of pointing and identifying that they had devised, and through it she had learned the name of her adoptive mother—White Cloud. The father's name eluded her, and she couldn't bring herself to call him *e-do-da*, father, as Straw Basket did, but she had easily fallen into the habit of calling White Cloud *e-tsi*, mother.

Both adoptive parents had welcomed her with quiet solemnness, calling her daughter. But the Cherokee word, *a-que-tsi-a-ge-yu-tsa*, was far too long and the words for "Mourning Dove" even longer. Priscilla consistently failed to recognize it. Straw Basket solved the problem by teaching her parents Priscilla's Indian name in English, and the resulting Mourning Dove sounded quaint but, at least, recognizable.

The patterns of family life were somewhat recognizable too, the main difference being far less time for leisure. Although she had yet to venture beyond the entranceway of the hut, Priscilla had seen some of the

45

children and men at play with stone-throws and stickball. At night, White Cloud sat by the fire, chanting softly as her fingers flew over some type of bead-work. Straw Basket, of course, used her spare time for the weaving that she loved, while her father joined his small family by the fire to whittle on what appeared to be a pipe bowl.

For the most part, however, daily life concerned the provision and maintenance of food, clothes, and shelter. Seldom did any members of the family eat together. Stopping, instead, they would scoop a chunk of bread or roasted meat or ladle up a bowl of vegetables or soup whenever hunger struck. By the time Priscilla breakfasted each morning her Indian father was long into the day's hunt for food.

She assumed, correctly, that other men in the village followed a similar routine of hunting for small game or fishing until their efforts were rewarded with catfish, bass, or brook trout. But if Bear Claw traveled among the men, Priscilla didn't know. Nor did she have any means of asking. Since she hadn't ventured out, she had yet to see a bear, or the claws of one, and until she did she had no way of pointing and identifying.

With her new language thus limited, she kept her eyes opened wider, taking in this foreign, yet familiar, culture. She was uncertain what her place in it would be, but it was fairly obvious now that her spiritual work could not interfere with the necessary physical chores required of every member of the village. She had to contribute *their* way before she could speak of *God's* way. She had to learn before she could teach.

Kaboom. Kaboom. Kaboom.

White Cloud moved her heavy pounder in unison

with the rest. Up, down, up, down, up. She stopped, her arms poised above her head, as Priscilla laid a hand on her shoulder.

"Let me help," Priscilla offered, pointing first to herself then to the pounder.

White Cloud shook her head.

"Please?"

The older woman laid down her large wooden mallet to feel the bit of muscle in Priscilla's thin arm. Then she shook her head again. But instead of continuing the job herself, White Cloud suddenly disappeared into the hut.

As soon as she was alone, Priscilla picked up the pounder and almost staggered under the unexpected weight. Still, she tried to lift the handle above her head as she had seen the other women do, but her aim went amiss. The mallet came down hard on the edge of the log, crushing not corn, but pride. More slowly she tried again, this time managing at least to hit the scooped-out center. But when she lifted the pounder, not a single kernel seemed to have suffered from her blow. Her third attempt succeeded in splitting a few kernels and in reminding her that she had unused muscles throughout her neck and shoulders. Then her fourth try had her wondering how anyone could keep this up for long!

Thankfully, Priscilla didn't have to. White Cloud returned with an empty vessel that she exchanged for the wooden mallet.

"A-ma," she said, and Priscilla nodded. Water. White Cloud wanted her to fill the clay pot with fresh water. A comparatively easy task, Priscilla thought.

Rather gaily, she set off in the direction of the stream toward which White Cloud had pointed. How good it felt to be outdoors in such beauty!

Around her, the village snuggled inconspicuously at the top of the hills below the mountains. Here, the smothering woods had been held at bay by fields of corn which, at the moment, bore only the stubby stalks remaining from the last harvest. As summer neared, the cycle of soil and seed, rain and harvest would begin anew, but now a far hillside blazed with a spring show of azaleas. Above that flaming slope hovered a smoky wisp of cloud, and beyond it, a blue, blue sky.

Priscilla inhaled deeply. Then, hugging the water pot to herself, she spun around slowly, her gray eyes sweeping the sky, the land, the village. This incredible place was her home. And there! That pole hut shingled in cedar was her house!

How small it looked from the outside. And yet, she saw, it was no different from the other huts scattered about the village, except that some had shakes of pine or hickory. One building, however, stood out from the rest. Built on a mound of earth, it had seven distinct sides which rose from the center of the village.

Priscilla stared at the strange structure, wondering at its purpose. The multi-fashioned sides must have some significance, she thought, and so must the building's placement at the heart of the humble town. A meeting place, perhaps. If so, then the layout was not unlike the towns she had always known. Why, it even had a plaza, a park, for ballgames and children's play!

She wondered why so few children were around. Back home, the plantation grew a prolific crop of black babies, like so much cabbage or cattle. Their status bothered Priscilla more after Sally Ann had gone because Papa forbade her then to have any

48

future contact with the colored children. Since she couldn't teach them to read, the Bible would remain a mystery to them, forever belonging to the white folks.

That troubled her deeply until, on a spring day like this, she had opened up the windows all around, allowing in the breeze, and on it blew a chorus of voices, singing in the fields. She had heard them before, but the Negro Spirituals she heard that morning touched her spirit as church hymns and rituals never had, and then Priscilla knew. The slaves on the plantation were freer by far than she.

How free was Charles, she wondered now? She had no more desire to join him than she had to join the field hands. Yet she hoped he was glad to soar beyond that cloud-smoked curtain of sky. Somewhere, somehow, a heavenly life was his.

She couldn't imagine Charles' being happy here. He had hunted awkwardly when he had had to, and he had fished to no avail. Priscilla admired him for his efforts, for his willingness to try, but she couldn't see him regularly following those pursuits. He would have disliked the bland food, too, since it consisted always of corn in bread or mush or soup. To the Cherokee, she had learned, that corn, *se-lu*, meant life. But Charles had never liked corn.

Ka-boom.

The ever-present heartbeat sounded in her ears as Priscilla hurried toward the stream that ran alongside the village. Here, women of various ages and size had gathered to fetch water or to scrub clothes on the large, water-polished stones. Since a warm breeze played, most of the women had shed their deerskin dresses in favor of cloth ones like Priscilla wore, but one stood apart with petticoats and a long dress of dark red calico.

Priscilla tried not to stare. Even at a distance, she could see that the girl, perhaps sixteen, was a beauty. Her blue-black hair glistened in the sun as she moved, doe-like, among the rocks. Then suddenly the girl stilled, as though she had felt eyes upon her, and, regally, she straightened, returning Priscilla's stare.

All around, smiles vanished; chatter ceased as the women became aware of the intrusion. The idyllic scene which Priscilla had witnessed from an upper bank took on a somber air—as lifeless and unmoving as a painted canvas— with her on the outside. The only sound was the creaking of a locust branch; the only movement, the gentle swinging of a baby carrier that hung from that low branch.

Priscilla halted. Hesitantly, she smiled, scanning the upturned faces in hopes of finding some response, then, cautiously, she took a step or two.

"*I-gi-do!*" Straw Basket called the greeting first, and her face broke into its familiar smile. Without it, Priscilla had not recognized her, and she wondered at its delay.

"Sister!" she answered now. "*I-gi-do.*" And with that call, the still scene sprang to life again.

With the clay pot under her arm, Priscilla scrambled down the bank. Most of the women had returned to their work, but two or three moved toward her with shy curiosity to touch her creamy skin and long blond hair. Both were commonplace back home, but here it was entirely possible that these women had never seen a complexion as soft and pale as the ivory-colored dogwood blossoms that heralded the spring. Or touched hair as silken and bright as tassles on the early corn.

Priscilla stood quietly, allowing the gentle strokes.

Then laying aside her water pot to free her hands, she cupped the face of the woman nearest her, looking steadily into the short-lashed brown eyes. This she did with each of the women who hovered around. Touching their hair and skin as they had touched hers, she fingered a thick braid and brushed a cheek which was reddened with paint. Each movement brought a fresh eruption of giggles from the women.

"Hair like corn silk is worth much," a voice said, and immediately all laughter died.

Priscilla whirled to face the speaker—the girl in the calico dress. This close, she appeared even more beautiful than she had from afar, and yet less so. A hardness narrowed the large brown eyes, and a pout tucked the fullness from the girl's lips.

"You are Mourning Dove," the girl said before Priscilla could introduce herself. "I am Dancing Water, daughter of the chief, daughter of the Wolf clan."

"The Wolf clan! Then we're like sisters!" Priscilla exclaimed. "I am in the house of White Cloud and Straw Basket, also daughters of the Wolf clan."

"White Cloud and my mother are from the same womb, but you are sister to no one." The girl's eyes narrowed more. "Some of our people do not want a white woman here."

"I'm sorry to hear that," Priscilla said truthfully, "but I hope you'll accept me in time. I mean you no harm."

"So you say! My people have heard those words before from your real brothers and sisters," the girl said ungraciously. "Your people take the land. Now you come to take what is not yours."

"It's not like that," Priscilla insisted. "I have come to give, not take."

"My people need no gifts from you," Dancing Water retorted. "You have come like the others. You have come to take Bear Claw."

Nothing could have astonished Priscilla more. Feeling her mouth drop, she consciously closed it. And how was she to answer? Apparently this girl had set her heart on Bear Claw, and that suited Priscilla just fine. Unfortunately, however, the matter wasn't that simple. Since she had been unable to communicate with her new family, she didn't know what would be required of her if she chose to stay here. God himself had brought her, and He had be the one to tell her when it was time to leave.

Unwilling though she was, Priscilla had to face the fact that she might indeed have to marry Bear Claw. She measured her words carefully, praying God would provide even those.

"I can promise you this, Dancing Water, I will not take what is not mine."

The brown eyes were mere slits. "Nothing here is yours."

"Oh?" Priscilla couldn't help but smile. "Then tell me, Dancing Water. If you have such distaste for me and my people, why are you wearing a white woman's dress? Why are you speaking my language?"

The questions went unanswered. With a heave of her petticoats, the girl sprang lightly up the side of the bank, heading back to the village.

Priscilla had no intentions of following even before Straw Basket placed a restraining hand on her arm. Mere words couldn't alleviate the jealousy, the animosity that Dancing Water felt until Priscilla had had time to demonstrate to the girl and the other villagers that she had truly come in love and peace.

52

She patted Straw Basket's hand, still resting on her arm. Until now, it hadn't occurred to her that this young woman and her family had placed themselves in a precarious position in the community by inviting her to stay with them. Dancing Water had made it abundantly clear that some villagers would not be so welcoming. Worse, some might look with scorn or ill favor on Straw Basket's family.

Priscilla sighed. She had meant it when she had told Dancing Water that she wished her no harm. She wished harm to no one. And it troubled her now that she might inadvertently bring reproach to those very people who had been so kind. Something had to be done. But, at the moment, her only recourse was to be an obedient daughter to White Cloud, a helpful member of the family, a loyal sister.

Carefully stepping onto the natural bridge of large, round stones, Priscilla bent to dip the clay pot into the fresh-flowing stream. Cool, clear, life-giving water poured in, filling the container and reminding her that she herself was a vessel. God's vessels.

"Fill me too, Lord, and bring good out of my presence in this place."

Then, having already taken longer than intended, Priscilla called a goodbye to Straw Basket, who had returned to scrubbing her clothes on the rocks. She smiled, too, at the other women who chanced a friendly glance. Then, cradling the full vessel against her, she climbed the low bank, sloshing water down her dress front in the process.

Back home there had been servants—slaves—to haul water from the spring pump, and now Priscilla understood why those people possessed such strength, such sleek, well-developed muscles. A filled water pot was heavy! Heavier than the books she had carried from Papa's library. Heavier than the samplers she had patiently embroidered. Heavier than the silver teapot from which she had poured tea for her guests.

She wondered if she would make it back to the hut. Each step seemed to unloosen more the joining of arm to shoulder, and so she paced herself slowly, avoiding, she hoped, a wrenching jolt.

"Whatever things are pure, whatever things are lovely . . . if there be any praise, think on these things."

Snatches of Philippians 4:8 came back to comfort her, and Priscilla thanked God for the strengthening power of His word. She wished she knew more of it, wished she had memorized it more faithfully when she had the opportunity, for now her beautiful, leather-bound Bible lay on the floor of the river.

". . . whatever things are lovely . . ."

How lovely the mountains were today. How peaceful the village. How snug the humble huts. She had thought the dwellings were single rooms, but looking now, she could see that each had a tiny addition toward the back. How much there was yet to discover.

How much her arms hurt. Oh, it was no use. She set down the pot before she dropped it. Then she gave her shoulders a brisk rub.

". . . if there be any praise . . ."

She had to think about it.

"Praise God for water. For two arms. For . . . Garth!"

His very real and very timely appearance filled her with thankful relief. She knew she shouldn't let him carry the water pot since she had to become accustomed to hard work on her own. But just today. Just until she could build up her strength.

Approaching her in steady, long-legged strides, Garth swept her with his eyes.

"You're looking fit," he remarked casually, as if it were a chance comment on the weather. "I see White Cloud has you doing chores."

"I wanted to," she answered testily, as if he had just implied that she would much prefer to lounge about all day on satin pillows.

Coolly, Garth lifted his left brow. "Then why are you standing here?"

"I'm resting," Priscilla snapped.

"I see." His dark eyes skipped across her, laughing, but his lips held no trace of a smile. "Do you suppose you could rest while we talk?"

"I might be able to manage that," she said sarcastically.

"Good. I need to know why you're here, Mourning Dove."

Something in his tone, his bearing, made her feel that she'd been set before a black-robed, white-wigged judge, and her answer would determine her future for all time.

"I—I don't know," she said evasively.

"Priscilla! You must know. He shook his dark head impatiently. "Good grief, woman. You don't travel weeks beyond civilization only to arrive and not know why!"

"My actions are not quite as irresponsible as you deem them," she said with a lift of dimpled chin. "You must understand, sir, that I had no way of knowing exactly what to expect when we set out."

Garth's stern gaze softened. "Of course not. Surely you didn't expect to become a widow enroute."

"I wasn't thinking of Charles," she admitted. "I was thinking of the people themselves—the Principal People. Why do they call themselves that?"

"Because they are. To the Aniyv-wiya, all creatures are 'people.' Even the creatures of the forest. But there are Animal People and Principal People."

"That's just it!" Priscilla said. "I had expected the Cherokee, the Aniyv-wiya, to be little more than Animal People."

"And now?"

"I'm discovering that civilization has many forms."

Garth looked pleased with her answer. "But you still haven't told me why you're here."

"Oh." She was hoping he hadn't noticed. "I'm sorry, Garth, I—I doubt that you'd understand. If you were a Christian . . ."

"But I am."

It was her turn to be pleased. "You are? Oh, that's wonderful! That's . . ." *Odd*, she thought, for Garth's face had hardened.

Lettie is a Christian, she reminded herself, but Lettie had not understood. Perhaps Garth wouldn't either.

"Let me see if I have this straight," he said now. "You came here— a do-gooder—to convert the savages to a civilized worship of God. But you found more civilization than you bargained for, and now you question your original purpose."

The cynical statement was close enough to the truth to make Priscilla squirm uncomfortably under Garth's harsh stare. While she fumbled for words, he went on.

"You could, of course, stick it out until the heat of

56

summer. Your civil sensibilities will glazen then for reform, Mrs. Prescott—I guarantee it. You see, the women get quite warm, working hard in the cornfields, so they're apt to strip down to their waists. Ah," he said unmercifully, "your cheeks are pink already! But it's the winters, madam, when you'll really blush."

Garth stopped and pointed to the tiny addition to the huts that Priscilla had noticed earlier.

"Do you see the *osi*? That's a winter house. It's small, airtight, and protected by the earth mounded around it. During the months of heavy frost and snow, the family of this hut will move into that *osi*, which is aptly called a 'hot house.' It's stifling inside at times. And then the family members, male and female, will shed all clothes when they enter that warm chamber."

Priscilla's lips parted, but no words came.

"What will you do then, Mrs. Prescott? Will you shed your own modesty as well? Will you wrap yourself in cloth and melt, while White Cloud and her husband enjoy the freedom in which they were born? Or will you convert the family—indeed, the village—toward your chaste roast, which is so unlike heaven? Or perhaps you could convince the people to remain in their summer quarters, wearing layer upon layer of animal skins. But I must warn you. If you choose the latter, you'll have to be most persuasive, for the Principal People are not inclined, as the white man is, to demand more from the Animal People than is truly needed."

Garth inhaled deeply. "So, madam? What do you propose?"

Priscilla stood frozen, immobile, horrified by his revelation of this culture so alien to her own. She had known, since the conversation with Dancing Water, that she could no longer burden White Cloud's family. Nor was she ready to leave when none of God's work had yet been accomplished.

Considering the picture that Garth had presented, Priscilla had no idea how she would cope. Regardless of his opinion of her, she had not set out to change the Cherokee culture. Instead, she had intended to adapt herself to it. But now! Naked in a hot house with Straw Basket and White Cloud and White Cloud's husband? God forbid.

"Mr. Daniels, I don't know what I'm going to do," Priscilla said frankly. "However, I have absolute confidence that the Lord who called me here will show me how I'm to minister. These people are His, and I mean to bring them Christ's name. But I haven't the faintest clue as to how I'll go about that. I'm sorry, but there's nothing more to tell."

"On the contrary, Mourning Dove, you've told me quite a lot. You've no intentions of going home yet, then?"

"That's correct."

"And I assume that you'll be most uncomfortable, come winter at least, if you have to live with White Cloud's family?"

"True. But, please understand, I've no wish to change their way of life, their means of survival."

"Understood," Garth said, and Priscilla thought she saw a glimmer of respect. "Then it seems to me that the only solution is for you to have a home of your own."

"Oh, I quite agree. But is that possible?"

"Not without insulting White Cloud and Straw Basket. Unless, of course, you should marry."

Priscilla sighed. "I was afraid of that, but it can't be helped. Until the Lord shows me that I'm to leave, I must stay, whatever the circumstances. Besides," she hesitated. "It seems that God has gone ahead of me in preparation."

Garth looked at her curiously. "What do you mean?"

"Bear Claw," Priscilla said, watching with some satisfaction at the startled expression on Garth's handsome face. "It's my understanding that Walking-stick brought me to this particular village because of Bear Claw. I've yet to meet the man, but apparently he's lost a wife. Since I, too, am widowed, Walking-stick seemed to think my marrying Bear Claw would be a good thing."

"He's probably right," Garth grinned.

"Well, you needn't look so amused, Mr. Daniels!" Priscilla felt annoyed. This was her future, her married life she was talking about, and for her, there was little humor in it.

"Forgive me, Mourning Dove. It's just that you're handling this unusual situation rather stoically, as stoically, perhaps, as an Indian princess."

"I'll take that, sir, as a compliment, though I'm not unmoved by joy or grief, and neither, do I think, is the Cherokee."

"Very perceptive of you."

"At any rate, I haven't met Bear Claw. I don't even know if he speaks English," she said, almost to herself.

"Set your mind at rest, madam. He speaks your language rather well." Garth seemed to be enjoying her dilemma.

Priscilla shot him a look of annoyance. "Good.

Now, what I was about to say is that it seems odd that I was intended to become Bear Claw's wife, but instead I've become Straw Basket's sister."

"Didn't you know? She was the same person."

"What?"

"Bear Claw married Straw Basket's sister about three years ago."

"Well, of course I didn't know. How could I? You didn't tell me," Priscilla said, exasperated. Then she wondered what else he hadn't told her.

"That's why you were taken to her family—to meet Bear Claw." Suddenly Garth laughed. "I wonder if Walkingstick realized that he was causing a stir when he deposited you here?"

"I don't find that particularly amusing, Mr. Daniels. We're talking about my presence being a source of trouble, which is not what I had in mind."

"Well, you'd better get used to trouble, madam, because Dancing Water may give you plenty of it."

Priscilla frowned. "I can handle her, I think. But what about her father? She said that he's the chief."

"So he is. But Blazing Sun is a fair man, predisposed to peace. This is a peace town, you know."

"I know, sir, only what you tell me."

Garth smiled. "There are around seventy towns in all. Some are designated as peace towns; some are war towns. From the city of Chota, the Principal Peace Chief presides in good times, and in turbulent times, the Principal War Chief has the final say over the entire Cherokee nation. But here, Blazing Sun is the local authority."

Garth pointed to the seven-sided building that Priscilla had thought was a meeting place.

"That's the council house where people come

together for political, social, and religious matters. Each side of the building represents one of the seven clans—Paint, Blue, Deer, Bird, Wild Potato, Long Hair, and, of course, the Wolf clan. Blazing Sun presides over all of it, sitting behind the sacred fire.''

"Then, he's almost like a king."

"Hardly," Garth scoffed. "Blazing Sun receives no birthrights, no inherited honors as do lords and ladies, knights and kings."

"It's not always like that," Priscilla said defensively.

"Often enough," Garth insisted. "But Blazing Sun had to earn his honor before the people would elect him to his position."

"Elect? You mean, the villagers themselves decided who their chief would be?"

Garth nodded. "Hard to believe, isn't it? The Principal War Chief and Principal Peace Chief are also elected. And not only that, but the women elect their most honored representative—the Beloved Woman of the Nation— who you may be interested to know, reigns in times of war or peace."

"Oh, my." Priscilla was having difficulty taking in all that Garth was saying.

"Mark my words, Priscilla," he added now, "someday our people will tire of handed-down kings we've never seen or heard. Someday we'll be *civilized* enough to elect representation for our own colonies. And then, we just might have a government as workable as the Cherokees."

"Perhaps, but I confess, at the moment I'm more concerned about representing myself to the chief."

"I doubt you'll have to. If Bear Claw wants to marry you—and I'm certain he will—he'll have the task of confronting Blazing Sun." Garth seemed to be laughing at her again.

"Laugh if you will, sir, but if I were the chief, I don't think I'd like having my daughter cast aside a second time by the same man."

"The first time Dancing Water was too young. And now . . . we shall see," Garth said. "But don't forget, Mourning Dove, the Aniyv-wiya marry by mutual consent, not by force."

"I didn't forget." Priscilla stamped her foot. "You never told me." Her glare didn't silence his chuckles.

At one point, she would have been overjoyed to hear that no one could force her into marriage. Only this morning, in fact. But now, Priscilla had determined to marry Bear Claw as her best solution for remaining in the village. It didn't help, then, to know that Bear Claw could withhold his own consent.

She sighed heavily and looked at the flies collecting on the brim of the water jug. If she didn't return the filled container soon, the water would be unfit for consumption.

"I suppose we should be heading back," Priscilla said. "White Cloud will be waiting for the water."

"So she will," Garth agreed as he picked up the clay pot. "I just hope you won't find it too taxing. We still have much to talk about as we walk."

Then with a smirk and a slosh, he handed her the heavy vessel.

CHAPTER 5

"YOU ARE NO GENTLEMAN!"

Garth laughed. "So I've been told."

"You might at least look ashamed of yourself."

"I might, but I won't." He fingered her hair, playfully at first then gently stroking it, much like the women had done by the stream. "I must say, Priscilla, that my eyes were hungry for a blonde."

"I'll thank you to keep your hands to yourself," she spat. "If my own weren't full—carrying this very, very heavy pot—I'd slap that grin from your face!"

"Don't ever try," he warned in a tone that showed he meant it. "The Aniyv-wiya don't take kindly to their people abusing one another."

"And what do you call this? I personally think it's abusive of you to walk along empty-handed while I'm still recuperating. And you're so big and strong and . . . ." She'd almost added "handsome," which had nothing to do with anything. It was just that ever since he had touched her hair, something within had quickened, some deep longing that she didn't understand and had tried to ignore.

"Don't take this personally, Mourning Dove," Garth said as she stumbled, wearily trudging up a slope. "You did say you wanted to be part of this village, these people, didn't you? Why, you're even willing to marry Bear Claw in order to stay. And he might be ugly and ancient, for all you know."

"Is he?" she asked, alarmed.

Garth chuckled. "Dancing Water doesn't think so."

"You're really no help," Priscilla said icily.

"Oh, but I am. I'm trying to point out that marrying Bear Claw is far more serious than carrying a water pot. Especially when the village women do all of the carrying and fetching. You'd better get used to it, Priscilla. The other women have. They know that their men must keep their hands free— to build, to hunt, to protect—even to kill if they have to."

She hadn't thought of that. What Garth said made sense, but that didn't stop her arms from hurting. She grimaced.

"Why don't you stop carrying that water pot like a white woman who's used to servants?" Garth said, sounding annoyed. "Here. Put it on your shoulder."

"I don't think I can," she admitted, and so he did it for her. Priscilla, however, withheld her thanks, feeling somewhat less than grateful.

"Tell me about Straw Basket's sister," she commanded rather sharply. She wanted to know as much as she could, and at the moment, she would be glad to have her mind elsewhere.

"Her name was Laughing Owl," Garth said in that soft voice, that special voice that made Priscilla think he had a heart.

"That's a lovely name. Was she beautiful?"

"Not like Dancing Water, but, yes, in her own way she was. Their mothers were—are—sisters, you know."

Priscilla nodded as well as she could with a clay pot on her shoulder. "Daughters of the Wolf clan. But what about Blazing Sun? Is he of that clan too?"

"Never. Members of the same clan are forbidden to marry," Garth said. "Blazing Sun is of the Paint People, but you might be interested to know that Nan-ye-hi, the Beloved Woman of the Nation, is a daughter of the Wolf."

"It seems I've been given a rather intriguing family," Priscilla said, delighted. "Oh, Garth, tell me about all of them!"

He laughed. "I will, but it'll take a long time."

Priscilla felt certain that the water jug had lightened with Garth's promise. Perhaps she was making too much of casual words, but her hopes leapt at his implication that they'd be seeing each other again. Then, just as quickly, her spirits sank. Bear Claw might not like the friendship that was forming between them.

Hesitantly, Priscilla broached the subject. "Garth, will Bear Claw object to our, uh, having contact with one another? Will he be jealous?"

"Hmmm." Garth stroked his clean-shaven chin thoughtfully, but the sparkle in his eyes belied his seriousness. "I should think, Mourning Dove, that that would depend on what you have in mind as contact."

"Oh, really, Garth. You are a dreadful man."

"Outrageous." Suddenly he stopped and whirled her around, catching the water pot before it drenched them both. "What do you want of me, Priscilla?"

"Want?" Her gaze shifted across his broad shoulders. "Why, information. Answers." She tried to keep her voice light.

Garth tipped her chin until he had captured her gray eyes. "And that's all?"

Her shallow breath came rapidly. "No," she admitted.

"What then? Friendship?"

She gave a feeble nod.

"Anything more?" His words pressed her as steadily as his hand.

"That's all there can be, Garth," she said and pulled away.

"I wouldn't be so sure, Mourning Dove," he said gently. "This is a different culture, a new world for you with fewer restraints. The men and women here have little time to win hearts. Or to hold them."

She wouldn't look at him again. Not with her chin quivering so.

"White Cloud has waited long enough for this water. Look, she's beckoning me to hurry."

Actually Priscilla thought her adoptive mother was waving flies away, but she had tarried long enough. Steadying the jug, she fled the spot where Garth still stood, but not fast enough to escape the laughter that he hurled against her aching back.

"Priscilla!" he called out. "Prissy! Bear Claw will be a most fortunate husband."

Oh, that man was outrageous. And yet, inside the dark interior of the hut, she couldn't stop herself from laying a cool hand against the dimpled chin he too had touched. The mere warmth of his fingers had sent ripples through her entire body—a sensation more foreign to her than the immediate surroundings of hearth and hut.

No, Bear Claw would not be a fortunate husband, she knew regretfully. Garth Daniels had seen to that. Although she had scarcely met the man, his magnetism drew her until she could not bear the thought of another man's touch. Not even Charles'.

Her alien emotions filled her with such shame, she sank onto the floor beside the fire and wept. She knew she was feeling sorry for herself, knew she wasn't trusting God's forgiveness or His love. But she cried anyway.

Maybe she had been mistaken all along. Maybe God had never called her here. Maybe she had only used the preacher's message as an excuse to get away.

And now that she was here, where could she possibly live? She would keep her eyes closed all winter if she had to. But she couldn't hurt Straw Basket or White Cloud by moving out, unmarried, when they'd been so kind. And yet she might hurt them more by staying. How terrible it would be if this family were ostracized by their own people because of her.

Oh, it was so unfair. But thinking about it only made her weep harder.

"Mourning Dove," White Cloud called softly, soothingly, as she padded across the dirt floor.

Priscilla sniffed and attempted a smile. "Oh, E-tsi, I wish we could talk; I wish you could understand what I'm saying. I just don't know what to do. Everytime I think I have an answer, I see that I haven't. And that dreadful man, Garth Daniels, confuses me even more.

"I don't want to hurt you by leaving," Priscilla went on. "Nor do I want to cause trouble for you by staying. I don't want to go home. But I don't want to marry a man who's not of my faith, a man I don't love, a man I've never met. Oh, E-tsi! What am I to do?"

The outpour of words lessened along with the sobs as White Cloud stood over Priscilla rubbing her sore shoulders and stroking her golden hair. The small, square hands brought comfort, just as Mammy Sue's larger, longer hands had done.

"Missy, no'un ever promised dat life wuz gonna be fair. But you has got de Lawd."

Remembering Mammy Sue's calming words, Priscilla smiled. Then she pressed White Cloud's rough hand against her cheek to let the older woman know it would be all right. Somehow, God would make clear what course was best. Until then, Priscilla knew the wisest choice was to trust God to work things out, to believe in the guidance He promised through His Holy Spirit.

With that decision consciously made, Priscilla laid aside her doubts, her fears, her confusion. The Lord had His work to do, and so did she—the most obvious being her need to master the chores required of a Cherokee woman.

Over the next few days, her language skills improved remarkably, but even without words, she learned quickly by watching White Cloud and Straw Basket. Step by step the women showed her the art of laying a fire, of cooking a meal, of carrying heavy burdens that weren't nearly so heavy, she discovered, when she knew what to do.

Using her head or shoulders or back kept at least one arm free for balance. Often she placed whatever needed carrying into a basket that hung down her back after being anchored with a wide strap across her forehead. This took some getting used to, especially since the weight thrust her forward as she walked.

Priscilla thanked God that she carried no living loads. The few women with children under a year or so were seldom seen without the forehead strap anchoring a stiff cradleboard across their backs. Or, if a woman didn't carry her own cradled infant, the burden fell to a grandmother or sister or aunt. Priscilla wouldn't want White Cloud or Straw Basket to be burdened thus, and she was still having enough difficulty taking care of herself!

Charles had been right to wait. No parent was ever truly prepared, but she was learning. When the time came, as she prayed it would, Priscilla hoped she would be ready enough.

Steadily, her strength increased, along with new knowledge and skills. As the weather continued to warm, she spent part of her daylight hours in the fields with other women and some of the men who had begun readying the soil for planting. Soon the Three Sisters would grow—corn, beans, squash. And, the Three Sisters would nurture the people of the village, sustaining them when the Animal People proved scarce.

With a freshly sharpened hoe, Priscilla upturned the dark brown earth, casting a wayward stone into a pile. Another downswing broke the clods into a finer texture just right for cradling seed.

When no one was looking, she knelt down to scoop up a handful of the dirt. Then she let it run between her fingers. She had seen Papa do so when he had stopped to admire his land, but Priscilla simply enjoyed the pleasure of being part of the earth's productivity. This land was God's.

The Principal People seemed to understand that, and Priscilla admired them for it. She had yet to learn by what name they called upon the Lord, but she had no doubt they did so, for chanting words and stances of uplifted hands showed a prayerful spirit evident in everyday life.

Once, she had tried to share with Straw Basket the good news of Jesus as Savior, but the experience had been frustrating to them both. Eventually, she had told herself, there would be no language barrier, and then Christ's name could take root as surely as the seed laid in a well-prepared field.

Meanwhile, Priscilla's actions spoke more eloquently than any language. With a jubilant spirit and a willingness to work, she had begun to gain a measure of acceptance—a nod here, a friendly gesture there. When someone had thrown a rock, hitting her on the shoulder, the people who witnessed the event shooed the boy away with a harsh scolding. Priscilla herself had intervened on the child's behalf, assuring the villagers with smiles and signs that she was unharmed. Yet it troubled her that Dancing Water had remained apart from the flurry with obvious malice marring that lovely face.

The girl had not spoken to her since the day of their meeting, and if anything, Dancing Water seemed more hostile. Priscilla couldn't understand such behavior. Nothing she said or did improved their relationship in the least, and she supposed that Dancing Water still considered her a threat. How ridiculous. Bear Claw had not approached her at all, much less asked her to marry him. If, however, he did, Priscilla knew what her answer must be.

She swung her hoe down hard. What a pity that the

people she had met thus far who spoke her language did not wish to be friends. Even Garth was avoiding her. She had seen him rarely in recent days, and then only from a distance. Arrogant man that he was, he probably expected her to race across the fields to greet him. Well, her heart did race. But, she had easily kept the rest of herself in check—probably because she'd spotted him coming out of Dancing Water's hut! Shortly thereafter, the girl herself had exited, wearing a conspicuously new, blue-gingham frock.

Dancing Water had on the same dress today, and Priscilla wondered if that meant Garth was still in camp. Probably. Seeking pleasure, consolation, passion? It was no business of hers what he and Dancing Water sought! Yet the more Priscilla thought about them, the faster she hoed.

She had to catch her breath when she saw Garth's familiar figure at last. What was it about that man that caused her own body to behave so unfamiliarly? Even her legs trembled beneath their leather strappings.

Unfortunately for Priscilla, Garth caught her staring across the length of the field. The sun flashed from his grin as he cocked his head and gave her a mock salute. Gladly, she could have wrung his neck when he hollered her name, calling attention to himself— and to her. Then, leaving her alone to face the resulting snickers, he slipped into Dancing Water's hut.

How dare he.

Priscilla threw down her hoe. Using more force than was necessary, she hurled the stones she had upturned, far beyond the perimeter of the field. Then she told Straw Basket she was going into the woods to gather kindling.

The cool forest air fanned the flush from her cheeks as she wandered down a deer path, carpeted with pine needles. Garth Daniels meant nothing to her, she told herself over and over again. Nothing, nothing, nothing.

Then why was he changing her into a person she didn't know?

"Look at me," she said to a chameleon, turning brown then green upon the forest floor. "We must be sisters."

The lizard darted away as Priscilla hurried up the path. Unconsciously, she headed toward her favorite retreat, a spot she had discovered when she first helped Straw Basket gather wood for the fire. She had gone back as often as she could since then until there was precious little kindling left.

Realizing this, Priscilla looked around until she found a stout limb that suited her purposes. Then she proceeded to clear the dead lower branches of a pine by giving them a sharp whack. That done, she advanced, club raised, on a promising-looking locust.

"Priscilla! Whatever are you doing?"

Club high, she whirled around to face Garth.

"You!"

"Would you put that weapon down before you hurt somebody!"

"I'm not finished," she insisted peevishly. "I've come to get kindling for the fire, and I'll not leave without it."

"Fine, but it can wait."

She eyed him suspiciously. "Why? What do you want?"

"To talk. That's all."

"How did you find me?"

He laughed. "Straw Basket pointed me in the general direction of your whereabouts, but the commotion you caused, getting a little firewood, could have alerted an army. Or a bear." Suddenly he sobered. "You shouldn't go into the woods alone, Mourning Dove."

"You needn't trouble yourself about my welfare, Mr. Daniels."

"Oh, but I must. Sit down Priscilla," he commanded, and she sat. "I've never really told you about Laughing Owl—what kind of person she was, how she died. I think it's time I did."

Primly, Priscilla sat on the rounded edge of a boulder, her fringe-covered knees tightly together, her hands folded expectantly in her lap. She didn't look at Garth, but gazed instead at the waterfall that had drawn her to this spot. The crystal beads of water rushed down a granite slope then settled peacefully into a moss-rimmed pool. Beside the mossy edge sprang the last of the spring violets, faded now from the warming sun.

"I want to know about Laughing Owl. Bear Claw too," Priscilla said. "And yet I—I don't."

"I'm not sure I understand," Garth admitted.

"Nor I!" She sighed. "Laughing Owl is my sister's sister. My mother's daughter. She's never been alive to me, Garth. If you make her so now, I'll only lose her. Or worse, I'll feel my new family's loss more deeply. I can't replace her, Garth."

"No one expects you to."

"Maybe not. White Cloud and Straw Basket have certainly welcomed me warmly as myself. But what about Bear Claw? What does he expect or need? The tremble in her voice surprised her. "It would make matters so simple for me to marry. To have my own home, to . . . Oh, you know the reasons. But I've thought about it often since we talked, and I—I just can't go through with it."

Garth observed her coldly. "Why not, Priscilla? Does the idea of a Cherokee spouse seem loathsome to you?"

"Garth Daniels! You've twisted my meaning altogether," she said hotly. "Oh, don't you see? Bear Claw is only a name to me, no more real than Laughing Owl. But he's alive! He's a person with feelings and—and needs. How unfair it would be for me to marry him when I have no personal feelings for him."

"Perhaps you will," Garth said. "Don't close the door yet, Priscilla. I'm still convinced that it's the best solution for you. And for Bear Claw."

"You really think so? You really think I'd be good for him?"

Garth gave her a half-smile. "The best," he said.

"All right then, I'm ready to listen. Tell me about Laughing Owl "

"She was killed by a bear."

Priscilla's eyes snapped to his. "Are you saying that to frighten me?"

Garth acted as though he hadn't heard. "She wasn't even alone that day. In fact, she seldom was alone." He dropped onto a smooth boulder beside Priscilla and ran a hand through his thick hair. The fingers she thought, trembled ever so slightly.

"In a way, she was like you, Mourning Dove. As soon as Laughing Owl married, she left the village life she had known, choosing instead to be at her husband's side, no matter where he went." He paused. "Some Indian women do that, you know. Nan-ye-hi, the Beloved Woman, even followed her husband into battle."

"I didn't realize. So, Laughing Owl followed her husband everywhere."

Garth gave her a hint of a smile. "Not into battle, but, yes, she went hunting with him, fishing, traveling from place to place as there was need."

"What about children?"

"They had not yet been blessed with a child," he said sadly, "But when she died, a child was on the way." For a moment, Garth seemed lost in his own thoughts.

"Yes?" Priscilla prompted.

"She was gathering firewood— *quietly*, I might add—not far from the spot where her husband was building a lean-to of sorts. He was pounding a stake into the ground, when her scream alerted him. She had probably screamed before, but he hadn't heard. She didn't scream again."

"Oh, Garth."

"He was right there, Priscilla. So close. And yet, he might as well have been miles away."

"What did he do?"

"He ran. But even the wind wasn't fast enough to reach her in time. He flew at that bear with empty hands until his face and arm were half-torn apart, but he was too numb to care, to feel the pain. Finally, he found his knife. And he stabbed and stabbed and stabbed until the creature was long dead."

"That poor man," Priscilla said, weeping. "To lose both his wife and child in a single instant."

Garth looked at her in wonder. "Why, Mourning Dove! You're crying."

Well, of course, I'm crying." She sniffed. "Wouldn't anyone?"

"There are few tears shed by the Cherokee. Life is often hard here, Priscilla, and death is a real part of that life. It has to be accepted before a person can go on."

"I suppose. But it couldn't have been easy for Bear Claw to accept the loss of Laughing Owl and her unborn child—not if he believed he could have saved them by acting in time. Believe me, Garth. I know."

"Charles?"

She nodded. "He was safe. He had latched onto a log and was moving downstream rapidly, away from me. I think I screamed; I don't remember. But I'll never forget his face when he turned and saw me. It was as though, for a moment, he had forgotten I was there. He looked startled. And then, treading water, he hurled the log upstream with a single hand. I remember thinking what strength that took, and I wondered how he had done it. It wasn't a big log, but Charles was of slender build. That effort must have cost him his last breath." Her voice broke into sobs.

Garth held Priscilla's hands in his own, saying nothing. When at last she had composed herself, she went on. "I had taught myself to swim, but my skirts weighted me down. I reached the log as quickly as I could, and kicking and paddling, I maneuvered it downstream. Somehow I pulled Charles onto it. Somehow we reached the shore. I collapsed, Garth. I couldn't move—even though Charles needed me."

"You did what you could." Garth put his arm around her until she stopped shivering.

"He was dead," she said simply, "with that same startled look forever on his face."

76

"Then that proves it. He didn't live long enough to reach the shore," Garth insisted quietly. "He made the choice, Priscilla, when he let go of that log. So you mustn't blame yourself or him. He wanted you alive. And so do I."

Sniffing, she shook her head. "I heard him groan. I know I did."

"Little Dove, you heard only yourself, not Charles."

The guilt unloosed its hold as Garth's words and arms enveloped her. Priscilla rested against his shoulder, listening to the waterfall— turbulent, yet peaceful, like her own heart.

"Did it occur to you, Mourning Dove, that God is bringing good out of two tragedies."

"Yes, but I don't see it yet," she admitted.

"In time you will."

His warm breath settled on her hair as she leaned, contented, against him. This was the way it should be, she thought, safe, secure, in someone's arms.

No, not someone's. Garth's.

Reluctantly, she pulled away. "I wish I'd known Laughing Owl," she said, feeling a need to break the too comfortable silence.

"You would have liked her. She was as kind as White Cloud, as attentive as Straw Basket, as spirited as Dancing Water. So bright, so alert, so alive." His voice softened until Priscilla had to strain to catch his words. "I've seldom met a woman like Laughing Owl."

"Why, Garth! You sound as though you were in love with her," Priscilla blurted out.

Immediately, she regretted her words as the color washed from his face.

"I was."

Ridiculous tears stung Priscilla's eyes as she stood abruptly. She had suspected all along that Garth enjoyed the company of the village women, Dancing Water among others. But she had never thought he would desire another man's wife.

"I—I'm sorry. I didn't know." She bit her lip. "I mean, Laughing Owl was . . . was married to someone else, and . . ." Her eyes suddenly widened. "Garth! She was, wasn't she?"

He shook his head. "No, Mourning Dove. Laughing Owl was married only to me." Lightly he touched the scar on his face, a jagged reminder of his futile attempt to save his wife and child. "I am Bear Claw."

CHAPTER 6

PRISCILLA FLEW AT HIM. pounding, kicking, sobbing. Garth allowed the blows until she sank into his arms, exhausted. Then he scooped her onto his lap, rocking her like a child until she had thoroughly quieted.

Tenderly his lips brushed her forehead, and a gentle hand stroked her hair.

"Marry me, Mourning Dove."

His tightened hold prevented her from lashing out again. She struggled to get up.

"Let go of me, Garth Daniels!"

"Not until you say you'll marry me."

Futiley, she pushed at his arms, his hands. "I told you I wouldn't marry Bear Claw!"

"Ah!" He gave her a squeeze. "Your reason, I recall, was that you had no personal feeling for the man. Surely you can't deny plenty of feelings, for *me*—even if, at the moment, they are angry ones."

"Quite." Deliberately, she stilled herself, back erect, chin lifted, as though she were a doll with no emotions whatsoever. Garth Daniels would not toy with her. She would not have it. No matter how long it took, she would sit here, she resolved—rigid, unmoving—until he wiped that smug grin from his face.

She couldn't stop, however, the heat that flushed her throat and crept slowly up her face. Nor could she stop her quickening heartbeat. A single finger touched the nape of her neck then circled her ear until it paused, maddeningly, on a telltale pulse. She held her breath.

"Don't try to fool me, Prissy. You're not indifferent to me, even though you may wish it."

She said nothing, but glared at him instead from the corner of one eye. The smug grin was gone, she noticed with satisfaction, but another look had taken its place. She turned to him more fully, and his lips came down, hard, on hers. His waiting hand captured the back of her head, and his other arm locked around her waist, gripping her in a smothering embrace.

She thought she had suffocated, but her quick breaths assured her she had not. What was she doing? Murmuring his name! What was he doing? Kissing her lips, her cheek, the tip of her nose! And how did her arms get there, around his neck? Abruptly, she pulled away.

"Don't get prissy on me now, Mourning Dove," Garth chided. Playfully, his lips tugged at her ear lobe.

Priscilla felt herself redden. One thing was certain. Garth Daniels' view of marriage would not be the same one held by Charles.

"You should know I'm not as *experienced* as you," she said hotly.

He chuckled softly. "And what, may I ask, does that mean?"

Priscilla glowered at him from beneath her long lashes. "I'm referring to the disproportionate number of European dresses floating around this village. They bear witness, I believe, to your—your escapades." She hated her priggishness, but continued snippishly. "Dancing Waters' blue gingham was especially fashionable."

To her surprise, Garth laughed outright. "Silly Priscilla, I believe you're jealous!"

He caught her hand before it reached his face, imprisoning it easily in a bone-crushing grip. "I warned you before—you'll not slap me. Do you understand?"

"I understand that you provoke me, Garth Daniels," she shouted. Yet despite her fiery words, her arm, her hand, went limp. Quickly she shut her eyes, barricading tears.

Garth wiped away the trickle that followed the curve of her cheek. "I'm sorry if I hurt you." His moistened finger slid to her lower lip, tracing it and making it tremble all the more. "Look at me," he commanded. Then, "Please."

She opened watery eyes.

"I'm a trader, Priscilla," he patiently explained. "My business is trading the items one would normally purchase in a mercantile—tools, iron pots, blankets, even dresses if a woman so desires." He slipped an arm around her. "Personally, I think the native clothing is more practical for the life encountered here. But regardless of my preferences, I trade what the people want for what they have. In return, I receive baskets, beadwork, furs and sometimes fa-

81

vors. But not, my dear, those favors that you suggest."

She wanted to believe him, but her own eyes made that impossible. "I saw you, Garth. Going into Dancing Waters' hut on more than one occasion. Each time she came out freshly gowned."

"Priscilla, as long as Dancing Water wants new dresses, I'll bring new dresses. But I wasn't visiting her; I was talking with Blazing Sun. I thought you understood that the good will of the village chief needs cultivating if you're to stay here."

"You mean you've been speaking to him on my behalf?"

Garth nodded. "Ever since your arrival."

"But I thought this was a peace town."

"It is. Much like the cities of refuge established by the Hebrews in Old Testament days." He cocked his head. "What? Are you astonished that I'm familiar with the Bible? Rest assured, my dear, my mother taught me well."

Garth shifted her scant weight on his lap. "At any rate," he went on, "you're safe enough in this place, but that doesn't guarantee the regards of those around."

"I'm aware of that," she snapped, "and I'm capable of earning that esteem."

"Are you?" He smiled at her as though she were a child. "That's splendid. Then I won't have to worry about you while I'm away."

"Away!" Priscilla exclaimed. "But, I thought . . . ." No, she couldn't tell him that she had hoped to see more of him if they married, not less.

"I seldom remain long in any camp, though you sorely tempt me to stay here forever, Mourning

82

Dove." His lips brushed the back of her neck. "Come with me."

"You know I can't," she said regretfully. "My work is here. The only reason I'm considering marriage at all is so I can remain here in peace and privacy."

Somehow that didn't come out exactly the way she had intended, Priscilla thought. She meant to suggest that she was too soon widowed to remarry just yet. Garth of course, would have little patience with such proprieties, but she doubted the truth would make him as angry as he appeared to be now.

"Don't use me, Priscilla."

"Don't expect me to be Laughing Owl."

"I m not."

"Well, I'm not using you either."

He raised a dark brow. "How can I be sure?"

She had merely planned to kiss him lightly, to show him her affection, her caring for him as a person. But the kiss deepened until nothing existed but his warm breath upon her cheek, his lips upon hers. His hands caressed her, his arms pressed her tightly against him until she, a willing captive, thought her head, her heart would burst. Then, without warning, he thrust her away from him. She could only stare, dumbfounded.

"You'd do anything to stay here, wouldn't you?" As he spoke, Garth rose, almost dumping her on the forest floor.

"That's not true," she said in a voice as shaky as her knees. "I wouldn't have kissed you if I hadn't wanted to."

"Wanted to what?" he asked, disgusted. "Wanted to stay here? Wanted to show me you would make it worth my while? Then you can save those innocent tears, madam. You have proven your point exceedingly well."

"But I didn't . . . ."

Garth's hand tore through his hair. "Let's not argue. You have your reasons for wanting to marry me; I have mine. We'll marry before the week is out. And may God help us both."

Stunned, Priscilla stood gaping after him until he was long out of sight. Then she sank into a heap, giving into the tears that had annoyed Garth so.

What had she done wrong? she wondered. She had only wished to demonstrate her caring, but instead he had practically accused her of harlotry. Well? Was she guilty? Priscilla wasn't sure.

She'd married Charles for the noblest of reasons: so that they, together, could commit themselves to God. Neither of them, however, had given much thought to their commitment to one another, Priscilla realized now. And, according to Garth's jaded view, she was about to do the same thing again.

No, he hadn't been quite so generous. Instantly he had assumed that she was enticing him in order to get her own way. The audacity of that man! Priscilla didn't know why she cared, but she did. In fact, his vexation arose because she cared more than she had dreamed possible.

"Why, Priscilla Prescott," she exclaimed to herself. "You're falling in love with that barbarous man."

Struck by this absurdity, she gave an ironic laugh. Lettie would have plenty to say if she were here, and Priscilla thanked God that she was spared, at least, that upbraiding. It was enough to recriminate against

the charges made by one's own self. Savagery—
that's what it was, wasn't it? Her savagely passionate
response to Garth had shocked her far more than it
did him, and she blushed again, just thinking about it.

He would never believe her admission of love.
Never. Unless . . . unless she proved her caring by
leaving the village, by going with him as Laughing
Owl had done.

At first Priscilla spurned the idea. She wasn't
Laughing Owl, and she had no wish to emulate her.
However, another consideration occurred that she
could not cast lightly aside: God had called her to this
territory, but not necessarily to this particular spot.
By traveling with Garth, she would come in contact
with many people in many areas. And, she would
have the advantage of remaining at her husband's
side.

The more she thought about it, the better she liked
the idea. With a lightened heart, she gathered the
firewood she had broken off earlier, laying it neatly
into a pile. As she worked, she hummed, her mind
singing lyrically of Garth.

"Mourning Dove."

Priscilla turned with a start. "Straw Basket! I didn't
hear you coming." She wouldn't have heard anything,
she realized.

"Bear Claw send. He say no good in wood alone."

"He did?" Priscilla was amazed. Even though
Garth had stormed off, he had still given thought to
her safety. She smiled. "Did he tell you we're soon to
be wed?"

Straw Basket shrugged, not comprehending.

"Marry," Priscilla said slowly. She held up one
hand, "Bear Claw." She held up her other hand,

"Mourning Dove." Then, bringing the two together with fingers intertwining, she said, "Marry."

Straw Basket beamed. "Marry. Good."

"Oh, I hope so," Priscilla laughed. "I sincerely hope so." She gave Straw Basket a hug, then gathered up her kindling.

When she had drunk in a last look of the waterfall, Priscilla headed back to the village with Straw Basket close behind. Indeed, her sister shadowed her constantly over the next few days until Priscilla began to wonder just what Garth had said. She would have asked him herself, but, once again, he made himself scarce.

She supposed Garth thought there was nothing more to discuss, although he could, at least, tell her what day they would be married! He had said before the week was out, but in this place, it was difficult to distinguish one day from the next.

Priscilla did have the assurance, however, that the wedding would occur as planned. For one thing, White Cloud spent every spare moment sewing beads on a soft white leather dress, fringed at the knees, which Priscilla presumed would be hers for the wedding. White Cloud had helped her try on the dress, satisfied then that it was a well-shaped fit. The thin leather molded itself nicely, smooth and supple against her own skin.

But it was Dancing Water's dress that convinced her that Garth's proposal had not been a dream. The girl wore new pink-sprigged cotton that Priscilla couldn't help admiring. Her husband-to-be, it seemed, had rather good taste in women's fashions, despite his disclamor that the native costume was best. But if he thought he could trade gowns for the girl's good will, Priscilla knew he was sadly mistaken.

86

Dancing Water's hostility had become almost tangible since the wedding news had spread throughout the village. Whenever possible, she directed harsh words or looks toward her rival until Priscilla wondered about her own safety. Straw Basket's constant presence reassured her, as Garth had obviously intended, but even a beloved sister was a poor substitute for Bear Claw's protective arm.

If only she could see him. A mere glimpse now and then wasn't enough. She longed to be with him, talk to him, let him know that she intended to go with him, wherever that might lead. But, when no opportunity presented itself, Priscilla decided to seek him herself.

The few times she had caught sight of him since their encounter in the forest, he had been coming from a section behind the osi, which she had yet to explore. Of late, other men had been in that area, a fact in itself that Priscilla found curious, especially when White Cloud's husband appeared among them. What, she wondered, was going on?

As soon as she could get away, undetected, Priscilla skirted around the hut and osi, away from the fields, the stream, and the favorite spot she had found in the woods. On the edge of the village, this parcel of land looked as though it had once been separated from the forest by a solid wall of log fence. Time had worn down the fortification, leaving only a partial barrier, but the semi-protected area was not forgotten. Men swarmed about on the freshly cleared land, building some kind of structure, and, as she had expected, Garth was among them.

Nearing the spot, Priscilla had an impression of a forest of legs, with only Garth's fully clothed. She wondered if she would ever get used to the breechclout that most of the men wore—the leather oblong that hung, front and back, from a strap tied about the waist. In warm weather, the scanty garment was certainly practical but, by her standards, immodest. She knew she was blushing even before Garth spied her.

Their eyes locked as he came toward her. "Did you want me, Priscilla?"

She glanced off toward the new building, rising rapidly before her. "What are you helping the men build?" she asked.

Garth snorted. "I'm not helping them build anything. They're helping me. That's your house, Priscilla." He waved an impatient hand. "Did you think it would just magically appear?"

"I—I hadn't thought . . . ."

"Obviously," he said. "Well, what is it you want? I can't leave the men at work while I stand about chatting."

"Tell them to stop."

"What?"

"You heard me. They mustn't build a hut no one will occupy." This was not the romantic scene she had envisioned, but now she had little choice but to blurt the truth. "I've decided not to stay in the village, Garth. I—I want to go with you."

He stared at her with aversion. "Oh no you're not. I wondered how long it would take for Dancing Water to get under your skin, but I must say I'm disappointed, Priscilla. I thought you would manage the girl somehow."

Priscilla couldn't believe this was happening. "I did. I can. I mean . . . ." She wrung her hands. How could she possibly avow her undying love when her intended spouse was standing, hands on hips, shooting daggered looks at her.

"Never mind," she said. "Forget I came." Hastily, she retreated, her back hiding a rush of tears.

"Priscilla!" he called out, but she broke into a run.

Thankfully, White Cloud and Straw Basket were doing chores elsewhere when Priscilla reached the sanctity of their hut. Breathless, she slipped inside the dark interior, then stood there trembling. Garth must certainly think her a simpleton now!

How different things might have been if she had responded positively when he had first asked her to come with him. But, no, she couldn't have done so then—not until she knew her own mind, her own heart. Now it was too late, the hut too close to completion to say she would not be needing it. But she *had* said. She had told Garth, and he had immediately assumed she had meant to escape Dancing Water's lashing tongue.

Admittedly, the girl presented problems that could intensify after the wedding. Garth would be gone, and Priscilla would no longer have the security of White Cloud's family. As daughter of the chief, Dancing Water could easily stir up resentments. Yet despite the hateful possibilities, Priscilla trusted God to protect and guide her. What she felt now was sheer disappointment. She and Garth would not be together after all.

He came to her at dusk, before the sky had purpled, drawing her into the blackening shadows behind the osi. Atop a small ridge, their hut stood silhouetted against the evening light. Garth pointed to it, his long finger curving with the arc of the winter house.

"We'll finish the osi tomorrow, Priscilla, and after

that . . . ." He stopped, his voice brittle. "Have you changed your mind?"

"Nothing's changed, Garth." *Only my awareness,* she added to herself.

She shivered, and he placed an arm around her. Priscilla stiffened beneath his touch, every sense alerted. She could tell he was still angry with her, the muscles of his arm tensed across her back. What would it be like after they married if neither of them let go of wariness, if neither yielded?

Deliberately, she rested her head against his chest as they stood gazing at the hut. Their hut. Slowly, she relaxed against him, breathing a contented sigh.

Garth froze. "What are you thinking about? Charles?"

She flung herself away from him. "Why do you ask that?" Her eyes narrowed. "Unless you were thinking about Laughing Owl."

He winced. "No. I was wondering why you had, I don't know, softened."

Priscilla lifted her dimpled chin in a vain attempt to stop its quiver. "Apparently I used poor judgment," she snapped.

In the gathering dark, she caught a glimmer of his smile. "Any mistake, my dear, was mine."

Tenderly, then, his arms went round her trembling shoulders, her tiny waist, and he held her to him, her head resting just beneath his strong chin. His warm breath stirred her silken hair, and his pounding heart awakened her own.

When his lips discovered hers, Priscilla tipped back her head eagerly, giving herself up to his kiss. She had had none like this delicate flutter, this winged search that sent her, a fledging, into flight.

Beneath Garth's moonlit eyes, she felt herself grow suddenly shy. "Tell me about the wedding ceremony," she asked, scarcely recognizing her own voice.

"You'll be there, and I'll be there," he teased, "as will the entire village."

"Everyone?"

"Of course. The Aniyv-wiya work hard, Little Dove, but that doesn't mean they don't like to play. Our wedding will provide a suitable excuse."

She laughed. "I didn't realize we were such an attraction."

A feathery finger traced her lips. "Ah, Little Dove, this is the attraction." He kissed her again, lightly.

"Who will perform the ceremony?" she asked a moment later.

His hands dropped to hers, giving them a reassuring squeeze.

"*We* will," he answered, matter-of-factly.

Shocked, Priscilla's gray eyes flew to his. "But—I—we . . ."

Garth let go of her hands, and his arms folded across his chest.

"Prissy, were you expecting the woods to yield a preacher or a priest?" he taunted.

"No. It's just that . . . ."

"That what?"

She didn't know. She hadn't thought about it until now. Oh, of course, she knew there would be no church organ, no satin gown, no waiting pews. But to marry without a proper clergyman . . .

"Is it possible to have a civil ceremony?" she asked, embarrassed.

"As opposed to an 'uncivil' one," he remarked

coldly. His eyes swept her pityingly. "Well, madam, would a judge do?"

"I suppose so," she said, hesitantly. Then with vigor. "Yes! A judge would be· fine," she added, bravely hoping that Garth had someone in mind.

"Splendid," he said, although his tone didn't correspond. "We'll marry the day after tomorrow then."

"And the judge?" she pressed him. "He'll be here then?"

"Naturally, I'll be here," Garth drawled.

"You?"

"I wasn't always a trader, Priscilla. For years, I studied law—even entered my father's firm." He looked away. I had a stroke of good fortune with other people's ill fortune," he said bitterly. "The results brought my name before a clamorous populace who wanted me for a judge. Those in authority listened, and the appointment came with amazing speed."

"Why, Garth, I'm impressed."

"Don't be. This life suits me better, Priscilla. I just pray it suits you."

CHAPTER 7

WITH NERVES ATINGLE, Priscilla slipped the leather dress over her blond braids. Today she would become Priscilla Daniels, Mrs. Garth Daniels. She repeated her new name over and over, savoring the sound. Judge and Mrs. Daniels, she thought, then waved a hand. No, he wouldn't like that.

Her pride in him seemed to annoy Garth, who had refused to discuss his background further.

"Get it through your head, Prissy. The person you see here is the man you're marrying," he had said. At the time, his abruptness had wounded her because of the ensuing chill, the remoteness she had felt return to their relationship. But today was different. Today they were to wed.

Somehow they had agreed that the traditional ceremony of the Aniyv-wiya would be followed by their own private vows spoken in the intimacy of their newly finished hut. Lettie would have a conniption if she knew, but Priscilla decided she had to pursue her own course.

Close at hand, however, her adoptive sister beamed. Straw Basket and White Cloud hovered over her, clearly expressing their approval and contributing in their own way. The beaded handwork sparkled on the leather dress, and now both women tediously threaded more strands of beads through Priscilla's hair.

"Pretty," Straw Basket pronounced when they had finished.

"Wa-do, E-tsi, I-gi-do." Priscilla twirled around. "Oh, I'm so nervous." At their questioning brows, Priscilla outspread her trembling hands. "See?"

White Cloud clasped the shaking fingers in her own warm ones, rubbing them in a calming, circular motion.

Straw Basket looked on with a grin. "Bear Claw good man," she said. "Mourning Dove good sister, good wife."

Priscilla's eyes misted. "I hope so." If love were enough, it'd be true.

But what about Garth? Would he come to love her, too, in time? She knew he found her attractive, perhaps even desirable. But would he accept and appreciate her as he had Laughing Owl? A shadow crossed Priscilla's face, and in that fleeting moment, she felt like running. How would she explain her unusual situation? He didn't strike her as the sort of man who could comprehend a celibate marriage, regardless of the noble reasons.

What have I gotten myself into? she wondered with gnawing apprehension. She had heard that some unchaste girls feigned innocence on their wedding night. Was it possible to pretend the opposite? If Garth taunted her, Priscilla thought she would die of misery.

94

No time to back out now. White Cloud solemnly laid a sheath of corn across Priscilla's quaking arms then draped a fresh blanket across her shoulder. The older woman nodded as Priscilla stepped hesitantly to the door.

Once outside, the small party progressed towards the large dome-shaped council house that stood in the center of the town. As she walked steadily toward it, Priscilla kept her eyes, trancelike, on the dome while all that was around her took on an ethereal quality. It was as though she walked through a painting of colored chalk, smudged by some giant hand that excluded the council house, leaving it alone sharply delineated. Smoky clouds cloaked the mountains. A fog-like veil muted the thatched huts scattered around and a smeary mist curtained the plaza where villagers had danced for her wedding and would dance again. And even the drums, the chants, the hissing shakers were slowly muted into silence.

This wasn't real. But there was Garth, his eyes softened by the dream, smiling handsomely as she floated toward him in the center of the town house. She had been told that the whole village would be there, but at that moment, there were only the two of them, caught in this alluring spell.

In a low voice for her alone, Garth was telling her how beautiful she looked. Then he was quietly instructing her on the trade of her corn for the leg of venison he held. The exchange, he explained, symbolized their obligation and their promise to provide for one another. Within the blissful cloud, his gift, her gift, exchanged hands.

And then, Garth slipped a blanket from his arm, and she, a shimmering mirror, followed his every move.

His fingers, her fingers, his blanket, her blanket touched, wrapped, knotted into one—a single unit, two halves made whole.

"This symbolizes our sharing the same bed," Garth said quietly.

The surrounding rainbow burst. Priscilla blinked. She looked around. Dozens and dozens of olive faces, berry faces looked back. Men, women, children sat, according to social status, on the bleacher seats circling the large room. Everyone stared, somber. Everyone had watched. Everyone had come to see the blankets tied.

"That's it," Garth said cheerfully.

"That's it?"

He nodded. "We're married, Mourning Dove."

"Married?"

And then, mortified beyond endurance, she fainted.

When her gray eyes fluttered open, the first thing Priscilla saw was stars coming through a hole. She closed her eyes quickly and opened them again, but the view didn't alter. She shifted, slowly becoming aware of thick blankets between her and a dirt floor.

Outside, the sounds of laughter, songs, and stomping feet filled the air, but inside all was quiet except an occasional shuffle, muted and low. Beneath the starry hole, someone had lit a fire that blazed now cosily, and silhouetted against the flame, a crouching man moved about.

"Garth?"

The darkened figure paused, then crept toward her. His hand settled kindly on her forehead, smoothing away the wisps of hair and stroking either temple.

"You're all right, Little Dove, though you've missed the celebrating on our behalf."

"Oh, Garth. I feel so ashamed." She rolled away, covering her face with her hands.

"What happened, Priscilla?"

"I don't know." She scooted onto an elbow and squinted up at him as her eyes adjusted to the dark. "It was like everything was a dream, all hazy and unreal. And then, suddenly, it wasn't."

Glad for the shadows to hide her flaming cheeks, she remembered that awful moment when an entire village witnessed her and Garth's intentions of physical union. No such thought had entered her mind when she had wed Charles, although she had had a vague notion of that being part of their married life, a small part of their glorious plans. Now, to have a whole town witness such intimate thoughts made her feel naked before them.

"Priscilla, when is the last time you've had something to eat?"

"Oh." She hadn't thought of food for at least a day.

When she told him so, he looked grim. "No wonder you fainted. Is this the way you're going to take care of yourself while I'm away?"

She didn't respond, and he gave an impatient snort. Then he rose, returning to the fire from which, she noticed now, good smells wafted.

"Eat this," he commanded, shoving a wooden bowl into her hands.

Steadily she ate, commenting on the discovery of yet another of his talents. The thick soup settled her stomach, but, more, it settled her anxiety. If Garth thought nerves and hunger had brought on a fainting spell, he wouldn't be inclined to probe further, she hoped.

When she had scraped up the last bite of vegetables

and drop of broth, Garth replaced the empty bowl with a cup of soothing herbal tea. Priscilla sipped it appreciatively.

"Did you know," she teased, "that if we only married by tribal law and custom, your name would have to be Garth Davis?"

"Don't let it go to your head." Playfully, he poked her, causing her tea to slosh.

"Now look what you've done," she scolded.

In mock exasperation, Garth slapped his forehead. "Spare me! A nagging wife already!"

She giggled. Then catching the odd look in his eye, Priscilla sobered.

"Having doubts?" he asked.

"Some," she admitted, not looking at him as she dabbed at the tea spill.

"I see." He sounded disappointed.

She looked up quickly. "Not about you, Garth. About me."

"You're stronger than you think, I expect." His voice held a note of relief. "I'm sorry I'll have to be away much of the time, but it can't be helped."

"I understand, Garth. You've no need to apologize."

"I'm not. I'm simply expressing my," he hesitated, "remorse." He tipped her face up to catch the firelight. "Don't fret, Priscilla. Blazing Sun is your ally—for now."

"What do you mean?"

"Times are changing. Our people are crowding in on the Aníyv-wiya, and a clash will eventually disturb even the peace towns. But I'll be out there. I'll know when a conflict erupts."

"Oh, Garth!" Without thinking, she squeezed his

hands. "Promise me you'll not place yourself in any danger."

"I wasn't planning on it," he answered dryly. "I'm well aware, Priscilla, that you're marrying me for protection, and I don't intend to let you down." Ignoring her small protest, he went on. "I can make no guarantees, of course, but I want to be able to come home to you and a passel of blond children."

Shyly, Priscilla lowered her lashes. "I make no guarantees either."

"Then how about dark brown hair and dove-gray eyes?" Garth teased.

Priscilla chewed her lower lip as he raised her face again to the flickering light. Was her chin trembling? Or was it his hand?

"No more mourning about the past, Little Dove?" His soft voice queried. "No more fretting about the future?" Then, satisfied by her small nod of assent he declared, "I want you, Priscilla."

"Enough to marry me," she answered with a trace of bitterness.

Garth sighed, not denying it, and she supposed she should be grateful that he found her so attractive. Perhaps in time he would come to love her as she did him, but they had so little time. She couldn't help but regret his lack of caring for her as a person, a companion, a wife. How much better it would be if they were partners of the mind and of the spirit as well as of the flesh.

"Are you ready to get on with our *civil* ceremony," he asked.

She took a deep breath and nodded, thinking that the tying of the blankets was the only part of any ceremony that interested Garth. His next words, then, surprised her.

"I've been thinking what might be special to you, Priscilla, and I'm ashamed to admit that it didn't occur to me until then that you've probably missed having a Bible. I assume yours was lost in the river."

"Yes."

"Well, consider this one yours," he offered. "But before you take it, I found some passages I thought were appropriate. If you like, I'll read them."

"Oh, Garth. Please do."

"Would you like a prayer first then the reading before we exchange our— our vows?"

'That would be lovely," Priscilla said, her heart suddenly warming. His boyish awkwardness astonished her as much as his unexpected thoughtfulness. Pleased, she smiled at him until his searching gaze brought a flush to her cheeks.

Silently Garth took the cup from her unsteady hand and laid it alongside his own. Then, facing her, he drew her to her knees while he, too, knelt. Their fingers intertwined, hers tingling, and when Garth bowed his head, Priscilla gladly followed suit.

"Father of heaven and earth," he prayed, "guide our words. Lead us in the true vows of wedlock in Christ's name." Her whispered 'amen' joined his.

"The verses I wanted to read are in Colossians," Garth said, "seventeen through nineteen."

" 'And whatever ye do in word or deed, do all in the name of the Lord Jesus, giving thanks to God and the Father by him. Wives, submit yourselves unto your own husbands, as it is fit in the Lord. Husbands, love your wives, and be not bitter against them.' "

Was Garth already bitter, Priscilla wondered, because she had refused to go with him as Laughing Owl had done? She had since regretted that hasty 'no,' but now there seemed no way of undoing it.

"Have you ever read the Song of Solomon?" Garth asked now, and Priscilla shook her head. But as Garth read from it, the words seemed prophetic.

"'My beloved spoke, and said unto me, Rise up, my love, my fair one, and come away. For, lo, the winter is past, the rain is over and gone. The flowers appear on the earth; the time of singing of birds has come, and the voice of the turtledove is heard in our land.'"

"Garth, I—I . . . ." What could she tell him?

"It's all right, Priscilla," he said with surprising tenderness. "Maybe someday . . ." His voice drifted away, and his eyes returned to the pages still opened before him. "Ah, here's a verse for you in chapter four. "'Behold, thou art fair, my love;'" he quoted, "'behold, thou art fair. Thou hast doves' eyes.'" Suddenly he closed the leatherbound book, capturing her hands, her eyes, her breath as his intense gaze drew her to him.

"Do you, Priscilla, choose to be my wife, to have and to hold from this day forward until death do us part?"

"I do." Softly, she inhaled. "And do you, Garth, choose to be my husband—"

"—to have and to hold from this day forward until death do us part?" he said. "I do, Priscilla."

"Well?" she prodded.

"Patience, Little Dove. I presume you want me to say something like, 'By the power of God, I pronounce us husband and wife.' There! Will that do?"

It didn't sound exactly as she remembered, but Priscilla nodded. "That'll do." Then she insisted that they record their names and date of marriage in the Bible that Garth had provided.

That accomplished, he asked, "Now, do I get to kiss the bride?"

Timidly at first, she came into his arms, welcoming his brief kiss.

"Mrs. Daniels," he murmured against her cheek.

"Or Mr. Davis?" she teased.

"We'll compromise. The Wolf clan here, and the Daniels' name elsewhere."

"Agreed."

"Hmmm, I like it when you agree with me, Little Dove." His face nuzzled her cheek as he repeated, "Little Dove," softly. 'I hope the name suits without 'mourning.' "

Settled snugly against his chest, Priscilla suddenly stiffened. She could not, would not call Garth 'Bear Claw'. Did he expect that?

Apparently, he sensed her dilemma. "You'll need a new name for me, I suppose. Something like 'Sly Fox' or 'Mighty Oak,' " he said with a glimmer of amusement.

Priscilla laughed. "My! You certainly have an elevated opinion of yourself, sir," she said.

Leaning against him she twisted in his arms until she felt his warm breath on her forehead. "How about Running Deer?" she suggested "so you'll hurry home . . . to . . . me?" Her voice became a whisper as she realized what she had said.

His lips, brushing her forehead, halted. "A man would be a fool not to rush back to you," he said, but the words sounded grim.

Turning her round to him, his mouth bore down on hers urgently, as though he had not moments to spare. Priscilla responded, half in joy, half in sorrow. This was where she belonged, she thought; this was where she wanted to stay.

When Garth sat up and unfastened his shirt, the

loosened clothing exposed a dreadful scar, a welted cord that encircled his arm and brutally etched his side. Priscilla gasped.

Garth observed her coldly. "Repulsive, isn't it?"

Mute, her head shook with denial. It wasn't revulsion that she felt, but fear. That scar, that awful scar, had reminded her of Laughing Owl and Garth's deep love for her, a love that had given no thought even for his own life. He had told Priscilla about it, but seeing the scar now made that relationship dramatically clear. How could their own one-sided love begin to compare with what he had known before?

Closing her eyes, Priscilla attempted to remove the scar's intrusion from her thoughts. Garth was her husband now. She was his wife. Nothing else, no one else must matter.

When Garth turned to her, he had a cold look in his eye, as though he was hurt and would force her to think differently. But whatever thoughts she had had were driven from her instantly by panic as he reached for her. Words of protest chocked her, as she tried in vain to free herself from him. And when he finally released her, a terrifying eternity later, she found she was sobbing.

Garth sat up on the edge of the blankets, his back to her. When he spoke it was in dry tones. "Why didn't you tell me, Priscilla?"

"What difference would it make?" she countered through her sobs. She hadn't meant to snap at him, but she felt so humiliated.

He turned to look at her, his voice almost a hiss. "Did you and Charles ever—?"

"What do you think?" she interrupted, unable to bear hearing him speak so.

Garth gave a derisive laugh. "What do I think?" he mocked. "I think you either lied to me about the fact that you were married, or you're one of those prudish women who makes a man's life unbearable. Either way, it's contemptible."

"And, of course, you'd know. You're a judge, aren't you? Tell me, your honor, do you always convict the persons before you on such little evidence?"

"Well, what do you expect me to think?" Garth shot back.

"I don't know," she admitted wearily. "But don't punish me."

"Punish!" he exclaimed. "I assure you, madam, that no woman in my arms has wished to be elsewhere—until now."

Hurt and angry, she glared at him until he had the grace to look away. When he spoke again, she saw only his grim profile.

"I suppose it's your business, Priscilla, how you kept Charles away from you—or why. But don't expect the same consideration out of me," he warned. "You knew I wanted you before you consented to marry me."

"Oh, yes," she said. "You made it abundantly clear that that was the only reason you were marrying me."

Garth scowled. "Is that what you think?"

"What else is there?"

"Trust, caring, companionship," he bit off. "Why do you look so surprised? I'm human, Priscilla, regardless of what you think. Keep that in mind, will you, before *you* go convicting *me* on such little evidence."

For a moment, her crying subsided, thinking about what Garth had said. Perhaps they both had mis-judged one another's motives and character, and, if so, their future held more promise than she would have dared believe. Hopeful, her eyes turned to him, flickering across his set jaw, his broad chest, his bare arm. There, her glance halted.

Garth followed it. "I'm sorry it bothers you," he said with disgust.

This time, however, Priscilla didn't look away. Instead she leaned closer, her hand reaching out to trace the reminder of his wounds, the reminder of Laughing Owl.

"You loved her very much," she said quietly. "I've never been loved like that."

"Good heavens! Is that what's troubling you?" Garth caught her hand. "Charles threw you that log, Priscilla. He cared."

"Charles never held me," she stated flatly, pulling back her hand.

Garth slid across the blanketed space between them and scooped her into his arms. "Forgive me, Little Dove," he whispered. "I thought my scars repulsed you. You're so exquisite, all that a man could hope for." His face nestled in her hair. "I didn't mean to hurt you." His low voice held unmistakable anguish. 'It never occurred to me that you . . . that this . . . It could be different," he finished awkwardly.

She believed him.

Toward dawn, she stirred, awakening to the charm-ing lilt of a songbird. The fire had died to bright coals, and she wondered if she could give it a poke without disturbing Garth. He looked so peaceful. She decided not to chance it, but she snuggled deeper against him, seeking warmth.

Almost immediately, his arm coiled around her, drawing her closer. Priscilla laughed.

"I thought you were asleep."

"I was. You make it impossible to rest long."

Lazily, he lifted his thick lashes as he spoke, and now he stared at her with such longing, Priscilla gasped. Could that be love she saw? Last night, she had made no effort to hide her feelings for him, though she had not put them into words. She had even begun to believe that her love was not as one-sided as she had feared, and his present look confirmed the hope she had dared to cherish.

"Garth, let me go with you," she said recklessly.

"Where?" he teased.

She made a face. "Wherever it is you go."

Thoughtfully, he studied her. "You mean that, don't you?"

"I meant it the first time I said it," she declared. "And don't leap to conclusions. I *want* to go with you."

"I believe you do," he said astonished. But to her dismay, he shook his head. "I was only thinking of myself when I asked you, Little Dove. Believe me, it would never work."

"Why not?" she demanded peevishly. "I learn quickly. I could be a help to you."

He sighed.. "You're not used to this life and its hardships."

Impatiently she tossed her head. "Honestly, Garth, I'm not made of porcelain."

"Hmmmm." He seemed to give the matter some thought. "No, you're much too soft for porcelain."

His lips met hers, and he held her close until daylight had broken in upon them. Their heartbeats seemed to keep pace with the rhythmic "kaboom" of the awakening village.

"You know, you're right," Garth said, as they rose to dress, "you do learn quickly."

"Oh? Then our lessons are complete," she teased.

"Never!" he exclaimed. Then, as though to show her, he leapt across the wavelet of blankets and swept her off her feet and into his arms.

CHAPTER 8

THEY BREAKFASTED IN COMPATIBLE SILENCE. stealing glances at one another, before they reluctantly parted to do the day's chores. Priscilla hummed as she pounded the corn and set soup to simmer by the fire. Later, when she saw White Cloud and Straw Basket, they responded to her glowing face with smiles.

Her bright mood stayed throughout the day, despite Dancing Water's hostile glares. Priscilla spied the girl by the stream as she dipped fresh water into her clay pot. Understandably, the young woman seethed with jealous anger, and while Priscilla felt a certain sympathy, she determined not to let the girl's attitude affect her.

She did, however, feel embarrassed by the giggles and curious stares of the villagers who had witnessed her collapse at the wedding ceremony. In time, she hoped they would forget, for surely no typical bride of the Aniyv-wiya would have behaved in such a fashion. The fainting spell had set her apart, which was the direct opposite of what Priscilla had hoped to achieve by remaining in the village. Well, it couldn't be helped, she told herself, and eventually she would gain their trust and love. But, then and now, she was who she was, and the people would have to accept that or reject her altogether.

Which would Garth do, Priscilla wondered. At the present, he was obviously enamoured with her, yet he still had little confidence in her abilities. He had practically said as much when he had denied her the right to stay with him, going where he must go. Unless his opinion altered, he would soon grow weary of her inadequacies, seeing her as a liability, a burden, rather than the helpmeet God had intended a wife to be.

No, Priscilla vowed to herself, she would not let that happen. She wished she could easily and quickly prove herself, but she had learned from past experiences that forcing a matter, prematurely, generally produced disastrous results. She would have to bide her time, she knew, learning all that she could as well as she could, then leaving the rest to God. He was with her; He would guide.

Was He guiding her thoughts even now? As she set fresh water on the fire to heat, Priscilla's thoughts kept returning to Nan-ye-hi, the Beloved Woman about whom she knew so little. Each time Garth had spoken her name, his voice, his tone, his expression conveyed the utmost respect for this daughter of the Wolf clan. Certainly, she was a woman to be admired, for had she not been elected to her sacred post by all the women of the nation?

Believing that Nan-ye-hi's life and character would hold a clue to the traits and manners most desired in a Cherokee woman, Priscilla determined to ask Garth about her. She sincerely prayed that she and the Beloved Woman of the nation would have something in common, something on which she could fasten her hopes of growing into the person, the wife Garth needed.

As soon as he entered their meager hut that evening, Priscilla demanded her husband to tell her all there was to know about Nan-ye-hi.

Immediately, Garth seemed amused. "Do I not first get a kiss?"

Priscilla blushed prettily and pecked her husband's cheek. "Now don't distract me, Garth," she scolded when he gathered her into his arms for a more thorough embrace. "I really want to know."

He laughed. "So I see." Yet he pulled her down with him on the blankets as he made himself comfortable.

Priscilla, however, was not to be deterred. "Didn't you tell me once that the Beloved Woman stayed by her husband's side, even in battle?" she asked with enthusiasm.

Nodding, Garth sighed. "But she isn't you, Priscilla."

"Of course not! But that doesn't mean we don't have some similarities. We're both of the Wolf clan," she insisted.

Garth snickered. "Yes, you are, Little Dove." Cradling her in his arms, he stroked her silken hair. "As a matter of fact, Nan-ye-hi was no older than you when she was elected to her position."

"Really?" Priscilla sat up, interested. "Tell me about it."

"It was about twenty years ago," Garth recollected, "sometime in the 1750's when she followed her

110

husband, King Fisher, into one of the bloodiest battles ever seen in these parts."

"Who was fighting?" Priscilla interrupted.

"The Aniyv-wiya and Muskogeans as usual," Garth said grimly.

"Not whites?"

Garth shook his head. "We've had skirmishes, of course, and undoubtedly will again, but the true warring occurs between the various tribes. Eventually, I expect they will annihilate—or betray— one another."

"I hope not!" Priscilla exclaimed.

"Time will tell," Garth injected. "At any rate, the Taliwa battle was a particularly dreadful one. King Fisher had five-hundred men in his war party, but they were showing pretty poorly. Nan-ye-hi remained in the thick of it, crouched beside her husband. As he fired on the enemy, she hid behind a log, chewing his bullets."

"What?" Priscilla couldn't believe it.

"It's an old trick, actually," Garth confirmed. "Chewed bullets mangle the flesh with deadly results.

Priscilla shuddered. "Go on."

Garth smiled at her response before continuing. "Apparently, King Fisher's men were flagging badly, then he himself was wounded and killed. Nan-ye-hi didn't hesitate. She grabbed her husband's gun, reloaded, and joined the fight."

"If you believe the stories," Garth drawled on, "her actions that day rallied the men. The Aniyv-wiya won, and the Muskogeans moved out of the territory. Until then, they'd been quarreling over that spot for nigh onto forty years."

"Incredible!" Priscilla exclaimed. "All that because of one woman's bravery."

Garth chuckled. "I thought you would believe the stories. Now don't look at me with those dagger eyes. I agree. It's probably true. Nan-ye-hi is a remarkable woman."

"You've met her then?"

Garth nodded. "In Chota. I imagine you'll see her there when the village goes during the Green Corn Festival."

Priscilla gave a little clap. "I'd love that. Does she speak English?"

"I certainly hope so," Garth said dryly. "Her husband, Bryant Ward, is an Englishman."

"Really?" For some reason that surprised her.

"They have a daughter, Betsy, in addition to the two children Nancy and King Fisher bore."

"You called her Nancy," Priscilla noted.

"Nan-ye-hi, Nancy. The sound of her name was easily Anglicized, so you may hear her referred to as Nancy Ward."

"An ordinary name for such an extraordinary woman," Priscilla commented.

"Indeed. It's uncommon for one so young to be elected to the highest position of Beloved Woman," Garth said. "Regardless of who is presiding— Peace Chief or War Chief—Nancy sits with them near the ceremonial fire."

"Ah, but do they listen to her?" Priscilla had to ask.

Garth chuckled. "I assure you, if she speaks—and she often does, especially on matters of peace and social concerns—you can be certain that the good chiefs listen. It's thought, in fact, that the Great Spirit will use the Beloved Woman's voice to address the nation."

112

"The Great Spirit? You mean God?"

Garth nodded.

"Perhaps the people are right," Priscilla said almost to herself. "Perhaps God will use a woman's voice to address this nation."

She said nothing more on the subject, but it didn't leave her mind. Without his knowledge, Garth had confirmed the fact that she and the Beloved Woman had more in common than Priscilla had dared to hope—their willingness to remain at their husbands' side; their willingness to speak the words given them by God.

Priscilla doubted, however, that she would enjoy chewing Garth's bullets. She couldn't help but wonder though if Laughing Owl had ever done so, and asked her husband if he had yet found himself in need of chewed bullets. His response was a hearty laugh that relieved Priscilla's mind more than mere words.

"You might chew the leather for my feet," Garth suggested, playfully, "the next time I need moccasins."

Priscilla scalded him with her eyes as she ladled up their pottage.

They ate in silence—a smile playing all the while on Garth's lips. When they finished, he commented on the aptness of her cooking skills.

Priscilla hid her pride in the accomplishment behind a scolding. 'You needn't be so surprised," she admonished him. "Perhaps I'm more capable than you think, Garth Daniels!"

"I shan't argue that point," he chuckled as she started off with a toss of her head.

Without warning, he pulled her onto his lap.

"Garth!"

"Hush, Priscilla, and kiss me proper."

And she did.

Priscilla was steeped in the wonder of it all. Even her most cherished dreams had been bland compared to the reality of laying in Garth's arms. If only it could last; if only she could be with him always.

Too soon he left her, saying he would only be gone an hour or two. The town council met, regardless of one's preoccupation with love.

As soon as he left, Priscilla mused over her husband's comment that he was eager to return home to a passel of children. She hoped not to disappoint him, although she preferred a dark-haired, dark-eyed baby to the blonds he had set his heart on. How strange it would be to have a dove-eyed infant peering at her from his cradleboard. Would such a child be out of place? Charles had feared so. And he had feared, too, for Priscilla's own well-being.

Odd that two men could treat her so differently and have such differing concerns while both were men of God. Charles had believed her safe while traveling in his presence, and that had proved to be less than true. Garth, on the other hand, believed his wife's wellbeing rested in the protection of the village. Would that also be untrue? She had encountered no threats here, other than the ill will of Dancing Water, but separation from Garth was threat in itself.

Priscilla shuddered. She could not bear to think of days without her husband. Or nights. Yet she supposed she was safe enough—safer, at least than if she traveled among bears and warring tribes. Right now she would be of so little assistance to Garth, she couldn't blame him for refusing her accompaniment, but, Lord willing, that would change. She had learned to perform housewifely duties enough to gain his compliment, and her normal strength had returned now, increased. In time, she would be prepared, she hoped, to journey with him, alleviating his burdens rather than adding to them.

Meanwhile, she wondered how soon Garth would have to go? When she'd put the question to him, he had been vague in his reply, leading her to believe he felt no need for haste. Yet she knew he couldn't remain in a place too long. Thus far, he had been in the village longer than she. A day, a week, or two, and he would be compelled to leave, she supposed.

Garth had assured her, however, of his intermittent return. As he traveled back and forth to the white settlements and Indian towns scattered throughout the mountains, most trips would require no more than a fortnight. Such a schedule was tolerable—and possible because her husband had had the foresight to build his stock adequately before their marriage. Priscilla appreciated that, but within the year, he would have to augment those supplies, taking a trip back East to do so. Then he would be away for months, instead of days, and even three months sounded a lifetime.

She wondered what Garth would say about her accompanying him on that long trip. She could see her family again. And meet his. The idea elated her the more she thought about it, and by the time Garth had returned from the council meeting, Priscilla was convinced her plan would suit him fine.

She presented it cheerfully, but his reaction failed to equal her optimism.

"We'll see," he said, noncommitally.

'But, Garth!" she pressed him. "You must consider the matter."

He raised a wary eyebrow. "Must I?"

She took no heed of his cautioning glance. "I want to meet your family." She stamped her foot. "And I want you to meet mine."

"Why, Prissy? To gain the favor of parental consent?" he asked, scornfully. "It's a bit late for that, don't you think?"

"Must you always twist my meaning?" she shot back. "I'm curious, that's all, and I thought perhaps that you'd be too."

When he said nothing, Priscilla's temper rose. "Pardon me, sir. I see I'm mistaken about your interest in me. Apparently, it's as I first supposed."

"What are you saying?" Garth asked darkly.

"I should think that would be obvious," she said haughtily. "You fancy me, and nothing more."

Garth sighed heavily. "You'll think what you wish regardless of what I say, Priscilla. I'm tired, and I'm going to bed. Are you coming or not?"

"Not."

"Suit yourself," he said, undressing.

"I'm too agitated to sleep."

"Well, you needn't be." Garth poked the fire before lying down. Immediately, he closed his eyes. "There's unrest among some of the white settlers, Priscilla. As long as you don't venture from the people of this village, you've no cause to worry." He spoke in a monotone. "I'll assess the situation again before I travel East. That's all I can promise you."

It took a moment for Priscilla to realize that was all she had asked— for Garth to consider the matter. She realized too that she had done the very thing she had intended *not* to do—force the issue prematurely— and by doing so, she had been rewarded with the

116

disastrous results she wanted to avoid. If only she had kept her lips sealed, she chided herself. By pressing the issue beyond a mere inquiry, she had goaded him and he her.

Silently, she watched his thick lashes fluttering against his cheeks before settling down to sleep. How handsome, how innocent her husband looked in his repose. He had seen no need to address himself to her accusation, and now Priscilla regretted making it. Garth did care; he did show concern for her far beyond fancy.

She supposed she owed him an apology. Or a word of gratitude for his promise to consider taking her back East. But he looked so peaceful, she didn't wish to disturb him.

Quietly, she prepared herself for bed, and she slipped beneath the blanket, snuggling close to him. Lightly, she kissed his cheek, a peace offering. Immediately, his eyes flew open.

"I thought you were sleeping."

"I thought you weren't."

Her apology slipped away, replaced with kisses.

Suddenly, Garth chuckled. "Careful, Mrs. Daniels," he said, "or I'm apt to think you fancy me and nothing more."

Priscilla made a face. "Do be quiet, Garth, and kiss me," she said. And he did, long into the starlit night.

CHAPTER 9

GARTH STAYED A MONTH LONGER. By then, the village fields had been planted, a task that taxed Priscilla's strength to the limit. Each night, she sank wearily into bed, and each morning, she awakened groggily.

"I think you'll be glad to have me gone a fortnight," Garth commented when she nearly fell asleep in his arms.

But she wasn't glad. She was miserable, and the sun rose with such burdens, she began to wonder if she were ill again. Her shoulders drooped, her steps lagged until even Dancing Water noticed.

"I see Bear Claw has taken away your heart," the girl sneered. "Do not say I did not warn you."

As she bent over her day's wash, Priscilla felt too tired to argue with the girl. Ignoring her, she scrubbed a spot on a garment against the flat-topped rock she had chosen by the edge of the stream. Her arms ached as she rubbed, and her head felt light.

Dancing Water drew closer, watching her until

118

Priscilla could feel the girl's dark eyes boring. Around them, the chatter of the other women quieted as though they were waiting for something to happen. Heedless, Priscilla scrubbed on.

"Have you nothing to say?" Dancing Water demanded. When Priscilla didn't answer, the girl went on. "I have words! We do not want you here. Bear Claw was mine, and you have driven him away."

Reluctantly, Priscilla glanced up at the malevolent face above her.

"Perhaps your spiteful tongue drove him away from you," she couldn't help but say.

Although true, the statement incensed Dancing Water. With a shriek, the girl lunged forward, knocking Priscilla into the stream. Panic assailed her temporarily, for she knew she was no match for the younger woman. Even if she were, she certainly did not wish to come to blows amidst the rocks.

Backing away, Priscilla threw out her arm, gesturing, "Halt!" before the girl could leap on her again. Dancing Water, however, paid her no mind. She charged ahead, pushing Priscilla to the bottom of the stream and holding her there until the other women yanked the girl away, scolding her.

Choking and gasping for breath, Priscilla sat upright, glad for the work-roughened hands that held her in place. Two other women held back Dancing Water, who strained and jerked within their grasp.

"Your friends will not stop me again," Dancing Water warned.

Priscilla flung her wet hair from her face and met the girl's icy stare that chilled her far more than the mountain stream.

"Harm me if you wish, Dancing Water, but you'll

only make Bear Claw dislike you more. And, if my blood stains your hand, you'll force him to bring you harm."

Angrily, Dancing Water glared at her. "He was mine until you came."

"Was he? Do not be so certain of that," Priscilla said with more calmness than she felt. "Regardless, he is not yours now. He is my husband, and you must accept that."

To her astonishment, the girl laughed. "Husband! In our village, Bear Claw has but to take his possessions and go to be done with you. Has he not already?"

"You know he hasn't," Priscilla retorted. "You know his work takes him away, just as your men must go during the long hunt. Besides," she added, "we are married not only according to your customs. We are married according to the laws that we uphold— laws that are not so easily broken."

The dark eyes narrowed as Dancing Water refused to give in. "I know something of your law," she smugly maintained. "I know of the civil ceremony that occurred when Nan-ye-hi married her man, Ward. She herself has told me. Did you have such a ceremony? Tell me. Did you?"

Shivering from something other than the cold water, Priscilla rose, unsteadily, from the stream.

"My husband is a judge, a man of the law," she said with dignity. "He performed our civil ceremony in the privacy of our home."

"Did he?" Dancing Water scoffed. "Then show me."

"Show you?" Priscilla repeated quizzically. "Oh, I see. You want proof."

120

It was a simple enough request, Priscilla supposed, especially if it would lay the girl's mind to rest. She would not, however, allow Dancing Water to bully her. "Very well. As soon as I have finished my wash, I will show you."

Without waiting for the girl's response, Priscilla splashed about in the water, until she retrieved the garment she had been washing. When she found it, she examined the cloth for damage with slow deliberation. Then she wrung out the dress and scrubbed it again until she was satisfied.

Dancing Water waited impatiently, but Priscilla did not give her a glance. Chin jutted forward, she scrambled up the bank, taking time to squeeze the water out of the dress she wore. Each twist and turn of the fabric calmed her further, and at last she headed toward her hut, not bothering to see if the girl had followed.

A series of splashes and chattering from behind told Priscilla that more than one woman had tagged along. Apparently those sympathetic toward her sensed the tensions that still existed and had come to lend their support— or enjoy a good fight. Regardless, she strode purposefully ahead until she had reached the entrance of her hut. There she stopped, turning to face Dancing Water and the other women.

"Wait here," she said, holding up an arm bent to stop their entry. This was her home, and she wanted no malice within its walls.

The faces peering in, however, did not bother her. Naturally, the women were curious about her, and it pleased Priscilla that they should find a well-kept hut, much like their own. The clay pots were scrubbed, the dirt floor swept clean, and the fire well-laid. The smell of bubbling soup filled the room as Priscilla crossed it, going to a corner shelf that Garth had constructed.

Atop the rough oak plank lay the Bible her husband had given to her on their wedding night. Carefully, Priscilla took down the leather-bound volume, pressing it tightly against her bosom. She had been so glad when Garth gave her the cherished book, but she had never expected such an unusual opportunity for showing it to some of the village women, especially not with Dancing Water, the instigator, among them. God certainly knew how to turn ill to good, she thought.

Smiling at the humor of the situation, she crossed back to the entrance of the hut.

"This is the Bible, our holy book." Priscilla held up the volume so that all of the women could see. "These pages are sacred to my people because they tell of the living God and His Son, Jesus. The book contains the laws of God and His promises, and it also has the stories, poems, and wise sayings of His people."

As she spoke, Priscilla directed her words to Dancing Water, who now interrupted. "Do not tell me that this book speaks of you and Bear Claw," the girl scoffed.

Priscilla smiled. "I was not going to say that, although the Bible does speak with such complete truth that every person on earth can recognize himself or herself in the stories. Even you, Dancing Water."

Seeing the girl's disbelief, Priscilla hastened on. "When a man and woman marry, it is our custom to write down the names and date in this holy book."

"Show me," Dancing Water commanded.

"As you wish," Priscilla said, opening the leather cover. How glad she was that she had insisted on recording their marriage immediately.

Leafing through, she quickly found the page, her fingers lingering over their inscribed names. Above them, someone had written the names of Garth's parents and their wedding date, and in between, his birth was recorded. The lower half of the page stood empty, awaiting future births and marriages to be penned in along the provided lines.

Priscilla held up the record for all curious eyes to see.

"You know, of course," she said to Dancing Water, "that Bear Claw has an English name, Garth Daniels, and mine is Priscilla."

The girl nodded slightly.

"Here. On this line, it says 'Garth Edlin Daniels married Priscilla Davis Prescott', and then it gives the date, in the year of our Lord," Priscilla explained, pointing.

"What is written there?" Dancing Water asked as she indicated a line above.

It says that Richard Garth Daniels married Elizabeth Margaret Edlin in 1733." Priscilla answered. "They are Garth's—Bear Claw's—parents," she went on to explain.

Suddenly, Dancing Water grabbed the leather Bible from Priscilla's unsuspecting hands, carelessly flipping the pages, almost to the end of the book. Then, she thrust the open volume back to its owner.

"Tell me these words," the girl demanded, stoutly tapping the thin paper with her forefinger.

"Very well," Priscilla agreed. She laid her finger on the exact location of Dancing Water's sound tap, following each word with the movement of her hand as she read.

"'Every good gift and every perfect gift is from

123

above, and cometh down from the Father of Lights, with whom is no variation, either shadow of turning.' " Priscilla read. "That's from the first chapter of James, and . . ."

Again Dancing Water yanked the book away. This time, she flipped the pages back where they settled on Romans, chapter thirteen.

"Say these words,"she insisted, giving the eighth verse a solid thump.

Calmly, Priscilla retrieved her Bible, reading once again with her finger underlining each word.

" 'Owe no man any thing, but to love one another; for he that loveth another hath fulfilled the law.' "

Dancing Water turned away.

'Wait!" Priscilla called. "Don't you want me to read more?"

"I have heard enough," the girl said, her proud face gleaming. "Your book speaks of love as law. That too is the way of my people. I love Bear Claw. He is mine!"

Triumphantly, Dancing Water marched off with the other women trailing behind. Stunned at this turn of events, Priscilla stood in the doorway, gaping after them. Whatever she had thought to accomplish with the girl had been defeated. And, worse, Dancing Water could interpret the scriptures any way she wanted to the others since she was the only one who had understood the language.

But she didn't understand! The girl had merely twisted the words of the Bible to suit her own purpose, and Priscilla felt dismayed—shocked—that she had been the instrument of such deception.

Feeling shaken, she retreated to the dark interior of the hut where she settled herself by the low-burning fire. With her Bible on her lap, she opened the book, leafing through until she located the seventeenth verse she had read aloud from the first chapter of James. That phrase "shadow of turning" had stayed in her mind, and she sensed now that the words had some message of comfort.

She read it again to herself and then again. And then she read the entire chapter to be sure she had understood the full context and meaning. The Father of Light does not vary from light to dark. The Father of Light is not overshadowed. The Father of Light sends only good.

Satisfied, Priscilla closed the Bible and cradled it against her. She had no idea what good gift could come from this day, but she knew now that it would. God was in charge, and He brought no darkness. Anything shadowed that would happen could be looked on as a temporary inconvenience, she told herself.

Trials, ill circumstance, misunderstandings, even death—they were all like a misty shroud that separated the known from the unknown, Priscilla thought. Until recently, she had perceived whatever situation she found herself in as being what was real, what was known. But as her faith in God had grown, her thinking had reversed. God was real; His love and power were knowable. And all that could be felt, seen, heard, touched, or tasted, was either a convenience or an inconvenience, great or small.

How simple it was during those times when veiled thoughts parted, giving her a glimpse of God's reality—His purpose—overtaking what *seemed* to be happening. Then, everything made perfect sense. At the moment, however, little did. And Priscilla could only trust that God knew what He was doing. She certainly didn't know! And Dancing Water *seemed* to be more of a problem than ever.

Over the next few days though, the girl attended to her own business, aloof but somewhat less hostile than usual. Priscilla felt relieved, deciding not to question the matter further.

During the daylight hours, she planned her work to coincide as often as possible with the routines of Straw Basket or White Cloud. Their companionship offered a kind of strength that helped Priscilla through the lonely time while Garth was away. From them, she also learned new skills that she hoped would please him—weaving, herbal cooking, gardening— the latter of which including flapping one's arms in the fields to scare away the *go-gv*, crow.

And so the days passed in waiting. Waiting for the Three Sisters to grow. Waiting for Dancing Water to make another move. Waiting for Garth to come home. Waiting for God's purpose to be made known.

Keeping busy helped Priscilla to fill the hours while keeping thoughts at bay. But, thanks to Dancing Water, one niggling worry took root, then grew: Were she and Garth really married? She honestly didn't know.

At the time, she had been so caught up in the drama of the day that any vows exchanged and scriptures read seemed more binding than merely trading ears of corn for the leg of a deer. Surely the promises they had made meant more than the tying of two blankets. But was that true? Did familiar customs make their marriage legal while unfamiliar customs did not? Somehow she didn't think so.

Unfortunately, Priscilla had never witnessed a civil

ceremony of marriage, so she had nothing with which to compare. Her own marriage to Charles had been under the auspices of the church with nothing unusual about the service except their haste in seeing it performed. Of course, her family members had been absent from that occasion, but Charles' uncles had deigned to give her away—his reluctance due to the inevitable wrath he'd have to meet when Priscilla's father returned from England. Understandable. But even so, the extraordinary circumstances of that day made it no less legal. She and Charles were securely married, according to the laws of God and of the crown.

Was that true now? Had she and Garth satisfied the laws which they esteemed? He had said he was a judge, but was he? This was a wilderness territory as far as their people were concerned, not a 'civilized' colony. Perhaps Garth had no jurisdiction here. If not, she had been living with a man outside of wedlock! Oh, what would Lettie say to that?

What would God say? Oddly enough, Priscilla didn't think He would mind. There had been no pastors or priests in the days of Abraham, yet he and other patriarchs of old simply took a woman for a wife. Jurisdiction belonged to God, if not to Garth, and surely He knew their vows had been sincere.

". . . for he that loveth another hath fulfilled the law."

Priscilla laughed, remembering the verse from Romans that had convinced Dancing Water that Bear Claw was hers. That same verse offered a measure of hope now. Even if she and Garth were not married according to the laws of the crown, their marriage could be binding in God's eyes, couldn't it? She loved her husband and had reason to believe he loved her. Under normal circumstances, that, of course, would not suffice, but these were not normal circumstances. The nearest preacher was in the Watauga settlement, if that good reverend had yet returned.

Priscilla wondered if one might find a justice of the peace there? Oh, why hadn't she thought of that sooner? She scolded herself severely, but that did nothing to alter the situation that, each day, seemed to grow worse. Garth had not returned to alleviate her fears, and she began to suspect that she had been deceiving herself as Dancing Water had done.

Her husband had said he would be back in a fortnight, and already it was beyond that. The corn had begun to grow, blades bursting through the well-tended soil, green leaves stalking daily towards the sky. Warming, the days had lengthened along with the corn until the spare hours of sunlight invited the villagers to play. Often, Priscilla collapsed onto her corn-husk mattress at dusk, falling into a restless sleep while the ground beneath her quaked with stomping feet, dancing as accompanying chants beat the air.

Usually, however, she fell asleep reading the Bible that Garth had given her. Over and over again she read the thirteenth chapter of Romans, then devoured the whole book before returning to dissect, word by word, the eighth verse. That then necessitated putting each piece back into context until she arrived at some conclusion, which, unfortunately, the next day, she would question. Exhausted by the effort, Priscilla finally turned the matter over to God, asking Him to instruct her and guide her, even as she slept.

The following morning, she awoke feeling more

refreshed than she had in some time, and three things had become immediately clear. The first thing was that God had created the law through Moses, and therefore He condoned it. The second was that God had created His Son to bring forth love into the world —forgiving, accepting, caring love that wished no harm on other people and therefore kept the law by its very nature.

Priscilla had no difficulty with either of those clear thoughts, but the third proved more weighty. Although she was convinced now that she and Garth were married according to God's laws and their own binding promises, that did not make them married in the eyes of others. As long as another person—be it Dancing Water or Lettie or a future offspring—had cause to doubt the validity of that ceremony, she and Garth were acting as a stumbling block. Love would not behave in such a fashion. Love would not cause Dancing Water to covet or Lettie to curse or a child to remain forever nameless!

She and Garth would have to repeat their vows, properly this time, with witnesses and a pastor or justice of the peace. She hoped he would understand that, and more importantly, she hoped he truly wanted her—Priscilla Davis Prescott Daniels—for his wife.

Priscilla wanted that for herself, of course, but she especially wanted that for her children, her child. It was much too soon to be certain, but she felt confident that Garth's wish would be forthcoming in the not too distant future. Blond and gray-eyed or brunette, a baby, Priscilla thought, was on the way.

CHAPTER 10

PRISCILLA PLUCKED A WEED from the garden and twirled it in her fingers. The color and shape of the leaves was so similar to the actual shoots of corn that a careless eye would be unable to discern the difference. Practice had taught her to recognize the quality, the texture of the genuine plant that would someday bear fruit and living seed. The weed, however, would propogate its own kind and nothing more, but left untended, it had the power to drain the needed nutrients from that which gave food and life to the village.

As she tossed away the deceiving plant, a movement on the far edge of the garden caught her eye.

"Garth!"

Immediately Priscilla straightened from the patch she had set out to hoe. Then, dropping her rough utensil of wood and stone, she sped across the garden and flung herself into Garth's outstretched arms.

"Miss me?" he asked, whirling her around until she was dizzy.

Her answer was a kiss that left her gasping for breath.

"Put me down, Garth," she pleaded when a little girl's giggles reached her ears. "No Cherokee wife would greet her husband so publicly."

Garth laughed. "I expect you're right, my love," he said, putting her onto unsteady feet, "but it's been too long since I've held you to exercise restraint."

"Where have you been?"

"Obviously detained," Garth said, dropping a light kiss onto the tip of her dirt-smudged nose. "Come on. Let's talk in our hut."

"But—but I have work to do," she hesitated.

"It's nothing that can't wait, dear wife. The garden will be here later, and so, no doubt, will the weeds."

"Go ahead, then. I'll just be a moment. I must fetch my hoe."

Her husband strode away as Priscilla hurried back to get the hoe. How lighthearted she felt, and so much the bride, now that Garth was home. Still, uneasiness tugged as she retraced her steps, for in the distance Garth stood talking to Dancing Water.

The discussion appeared animated. Not wishing to disturb it, Priscilla slipped around the edge of the village, swiftly reaching the sanctity of her home. Home! Barren, mud-plastered walls and a roof with a hole in it. But as long as she and Garth shared the dwelling, their life and their memories made the meager place special.

She wished he would hurry to her as she had to him. But now she paced the room, clasping and unclasping her hands as she waited for her husband to appear. When he did come in, he was scowling.

"Prissy, did you tell Dancing Water that we're not married?"

"What?" It seemed impossible to think with him frowning at her so!

"Did you?" he repeated.

"Of course not!"

"Well, for some reason," Garth said, "she has it in her head that I'm free to commit myself to her."

"That's ridiculous, and she knows it," Priscilla said, frowning. "What did you say?"

"I told her I had a wife and that was that, but she didn't seem to take me too seriously," Garth admitted. "I don't understand what brought on her bold display of affection, Priscilla, but I assure you, I did nothing to encourage her."

Priscilla smiled in spite of herself. Dancing Water's behavior was no laughing matter, but her husband's bewilderment was charming—almost the air of an innocent child falsely accused.

"I believe you, Garth," Priscilla said. "If there are confessions to make, I fear it is I who must make them."

As lightly as she could, she skimmed over the incident at the stream that precipitated the need to provide Dancing Water with proof of their marriage.

"I felt the Lord had arranged that very moment as an opportunity for me to share His name," Priscilla went on, "for the other women followed us here out of curiosity. I explained briefly what the Bible is and how it was our custom to record marriages within its cover. I showed Dancing Water our names, and then, before I knew what was happening, she had jerked the book away and was demanding that I read to her the verses to which she pointed."

Even before Garth asked, Priscilla headed toward the oak shelf. Then, getting down the Bible, she read the verses to him. When she finished, she looked up and found her husband staring thoughtfully into the fire.

"Hmmmm. I believe I understand," he said at last. "Dancing Water is also one to take full advantage of an opportunity"

"If that's meant to set me in my place," Priscilla said, feeling admonished, "I assure you it's not necessary. I've rued the moment more than you'll ever know. In fact, it's caused me no little distress."

To her surprise, Garth took her into his arms. "I've no wish to accuse you, Priscilla," he said, his lips brushing her forehead. "I'm sorry you've suffered over this matter, but I believe it will work out for the best, as you first intended."

"I hope so," she said glumly.

"Trust me. I'll take care of Dancing Water," Garth promised.

Tilting up her chin, he kissed the dimple he found there. "You're trembling," he said. "Is something else troubling you?"

Priscilla chewed her lower lip. She had waited for endless days for her husband's return, and now his very presence set her aquiver. But the concerns that Dancing Water had stirred up needed to be laid to rest.

Reluctantly, she freed herself from Garth's embrace.

"There *is* something disturbing you," he said.

Priscilla nodded. "It's about the legality of our marriage," she said, haltingly. "Dancing Water's questions made me wonder, well . . ."

Her explanations stopped as she saw the tightening of Garth's jaw.

"I thought you were satisfied," he said almost coldly.

"I was! I mean, I am. But there are other people to consider."

A dark eyebrow rose in disdain. "Prissy, did it ever occur to you that you concern yourself entirely too much with what other people will think?"

"Perhaps one of us should," she returned hotly. "I suppose it makes little difference to you, Garth, but I prefer that our marriage be a witness, an example rather than a stumblingblock."

Garth seemed somewhat amused. "And who, pray tell, is stumbling on our account?"

"Dancing Water, for one."

The amusement vanished. "I told you I'd take care of her."

"What about our families, then?"

"Ah! I thought as much." Garth gave an ironic laugh. "Are they your conscience, Prissy? Are they looking over your shoulder these many miles away?"

"Don't be ridiculous. I'm quite capable of making up my own mind."

"Really?" His dark eyes swept over her. "Shall we put a wager on that?"

She frowned, not knowing what he meant.

"Before the year is out, I shall seek your father's permission for your hand. I'll ask his blessing on our marriage. But," Garth went on, "if such is not forthcoming, Priscilla, I wager that you'll be gone before I can say farewell."

Priscilla stared at him, incredulous. "Is that what you think? Seek what you will, but Charles and I had no such permission or blessing."

"What?" Garth did not believe her.

"It wasn't as I wished, of course," Priscilla explained patiently. "Papa was away, Mama was abed, and Lettie refused to come to the wedding."

"But why? I thought you and Charles had known one another all your lives."

"We had. We were the best of friends."

"But nothing more?" Garth finished for her.

"That depends on how you view it," Priscilla said. "We felt the Lord was calling us here, and little else mattered."

"And so you submitted yourself to a marriage of convenience." Garth said wryly. "How very noble of you, Prissy."

"Oh, be quiet," she said. "You don't know what you're talking about."

"I know that it's perfectly natural for a man and woman who are married to desire one another, my dear. God Himself ordained it. Perhaps you and Charles should have considered that aspect of marriage before you leapt into wedlock."

"You make our vows sounds paltry. It wasn't like that at all, Garth Daniels. For your information, Charles was quite interested in me, but being a man of scruples, he had no wish to burden me with a—a child in the middle of a wilderness."

To her astonishment, Garth gave a slight bow. "If Charles were here, I'd beg his pardon for questioning his mettle."

"And well you should," Priscilla exclaimed. "Charles at least gave a care to the welfare of his family."

"What's that supposed to mean?" Garth asked darkly.

"That you should do the same, perhaps." Priscilla

flung her hands about as though to whisk away Garth's anger. She had not intended to ignite his temper, but even now she couldn't let the subject drop—not when the consequences held such significance.

"What if we have children, Garth?" she asked at last. "Is it enough for us to tell them that we're married? Or do we owe them that assurance legally? It's not for myself, you understand," she hastened to add, "for I believed then and now that our vows were acceptable. But I question the legalities of our ceremony. Surely even a judge has limited jurisdiction."

"I never said I was a judge, Priscilla."

"You—you what?"

Garth sighed deeply. Then he sat down, his elbows on his knees, his hands wearily clasping his forehead.

"The appointment came, but I didn't accept it," he said. "If you'll recall, I never said that I did."

"You knew very well that I would assume so!" Priscilla exclaimed. "Oh, Garth, how could you?"

"How could I what?" he responded with feeling. "You would never have married me otherwise, and I couldn't leave you alone here unless you did."

"Have I no say in the matter? How dare you make such a momentous decision for me without consulting me, without supplying me with the facts!" Priscilla wrung her hands. To think she had trusted him. For what?

Saying nothing, she paced the room. With each step, the agony and frustration mounted until she thought she would scream. She wanted to hit him, to throw something, to tear this hut apart.

"Calm down, Priscilla," Garth said at last.

She stopped her pacing and looked at him. "Calm

down? Oh, really, Garth, you're the most obtuse man I've ever met. Have you no heart? You've just informed me that our marriage is a fraud, and then you expect me to react calmly?"

"Of course not, but you needn't be so shocked. You yourself questioned the legality of our ceremony."

"Only from the standpoint of others," she returned. "As for myself, I thought, I thought . . . ." To her dismay, she sank on the corn-husk mattress and burst into tears.

Garth neared and slipped an arm around her, but Priscilla wrenched away from his touch. She found no comfort now in his embrace.

Slamming a fist into the mattress, Garth backed away. "Tell me what you thought," he demanded.

Without looking at him, she asked, "What difference does it make?"

"I don't know," he answered truthfully. "But tell me anyhow."

She sniffed, still refusing to meet his gaze. "I thought our vows were genuine and well-intentioned. It never occurred to me that yours were spoken with full knowledge of deceit."

It was like the weeds growing beside the Three Sisters, Priscilla thought —so similar to what was real, so convincing, and yet nothing good could ever come of the deception. Was their marriage also to be recognized as mimicry with no hopes of becoming a genuine union, fruitful in love?

She held her breath, waiting for Garth's reply, for it seemed that he had the power to pluck and twirl and toss away their marriage far more than she. She had committed herself to him in thought and vow and deed, and now there was no turning back, especially if a child were on the way. Regardless, she had loved him—still loved him—and would love his child fiercely, proudly. But if unwed in his eyes she would not allow this man to touch her again.

Garth's voice cut into her thoughts. "I meant our, vows, Priscilla. I doubt that you'll believe me, but I had only your best interests at heart." He stopped himself. "No, that's not precisely true. I had my interests in mind, too, but I never wanted to deceive you. Oddly enough, though you may not believe me, I merely wanted to relieve you of worry, to assure you that you had a home, a husband, a place here in this village where you seemed so determined to be.

"I confess, however," he continued, "that I lack Charles' foresight. I want a family. I've told you that. But I gave no thought to a reversal of our situation should we ever return to society. Our children would be the object of ridicule and confusion if we were not properly wed. I should not want them or you to be subjected to such ill treatment, Priscilla, any more than I wanted you to be subjected to it here."

Priscilla supposed she should be grateful for her husband's willingness to protect her, but her eyes misted as she sought his face. He had spoken sincerely; of that she was sure. But he had failed to mention the one quality she had most desired—love.

"Will you forgive me?" he asked.

Unable to trust her voice, she merely nodded.

"What would you have me do now, Priscilla? You need only to toss my possessions outside of this hut, and the villagers will no longer consider us wed. You would be free then to do as you like."

"And what would you do?" she asked as soon as she had found her voice. "Marry someone else?"

"No." He sounded annoyed. "There's no one else. I thought I had made that clear, Priscilla. I want you."

"Then I'll not turn you out," she stated firmly. "Let the Aniyv-wiya think we're married. The arrangement suits me—as you knew it would."

Garth moved toward her, but Priscilla put out a staying hand. "Please don't touch me," she begged.

"Why not? I thought you had forgiven my poor judgment."

"So I have. But we must think ahead."

"Priscilla, I only wanted to hold you."

"I—I'm sorry, Garth. I thought—"

"I know what you thought. But let me tell you something, Prissy. As long as we're in this camp, we are indeed legally married. The laws here are the ones we must submit to, not those someplace else. So unless you're willing to throw me out of this hut I have every right to expect you to act as my wife. Do I make myself clear?"

"Perfectly."

"Good. Then I'm going for a walk." He went out without another word.

Priscilla sat staring at his retreating back. He was right, she knew, though she didn't care to admit it. She wanted it both ways, which was not exactly fair to Garth. He had said, of course, that he had no intention of marrying anyone else, and Priscilla had no doubts that he did want her in the strictest physical sense. But was that enough for either of them? In time, she expected, emotions would ebb. And then what? Bitterness? Resentment? The frustration of feeling trapped in a loveless marriage?

Shamefully, Priscilla knew now she had had no business marrying Charles without loving him as a person, a lover, a friend. Anything less would sour eventually. Theirs had been a marriage of convenience, regardless of their purposes, and she could not—would not—repeat such a mistake with Garth.

When he came home that evening, silent and withdrawn, she quietly prepared his meal of ga-du, soup, and fresh-picked berries. Then she moved slowly to his side, wrapping her arms around him.

"Priscilla, what are you doing?"

"Acting as your wife!"

"Well, stop it."

"Stop? But you said—"

"I know what I said," he cut in, "but forget it. Get some rest, Priscilla. I'll be gone in the morning."

"Gone? For how long?"

"I don't know."

"But why?"

"It's best this way, don't you see? Being near you is torment."

"But I've been thinking about what you said, Garth, and you're right. The law of the Aniyv-wiya is the only law we have at present."

"At present, yes, but there's the future to consider, as you so aptly pointed out."

"So where does that leave us?" she asked bitterly. "With a marriage of convenience—for my sake? Well, I won't have it—for you or me, Garth! God forgive me for ever thinking otherwise."

It was hard to see with tears salting down her eyes, but heedless, Priscilla stumbled about the room, snatching up one of Garth's garments, then another.

"What are you doing?" Garth demanded.

"What does it look like?" she snapped as she began to throw his possessions out the door.

"You can't do this!"

"Can't I? Watch me," she said, grabbing up his pouch and hurling it, too, outside.

"Stop this, Priscilla!" he commanded. "You don't know what you're doing."

"I know exactly what I'm doing," she raged as she tossed out the last of his belongings. "I'm freeing us, Garth—both of us—to have a *true* marriage based on commitment and love. That's the way it has to be. Anything else is a fraud."

"Listen, Priscilla," he said in a voice that seemed, to her, patronizing. "It's not too late to restore appearances here."

"Appearances! How dare you talk to me about appearances, Garth Daniels. You've done nothing but ridicule mine ever since I've been here. Calling me Prissy, mocking me, questioning my motives, criticizing my background. Well, I'll not have it, do you hear? Whether I'm at home or in this village, I do the best I can to accept my surroundings, regardless of personal feelings or discomfort, and you might give some credit instead of—of *sniggering* at me."

"I've never sniggered," Garth said, while a smile played havoc with one corner of his mouth.

"Then stop accusing me of caring too much what other people think, on the one hand, and cautioning me about appearances on the other."

"That's not what I meant," he said, exasperated. "When I leave here, I want to know that you have the protection of our marriage. Can't you at least give me that peace of mind?"

"Why should I?"

"Because," he answered carefully, 'I think you love me. Tell me, Priscilla. Am I wrong?"

Garth stood in the doorway, complying with her need for distance. He had spoken softly to the back that Priscilla had turned to him, but when she did not respond, he repeated sharply, "Tell me if I'm wrong."

Priscilla wheeled around. "No, you're not wrong, and you know it! There. I hope you're satisfied, Garth Daniels, because I'm not. Yes, I love you. I've said it, and I want nothing less from you. So just go away— please —and leave me alone before I scream and bring down the whole village."

"That would be most unwise," he cautioned, "because then we would have to go through the entire ceremony again before I would leave. Close your mouth, Priscilla. I mean what I say! That's better. I'll gather my belongings now and be off before anyone is the wiser, and you'll give me the peace of mind I so desire while I'm away. Understood?" He waited for her answer.

"All right! Now go."

"I'm going, though I detest leaving you when you're quite beyond reason. Perhaps when you've soothed yourself, you'll realize that—"

"Garth! Would you just leave?"

"I'm leaving," he assured her calmly. "But believe me, Mrs. Daniels, I will be back."

CHAPTER 11

Priscilla stood in the doorway of her hut, looking in the direction of the mountains. Today their gentle peaks hid behind layers of smoky clouds that obscured the view she knew was there. How often she had gazed upon the summits and watched their subtle change from the new yellow-green of spring to the deeper, richer colors of summer. Yet despite the changing shades and hues, the majestic peaks remained the same, regardless of the seasons or the clouds or the fickle weather, and from them Priscilla had drawn strength.

God, too, remained the same. His strength, above all, could be trusted. The peaks of His power, the summits of His love would not be long obscured.

At the moment, however, they were. At the moment, that dreary veil had draped itself once again between the knowing and the not knowing, the believing and the not believing that all would be well. All *was* well, she reminded herself, whether it seemed to be so or not.

143

Even that reassurance, however, failed to banish the clouds. They still hovered, and she still hurt. Although she had no doubt that God was there working good in her life, she could not help the bleak feelings and the heaviness of her heart. Garth was gone, she wasn't married, and she would be a mother before the next breath of spring.

A fine kettle of fish, Lettie would say. Priscilla supposed it was that and more. Admittedly she had gotten herself into these circumstances, yet she couldn't believe she acted totally on impulse or totally alone. She had sought God's direction for her life in openness and good conscience, and even though she felt miserable and alone, she couldn't regret her choices. She loved Garth; she was glad she married him; and she was glad she carried his child.

In the weeks since he left, she was especially glad that he had protected her from her own rash behavior in tossing him out—although, at the time, she felt that, too, was right. She had wanted him to understand clearly, once and for all, that she never had intentions of using him. She supposed she had made her point, for Garth at least accepted the fact of her love. But the misery of not knowing if that love were returned had surrounded her ever since.

She allowed herself some comfort in his parting words, assuring her that he would be back. And occasionally she reminded herself that he called her Mrs. Daniels, although that could have been a slip of the tongue. She preferred to think that it wasn't, that he deliberately used the term to reassure her of the reality of their marriage, regardless of its legality. But she didn't know, and the last thing she wanted was false hopes.

No matter how despicable it seemed, Priscilla preferred the truth. If Garth didn't love her, so be it. She would learn to live with that. If only she knew! But that was impossible. He was gone, and there was no knowing when he would be back.

She hoped he wouldn't come while she herself was away, although if he did, Priscilla assumed he would know immediately where to find her. He himself had been the one to tell her of the annual Green Corn Festival in Chota, and he would surely recognize that the season was now upon them.

Straw Basket had been chattering excitedly about it for days, managing at last to arouse some of Priscilla's initial curiosity. By canoe, they would travel to the larger village, where they would stay until the festivities ended, and if Priscilla understood her adoptive sister correctly, they would go to Chota twice more before the year was out. Garth hadn't mentioned the other festivals, yet she felt certain he was far more familiar with the gala events than she.

Prior to her coming, the Aniyv-wiya had collected in the capital town for celebration of the Feast of the New Moon. And since then, local celebrations had accompanied the planting of the corn. On the night before, the villagers had danced to the Old Woman of the Corn, with men and women pouring meal from one basket to another. The next morning, when the planting had begun, the magicians had stomped their feet and chanted prayers for rain. Turtleshell rattles called to the Thunder Man, and bird feathers laid near the stream beckoned to Big Brother Moon.

At the time, Priscilla had thought the customs quaint. She was enamored of Garth and failed to see the significance of the chants, the dance; but now she recognized them for the religious occasions they really were. In fact, she had begun to see how very much of the Aniyv-wiya's life was tied to prayer and praise and other forms of worship. Every act, every chore acknowledged the presence of spiritual beings at work, and Priscilla had no wish to alter the thinking that, she thought, was superior to the acknowledgment of a Sunday-only God.

And yet she felt she had failed in her reasons for coming to this place. She had hoped to share with the people the God of gods, the Light of lights, the Supreme Being who was and is above all others. But how? So far she had merely indicated that such a God did indeed exist, and even then she felt she botched it.

As she looked out over the cloud-obscured mountains, she prayed that God would right this situation, too. Then, reassured that He would, she turned back to the task at hand—getting ready for the trip to Chota. Perhaps the change of scenery would do her good, she thought as she rolled up the garments and packed the few supplies that she would need.

It had been decided that she would travel with White Cloud's family, and so, when Priscilla heard soft footsteps padding into her hut, she assumed Straw Basket had come to fetch her. Looking up from her preparations for the trip, she saw that the girl who had entered her house unannounced was not her adoptive sister.

"Dancing Water! I didn't expect to see you here."

For some reason, the girl had left Priscilla alone since Garth's departure, but now she strode purposefully across the hard-packed dirt floor as though assured of her welcome.

"The trip to Chota is too long," Dancing Water

complained. "You will come with us and say more words from this book." Without hesitation, the girl snatched the Bible from its shelf. Then she glared at Priscilla as though daring her to object.

For an instant, Priscilla reacted with astonishment, then amusement, which she promptly hid. Boredom seemed an odd reason for turning to the Word of God; but the Lord, no doubt, could work through the slightest opening.

"All right," Priscilla agreed. "I'll come with you, if White Cloud doesn't mind. I don't want to offend the family that has been so kind to me."

"I will speak to White Cloud," Dancing Water said, and flounced off apparently to do just that.

Priscilla followed after. The prospect of spending a long canoe ride in the company of Dancing Water was not the way she had wished to spend the day. Of late, she'd had so little time to be with E-tsi and Straw Basket that she had looked forward to some relaxing hours with them on the trip. Yet despite her disappointment, Priscilla thanked God for this unexpected opportunity. Surely it was an answer to her prayer.

"Why do you go with me?" Dancing Water asked when they received White Cloud's approval.

Priscilla didn't hesitate. "Because I think you're an unhappy girl, and the words of the Bible can bring you joy and peace."

Dancing Water frowned. "Do not the words bring love?"

Priscilla couldn't help but smile. "Yes, of course. God is Love, so naturally the words of His Book will bring love. But it's up to you, Dancing Water, to accept the love or refuse it."

The girl nodded thoughtfully. "Bear Claw says the same."

"Bear Claw! You spoke to him about this?"

Dancing Water shrugged.

"Tell me," Priscilla insisted. "What did he say?"

When it looked as though the girl would not comply, Priscilla stopped on the path to the stream. They had neared the low bank where the canoes rested, waiting for the journey to Chota, but Priscilla decided she would not take another step until Dancing Water answered—even if she alone were left behind.

"Are you coming?"

Priscilla shook her head. "Not until you tell me what Bear Claw said."

For a moment the two young women stared at one another, unblinking, as their wills clashed. Finally Dancing Water turned away. "The canoe is ready," she said.

Priscilla didn't answer. Shoulders braced with determination, she wound back up the path from which they'd come. She hadn't gotten far when the girl's shout of "Wait!" halted her.

"My father is the chief," Dancing Water said proudly.. "He will not be pleased if you delay him."

Priscilla's smiled at the girl's tactics. "If I do not go with Blazing Sun, then I cannot delay him, can I?"

Dancing Water made a face. "What is it you wish to know?" she asked.

"You tell me."

The girl sighed her displeasure. "Bear Claw says that your Book tells about the Father of All Loves. He says that the Great Spirit is that Father."

"And that's why you want me to read the Bible to you," Priscilla asked, "so that you will know better the Father of All Loves?"

Dancing Water stomped her foot. "The Book has special powers!"

148

Priscilla's eyes narrowed. "What kind of powers?"

"Do not pretend you do not know!" Dancing Water's animosity flared now, unconcealed. "Bear Claw loves only you. He says that he asked the Father of All Loves to bring you to him, and that is why you are here. He says that the power is so great that he can never love another woman. He is yours for all seasons."

Priscilla closed her eyes against the sudden swell of tears. How very like the Lord to fill her heart with hope when she was most in need of it. She had thought it was impossible to be reassured of Garth's love when he was gone. Yet that reassurance had come—and from the last person she would expected. She chuckled softly.

But Dancing Water misread her chuckle as amusement. "You laugh now, but I will hear the words of the Book. Then I too will have special powers."

"I do not laugh at you, Dancing Water," Priscilla said, opening her eyes. "Come along. Blazing Sun is waiting."

The girl seemed surprised that Priscilla was still willing to read to her, but doing so proved more difficult than either of them had expected. As they rested in the flat bottom of the dug-out, Priscilla had to keep her voice unnaturally low. Even then, her whispered readings were occasionally interrupted by the sharp jab of Dancing Water's elbow when one of the other occupants of the canoe warned them to be quiet. One such interruption lasted so long that Priscilla fell asleep, and later she wondered how she could doze when threatening enemies lurked about.

As they traveled, however, she felt a perfect calm that came from knowing she was in her Father's hands. Clearly He had arranged this time for the sharing of His Word, and Priscilla didn't doubt He would see her through it, regardless of the interruptions.

She decided to start at the beginning because that was usually the best place to begin. If Dancing Water had had prior knowledge of God, the New Testament, perhaps the Book of John, would have been a better place to start. But the girl's concept of myth and magic might make Jesus seem just another god, Priscilla feared. Genesis, she hoped, would leave no doubt about the supremacy of God. All she could do, however, was read. The results were up to Him.

And so she read, "In the beginning, God . . ." until she herself was caught up in the poetry and wonder of the creation account. Although familiar, the passages never failed to move her with fresh understanding and insight—a true mark of the *living* Word. Whether or not Dancing Water was similarly moved, Priscilla didn't know. The girl asked no questions, which seemed odd. It was as though she waited to receive some mystic power without giving even curiosity in return.

Except for her brief nap, Priscilla used the moments of silence to pray. She sought the Lord's counsel for Dancing Water and herself, asking Him to provide her with any explanations needed. Then, when none were required, she read straight through.

She had finished Genesis and enough of Exodus to include the commandments given to Moses when she felt compelled to stop. Her parched throat ached—a sign that she had exceeded her limits—and she didn't believe that God expected her to develop laryngitis by continuing on! He would accept her limitation, even if Dancing Water would not.

"Why do you not tell me more?" the girl complained as soon as Priscilla had closed the leather cover.

"It's not that I don't want to, Dancing Water, but I can't just now."

"So you say." The girl's eyes narrowed suspiciously. "You are afraid I will have more power than you."

"Believe me, nothing would please me more." Priscilla responded sincerely.

A quietening hand cautioned them, and in the silence that followed, Priscilla realized the obvious solution. She would teach Dancing Water to read!

As soon as she could, she told the girl her plan. "Don't you see, it's the perfect answer!" Priscilla exclaimed with such enthusiasm that she was promptly shushed. She lowered her voice to a whisper. "If you will learn to read, Dancing Water, then you will not have to depend on me to read to you."

The girl didn't bother to hide her skepticism. "Why will you do this for me?"

"Because I want you to know the loving God, the Father of all."

Dancing Water gave an uncertain nod.

"Perhaps you'd like it better," Priscilla went on brightly, 'if Straw Basket were included. You could learn to read together. Of course, you'll need to be patient with her since she doesn't know the English language nearly as well as you."

The idea of progressing more rapidly than her cousin seemed to appeal to Dancing Water. This time she nodded briskly. "We will learn today."

Priscilla bit back a smile. "Learning to read may take many days, but it's worth the effort. Once you have learned how, you will know it forever."

"Then I will do this," the girl affirmed.

"You won't be sorry, and—oh! Dancing Water! As I teach you to read, you will also learn how to write down words for yourself. Then other people who can read will see the markings and know what you say."

The girl's eyes widened like black walnuts. "Yes. That, too, is power. We will begin."

"I don't know if we can start the lessons today or not," Priscilla said regretfully. "Remember, I've never been to a festival in Chota, so I don't know what to expect."

"I will tell you."

Priscilla concealed her surprise as Dancing Water, in a low and melodic voice, began to tell her about the Green Corn Festival.

"When the new corn is sweet, the High Chief sends out seven hunters," the girl explained. "The hunters go into the forest to get deer for the feast. One of the hunters wears a mask like the head of a deer. For six days these men remain in the forest.

"The High Chief also sends out messengers," Dancing Water went on. "The messengers go to seven towns and bring back an ear of the new corn from each town. No one picks the corn until then. No one eats it. The messengers call the people of the seven towns to come to the feast. On the night before, the hunters bring in deer; the messengers bring in corn."

"Is that tonight?" interrupted Priscilla.

Dancing Water nodded. "The people will dance the New Green Corn Dance in the town square."

"And tomorrow?"

"Tomorrow you will eat plenty of deer meat and corn," Dancing Water said, laughing, and Priscilla joined her.

The girl's remarks proved true. Throughout the evening, the steady beat of drums kept the people in unison as they danced in an up-down motion, stamping their feet. Priscilla could detect no variation in the simple pattern, but movements of the hands made each dance unique. With a playful quality, the men and women seemed to imitate the world of nature or act out a village scene. But one delightful dance seemed to be a game of follow-the-leader.

Priscilla wondered at their tirelessness. Each step occurred, not by stamping the feet alone, but by lifting and dropping the entire body. Just watching exhausted her, so when Dancing Water told her to try the step, Priscilla declined hastily. "Oh, I can't." And unconsciously she rubbed the imperceptible swell of her abdomen as she spoke.

Dancing Water stared at her intently, her dark eyes growing darker. "Do you carry Bear Claw's child?"

Priscilla compressed her lips. She'd told no one— not even White Cloud or Straw Basket—and it seemed a shame that Dancing Water would be the first to know. Still, she couldn't lie, and so she answered by way of a nod.

"Will you keep my secret to yourself for now?" she pleaded.

The dark eyes gleamed. "I will tell no one," Dancing Water promised.

Instead of relieving Priscilla's mind, however, it gave her a sudden twinge of anxiety. Or was it fear?

She hadn't intended to exclude her adoptive family from the knowledge of her happy news, but Priscilla simply didn't want them making a fuss over her at such an early stage. There was plenty of time, she told herself, and, besides, she rather hoped that Garth would soon return and be the first to know. Now that was no longer possible since Dancing Water had been so quick with her deductions. Too quick?

By the following day the episode was crowded from her mind as preparations for the feast began. The smell of venison drifted about as she joined the others in the council house. From the altar in the center of the room, a fire sparked, and upon it the High Chief laid the seven ears of corn. Priscilla couldn't understand many of the words he chanted, but he appeared to be giving thanks to the Old Woman of the Corn.

This done, the people fell upon the feast, oblivious to the gray eyes watching as Priscilla took it all in. Since arrival, she had been on the lookout for Walkingstick and Little Spoon, but had caught not a glimpse of the medicine man or his apprentice. So many people mulled about that she had difficulty keeping track of her adoptive family and Dancing Water, though that didn't alarm her. Most of the faces were friendly in their solemn way, and a few of the women had sought her out, wanting to touch her hair and skin.

Recognizing one of the women, Priscilla gave a warm smile. Every person was so different from every other that she chided herself for thinking otherwise. The majority of men wore deerskin breechcloths, but some wore shell necklaces, some wore beads, and some tied various kinds of feathers in their scalp lock. Feathers also adorned the weaving, here and there, of women's skirts, and some women wore scarves woven of mulberry bark about their shoulders. Red and black appeared to be the favorite colors, though Priscilla wondered if that was due to the easy accessibility of those dyes.

One woman wore a fringed dress of softest deerskin. Around her trim waist was fastened a wide leather girdle decorated with shells, and above it hung a large medallion, handcrafted in silver. A claw necklace hung from her slender neck, and around her high forehead a beaded strap held two feathers in place. The woman carried a staff, feathered at one end, and both of her wrists were encased in silver. From the wider silver band on the left arm rose the tiered spread of a white wing, halted in flight.

Priscilla had wondered how she would recognize Nan-ye-hi, and now she knew. Not only was the woman's dress unmistakably regal, but so was her bearing. Taller than most of the women, her queenly posture dignified her honored position, and even more majestic was her beauty. She had no need for the reddish paint that was often worn cosmetically, for the natural tint of her skin was the pinkish hue of the silky wild rose. Indeed, before the feast was over, Priscilla heard someone call the woman by her appropriate name.

Seeing the Beloved Woman now, Priscilla realized how presumptuous she had been in hoping for a word with her. Really, she had nothing to discuss— nothing specific, that is. She had merely wanted to draw from the courage and wisdom of this outstanding person. It was with tremendous surprise, then, that she realized Nan-ye-hi was returning her stare.

Slowly, gracefully, the woman approached her, her large black eyes piercing Priscilla's own gray ones. Then, holding out a hand in a gesture of peace and friendship, Nan-ye-hi smiled, instantly transforming the regal face into one of incredible kindness.

"Welcome, Mourning Dove."

"You—you know me."

The smile deepened. "How could I not know you when Walkingstick and Little Spoon tell me of your courage?" The beautiful face grew more serious. "You will need much bravery to remain long in this land, Mourning Dove. Troubles come from far and near, from your people and from mine. We must speak to them the words of truth until they listen. We must show them that both peoples have much to learn."

"I couldn't agree with you more, Nan-ye-hi. Tell me what to do, and I will follow your counsel."

The lovely smile returned. "You are young, Mourning Dove, but the Great Spirit gives you wisdom. To me, he says, teach my people the white man's ways of farming and raising livestock. To you, the Great Spirit gives other instructions, but you will know. Bear Claw says you hear E-do-da's voice."

"You have seen Bear Claw recently?" Priscilla asked, her heart thumping at the mention of his name.

"It has been two moons or more. He did not remain long in Chota."

"Do you know where he was going? Or when he will return?"

"I cannot say, but he travels like the eagle toward the rising sun."

"East?" Priscilla queried, dismayed. "He didn't tell me that he was going back East so soon." And now that she knew, Priscilla dreaded the lapse of more weeks before his return. Her spirits sank.

"Be not troubled, Mourning Dove, about Bear Claw," Nan-ye-hi said. "He is with you even now. But you must be wary of serpents. Give kindness to all in equal measure. And do not let your enemies deceive you."

Thinking about the conversation later, Priscilla realized how unusual it was, although she had expected no less from the Beloved Woman. Nan-ye-hi spoke with almost prophetic wisdom. Yet even so, it did not occur to Priscilla that she had anything to fear.

CHAPTER 12

IN THE WEEKS FOLLOWING the Green Corn Festival, the reading lessons progressed remarkably well. As anticipated, Dancing Water proved to be the quicker student since her command of the English language and her strong motivation kept her going when Straw Basket was ready to quit.

Some days Priscilla would have preferred a shortened lesson. When she had suggested the idea of reading lessons, she did not realize how taxing it would be, bending over with a thickened waist to scratch letters and short words in the dirt. But she couldn't give up when Dancing Water was so eager, and not when the only book available was the precious copy of God's Word.

It was Priscilla's fondest hope that the message itself would stir up Dancing Water's mind and heart, giving the girl a true desire to learn about God. Dancing Water had not mentioned again her wish for greater power, and Priscilla was encouraged that the spirit of the Gospel was beginning to take hold.

Straw Basket, however, with her faltering speech and labored pronunciations, was the one who began asking questions, and Priscilla rejoiced in the interest shown by her adoptive sister. The Book of Psalms had proven a particular favorite, and after one such passage, Straw Basket looked up quizzically.

"This God has made all that there is, and yet He speaks to His people."

"That's right," Priscilla said. "And if you but ask Him, Straw Basket, He will speak to *you*."

"How will I know this?"

Priscilla leaned against a stout oak, her weary back glad for the respite as she thought how to answer Straw Basket's question. In the distance rumbled the waterfall, for the three women had agreed to have their instructions in this favored spot.

"First, there's the law," Priscilla responded at last, while her sister listened intently. "Remember, we read the commandments that God gave to Moses in one of our lessons. Well, those laws are for us, too, and nothing God says will conflict with them."

"Conflict?"

"Go against them," Priscilla explained. "But God's Word is not only law, it is love, and if we want to know the way of love, the truth of love, the life of love, then we must look at God's Son, Jesus.

"But there's a problem," Priscilla went on. "No matter how hard we try, we cannot possibly be as kind or as loving as God. Someone has to pay for our mistakes, and so God sent His own Son to do it. Actually, you could say He sent Himself."

"I do not understand," Straw Basket admitted.

"Nor do I," Priscilla said. "It's too wonderful to understand completely. But we can believe that it happened, that part of God became a man named Jesus, simply because His love for us was so great."

"He would do this for me?"

Priscilla smiled. "He *did* do it for you, Straw Basket. And He would have done so even if you were the only person on earth."

"And this Jesus. Does He still live?"

"He died, yet He lives again. It is Jesus who will speak to you now. He will comfort you when you are sad. He will encourage you when you feel disheartened. He will teach you what you need to know when the time is right. But He will never deceive you, He will never lie to you, and He will never accuse you or make you feel bad about yourself or other people. You can trust Him, Straw Basket, for He is perfect love."

"Where will I find Him?"

"Everywhere. But mostly in the people who open themselves to His love."

"Then I will speak with Him." Straw Basket spoke so decisively that Priscilla had no doubts her sister meant it.

What a beautiful day that was, Priscilla thought later, with even the surroundings contributing to its glory! The cool spray of the waterfall fanned the crisp autumn air, and a choir of birds spanned the cathedral ceiling of yellow oak and red maple leaves. Acorns and an occasional pecan tithed their offerings, and late-blooming black-eyed susans adorned the altars of mountain rock.

Only the attitude of Dancing Water had shrouded the bright moment, and Priscilla prayed that nothing would act as a stumblingblock to hinder the girl's progress. Although she was reading exceptionally well for such a short time of instruction, she gave no indication that she comprehended the readings. Only once, in fact, did Priscilla perceive special interest on Dancing Water's part, and that was when they'd read the fourth verse of the eighty-ninth Psalm: "Thy seed will I establish forever." Oddly, Priscilla recalled, the girl had frowned.

Generally, however, Dancing Water reacted impassively, her enthusiasm reserved for the task itself, although Priscilla couldn't help but notice that the girl sought her out more and, in her own way, tried to be of assistance.

"Your back hurts," Dancing Water commented at the end of one particularly lengthy lesson. "I will make a soothing tea."

"Why, thank you," Priscilla exclaimed, delighted that the girl had exhibited this measure of unexpected caring. She chose to ignore the odd tone in her voice.

Rather thick for tea, the beverage tasted good, sweetened as it was with wild berries, and Priscilla expressed her appreciation even more profusely. Dancing Water seemed pleased.

"I will make it for you each day," she promised.

Accepting this hospitality, Priscilla had to laugh. It was rather like the time she brought Mammy Sue's pecan fudge to her tutor, hoping to win favor. Apparently Dancing Water sensed the strong attachment between her own tutor and Straw Basket and hoped somehow to gain more attention for herself. Well, Priscilla thought, there was no harm in that. After their lessons, Straw Basket preferred to get back to her weaving, and Priscilla supposed the extra moments alone with Dancing Water were well-spent.

The girl had not mentioned Garth again, which

made their private times more companionable. Priscilla missed him dreadfully. She hoped he would return before the first flutterings of the baby's movements, for she was certain he would be as excited about it as she. Once or twice she felt a ripping sensation across her abdomen, which she thought might be their child astir, but she wasn't sure. Perhaps she even wanted to postpone that moment for Garth to share, yet by doing so she failed to share it with her loved ones at hand.

Since Dancing Water was still the only soul to know Priscilla's secret, she was the one in whom the mother-to-be confided one afternoon. They ended lessons early because of Priscilla's discomfort, which Straw Basket attributed to a stomach ache. She had seen Priscilla to the hut, then left her there, having extracted from her a promise to rest. And obligingly Priscilla had closed her eyes. But a sharp contraction caused them to fly open once again. As she looked frantically about, Dancing Water appeared in the doorway.

"Oh, I'm glad to see you! Something's wrong, I think."

Quickly the girl prepared the sweet beverage that Priscilla had come to like, but now she pushed the tea away.

"I don't think I can drink anything," Priscilla apologized.

"You must," Dancing Water commanded. "Here. Drink this while I gather roots for you. Then you will never have these pains again."

The girl's soothing promise failed to comfort, however, as Priscilla gasped beneath a thrusting pain. Although she did sip the sweet liquid, her deepest

162

instincts told her to get up, to seek White Cloud's aid. But her body could not comply. The pains had worsened—so intensely that Priscilla found it impossible to walk. Beads of perspiration adorned her forehead.

The beverage had done little good by the time Dancing Water returned, and Priscilla felt queasy.

"The pain is worse—much worse. Please bring White Cloud to me."

"I will," the girl agreed. "But you must chew this root and swallow it. Then I will bring White Cloud."

With no one else to aid her, Priscilla did as told.

"Do you feel better?" asked Dancing Water in a voice no longer benign.

"I—I feel dizzy. What's happening to me?" Priscilla asked. But she never heard the answer.

When she awoke, White Cloud was kneeling over her, stroking her forehead with a cool cloth. The scent of herbal water reached Priscilla's nose, but only a whiff, for the overpowering smell was one of death. No words were needed as her eyes, large with pain and fright, searched E-tsi's face. The older woman shook her head sadly and laid a gentle hand on Priscilla's abdomen.

Priscilla thought her heart would break. This child whom Garth had wanted most dearly, whom she had loved so well, was not meant to be. *No!* Priscilla told herself. That wasn't true! God was the Father of love, the creator of life. He was certainly not responsible for the death of her child, even if He had permitted it to happen. Besides, had He not warned her? Did He not speak to her through Nan-ye-hi? Priscilla railed against herself. If only she had understood the message . . . .

No. That was the voice of the accuser, Priscilla knew, and not God. Yet guilt deepened her grief in the following days until she asked the Lord to help her forgive herself for being such a fool. Then, as she prayed, it seemed incredible that she could have trusted her baby's life, and even her own, to a girl who wished her nothing but harm. For Priscilla was coming to suspect a terrible truth—that what had proven fatal to the child was the lovely "tea" and the root. She shuddered thinking about it.

To her relief, she caught no glimpse of Dancing Water as she lay abed, recuperating. At first she wanted to lash out, to tell everyone what she suspected the girl had done, but no good purpose would be served. She kept quiet, which at last brought Dancing Water to her door.

"You have not spoken ill against me," the girl said as she stood in the entranceway to the hut.

"Would it bring back my baby?" Priscilla asked, chilled.

When Dancing Water did not respond, Priscilla coaxed her into answering the one question she wanted most to know: "Why?"

"I did not try to kill you," the girl responded at last with a haughty snap of her head. "It was the child, which your Book told me I must not allow, or the seed of you and Bear Claw would be established forever."

"How dare you use the Bible for your own selfish purposes!" Priscilla exclaimed, though she knew it wasn't the first time such a dreadful thing had happened.

Priscilla sighed. She supposed she was negligent in not telling the girl about the presence of another power—a lesser, but evil power, and now she did so briefly.

164

"You must be careful, Dancing Water," she went on to explain, "to shut out the voice of the evil one. It will bring you no good, and the Great Spirit within you will get smaller and smaller until it no longer exists. My words are not meant to frighten you, Dancing Water. But you must decide which power you will follow—the greater or the lesser, the good or the ill. It's up to you."

For a moment Dancing Water said nothing, contenting herself to stare at some unseen object on the floor. Then she burst out, "The hemlock root you chewed was meant for other seed, too."

"What?"

"You heard," the girl said defiantly. "But you must chew and swallow the root for four days before all seed will die. I gave you too much. I will not have your blood upon me!" Dancing Water declared, then rushed away.

Sickened, Priscilla lay back down and closed her eyes. She couldn't have understood Dancing Water correctly, could she? Yes, the girl *had* admitted that Priscilla's suspicions were true; the thick tea was indeed responsible for the death of the unborn child, simply by bringing it far too prematurely into the world. But the malice didn't end there, Priscilla realized now. The hemlock root that Dancing Water had given her to chew and swallow was not meant to poison her. It was part of a treatment—a murderous attempt on all of the children Priscilla had yet to conceive!

Had the hemlock worked? Was all future seed now dead, poisoned by a poisoning spirit of hate and covetousness? Dancing Water had said the treatment for such sterility required four days to succeed, and knowing that much time was not available, she merely increased the dose. Apparently the girl became frightened when she thought Priscilla herself would die, and so she had fetched White Cloud after all. Priscilla lived. But was all hope of a family dead?

Now unanswerable, the question tormented her. She could neither eat nor sleep, thinking about it, and her daily chores were soon forgotten. Stale water sat about in a clay pot, collecting dirt, and the ashes on the fire went cold, while Priscilla didn't care. She didn't even notice.

She began taking long, aimless walks into the forest, alone, unmindful of her safety. Garth would be better off without her, she decided. Even though he loved her—*because* he loved her—she didn't want to bring to him a fruitless marriage. He deserved more, needed more.

Without realizing where she wandered one day, Priscilla ventured along the path that led her to the waterfall. The thunderous spray burst upon her reverie as she saw where her treacherous footsteps had taken her. This was the place of solitude she had loved. This was the place she had first realized her love for Garth, where he had asked her to marry him. This was the place where she had painstakingly scratched out the letters of the alphabet, where she had told Straw Basket about a living God, a loving Savior. And this was the place where Dancing Water's evil scheme had been conceived.

The stick she used to scratch the dirt lay discarded now against a boulder, and Priscilla snatched it up as though it were a serpent. With furious loathing, she beat and beat the stick of wood against the rock until it split and splintered. Gone were the lessons. Gone

166

were the dreams. Gone were the angry tears she had stored in bitterness. She wept, and her sobs broke louder than the thundering falls.

"O God, I can't go on like this!" she cried. Then the intensity of her anger and hatred toward Dancing Water frightened her, and she sat down on the rock, subdued.

She hated the girl—she admitted it—and she never wanted to see her again. Yet even knowing she was justified in her feelings toward Dancing Water brought no comfort. But were such feelings ever justified? Shivering, she wrapped her arms around herself. Somehow the hatred had to stop; somehow she had to break its hold upon her.

There was no way of knowing right now if Dancing Water had succeeded in her malevolent mission. But neither was there any way of knowing if Priscilla had succeeded in her mission of benevolence and love. In the final revelation of the matter, which force would overcome, good or ill? And which, Priscilla wondered, would she herself represent? As long as this awful hatred had its hold. . . .

She shuddered. Dancing Water's actions were murderous, but so were her own reactions.

"Heavenly Father, Lord of all, I need Your saving power. I could murder, too," Priscilla choked out in prayer. "Forgive me, Lord. And Father, I *choose* to ask You to help me forgive Dancing Water. Send Your saving grace upon us, and let the overcoming be in Christ's name. Amen."

She blinked. Incredibly, God's response was instantaneous, for Priscilla had already drawn the first peaceful breath she had had in days. A calmness, inside and outside of herself, prevailed, and she knew beyond a doubt that whatever happened, it would be all right. With the hatred and unforgiveness removed, God was again with her. No, He had been there all along, but choked off by darkness, her spirit had been unable to receive Him. Prayer had loosed her from the clutches of all that would harm her in body, mind, or spirit.

It was then she realized she had no business being in the forest alone, and she thanked God for protecting her—not only her, but Garth. Whatever would it do to him to have her, too, torn apart by a bear or some other wild creature?

Hurriedly, she scrambled down the path to the village. Soon dusk would fall, with only the spark of a fire and the sediment-ridden water to see her through the night. She hurried along, stopping only to grab pieces of firewood that lay here and there beside the path. Even those, she thought, must be providentially supplied.

Priscilla was so intent on completing her belated chores that she didn't notice the girl in the field until she came quite near. When she saw it was Dancing Water, she supposed she could turn around or change her course, but at the same moment it occurred to her that God's timing was at work. She wouldn't be surprised if He had actually planned their meeting.

Maintaining her pace, Priscilla approached the girl warily. She could not—would not—pretend a liking for Dancing Water, but neither did she wish the girl ill any longer. Praise God for that, she thought, for it certainly was not of her own doing.

A few steps away, she struggled with what she would say. And then, suddenly, the healing words were there.

"God be with you, Dancing Water."

Priscilla did not pause, in word or step, but the greeting had its desired effect. Both Dancing Water and Priscilla knew that the girl was forgiven.

Dusk fell on a rekindled hearth, and when Priscilla slept, she rested more peacefully than she had since Garth's departure. It would take time to heal her body completely; time to ease the grief of losing a child; time to convince and convict Dancing Water of a loving God. But knowing He did not slumber, she could rest. And when she awoke, Garth was there.

Priscilla stretched. "I must be dreaming!"

"A nightmare is more like it," Garth said, scooping her into his arms. "I wish you had told me you were expecting a child. God forgive me for not being here when you needed me."

"Darling, you mustn't blame yourself," Priscilla said, her soft lips brushing his pinched face. "You thought I would be safe in the village, and I would have been if I'd heeded Nan-ye-hi's warning and not allowed myself to be deceived."

"I don't understand." He pulled away, his dark eyes tormented and confused. "When White Cloud told me you lost the baby, I assumed you had overdone. Now don't look at me that way, Priscilla. I know you're not made of porcelain, but neither are you cast in bronze."

She allowed herself the hint of a smile before she sighed. Garth would have to know the truth, yet she feared for his own safety. Dancing Water would never harm him physically, of course, but how much harm would the girl do to his spirit if he refused to forgive her? God only knew.

Priscilla shut her eyes as she asked the Lord to guide her in telling Garth what had happened. And then the words flowed as she lovingly explained, her eyes now meeting his.

"You could blame her," Priscilla finished, "but what good would it do? It wouldn't bring back the baby. And you could blame yourself for not being here. Or you could blame me for being such a—a simpleton! But I hope you won't do any of those things, Garth. I hope you'll ask God to forgive—her, you, me—all of us."

"Good grief, Priscilla. Do you know what you're asking?" Then, seeing the pain in her gray eyes, he quieted. "Yes, I guess you do know."

Rising, he paced the room. And when he halted, his dark eyes glistened with tears. "Why? Can you tell me that? Why did this have to happen?"

"I don't know," Priscilla admitted. "I've asked, but it did no good. Garth, please let go of it. We must ask God to help us forgive even Him, if need be! If you feel as I did, you probably don't want to do even that. But it's a choice. Forgiveness is a choice."

His shoulders slumped wearily. "How? What do I do?" he asked. Then, for the first time since their wedding ceremony, they agreed in prayer. God would forgive and be forgiven. God would heal. God would bring good out of evil.

When the prayer ended, Garth gathered Priscilla in a tight embrace. "I love you, Little Dove," he whispered.

Wryly, she smiled. "It was Dancing Water who convinced me of that."

He grimaced. "I suppose I should be grateful. I didn't know how to convince you myself. Do you realize how difficult it is to prove you love someone?" he added thoughtfully.

Priscilla gave a laugh. "Indeed I do! I knew I had fallen in love with you that day by the waterfall, but it was too soon to tell you. You would never have believed me then."

"We'll never know, will we?" He tipped her face to catch the morning light filtering through the hole in the thatched roof. "But, Little Dove, I loved you from the moment you opened those big gray velvet eyes and set your lashing tongue on me. You had the spirited strength to match your beauty, and as soon as you met Straw Basket, I knew you were loving, too. You had been through a shock, and yet you handled yourself with intelligence and humor. And as I came to know you, I saw that your gentility was tempered with a giving nature that you couldn't hide. What more could a man ask for, Priscilla? You were, quite literally, the answer to a prayer. But then I couldn't believe God had actually done it. I kept thinking it was all a mistake, and you would leave as soon as you found out."

"Oh, Garth! Is that why you led me to believe you were a judge?"

He nodded grimly. "I couldn't bear to see you go."

"Nor I, you."

"Forgive me for not trusting you or God to work out the matter, for not having enough faith in His love or ours. And then, when it *did* work, I thought you only wanted to use me."

"You know I love you," Priscilla said softly.

"Until this happened," Garth went on, "I never realized how much fear can destroy faith. That in itself is rather frightening."

Priscilla bit her lip, nodding. "I'm afraid now, Garth."

"Of what?" he asked gently.

She looked at the floor, drew a deep breath and let it out with the words, "That we'll never have the family you so wanted."

Garth pulled her chin up firmly until she again looked him in the eyes. "Priscilla Daniels, you *are* my family! Don't you know that?"

"But Garth—"

"No but's. We'll take what comes—together—you and I and God."

Her dimpled chin quivered in his loving hand. "Then we're back where we started—with no more means of having a proper ceremony than we had a few months ago. Don't misunderstand me, Garth," she added quickly. "In my mind, we are as married as two people can be . . . ."

"More."

"All right—more." She smiled fleetingly. "But if we had come here to live and not had a ceremony acceptable to the Aniyv-wiya, that would have been offensive. And if we live elsewhere without a legal ceremony, that too would be offensive. Love doesn't offend," she ended simply.

"Nor does it *take* offense easily," Garth added wryly. "Perhaps you'll remember that, too. Nevertheless, there's nothing for you to worry your pretty little head about, Priscilla." Folding his arms across his chest, Garth looked at her with a smile. "Do you recall, per chance, a Reverend Jones?"

Priscilla's lips parted, but for a moment no sound came out. "Is—is that why you traveled east? To fetch him?"

Garth laughed. "Or any other minister of God who would agree to accompany me. But it was the good reverend I found, and not too far from your home."

"You went without me!"

"Don't fret, Little Dove. We'll go back soon."

Priscilla's eyes narrowed. "Garth Daniels! You were afraid if you took me with you, I wouldn't come back," she accused him, and he did not deny it. "And here I thought you didn't want me to be part of your family or you of mine! I thought you'd accept me only if I were truly part of the Wolf Clan." Lightly she touched the jagged scar, pink against his cheek.

"Silly Priscilla," he said, so tenderly she didn't mind. "Neither of us, it seems, has had reason to fear that our commitment was genuine. It is, you know." Then he looked exceptionally pleased with himself. "And you'll be happy to learn that I've succeeded in gaining your father's blessings."

"Oh, Garth!" she said, her large eyes even wider. "How on earth did you manage that?"

"I expect it wasn't earthly powers that triumphed," he admitted. "Your father proved as difficult to convince as you. All he wanted to know was that you were cared for and cherished, Priscilla. He loves you very much."

She nodded, teary-eyed. "Sometimes he has an odd way of showing it."

"Don't we all," Garth said, drawing her close, his lips brushing the top of her silken hair. "You'll be glad to know, however, that the Lord provided me with an ally from the start."

Priscilla tipped back her head. "Who?"

"Your sister, of course. For some reason she took an immediate liking to me and sized up the situation rather astutely."

"Lettie?"

Garth gave a dry laugh. "You needn't be so stunned. I can behave nicely—except when I'm with you," he added smiling.

Priscilla stilled his distracting hands. "Garth, are you saying that Lettie actually approved of you? Approved of our marriage?"

"Why shouldn't she? I made it clear to her that I love you, and she could readily see why you're equally smitten with me," he teased.

"Oh." Suddenly Priscilla felt ashamed.

"You're thinking of Charles," Garth said, serious now. "Lettie was upset with you for going off with him when there was no deep love between the two of you, Priscilla, but I think she understands now your reasons. She admits she was rather hard on you."

"I deserved it. Oh, Garth, Charles' family! Did you—"

"They know. Naturally they were distressed to hear of his death, but oddly enough they didn't seem surprised," he added. "It relieved them greatly to know you were well—and loved."

"I'd like to tell them that his bringing me here has already born fruit," Priscilla said wistfully. She told Garth then about the reading lessons and Straw Basket's acceptance of the loving Father made manifest in Christ. "I still have hopes for Dancing Water, too," she ended shyly.

Garth sighed. "So have I—but only because God can work miracles."

Priscilla smiled. "He's certainly revealed a number of them today! Oh, Garth, I'm so pleased my family likes you. And Lettie! I never dreamed she would approve."

"Perhaps," Garth drawled, "she's presently inclined to discern a romance when she sees one. She's getting married herself soon."

"Lettie? Married?" Priscilla exclaimed. "To whom?"

"A young man who's just come over from England, I believe. Nice fellow. He and Lettie seemed quite taken with each other."

"But she said she would never marry. She said she'd take care of Mama, and . . .Garth! Is my mother—?"

"She's fine. As well as ever, that is, and you've no cause to worry. Lettie will still see to her. Although I must admit, it's plain that your sister has difficulty remembering that others are around when her Lord Chaucey is present." He chuckled.

"Lord Chaucey? From England, you said?"

Garth nodded, and to his surprise, Priscilla burst into giggles.

"Have I missed something?"

"No," Priscilla laughed. "I have. Papa fetched him for me. Now don't pout, Garth! It's worked out rather well, don't you think? My father never would have set out to make a match for Lettie. And it seems," she said, snuggling close, "that I've done just fine for myself."

"So have I," he answered. "We truly are blessed, Little Dove."

"I know."

The kiss she had waited for in solitude came swiftly and lightly, its feathery touch stroking, coaxing the beat of her heart. Contented, Priscilla sighed. Then she caught her breath as Garth's lips pressed harder, more demanding, against hers.

"Oh, I love you, Little Dove," he said, his voice muffled against the hollow of her throat.

His name became her breath as she quivered beneath his touch. "I love you, Garth—completely."

Suddenly he was pulling her to her feet. "I'm going to make you a respectable woman." He kissed her forehead then with his dark eyes looked lovingly into hers.

"Get dressed, Priscilla darling," he commanded. "The Reverend Jones is waiting."

EPILOGUE

IN THE SAME YEAR of their marriage, 1773, Garth's prediction that the colonists would eventually tire of having no say in their government came true. On December 16, a group of protestors dumped tea in Boston Harbor. Upon hearing of the matter, Garth laughed. He was not amused that the colonists wanted to elect their own officials, as the Aniyv-Wiya had had the privilege of doing, but he chuckled over the disguise that the colonists had used for the occasion. Hoping to lay blame elsewhere, the men had dressed themselves as Indians, not realizing perhaps how ridiculous a choice they had made.

By the time the news of the incident reached the region of the Smoky Mountains, Dancing Water was living in Chota, having married a distant relative of Bryant Ward. Since Priscilla was by then traveling with Garth, she never saw the girl again. Yet she included her in her prayers, remembering her especially when she mourned the absence of her child.

Although Priscilla and Garth felt they were complete together, their family did eventually grow. Lettie was the first, however, to present her parents with a grandchild, a son; and after his birth, Mrs. Davis was coaxed by the infant's wails out of the enveloping cloak of withdrawal. She was, in fact, almost like the person Priscilla had known from her early childhood when they returned home, at Garth's insistence, after the birth of their own baby girl.

Straw Basket, who had not married, dubbed her blond-haired, brown-eyed niece Corn Tassel, a fitting name that Garth promptly shortened to Tassie.

The following year, a son entered the world with a thatch of black on his head and a pair of enormous gray eyes that took in everything as he swung from his cradleboard. Priscilla and Garth agreed that the child should be called Charles Davis, but somehow neither name stuck. And so it was Chad who later roamed the woods with his pleased papa, and who asked again and again to hear the stories of the bear—and how his father had won.

Moon for a Candle

Maryn Langer

CHAPTER 1

1892

ALEXA SPENCE STOOD ON THE COVERED PORCH of the two-story Victorian house—stood staring at the slender brass key lying in the palm of her black leather-gloved hand. The key looked well-used and that seemed strange to her. Back in southern Illinois folks seldom ever locked their doors. What was so different about northern Idaho that houses should always be locked when one left home? A slight shiver of apprehension prickled through her and, for a moment, she considered not unlocking the door. Maybe she should climb back in the buckboard, return to Rathdrum, and take the train back to Mt. Vernon. Maybe she should go on being a telegraph operator and living with Aunt Cassy.

No! Most definitely not! Her bachelor uncle, Clyde Grant, had left her his ranch, and she was going to claim it. With a tenuous motion, she reached out and fitted the key into the lock. A little click told her the lock had found its resting place. She withdrew the key and dropped it into her purse.

7

Drawing a deep breath in an attempt to calm her heart, she gripped the carved brass doorknob and slowly turned it. The varnished pine door with its window of stained glass swung open on well-oiled hinges. A slight musty smell from a house shut up for several months greeted her as she stepped from the bright sunshine of an early June morning into the dim entrance hall.

She stopped and waited for her eyes to adjust before moving further into the unfamiliar rooms. Why did she have a feeling that someone was watching her? Deep inside the house, boards creaked and Alexa, muscles tensed, jumped at the unexpected sound. Standing at the entrance, but leaving the front door ajar, she slowly removed her gloves.

There it was again! Did empty houses squeak and groan of themselves? In her twenty-three years, she couldn't remember ever having been in a house alone. Aunt Cassy had eight children of her own and five strays like Alexa whom she took in as she would kittens to feed and tend. The loving woman couldn't turn away homeless children or animals and, as a result, her Illinois farm resembled a combination of orphanage and zoo.

But Mt. Vernon was no longer home. Now Alexa possessed her own place— a ranch in northern Idaho. It was time she stopped letting her imagination run wild and explore her new residence.

Alexa had a choice of two doors leading off the entrance hall. Deciding on the one to her left, she carefully opened the door. Again the musty smell assailed her nostrils. At last satisfied that she could breathe comfortably, she crossed the pale gray carpet, patterned with bunches of roses and green leaves, and pulled up the window shades. Sunlight diffused by white lace curtains streamed in to the room. Alexa trailed her fingers along the leaf-green silk brocade and noted with approval the lambrequins that hung from gold cornices. This obviously was the parlor, its sheeted furniture standing protected against the dust, like deformed ghosts.

She examined the crystal chandelier fitted with coal oil lamps hanging in the center of the room. Its faceted prisms and chimneys, dulled by dust and smoke, remained lifeless even in the sunlight.

Passing a large rectangular looking glass in a gold leaf frame that hung lengthwise on the white painted wall. She paused and examined her reflection. "I suppose I could take off my hat since I'm planning to stay."

Raising her arms, she started to remove the hat pins. When the reflection of a definite movement of the draperies behind her caught her eye. She whirled about, hands still suspended.

"Who . . . who's there?" she stammered, fright turning her tongue to wood.

The only answer was a squeaking board on the stairs going to the second floor from the front entrance hall. Alexa unconsciously wiped sweaty palms on her Melton cloth cloak as she looked about the room for a weapon. Spying a poker among the fire tools standing next to the little Lady Franklin stove, she dashed across the parlor, grabbed it and ran into the hall, brandishing the black, hooked iron piece over her head like a sword. She was stopped short in her charge up the stairs, however, by a gangly adolescent cat that managed to get tangled in her flying skirts.

"Meeeoooow!" the light gray-and-white animal screeched. It jerked itself free and pranced sideways. Back arched, with tail stiff and straight in the air, it continued to hiss.

Collapsing onto the stairs in relief, Alexa laughed. "So you're the villain who invaded my house and scared me witless. Well, you're very welcome if you'll be a nice kitty and stay out of the curtains." She reached out a hand and curiosity overcame the little beast. "Come here and let's get acquainted." It came to sniff and she scooped it up into her lap.

After a thorough scratching around the ears and under the chin, the cat was convinced that Alexa meant no harm and curled into her lap to take full advantage of the warming sun.

"You need a name," Alexa said. "I think Tiger's appropriate even though you're the wrong color. It fits your nature. Now, down with you. I have more house to explore now that I know you're the cause for my mysterious noises."

She dumped Tiger on the floor, retrieved the poker, and placed it back in its stand. Opening the door next to the mirror, she entered the dining room.

The long table, covered with an elegant lace cloth and the eight chairs set around it occupied much of the room. "My goodness, Tiger, it looks like I shall be expected to entertain. And in a grand style, too, from the looks of the china and crystal in the cupboards." Small shivers of anticipation ran down her spine as she thought of her new life. Bless Aunt Cassy. She had trained Alexa well, always insisting on the observance of proper etiquette and the best china and linen for the elaborate Sunday dinners she served each week.

Next, Alexa, with Tiger continually rubbing against her skirts, found the big kitchen. It had a galvanized steel sink with a pitcher-spout water pump. Did the pump actually draw water or was it just a decoration? She gave the handle a couple of pumps, but nothing happened. If it did provide water directly into the kitchen, it had lost its prime from disuse. No matter. There was time enough later to find out. The walls were lined with tall cupboards reaching from floor to ceiling, packed with all manner of cooking utensils. A great range handsomely ornamented with nickel trim and sculptured iron stood against the outside wall. It had both a high warming closet over the six hole stove

10

and low warming closet under the oven. The over-sized water reservoir on the side was mounted with brass couplings. A full woodbox was placed conveniently next to it.

"What a lovely kitchen! I have arrived in paradise," she said, and clapped her hands with the joy of it. But if it was paradise, she was sharing it, for again she had the feeling of being watched.

She hurried out into the hall and entered a room behind the kitchen. The sitting room, convenient and private, was decorated with walls painted a soft green. Pushing aside the lace Nottingham curtains, she opened the windows to provide some cross ventilation.

"The sooner we get this place aired out, the better," she said to Tiger.

Alexa walked to the corner where a tall, black, nickel-ornamented heating stove stood. In the ceiling above the stove, a register had been cut that allowed the heat to rise and warm the room above. She crossed the room and looked up into the register. A shadow moved. She was sure of it. The hair on the back of her neck stood up, and her heart surged into her throat. Another creak! She froze and managed not to cry out only by exerting the greatest control.

Trembling knees barely carried her to the nearest chair, and she collapsed into it. Tiger leaped into her lap and she sat, absent-mindedly petting him, while she tried to recover her composure. "What are we going to do?" she spoke softly to the cat. "There isn't anyone around for miles who can help us." She looked about the room and noticed a cabinet in which rested a wide variety of guns. "There's a veritable arsenal, but I've never fired a weapon in my life." Alexa hugged the cat to her. "Oh, Tiger, I'm so frightened."

Another creak from overhead! A small involuntary cry escaped. Never in her memory had she faced a crisis alone. And she felt defenseless.

11

Slowly rising, she made her way to the gun cabinet. Selecting one of the smaller rifles. She took it from the cabinet and placed it to her shoulder as she had seen Aunt Cassy's boys do. If she could find some ammunition, she might even be able to load and shoot it. Then, she stopped her rummaging. Did she really think she could shoot someone? She, who cried all the time she was skinning the wild birds the boys brought home for roasting?

She started to return the gun to its resting place in the cabinet. *Now, wait a minute. Whoever is in this house doesn't know anything about me. I could be a regular Calamity Jane for all he knows.* Alexa laid the gun on the table and removed her hat. She draped her cape over a chair and knelt to pray. "Dear Lord, I can't remember when I've needed You more. I ask You to be with me so I won't do something foolish. Please don't let anyone hurt me—and don't let *me* hurt anyone in panic. Give me courage. I'm in great need of courage. I'm scared—so scared. Worse than ever before in my life." Alexa continued to kneel, trying to quiet her racing heart and collect her wits. Finally, she felt a calmness flow through her. "Thank you, Lord. Amen."

Standing, she nervously picked up the gun and cradling it in her arm, marched into the hall and up the stairs.

The first door at the top of the stairs opened into a lovely bedroom. Alexa could quickly see, even in the dim light coming through the window shade, that the room was empty. Unless someone was hiding in the wardrobe. She didn't intend to open it to find out.

"Come on, Tiger," she called softly as she stepped back into the hall, closing the door behind her.

The door into the next bedroom stood ajar. Raising the empty gun to her shoulder, she kicked the door open with her foot, stepped through the doorway, and pointed the gun into the empty bedroom. Whoever had been there earlier had slipped away.

"Do you suppose he went downstairs and out the open front door?" she asked the cat. Satisfied that that was indeed the case, Alexa lowered the gun and stepped back into the hall.

From the second floor, the stairway turned into a spiral leading to the attic. "I guess we can leave the attic for a bit later," she said, but Tiger disagreed. He bounded up the stairs and stood clawing on the door.

"Very well, if you insist."

This door didn't open easily as the others had, but by pushing with her shoulder, she forced it. Something slid across the floor as she pushed the door partially open. Looking behind the door to see what had blocked it, she found several boxes had been stacked against it. Now, wariness turned to fear.

She whirled and started downstairs, but reason returned before she had gone far. This was her home, and she wasn't going to abandon any part of it to an unknown person. With a deep sigh to cover her fright, she turned back up the stairway. She stepped into the attic hallway, swallowed her panic. The light from one small window revealed a hall and two doors, one directly across from the other.

Her heart pounded in her ears and she licked lips that had suddenly gone dry.

"Which door, Tiger?" she whispered.

As if he understood, the cat padded with great certainty to the door on the right. Alexa followed, but her hands trembled and she fumbled at the doorknob. Tiger gave a little meow, as though asking her what was taking so long.

She swung the door open and raised the gun into shooting position. It didn't give her much confidence, though, when she looked down the shaking barrel.

The room in front of her was shadowy, but Alexa could see it was a tidy storage room. Everything was neatly boxed, wrapped, stacked, and labeled. A large floor-to-ceiling wardrobe occupied one full wall. If

13

someone were here, he must be hiding in that wardrobe. Alexa gulped and backed toward the door.

"Meow," Tiger commanded as he stood in front of the wardrobe, looking at her.

"Oh, dear Lord, please, please, help me," she pleaded softly.

Resting the gun on her hip, she edged toward the cupboard. Tiger gave an impatient scratch on its door. Pricks of fear ran from Alexa's head to her toes. Did she really want to know who was behind that door? She had no choice. She must assure herself that this was not someone who might murder her in her sleep or . . . worse.

Alexa grabbed the handle and pulled the door open. Nothing! The cupboard hung full of winter clothing, and the bottom was stacked with boxes. Using the gun barrel, she poked through the clothes, testing the space to the back of the closet. Each time she heard a solid thump against the back wall, she became more confident that this whole episode was a figment of her imagination. And then the barrel rammed into something soft and fleshy-feeling.

Alexa raised the gun to her shoulder. "Co—co— come out of there." It sounded more like a plea than a command.

The clothing stirred, and two hands and the top of a head appeared.

"Please, don't shoot," the frightened woman begged. Straightening before Alexa, her hands in the air, she continued in a trembling voice. "I didn't mean no harm. The house was empty, and I needed a place. Ain't done nothin' but good." She talked rapidly as though hoping if she explained fast enough, Alexa could be persuaded not to kill her on the spot.

The woman looked to be in her middle thirties, maybe older. Her coarse dress and shoes, unstyled hair, and work-calloused hands were mute testimony that her life hadn't been easy.

14

Lowering the gun, Alexa said, "Put your hands down. I won't shoot you. What's your name?" Her voice sounded firm, helping her to feel in control of the unusual situation.

"Emmie. Emmie Dugan." She winced, speaking barely above a whisper.

"Is that supposed to mean something to me?"

"My husband's the outlaw, Luke Dugan."

"If you have a husband, then what are you doing hiding out in an empty house?"

"The law's got 'im. Holdin' 'im in Coeur d'Alene. Aimin' to put him behind bars permanent, down in the penitentiary at Boise City. Maybe even hang 'im. I ain't got no money and no place to go. Don't know what I'm gonna do." She hung her head and stood, shoulders slumped, a picture of despair.

An idea crossed Alexa's mind. "What are you fit to do?" She moved toward the door after shutting the cupboard.

Emmie followed, keeping a safe distance from the gun. "I kin wash clothes, clean, cook. Things like that's about all. Don't nobody rich want someone that looks like me for the likes of that, though."

Alexa had to agree the missing front tooth and uncorseted figure didn't present a particularly appealing image. But Aunt Cassy would never have turned away such a pitiful person.

Accepting the challenge, Alexa said, "Well, I must have help doing the very things you mentioned. I was wondering how I was going to manage all this house and run a ranch, too. If you'll stay, I'll pay you twenty dollars a month and your room and board."

Emmie's face lit up like the sun breaking through storm clouds. "Ma'am, you won't be sorry. I'll work real good for you. And I'll stay as long as you like. My Luke's done got hisself in a peck o' trouble this time. Worst part is, he's innocent. Done plenty of wrong in his time, but he didn't do none of this."

"None of what?" Alexa asked as she led the way down the spiral staircase.

"None of the train robbin' and killin' the guard, and him bein' charged with the whole thing. Luke's a lot of things, but he's no killer. He wasn't near that train. We moved from Colorado and found a little cabin in the Selkirk Mountains up near the Canadian border. He was huntin' us some fresh meat, and he don't have no alibi. Witnesses say it was him held up the train, but they got him mixed up with someone else. We come here for a fresh start. Funny how things work out." She sighed. "Can't afford a lawyer, so he plans on hangin'."

Her voice sounded so tired and defeated it hurt Alexa. "It should give him some comfort to know you're being taken care of, at least."

"That's the last thing he said to me. 'Emmie, what's to become of you?' he said. He's a good man in a lot of ways. He's served the time to pay for his past sins and he was workin' hard at stayin' out of trouble. We ain't been married so long, but he settled in just fine. Wanted a permanent job with stock. He's real good with animals."

Emmie trailed Alexa downstairs. In the kitchen. Alexa stood the gun in the corner and asked, "Emmie, do you believe in the Lord?"

Emmie looked shocked by the question. "Yes'm," she said slowly. "My ma, God rest her soul, always read to us out of the Bible every Sunday. But I ain't talked with Him in years. Lord don't know the likes of me exists anymore."

"Oh, yes He does. We'll get down on our knees and do some talking to Him, and a way will come to help your Luke. I know it will."

"I wish I could believe that, ma'am. I truly do."

"You can truly believe that. Come, kneel here with me and I'll pray with you. He's the only one to trust with a problem like yours. He'll know exactly what to do about it."

16

Alexa grasped the work-worn hand, gently pulled Emmie to her knees, and prayed, "Dear Lord, we give thanks for Your great compassion as You seek the lost lambs. Today we come to You with a special request to help Luke Dugan. We know that if it is Your will, the truth will be made known about him and he will be set free. Comfort Emmie's heart and let her feel that, with faith, all things are possible."

As they said their final amens, the voices of men shouting greetings carried in through the open front door. Emmie leaped from her knees and raced across the hall to hide in a room Alexa had yet to explore.

Alexa advanced to the front porch where she could see a cloud of dust rising along the road. Over the rattling of an approaching buggy, she heard the hoofbeats of more than one horse as they came pounding toward her at a hard gallop.

Who would come calling at such an early hour? Nobody even knows I've arrived.

17

CHAPTER 2

ALEXA STOOD IN THE OPEN DOORWAY and watched as a buggy with a man and a woman clattered up the rutted road, accompanied by a horseman riding alongside on a shining silver-gray horse. The man in the buggy, whom she guessed to be in his late twenties, swung the shiny black vehicle about. Turning the high-spirited horse too late for safety, he nearly annihilated the red hollyhocks blooming profusely at the foot of the wide covered porch that encircled the house. His speed was such that he narrowly missed the wagon in which she had arrived. Alexa grew highly anxious for the well-being of the occupants before the buggy slid to a stop next to the porch steps, leaving clouds of choking dust in its wake. What manner of speed demon controlled the reins, she wondered? He must be slightly mad to drive so wildly with the delicate appearing older woman as a passenger.

Land, did people in the West always come calling so early? Anxious that she present a reasonably proper appearance, she nervously fingered the nape·of her neck in search of escaped tendrils from the curls

18

in the upswept hairdo. She didn't wish to appear disheveled before her visitors, even at such an hour. First impressions lasted, Aunt Cassy always said.

Alexa did not respond well to the unexpected, perhaps because there had been so little in her life that hadn't been thought through and carefully planned. As a result, Alexa found it difficult to keep her composure at this moment.

The rough-looking man on horseback pulled up at a distance behind the buggy and appeared in no hurry to state his business. The woman, clearly a breath-taking beauty in her youth, and still quite stunning, shared the single seat with the tall, faultlessly groomed driver of the buggy. Alexa felt for a moment transported from this wild land back to the civilization of Illinois.

"How do you do, my dear," the smiling, silver-haired woman called. "I do hope you'll forgive our manners. This isn't a formal call."

Alexa breathed a sigh of relief at the bit of news and relaxed perceptibly.

"David and I were on our way to town and noticed an unfamiliar wagon here. We thought it best to stop in case strangers were making themselves at home."

She spoke with a New England accent and her bearing affirmed breeding and polish. Alexa wondered how the woman happened to be so far from her roots. "Thank you for keeping watch. I'm Alexa Spence."

"I thought you might be. We've waited anxiously for your arrival. I'm Jane Hornbeck and this is my son, David. We own the ranch bordering yours on the west."

Such lovely, gracious neighbors. Alexa welcomed this kind of surprise. She walked to the edge of the porch and extended her hand in greeting. From that vantage point she also noticed David Hornbeck's clear tanned skin and an impeccably trimmed blonde mustache.

Alexa spoke in the formal language of first acquaintance. "How do you do," she said to Mrs. Hornbeck. "It is a great pleasure to be here. I, too, have anticipated this day for several months."

Alexa couldn't recall ever having received such unabashed approval, and she felt herself blush.

"Have you ever been on a western ranch?" Mrs. Hornbeck asked.

Managing a bare minimum of control, she struggled for a coherent answer. "Not on a ranch. I was raised on a farm."

"I daresay you'll find ranching quite different. Are you planning to run it yourself?"

Alexa could almost hear the sniff of disdain beneath the words. Apparently Mrs. Honrbeck regarded ranching considerably above farming.

"Yes. Aunt Cassy says I'm a natural manager and this ranch should finally give me a challenge," Alexa replied. "But I'm sure I shall need guidance while I learn."

David's full lips parted in a smile that revealed nearly perfect white teeth, and his eyes creased deeply at the corners. She had trouble breathing as her rapidly beating heart seemed to take up far more than its alloted space.

Doffing a soft tan Stetson, and uncovering thick carefully barbered blond hair, he said, "A great pleasure to meet you, Miss Alexa." His voice, a fine, smooth baritone stroked each syllable of her name. "I would be more than happy to offer you my assistance any time you wish to begin."

At that moment the large saddle horse standing next to the wagon shook its head impatiently, and the jangle of the bit rings broke the spell. Alexa forced her attention to the other guest. He sat astride the striking gray stallion fitted with expensive tack. Alexa didn't know a great deal about fine riding horses or their equipment, but she knew quality shen she saw it. Even though the rider slouched in his saddle, she could tell the man was tall. A wide-brimmed black Stetson sat well down on his mop of dark curly hair that had not seen a barber in far too long. Dark eyes above a full, black beard pierced hers, and his look held no welcome.

Mrs. Hornbeck turned and gave the man a decidedly cool smile. "Alexa, this is your neighbor to the east, Martin Taylor. He operates a logging operation that is rapidly scalping the land of its beautiful trees."

Holding out her hand to him, Alexa said, "How do you do?"

His only reply was a curt nod.

Anger flashed through her. *How rude*, she thought. Alexa quickly retracted her hand and clasped it together with the other one in front of her. She felt an immediate and intense dislike for the unmannerly clod.

Mrs. Hornbeck let her enjoyment of the little scene show in her twinkling eyes. "Well, my dear, we shan't detain you. You must have many things to do. When you've had a bit of time, we'll make a proper call. In the meantime, though, please don't hesitate to let us help you if we can." She smiled and gave a little wave of her leather-gloved hand. The gloves, Alexa noted, were the same shade as the beaver fur trimming on her cloak. Tying a piece of ecru netting over the toreador-styled hat, Mrs. Hornbeck looked fondly at her son. "Shall we go, David?"

David nodded in acknowledgment, but continued to let his gaze rest openly on Alexa's face, making no attempt to mask his pleasure at meeting her. "We're glad you've arrived safely," he said in a normal voice. "I shall call back this evening, to be certain everything is in order and make myself available in the event you need any help. I would be very glad to share my ranching experience with you."

"Thank you, Mr. Hornbeck. I shall look forward to that."

He smiled and nodded, then returned his hat to his head with a flourish. "Be sure to save the wood-cutting until I come." Gathering the reins, he expertly swung the buggy around, and clattered out of sight down the dusty road.

Alexa, much to her annoyance, was left alone with the unmannerly horseman. Even his dress irritated her. He wore a bulky red and black plaid shirt that could not hide his broad muscular shoulders. Dark gray pants tucked into work-scarred knee-high boots completed the clothing that spoke his occupation. Leather-gloved hands holding the loose reins rested lightly on the saddle horn. The gun in a holster strapped around his waist disturbed her. She wished he would state his business and leave, for he obviously hadn't come to greet her. But he would have to talk outside. She had no intention of inviting him in.

"Miss Spence," he began very formally, "as Mrs. Hornbeck pointed out, I own the land to the east of your ranch. Your uncle and I agreed that we would mutually maintain the fence separating our property. I have been handling it all myself this spring."

Alexa opened her mouth to defend herself, but Mr. Taylor left her no opportunity.

"I have been willing to do this under the circumstances, even though it has taken men from my logging crew, slowing down my operation. However, there was another part to the agreement. Your uncle agreed that while his cattle were on the open range he would prevent them from grazing in the section of the forest where we were cutting. When cattle get in the way, it is hazardous to both animals and man. The woods where we're cutting are full of your stock this morning. I am *not* going to tend your cows any longer. I would appreciate it if you would take care of the problem."

Alexa drew herself up to her full five feet. "Sir," she began in a cold regal voice. "I have only just arrived. I do not see how you can expect me to be knowledgeable regarding the situation you describe, nor expect me to solve it immediately."

"That is why I explained the problem in some detail, so that you *would* be knowledgeable. Now, with your permission, I'd like to try to find that lazy bum who's supposed to watch the herd and get him out to round them up. There's plenty of good grazing all over the forest, but the beasts seem to like human company. Unless they're checked on frequently, they'll gravitate to where we're cutting every time. I don't relish cleaning up a flattened cow if one of those big cedars falls on it."

Alexa shuddered at the mental picture he drew. The man was a course individual, and he offended her sensibilities.

Standing in the high-noon sun, she was growing uncomfortably warm in her fully lined, woolen traveling suit. If this conversation didn't soon end, much as she resisted the idea, she would be forced to invite him inside for her own comfort.

"Am I to conclude that this negligent person is somewhere on my property?"

"He's probably passed out cold in the bunkhouse. If that's the case, I suggest you fire him and get a responsible cowboy. There are plenty around looking for work. In fact, I turned one away just this morning. Wanted to hire on as a logger. And what I don't need is a cowboy who thinks all you do is rope a tree and saw it down."

Even shaded as they were by the brim of his hat, she could see the glint of humor in his eyes. "Does it amuse you to find a lady in such a predicament?" she asked, keeping her voice cold and distant.

His expression immediately grew inscrutable and his voice a bit warmer. "No ma'am, it doesn't. But I believe in solving problems. It creates real hard feelings and misunderstandings when they're allowed to drag on." He shifted his weight and swung easily out of the saddle. "Mind if I tie the pony to your porch since there isn't a hitching post? I'll go with you to the bunkhouse. See if that miserable excuse for a cowboy is sleeping one off."

She looked down at her outfit. She wasn't going out through the weeds and brush in this suit. "The cattle have been in your way all morning. A few more minutes won't matter. If you'll be so kind as to help me carry in my luggage, I'll change, and we can go searching for my reluctant employee together."

Alexa wanted to laugh. The look on Mr. Taylor's face indicated he'd much prefer to find the errant cowboy, deliver his lecture, and be on his way. But there was no way she and Emmie could carry those heavy trunks and traveling bags. He was an opportunity sent from heaven, and she had no intention of letting him slip away.

He walked over and looked in the wagon. "You need all these?"

"Mr. Taylor, I would not have brought them all the way from Illinois if I had not. And as you can see, I can't possibly lift the trunks, much less carry them. If you would like, I'll take one end, for I know they're quite heavy."

His answer was to reach in and grasp a thick leather handle, testing the weight of the largest trunk. It was a square box made of basswood and covered with extra heavy duck cloth. Three evenly spaced hardwood slats ran the length and width of the trunk to give added strength. Its corners were bound with heavy brown leather and two thick leather straps banded the trunk and buckled in front. He turned to her, a heavy scowl darkening his face. "Tell me one man put this in here," he said in a way that let her know he'd recognize the lie if she answered yes.

"No. It took two people, huffing and puffing rather pathetically, as I recall." Then she added wickedly.

"Of course, one looked to be about seventy and the other was a boy."

He shot her a deadly glance, tipped his head, and hoisted the trunk over the side of the wagon and down to the ground. He did it so quickly and with such apparent ease she would never have known the effort put forth if the muscles and veins in his neck hadn't stood out dramatically under the strain.

"Where do you want this—second floor or the attic?" he asked, making no attempt to keep the sarcasm from his voice.

If he carried it up the steps and into the entrance hall without acquiring a rupture, he'd be lucky, but she intended to make his life as miserable as he was making hers. At least, for a few more minutes. "Attic," she answered curtly.

He re-set his hat, rubbed his gloved hands together, and grasped the leather handles on each side of the trunk. Even through his pants she could see the muscles in his legs distend as he lifted the load.

Suddenly, feeling guilty, she offered, "Here, let me take one end," and started down the steps toward him.

"Get out of the way," he growled.

It became abundantly clear she had pushed him almost too far. She ran into the house and without having any idea what was behind it, threw open the door across from the parlor entrance. "Thank you, Lord," she breathed as she stepped into a large bedroom. From the pipe still resting on the bedside table and the faint scent of bay rum that lingered, Alexa concluded this bedroom had belonged to Uncle Clyde.

She stepped back into the doorway as he entered the hall. "In here," she instructed briefly, her voice cool and distant. She had no intention of letting him know how badly she felt at having asked him to carry that terribly heavy piece of luggage. "Set it over by the window out of the way. I'll unpack it later."

She watched muscles ripple over his back as he carefully placed the trunk where she had indicated. Then without a word, he turned and retraced his steps to the buckboard for her other things.

When he reappeared with the suitcase containing her everyday dresses, she quickly opened it and selected a royal blue calico and a gingham-checked apron to match and laid them across the bed. Looking about for somewhere private to change, she noticed a door at the far end of the long room. Hurrying, she opened it and found herself staring into the most elegant bathroom she had ever seen. A six-foot copper-lined bathtub and an enamel wash basin set in a marble-topped oak cabinet drained to the outdoors. A commode of polished solid oak fitted with a galvanized bucket completed the elegant fixtures. Uncle Clyde had spared no expense in building or furnishing his home, she was rapidly discovering.

As she crossed the room for her things, Mr. Taylor, face red and shiny with sweat, came through the door with arms and hands loaded. "This looks like it, unless you have a freight wagon coming with the rest." His voice sounded much less angry. Perhaps he'd worked out his irritation at her.

Alexa gathered her dress and apron into her arms. "Excuse me, and I'll get into some work clothes. When I've changed, you can show me where the bunkhouse is, and we can see about my wayward help."

He nodded. "Mind if I get a drink?"

"I haven't had time to carry in fresh water. Do you know where the well is?"

"It's under the house. You have water indoors and a pump in the kitchen. In fact, there isn't a modern convenience Jane Hornbeck overlooked when she supervised the building of this house. Thought it was going to be hers." He disappeared through the door and she could hear his booted feet thudding down the

26

hall to the kitchen. Alexa dressed quickly and went to find her neighbor. He sat in the shade of the front porch, slouched in a rattan chair, casually picking his teeth with a straw. *Honestly*, she thought, *he has the manners of a goat.* Trained, however, to show the utmost courtesy to company, she put on a polite smile and said, "Are you ready?"

"Just waiting on you, ma'am," he answered casually, and languidly unfolded himself from the chair.

For a man who had been in such an all-fired hurry earlier, he surely took his time now, she thought as she watched him. He moved with a slow cat-like grace that fascinated her and only by exerting the greatest effort could she unfasten her gaze from him.

He led the way around the house and down a well-used trail that skirted a large clump of trees. He walked easily but steadily and his long legs covered a great deal of ground. Alexa found herself trotting behind him to keep up. She arrived breathless at the hired helps' gray weathered quarters that stood a discreet distance from the house.

Mr. Taylor didn't bother to knock. He flipped back the latch and threw open the door. His huge frame filled the doorway so she couldn't see a thing.

'What's there?" she asked.

"Just what I expected." He didn't move, as though deciding what action to take.

Alexa stepped closer to the doorway and a sour smell filled her nostrils. Before she could request he move so that she might see, he stepped back out and pulled the door shut.

"Why did you do that? Is there someone in there?"

"He's in there, all right, but it's no use trying to wake him now. The place is a mess and needs a thorough cleaning."

"Let me see."

"No." He set his body across the door. "I'll come back later and see that he cleans it up before he leaves. I really hate to fire the old boy. He's been on the ranch for years, but he's taken to drinking something fierce ever since Clyde died. Can't depend on him for a thing. Almost as bad— he's drinking up all his savings. Don't know what'll become of him." Compassion filled his voice, and Alexa realized that Mr. Taylor really liked the old man.

"I appreciate all your help, Mr. Taylor, but you don't have to fire him. He's my problem. I inherited him along with the rest of the ranch. Has he always had trouble with drink?"

"Not really, Miss Spence. He ties one on a couple of times a year, usually after the round-up and on New Year's. Never let it interfere with his job before, though. He's worked for Clyde since he started the ranch and can't seem to get over his death."

They started walking back to the house, but this time Alexa led the way.

"Won't you come inside?" she invited. "We still haven't settled the issue of my cattle in your forest."

He untied the reins and gathered them preparatory to mounting. "I'll have my men run 'em back into the hills. In the meantime, I'll keep an eye out for someone to help you." He swung easily into the saddle and adjusted the reins. Then he sat, not signaling the horse to move.

Alexa wondered what she should do now. Had she missed a cue? Was he waiting for her to say goodbye, thank him again for unloading her luggage? Remembering the rebuff earlier, she reluctantly extended her hand again, and walked up to the mounted rider. "Thank you so much for your help, Mr. Taylor. I also appreciate your patience in dealing with my wandering stock. I hope I am soon able to resolve the problem of the cattle so you can get on with your work without fear of wiping out my herd."

He looked down at her, his granite gray eyes glowed with a soft patina as they scanned her upturned face. "Mind calling me Martin?" he asked, his voice deep and rich with overtones.

She felt the vibrations of his voice penetrate and pulsate through her. Felt his look pin her to the spot. Felt impaled by the emotions that surged through her. In the turmoil, she forgot he had asked a question.

He removed his glove and, leaning over the saddle, took her hand. His palm was warm and surprisingly uncalloused, but his strength flowed over her, leaving her renewed through its force. She ran the tip of her tongue over her dry lips, then dared to raise her eyes to his.

. "You should never wear any color but blue. Turns your eyes to sapphires." His voice became a low throb that scattered her thoughts like rose petals in the wind. She stood dumb, her hand still resting in his, caught in the trance he induced so expertly. "I'll be back this evening to look in on our friend in the bunkhouse and chop you some wood."

She swallowed and hoped her voice wouldn't reveal the disquiet inside. "That's very kind of you, but I can attend to the poor man when he awakens, and Mr. Hornbeck has offered to stop by. I've put you to enough trouble for one day."

Martin's grip loosened, and he dropped her hand most unceremoniously. She watched his face grow hard and opaque, the eyes turn to slate. He pulled his hat hard over his eyes, set his mouth in a tight line, and wheeled his horse about. Without further words, he bent low and raced down the road at a full gallop.

Alexa stood dumb founded. What on earth had she said to bring about such a complete change in him? She would think more about it later, but right now she had a house to put to rights and a hired man to sober up.

CHAPTER 3

MUCH TO ALEXA'S DELIGHT , she found Emmie to be a hard worker. The woman learned quickly how Alexa wanted things done and strove mightily to do them that way. The clotheslines soon hung full of airing linens, and most of the windows in the house were thrown open to drive out the musty smell. By late afternoon the inside of the house had taken on a shine produced by vigorous scrubbing, dusting, and polishing.

Finished, they collapsed into chairs in the sitting room. "We have earned our keep this day," Alexa said, rolling down the sleeves of her dress and buttoning them at the cuffs. "Let's rest a minute and then while you start supper, I'll go up to the bunkhouse and see about that poor man. If he's well enough, I shall bring him down to eat."

Alexa laid her head against the high back of the rocking chair and relaxed. Her eyelids grew heavy, and she drifted off into unbidden sleep. Five chimes of the rosewood grandfather clock across the room wakened her. Stretching thoroughly, she drove sleep from her body so that she might be up and about her tasks. She could hear Emmie already busy in the kitchen.

Alexa stuck her head through the kitchen door. "You'd have let me sleep the night, wouldn't you?"

Self-conscious over the missing front tooth, Emmie flashed Alexa only a quick, flawed grin. "No, I'da made you eat, then sleep again. You're plumb tuckered, what with travelin' night and day and then doin' work in one afternoon that woulda took other folks days."

"I feel wonderfully refreshed by the little nap. Now I must go and see to our man. I shall be back in a few minutes. Be sure to set three places."

Alexa made her way across the freshly scrubbed pine plank floor, brightened with small multi-colored rag rugs and out onto the porch. A slight breeze brushed her cheek and brought the fragrance of wild roses growing in big scraggly bouquets about the yard.

Alexa walked slowly along the path, enjoying the view across a lovely meadow she had missed earlier as she trotted after Mr. Taylor. Several fine horses grazed there on grass already grown two feet high. Such an abundant stand would make good hay if she was able to find someone to cut and stack it. And if she could get two crops, she would have no worry about feed this winter.

Alexa raised her eyes to the sharp-edged mountain ridges twisting and turning in the distance. They might have been formed by gargantuan loggers, running among swinging huge axes, chopping ridge from ridge, and then with their hatchets, carefully trimming the high parts of the ridges into separate peaks. However, the appearance of all but the tallest mountains was softened by a mantle of deep perpetual green – the thousand-year old evergreen of trees—white pine and red cedar. The trees Martin Taylor was stripping from the land.

31

She arrived at the bunkhouse that stood shaded by tall firs, their rough bark moss-covered on the north. Standing with her hand on the latch, Alexa felt reluctant to face what she had only smelled previously. At last, determination won, and she knocked on the slab door. There was no answer and not a sound from inside to indicate anyone was there. She knocked again. Nothing. Lifting the latch, she pushed the door open a few inches, enough to stick her head through. The odor was gone, replaced by the unmistakable smell of strong lye soap. The place had been scrubbed, the bed made, and despite the somewhat crude, homemade appearance of a small unpainted table, four upright chairs, and a rocker, the room had a comfortable, lived-in air. But it was empty.

Pushing the door open all the way, she stepped up into the room. Behind the door she found his clothes hanging on pegs along the wall. Beneath these on the floor, stood a collection of cowboy boots in various stages of wear, from nearly new to ancient. *Well, if he's gone, he's traveling extremely light*, she concluded.

She felt the cookstove in the corner. It was cold, and there was no wood in the woodbox. She could find very little food in the cupboard, certainly not enough to prepare any kind of a meal. What had the old man subsisted on? Obviously, from the collection of bottles in the trash, his diet for some time had been mainly liquid. He must be a physical wreck and feeling wretched. Poor man!

Leaving, but making sure the door was securely latched behind her, she stood, hands on her hips, wondering where he might be. She would feel much more comfortable if she could locate and speak with him. In his present condition, he probably wouldn't prepare a suitable meal even if he had supplies. She wanted to be sure he had a proper supper.

It suddenly occured to her that she hadn't seen any

barns or other out-buildings. A ranch had to have a barn. Looking about, she located a well-used path leading through the trees. *Probably goes to the outhouse.* But since it was the only trail she could see, she started up the path anyway. A short distance into the woods, it forked. Having a tendency toward left-handedness, she chose the left fork and continued. The trail broke through the trees abruptly, and she was again in the meadow.

Now, however, instead of grazing horses, she faced two large red barns and several smaller buildings, also painted red and white. Beyond were numerous corrals and chutes.

Suddenly she realized the extent of the wealth Uncle Clyde had left her— not just the fine house and cattle—but this wide open space—to breathe, to be! She took a deep breath and threw out her arms in a spontaneous gesture.

Aunt Cassy had given her a rich heritage too— albeit one of learning to share too little with too many. Now, here in Idaho, she could build on that foundation—could grow, mature, and with God's guidance, begin to repay her great debt by helping others as she had been helped.

As she stood absorbed in her thoughts, a bent old man tottered out of one of the buildings and, carrying a small bucket, hobbled into the barn nearest her. Galvanized to action, she hurried down the path and through the door he had entered.

It took a few minutes for her eyes to grow accustomed to the hazy, subdued lighting of the interior, but when she could see, she found him scattering grain to clucking, red-feathered chickens gathering around his feet. He talked softly to them and then when he finished, he sat down on a stump and watched them feed.

Alexa felt like an intruder as she watched the intimate moments, but the longer she looked, the more her desire grew to help this poor old man suffering such deep grief and distress. She cleared her throat and gave a tiny cough. He looked up quickly and, upon seeing her, struggled to his feet.

She stepped forward. "I'm Alexa Spence, Mr. Grant's niece."

He nodded and bowed slightly. "I'm Jake."

His answer, so brief and curt, caught Alexa by surprise. She had anticipated an explanation of his earlier behavior—perhaps even an apology. Why had she thought he would oblige her with all the information she wanted? Obviously, she was going to have to dig it out of him.

"Are you Uncle Clyde's hired man?"

"Yep."

He was being less than cooperative. To cover her increasing discomfort she asked, "How are you feeling?"

"Fine."

Well, this wasn't getting her anywhere. Perhaps if she could get him into more favorable surroundings, she might learn something of him and the ranch. He was the only one who could really tell her about the daily routine. "I would like you to come to the house for supper," she insisted. "We need to talk about your plans, which I hope include continuing to work for me."

He looked extremely uncomfortable. "Don't eat at the big house. Eat in the bunkhouse," he mumbled.

"It would please me greatly if you'd consider making an exception tonight. I need to know the details of ranching and I am at a loss to know where to begin."

He stood shuffling his feet and clenching and unclenching his hands. Finally, as she was about to give up, he said, "Guess I can, this once, seeing as you're in need of help."

"Thank you. I appreciate your accepting the invita-

34

tion. We'll eat in about a half an hour." Alexa turned and nearly ran out the door before he had second thoughts and changed his mind. She hurried back along the path to the house, her thoughts on how best to get Jake to talk to her. If he had been with Uncle Clyde all those years, this must seem like home to Jake. She wanted him to continue to feel that way. Move on when it was his choice, not from having to. But how could she get him to stop drinking? She would not put up with that. There were too many things needing attention. In fact, it seemed to her, she needed more help. She and Emmie could take care of the house and garden, but the ranch itself was too large for one man to run properly. And an old, drunken one at that.

Arriving in the clearing where the house stood, she paused. Tied to the front porch stood a fine pony fitted with a well-used saddle and a bedroll strapped across the back. Sitting on the front steps was a middle-aged man dressed much as she had seen Jake, the boots with specially designed heels to keep the feet from slipping through the stirrups, denims, and a slip-over cotton shirt. A famous western-cut Stetson hat was pulled far over his eyes. It took a couple months' wages to buy a Stetson, but she knew no self-respecting cowboy, no matter how poor, would be seen in public without one.

The stranger sat rolling a stick between his fingers and apparently looking at the step between his feet. When he became aware of Alexa, he leaped up and removed his hat. "Afternoon ma'am. You Miss Spence?"

Perhaps this was the cowhand Mr. Taylor had promised to send over. He had left in such a state, she wasn't sure that he would remember his promise.

"I am," she said and moved quickly to the steps. Alexa liked the no-nonsense look about this man. He stood less than six feet, but his erect bearing made him appear taller. He didn't seem to limp or favor any part of his anatomy as she had seen so many cowboys do as they got off and on the train during her trip west. She scanned the stocky, well-muscled body. He would be able to throw a cow to brand and do the heavy work. Hopefully, he didn't drink to excess.

"Martin Taylor sent me over. Said you could use an extra hand."

Thank you, Lord, for knowing what I needed before I did and for providing.

So, Mr. Taylor had sent him. Did that mean he had forgiven her for whatever it was she had done to make him angry? She hoped so. She didn't want trouble with a neighbor. "Yes, I need a permanent extra hand, one that won't pick up and leave just before round-up. One who can handle a crew."

"I can do that, ma'am. And I'd like to try out that permanent arrangement. I ain't been permanent no-where for so long, I can't remember when the last time was. Name's Bill Smith."

"Pleased to have you here, Bill. The bunkhouse is over through the trees. You'll be sharing the space with Jake. He's a fixture around here. Going through a bad time since my uncle died."

"Taylor told me a little about the place and the situation, you being new and all. I'll make peace with Jake. You'll have no worry."

"Good. Supper'll be ready in a few minutes."

He looked stunned. "Ma'am, not meaning no offense, but I'm not used to eating in the big house. If there's a stove at the bunkhouse, I can stew up some satisfactory vittles."

"There's a stove, but I don't think there's anything to stew up. When I return the wagon to the livery stable in town tomorrow, I'll do some grocery buying. Emmie found enough canned things to make supper tonight, and Jake's coming down."

Bill looked puzzled. "Emmie?"

36

"Her husband's . . . well, she needs a place to stay right now. She's going to be my housekeeper."

"Real nice of you to do that for her, ma'am. Real nice."

Why does this stranger care about Emmie? Oh, it's probably not Emmie. He figures I've a soft heart good for a loan or something. "She's doing as much for me. I need her help with this big house to run and the ranch to oversee."

He peered over his shoulder and strained to see down the porch. Alexa wondered at his action, but before she could inquire, he gave a shrug and mounted his horse. "See you at supper," he said. As he trotted off in the direction of the bunkhouse, Alexa noticed that he continued looking back over his shoulder. *What is he looking for?*

Alexa insisted that dinner be served in the dining room despite Emmie's timid objections. She had thought Emmie didn't want the bother, but after a quiet awkward meal during which the men spoke briefly only when spoken to, and then left hurriedly after, she realized Emmie knew far more about these people than she.

She helped Emmie with the dishes and then went to sit on the porch. Emmie disappeared immediately afterwards on her own errands, and Alexa was truly alone for the first time that day—alone to think and plan. She decided it would be wise to pay more attention to Emmie's instincts. She seemed to possess a primitive wisdom. Tonight, Alexa had learned absolutely nothing about either of the men or any details of running the ranch.

Since she hadn't been able to visit with Jake, she was going to have to devise another plan to reach him. Tomorrow, she would go to the bunkhouse and talk with them both, maybe even have supper there.

Tiger jumped into her lap purring contentedly, and

she rocked slowly in the man-sized cane and mahogany rocker and wondered if this was how Uncle Clyde spent his evenings after the day's work was finished. Looking down, she noticed a worn spot where her feet rested and knew he had.

Relaxing against the chair, she watched the red-orange sun drop slowly into its nighttime pocket in the mountains to the west. The air filled with bird calls, and in the distance she could hear her horses whinny. There was an answering neigh close by, and she looked to see David Hornbeck riding up on a shining chestnut.

"Hello!" he called.

She rose quickly and went to meet him at the front steps. "Hello, yourself. This is a nice surprise."

When he dismounted and came to stand next to her, she saw he wasn't as tall as Mr. Taylor, though he stood close to six feet.

"There shouldn't be any surprise. I told you I'd be back this evening." His dark brown eyes roamed at will over her face, and he made no attempt to hide the pleasure he received at what they saw. "I always keep my promises," he said, his voice warm and intimate.

Suddenly flustered, Alexa fumbled with the collar of her dress and smoothed the hair at the back of her neck. "But it was growing so late, I thought perhaps something had come up to detain you." She led the way to the spot on the porch where she had been sitting.

"Unfortunately, something did come up, but I have good men and they took care of it."

She indicated the chair next to hers. "What sort of problem did your men have at this hour?" she asked, genuinely interested in the answer. Soon, she must learn all she could about ranch affairs.

He moved the chair so he could see her clearly and sat. "The spring runoff is slowing and some of my cattle were out of water. We had to move them onto the public range. They'll be grazing alongside yours now."

The tone of his voice was far from conversational and each syllable sent little pulses of excitement through her. Learning about ranching from him was going to be an experience to look forward to. One small thing bothered her, though. Withhighly polished boots, white shirt, and ever present tan Stetson he appeared to be a very prosperous cowboy yet his hands didn't look like he had ever done a day's work in his life. He was a puzzlement.

The sun was now safely stored for the night, and a soft pink-orange afterglow filled the western sky. Alexa and Mr. Hornbeck sat silent, listening to the birds begin their subdued evening chirping.

"Between the dark and the daylight, when the night is beginning to lower, Comes a pause in the day's occupations, That is known as the Children's Hour," he quoted softly.

Alexa turned to face him. "I, too, love Mr. Longfellow's poems and you have quoted one of my favorites."

"Mother used to entice me from my play with that verse. Then she would read to me, and we would play games before I prepared to retire. It's a rare evening that verse doesn't still run through my head."

He turned, smiled, and met her gaze. She was unaccustomed to such a frank display of esteem and it flustered her. She quickly raised her eyes to the deepening sunset. "Uncle Clyde has a wonderful collection of books. I've only just scanned the titles, but I'm anxious to begin reading them." Her voice came out in a breathless rush.

"I've shared many of those books with him," David Hornbeck nodded. "He and I exchanged reading material on a regular basis. I'd like to begin sharing them with you. However, I came to chop some firewood for you tonight. I'd better get to it before it gets too dark." He stood up as he spoke and walked toward the wood pile a short distance from the house. Obviously, his offer had not been an idle one. Having recovered her poise, Alexa rose and hurried to his side. "Oh, please don't bother! The woodbox was full when I arrived. And now that I have a new hired man, he can cut more tomorrow."

Thus reassured, David Hornbeck returned to the porch. "So you fired old Jake?"

He sounded almost glad at the idea. This also bothered Alexa. There were many undercurrents here that she could feel, but couldn't yet make sense of. She began to realize, however, that she was going to have to keep her wits about her until she learned what was going on.

Working to forget her annoyance, she answered in a soft voice, "Oh, my no. I couldn't do that. Poor man is heavy with grief. He's been behaving badly, I know, but he'll get straightened out. With Uncle Clyde gone, there's too much work for one man. The new man Mr. Taylor sent over will be a help to us both."

"Taylor sent him over, did he?" A cutting edge crept into his voice. "Taylor has no business interfering in the running of your ranch. He'd do well to tend to his own operation."

His voice, hard and sharp in contrast to the earlier warm vibrant tones, pierced her, leaving her cold. Was it possible these two men were jealous of each other? Each had reacted when the name of the other was mentioned. It seemed a highly likely supposition, she decided, given that each man was unmarried, ambitious, and in an occupation that, if expanded, could destroy the other.

Mr. Hornbeck stood suddenly. "I must be going. It will be dark soon and I have no light." He didn't even wait for her, but stalked along the porch, his steps echoing in the still evening air.

40

Dismayed that she might have offended him in some way, she hurried after him. "I'm sorry you have to leave so soon, but I fully understand. Thank you for coming all this way to chop my wood. I apologize for the inconvenience I've put you to," she said when she caught up with him.

He stopped on the second step and took her hand, rubbing the back of it with his thumb as he spoke. "Forgive me, Miss Alexa. I was rude just now. Your uncle talked of you so often that I felt I knew you well enough to share my deepest feelings. Martin Taylor is calloused and insensitive, intruding on everyone's lives in the valley. I find myself vexed whenever his name is mentioned."

Now he slowly turned her hand palm up, bowed, and pressed his lips into it. Her hand trembled as she felt the warm flesh of his lips and soft mustache brushing the cup of her hand. In Illinois, this would be frowned upon as fast and loose, but it seemed perfectly normal under the bright evening star rising in the pale blue afterglow of an Idaho sky.

She leaned against the porch railing to steady her weak knees. Then, gently he placed a parting kiss on the inside of her wrist. How glad she was she had taken a minute to dab a bit of persian lilac cologne there.

"Thank you for a special time. I will be over soon again," he promised. Mounting his horse in one flowing movement, he doffed his hat to her, and then galloped away.

She sat down on the steps and hugged her knees. She wanted to capture forever the lovely feelings running through her.

Later, as she undressed for bed, she could still feel the soft brush of his mustache and the imprint of his lips tingling in the palm of her hand. She lay sleepless with her hand open on her pillow. She felt the soft full moon steal the special tingle from her hand and seal it into her heart.

CHAPTER 4

LIFE ON THE RANCH QUICKLY settled into a routine. Jake, too crippled with arthritis to ride a horse with ease, tended the chickens, chopped wood, and became general handyman. He built the hitching post Alexa wanted, and a fence around the yard. She then instructed him in how to plant flowers and a garden.

Bill took over the range stock, haying, and the heavy work of the ranch. Martin Taylor had a good eye for men. Bill proved to be a hard worker, steady and dependable. He even gave Jake a powerful talking to about the evils of drink and refused to let him have a bottle. Alexa had happened to overhear this particular discussion and the intensity with which Bill spoke lingered with her. She hoped an opportunity would present itself to ask him about his experience with liquor.

Emmie and Alexa shared the housework, cooking, and gardening. Alexa set the table in the sitting room and insisted the men eat their meals at the big house. They worked long hard hours and she felt it was too much for them to prepare substantial meals. She could have hired a cook, but that seemed foolish for just two. When it came round-up time and there was a big crew, then she planned to have a full-time cook for the bunkhouse.

Alexa found herself with more and more work, and less and less leisure time. In fact, one morning a couple of weeks after her arrival, Alexa mutinied and stayed abed. She realized that she had trapped herself with all her plans. It occured to her that she had seen very little of her ranch. She had no idea what lay beyond the fenced meadow or how far her holdings spread. Today seemed a fine time to do some exploring.

There was just one small problem with her idea. She didn't know how to ride a horse, at least not very well. Aunt Cassy had declared such a pursuit unlady-like, and with Alexa alone among twelve boys, she was raised to be a lady. A very proper lady who didn't play tennis, ride horseback, square dance —anything "common" people did. Bless Aunt Cassy. She thought she was doing the right thing, but many times Alexa had chafed under the restrictions laid down by the dear woman.

Well, she couldn't blame her bondage on Aunt Cassy any longer. Hurriedly, she dressed in an old flowered calico dress. If she took a tumble or soiled it beyond washing clean, there would be little loss. Gulping down hot cereal kept warm in a double boiler on the back of the stove, Alexa bade Emmie goodbye and in her eagerness, flew to the barn.

As she entered the barnyard, she saw the chickens, and they reminded her of the blue ribbon Rhode Island reds she had raised back home. Even in her rush, she had to stop a minute and watch them scratching and clucking contentedly. As she stepped into the dusty, dimly lighted barn, she savored the smell of sweet hay, remnants of which still remained in the loft above. She must get a cow. She did miss the fresh milk, butter, and cream. Canned milk would do in a pinch, but as a steady replacement, it fell short. She began a serious hunt for the tack room in search of a side-saddle. She found the room without much trouble, but look as she would, there seemed to be no woman's saddle. This was frustrating for it would delay her investigation of her holdings. Hopefully, there was a store in town that carried sidesaddles in addition to their regular line of stock saddles. She decided to catch a buggy horse, drive in, and find out. Grabbing a bucket of oats and a halter, she started out through the meadow toward the peacefully grazing horses. She hadn't quite reached the herd when she became aware of an approaching horse, its shod feet and jangling reins disrupting the quiet.

She looked about until she spied the horseman. "Mr. Hornbeck!" she gasped aloud. Her eyes dropped to her faded old dress. What would he think? But he had seen her and was already riding in her direction. There was no escape.

When he was close enough, he called, "Good morning, Miss Alexa. What are you up to, standing way out here holding a bucket of oats? Have I interrupted something?" He dismounted, dropped the reins so his horse could graze, and walked over to her.

"I was on my way to catch a buggy horse and drive to town. I very much want to learn to ride a horse and there seems to be no appropriate saddle in the barn. I thought perhaps I might be able to purchase one." He stood so near she could smell the clean, warm scent of him, fresh starched clothes mingled with the pungent odor of leather.

He flashed a wide smile. "You won't find a sidesaddle for sale in town. Don't stock them. It has to be ordered from a saddle maker and then he has to have to time to make it. Takes awhile for a new one, but we have several well-used models at the ranch. Let me help you bring in a good horse. Then, I'll go back to the ranch and pick up a saddle. It would give me a great deal of pleasure if you'd allow me to teach you to ride."

"That seems a considerable amount of trouble," she objected politely, secretly delighted at his suggestion.

"No trouble at all. I came by to see if I could be of help in some way. Also, Mother wanted me to find out if you were ready for a formal call."

Alexa thought a moment. "Would you ask her if next Tuesday is convenient?"

"I'll relay the question."

Alexa kept her distance as David took the oat bucket and halter and expertly captured a fine-looking sorrell grazing nearby. Leading the horse back to her, he said, "I seem to remember this mare as being tame. Don't want to start you out on something eager to cut for the hills."

They walked slowly together toward the barn. "I'll be back in about a half hour with the saddle. That'll give you time to get acquainted with the old girl."

"And how do I make myself known to a horse?"

"By grooming her and talking to her while I'm gone. The two of you should be good friends by the time I return.'" He tied the horse in a stall, waved, and disappeared through the door.

Alexa stood outside the stall, eyeing the huge animal. "You certainly look a lot bigger inside than you did out in the pasture. I do wish Mr. Hornbeck hadn't tied you in here. I have no desire to walk past your heels to get to your head." Alexa found the curry comb and brush in the tack room, but how was she going to get next to the mare to brush her?

She decided to climb the wall of the adjoining stall and reach over into the mare's stall. When Mr. Hornbeck returned, Alexa, sitting on the divider between the stalls, had overcome her initial fright and was visiting happily with the docile animal as she brushed her.

45

Mr. Hornbeck set the saddle on a sack of grain. "I realized after I left that I should have tied her outside. You're a bit small to reach her back easily."

Alexa jumped down. "But as you see, Mr. Hornbeck, the problem is easily solved."

"Yes, Miss Spence, you are a clever woman." He untied the horse and brought the animal to stand next to the saddle.

He had called her Miss Alexa earlier, and she found this return to formality distressing. "Mr. Hornbeck, since we are neighbors and bound to see a great deal of one another, I would be pleased if you called me Alexa."

"Thank you, Alexa," he said, and then turned laughter-filled eyes on her. "I've longed to drop the formality myself."

The few dates Aunt Cassy found suitable for Alexa had been with gangling farm boys whose manners were bungling and whose speech seemed limited to words of one syllable. David's manners and maturity filled her with delight, and just gazing at him gave her pleasure.

She held the halter rope while David put the blanket and saddle in place. "I'm sure I could never lift that saddle," she said as she watched him swing the awkward-looking contraption to the back of her horse.

"I'm sure you couldn't. You'll need help when you want to ride. You have only to inform me of your plans, and I shall be right over." His dark eyes locked into hers and she felt an unwelcome blush rise. "You blush more beautifully than anybody I've ever seen," he said as he took the rope from her hand and replaced it with leather reins.

Alexa lowered her head and David responded with a chuckle, soft and rolling. She escaped the emotionally charged moment by leading the mare outside. There she met Jake as he came from around one of the buildings. "Howdy," he greeted them. "See you gonna give old Molly a workout. She needs it. Just been growing fat and sassy out there in the pasture."

"With David's help, I'm going to try," Alexa said.

"Looks to me like you're a mite short in the limbs," Jake said as he appraised Alexa. "There's a stump over there you can use to board her."

"Come on, Molly, let's you and me get started on this lesson," Alexa urged as she pulled Molly toward the stump.

"What do you know about riding?" David asked.

"Precious little."

"I do hope you'll forgive me, but it is necessary to refer to certain parts of your anatomy. I shall attempt to be as delicate as possible." He waited for her to digest his warning and give her permission.

"I trust your judgment."

"Thank you." Clearing his throat, his face took on an impersonal look and his voice became crisp and business-like. "You mount and dismount on the left side. The upper crutch is a few inches to the left of the center line of the saddle and curved upward so as to hold your right limb in a secure and comfortable grip."

Alexa nodded her head, controlling the waves of shock at the mention of her limbs. While she knew nothing about a sidesaddle, she already doubted his casual remark that she would be secure and comfortable.

"The downward curving horn fitted to the saddle below the upper crutch is called the leaping-horn. It curls down and holds your left limb in place. In a crisis, you can stay in place by gripping downwards with your right limb against the upper crutch while drawing your right foot back, and pressing upward with your left limb against the leaping-head."

He said it all in such a nonchalant manner, Alexa knew he had never sat such a saddle. She wished for a woman to tell her how she could perch on that ridiculously small piece of leather, with her legs wrapped around two proturberances, and not fall off the moment the horse moved.

"Let me hold the reins and you get up on the stump. Put your left foot in the stirrup and rise into the saddle. Tuck your right extremity around the upper crutch." He pointed to the v-shaped object jutting out high on the front of the saddle.

She placed her foot in the stirrup as he directed, but when she tried to set her weight on the saddle, it moved. "Oh," she gasped, retreated immediately to the stability of the stump, and glanced wildly at David.

"If I cinch the saddle so tight it won't move, Molly will feel cut in half. Don't worry, it won't slip off."

Reassured, Alexa tried again. This time she succeeded in getting into the saddle seat and her leg hooked up over the crutch. *What an uncomfortable arrangement.*

"Bring your left extremity up against the leaping-horn," David instructed.

She did as he told her, then watched as he shortened the stirrup until her thigh was in contact with the underside of the leaping horn. She felt like a pretzel.

"The big problem with sitting a sidesaddle is both rider and saddle are fundamentally unbalanced. You must keep your weight positioned directly over the horse's spine, or the horse will develop a sore back. To compensate for everything being on the left side, you must consciously put most of your weight on the right. Imagine there is a tintack sticking up on the left side of the seat of the saddle, and you must avoid sitting on it."

Alexa pictured a large sharp point rising from the left of the saddle and immediately rose away from it.

"Splendid!" David cheered. "One more thing, and

you'll be ready. You must sit as squarely in the saddle as possible, with your body and shoulders facing perfectly forward."

Alexa squared her shoulders and shifted her hips to the front. This made a terrible kink under her left rib cage as she stretched away from the tintack and faced forward.

"You look wonderful. You're going to be a natural at riding," David praised.

She smiled at his encouragement, but she watched with envy as David swung easily onto his stock saddle and settled himself astride his horse. Why was she nested on top of Molly like a fashionable hat? And she wasn't even anchored with hat pins. She looked with longing at his saddle horn. She had nothing to hold on to, and she desperately wanted to clutch something as David commenced leading the horse around the barn yard and corral.

She began to feel the gait of the steady mare and let her body rock with it. Round and round they went until Alexa felt not only comfortable, but bored.

"Are you ready to try your own reins?" David finally asked.

"I think so. I'm going to sleep, sitting up here and rocking along."

He handed her the reins but continued to hold the halter rope as a precaution. "You gently pull the rein on the side you want the horse to go," David instructed.

"No need to pull," Jake, working nearby, spoke up. "She's neck broke."

"So much the better," David answered. "Then you lay the rein across her neck on the opposite side. Here, give it a try."

David reached up and pulled the rein across the right side of Molly's neck. The horse turned her head to the left. Alexa understood, so she clucked Molly into a slow walk and practiced reining her. She and the horse soon understood each other very well. But this saddle was a torture device developed, she was sure, by a man who wanted to get even with women.

"Do women ever ride in saddles like yours?" she asked David.

His head swiveled and his mouth dropped. "Women, I suppose, but no lady does."

"Well, this lady thinks this sidesaddle is terribly uncomfortable."

"You'll get used to it. Mother spends full days riding sidesaddle. My western saddle isn't rocking-chair comfortable, either, when you're first starting out."

So much for the idea she might ride astride. Yet, it wasn't only the comfort she craved. She simply didn't feel in control of the horse. If she had both knees around Molly and a saddle horn to grasp, Alexa knew she would have more control.

"Well, I think you've had enough for one day. You'll be stiff and sore tomorrow if we don't stop now." David guided Molly to Alexa's mounting stump and extended a hand to help her off.

Obediently, Alexa allowed him to unsaddle Molly and turn her back into the pasture. All the while he worked, she felt as she had with Aunt Cassy. Her life was being run by someone else. When was she ever going to have control, to do what she wanted, when she wanted, where she wanted? She hadn't planned to take her first riding lesson by walking around and around the barn yard. She had seen the barn and corrals, many times. She wanted to see her ranch.

"Are you going to be busy tomorrow?" she asked.

He hoisted the saddle onto his hip. "I'm sorry to say, I am. We have to move cattle. Probably take us the better part of the week." He must have noticed her face drop, because he added. "I'll have some free time next week if you'd like another lesson," he said before starting into the barn at a brisk pace. He

50

stopped and turned as though just remembering his message. "By the way, Mother would like to come calling next Tuesday, if that's agreeable with you."

She caught up with him at the tack room door and followed him inside where he put the saddle on a V-shaped rack protruding from the wall. "I'd be delighted!" But Alexa was thinking, *A whole week to sit and clean and weed,* and she narrowly prevented a deep sigh from escaping.

She didn't want David to leave. They were just beginning to feel comfortable together. "Won't you stay for dinner?" she asked, hoping that they could continue the lovely day.

He turned to face her and taking both her hands, drew her close to him. "I can't think of anything I'd rather do, but I have to go into town. Promised the bank I'd stop by and sign some papers. Then it's back to the ranch and herding cattle."

"It seems you spend a great deal of time with your cattle. Unless Bill isn't telling me something, all he does is keep mine away from Mr. Taylor's lumbering operation. Am I doing something wrong?"

"No. You don't have any problems. You have the best meadow land and water of anyone around. The rest of us in the valley are very envious of your situation." He tucked her hand into the curve of his arm, and they walked out into the sunshine.

"How many people live in our valley?" she asked as David gathered the reins of his horse and led him as they strolled slowly toward the house.

"A surprising number when you count the loggers and miners. The ranch folks and town people don't do much socializing with them, though. They're a rough unmannerly lot for the most part and prefer their liquor and women to our square dances and socials."

Alexa was having a hard time concentrating on what he was saying. All her senses were tuned to the feel of him next to her. He seemed to radiate security and protection. She knew she would never have to worry about anything with him around. The sound of his cultivated voice enfolded her like a cocoon, making the words he spoke seem of little importance. He brought her to a stop at the foot of the back door porch steps.

He turned her about so she stood opposite him. "I don't want to leave. I'd very much like to stay for dinner. I hope you understand that."

She looked into his sable brown eyes, soft and inviting, like magnets drawing her helplessly into their depths. She found herself inwardly straining toward him, knowing her eyes were begging him to kiss her and powerless to control their message. In her mind Alexa knew this was inappropriate behavior; her heart *refused* to let her behave properly. She had grown bored playing coquettish games with boys she cared nothing about. David was a man with everything she had ever dreamed of. They had so much in common, from bordering ranches to a love of poetry and literature. It seemed dishonest to deny her feelings.

She closed her eyes and allowed him to gently cup her face in the palm of his hand. He bent low over her, taking her waiting lips in a brief tender kiss. The emotion he stirred flowed through her like warm honey, leaving her unsatisfied, wanting more. Opening her eyes and searching his face, she saw a longing for her change the planes of his face.

Still holding her face, letting his thumb caress her cheek, he watched her intently. Clearing his throat before he spoke, he said, "There's a valley square dance a week from this Saturday at the schoolhouse. There'll be bidding on box lunches to raise money to remodel the teacherage. Would you do me the honor of attending?"

"Oh, David. That sounds wonderful! Our box socials in Illinois were such fun."

"They are here, too." His voice and the way he looked at her held future promises.

David seemed reluctant to let her go, but at last he released her and mounted the patient chestnut. "I'll see you before then. I'll try to bring mother when she comes to call on Tuesday. If I can't make it, I'll ride over some evening." He paused as if suddenly realizing she had issued no invitation. "That is, if it's all right with you."

She reached her hand up to him. "You know it is, David. Anytime."

He took the proffered hand and kissed the palm the way she remembered. The tremors again flocked through her, sending her heart into unrhythmic beats and leaving her breathless.

"Goodbye," he whispered softly as he folded her fingers over the kiss to protect it. "See you soon. Maybe sooner than you expect." With those words, he turned and rode away. This time, though, he kept looking back over his shoulder to where she stood with the hand holding his kiss closed tightly.

CHAPTER 5

THE REST OF THE DAY, whenever Alexa thought about David, she could feel his kiss on her mouth and in her hand. She would have floated totally out of control had not a hard little rock of uneasiness kept irritating her mind. She refused to let it surface, but it remained tenaciously disturbing.

After supper, when she and Emmie were finishing the dishes, Alexa took courage and mentioned an idea that had been forming all day. "Have you ever seen a lady ride a western saddle?" she asked, trying to keep her voice casual.

Emmie peered at her from under heavy dark brows. "Not what *you're* meaning by a lady."

Alexa was confused by Emmie's remark. What other kinds of ladies were there? One was either a lady or one wasn't. "Then you *have* seen ladies ride them. What kind of ladies?"

"Outlaw ladies," Emmie said curtly, and gave the dish towel a resounding snap before she hung it to dry.

"Oh," was all a subdued Alexa said, her hopes thoroughly dashed.

Emmie cast Alexa a disapproving look and stomped out of the kitchen on her nightly errands, whatever they were. Alexa walked slowly out onto the porch and sat down in her rocker. Tiger, waiting for his evening stroking, jumped into her lap and curled up. "Tiger, do you know I have never, never in my whole life done something I wanted to do if there was danger of censure. I have been the best, most obedient, dutiful person I know. And I'm sick of it!"

"Meow," Tiger responded.

"I quite agree. It's about time I started doing some of the things I want to do. Before I know it, I'll have lived my whole life and never been me. What I've been is a coward, afraid of risking someone's rebuke."

Tiger stood up, stretched, licked her hand, and laid back down.

"You're absolutely right. I've been licking hands long enough. I am not going to ride a horse on that miserable sidesaddle. If the whole valley wants to talk, they can. Give them something to chew on."

Gathering Tiger up in her arms, she marched through the house and up to the attic. She hadn't returned there since her first day when she had found Emmie hiding in the clothes cupboard. It was about time to explore its secrets.

She put Tiger down and he immediately started sniffing likely mouse retreats. Alexa opened the cupboard. A thorough examination revealed a collection of expensive men's clothes. These must have been placed here after Uncle Clyde died. Undoubtedly Mrs. Hornbeck had seen to it. However, there was nothing Alexa could wear or even make over.

The boxes placed under the eaves, labeled and stacked carefully, might produce some fabric or even some women's clothes. Alexa turned to these, but it was growing too dark to see. She could get a lamp, but if it accidentally tipped over or dropped, there was a good chance of burning down her house. Nothing was worth that risk. She couldn't do anything about a riding costume tonight, but that would be her first project in the morning.

When Alexa awoke, her back had a painful crick to remind her of yesterday's horseback ride. It also reinforced her decision to make a riding skirt and sit astride Molly.

Alexa found Emmie weeding the garden, a large poke bonnet hiding her face from the sun. When she heard Alexa, she raised up. "You know, Miss Alexa, if you'd quit tearing around in the hot sun without a bonnet, you wouldn't grow such a crop of freckles."

Her remarks and tone of voice stopped Alexa short. Emmie sounded just like Aunt Cassy. "I wore a bonnet everywhere I went for years. It didn't help that much. Besides you can't see but straight ahead when the poke sticks out so far."

"Turn your head, 'lessen your neck won't twist," Emmie said in a sour voice, and went back to her weeding.

Alexa bent to help Emmie, but her mind kept returning to her riding skirt. And she wasn't going to wear a bonnet, either. She pictured herself on Molly, riding across the meadow wearing a lace-trimmed flowered bonnet. She almost laughed aloud at the scene.

"You eaten anything?" Emmie asked.

"No, but I'm not hungry. I'll be fine until dinner. What do you want me to do now?"

Emmie picked up the hoe and leaned on it. "I hate to say this, and I don't mean no offense, but I'd be a lot happier if you'd find something else to use your time and stay outta my kitchen. I ain't used to help. Just keep tripping over your skirts." Emmie ducked her head and tightened her body as though waiting for blows to fall for having been so forward.

This was the longest speech Alexa had heard Emmie make and she hadn't known that Emmie had it in her. Likewise, she hadn't known she wasn't wanted as a helper. Alexa hugged her. "Thanks, Emmie. I really don't like housework or cooking. I was doing it because I thought I should. I can find a lot of things more to my liking."

Feeling like a child given a reprieve from chores, Alexa dashed off to the house and up the stairs to the attic. Throwing open the clothes cupboard, she found the boxes labeled hats and began opening them. They were filled with different colored Stetsons, some new or nearly so, and some well-worn.

She took out one of the new ones and tried it on. With a little padding inside the headband, it would fit. It had a number of colors and would go with any outfit she might choose to wear and keep the sun from growing so many freckles on her face. She didn't like admitting it, but Emmie was right. Alexa was beginning to produce a prize-winning crop as a result of her open rebellion against protecting her skin, either with parasol or bonnet. Aunt Cassy would have a fit if she could see her.

Setting these aside, she turned her attention to other boxes. Examining the labels, she finally located one marked fabric. With trembling hands, she unstacked boxes until she reached it. Excitement turned her fingers to thumbs, and she fumbled badly in her attempts to untie the twine. At last, she lifted the lid. There, folded in neat piles, lay an assortment of linen, cotton, velvet, and calico fabric. No worsted. She couldn't imagine riding with a calico or linen skirt. Velvet would look lovely, but not for long.

She left this box open and continued reading labels. No more fabric. Discouraged, she returned to the open box and began taking out each piece, testing the weight and weave for suitability. She was nearly ready to give up. Only a few pieces remained, and they all looked to be velvet. "Oh well," she sighed aloud. "You've come this far. You might as well empty the box and re-pack it." A dismal gloom rapidly replaced the sunny spirit of Alexa's revolution. She felt forever doomed to being proper, lest someone not think she was a lady, to be what others wanted her to be. At this rate, she would become more and more stifled by propriety until she grew so lost she would never find herself.

She wanted to cry at the death of her first little revolt. Then, folded flat across the whole bottom of the box, she spied a large piece of brown corduroy. "Oh, Lord," she cried. "Thank you." She took the find as a sign of His approval, and her smile was back in place.

Lifting the treasured piece of material, she quickly replaced the remainder of the fabric, tied the box securely, and returned it to its proper stack.

She hurried downstairs to the small alcove off the sitting room where the treadle sewing machine stood. It hadn't been used since Alexa arrived, but now she took off the lid to reveal a brand-new machine. In one of the cupboards, she found a basket containing threads of many colors, scissors, thimbles, needles, and pins.

Alexa laid the material out on the floor and folded it in half. Another of the skills Aunt Cassy had insisted she learn was sewing. Alexa hadn't been particularly thrilled with the idea, but as usual, had learned in spite of her own desires. Now she was thankful she had.

Without benefit of a pattern, she quickly designed and cut out her riding skirt. Threading the machine, she began sewing the pieces into a gored skirt, split so that when she stood it looked like a normal skirt. When she wanted to ride, though, she could swing her leg over Molly, sit astride, and still be fully covered.

By dinner time Alexa had finished her creation,

58

pressed it, and laid it across her bed to wear after she had helped with the dishes. She was going horseback riding this afternoon and not around the barnyard, either. Jake could tell her what she needed to know, then she could be on her way to look over her ranch.

Alexa was too excited to eat much, and it was hard to sit while everyone finished eating. Afterward Emmie seemed unusually picky about the clean-up, but at last everything was tidied to her satisfaction, and Alexa felt free to leave.

She rushed to her room and changed into a pale blue cotton blouse with long, full sleeves and her new brown corduroy split skirt. Wearing Uncle Clyde's brown Stetson, she didn't look like anyone she had ever seen. Nevertheless, she was pleased with the combination, and felt like a ranch owner for the first time. Alexa resolved to make more of these skirts. She even considered making jackets or vests to match and ordering some cowboy boots to replace her thin buttoned boots. Might as well go all the way if she was going to break with tradition!

Emmie usually rested after diner, so Alexa, putting on her cowboy hat and leather gloves, tiptoed out of the house and hurried to the barn. Taking a bucket half full of oats and a rope halter, she quickly snared Molly and brought her back to the barnyard. Tying her near the mounting stump, Alexa searched the tack room for a small saddle. There were several to choose from so she took the one with the highest pommel; more to hold on to. She could even lift it. Grabbing a saddle blanket and bridle, she lugged everything out to the horse.

Standing on the stump, she spread and smoothed the sweat-blanket, then tried to hoist the saddle onto Molly's back. Molly kept backing away, and Alexa missed the target each time. Perspiration beaded on her face and rolled down her back where the sun shone hot.

Exasperated, Alexa stormed, "Molly, you stand still, or I'll hit you over the head with this bucket. Hear?"

Something in the tone of her voice must have communicated. Molly stood still and allowed the saddle to be placed on her back. Alexa paused, baffled by the next steps. There were leather and webbed straps everywhere, and she didn't know which went where. She had no idea how to go about fastening the saddle securely enough to mount.

Molly turned her head and looked directly at Alexa. She rolled her eyes and shook her head as if to say, "Go away and leave me alone."

"I am not going away," Alexa retorted. "I intend to learn to saddle and ride you properly."

"Need a little help cinching up the girth, Miss Alexa?" Jake asked as he magically appeared at her elbow.

"If you'd show me how so I can do it by myself, I'd be enormously grateful," she said.

Jake stood eyeing the saddle. "Sure you got the right saddle?"

"I'm sure. I have no intention of riding on that cleverly designed torture device."

Jake shrugged and reached under Molly's belly for the girth, a webbed strap with a ring in the end. Then he made four loops with the leather strap in front of him. "Now make sure the cinch is close to the forelegs, not across the horse's belly," Jake instructed. "Work the cinch tight."

She watched as he kept working out the slack in the leather strap and pulling the cinch tighter and tighter. "Aren't you making it awfully tight?"

"Horse always holds air. Won't be too tight when she starts breathing normal again. In fact, if you was to do some fancy riding and roping you'd have to stop and cinch the saddle tighter." Jake wrapped the strap around the loops of leather and slipped the end

60

through the top ring holding the strap. Then he
brought it back through itself, making a fine flat knot.
"There. That's all you do," he said, and patted
Molly on the rump.
"If you have time, I'd like to practice."
"You're the boss," Jake reminded her.
She liked the sound of the words and as she undid
the saddle, she savored them over and over. After she
had saddled the horse several times, she was finally
given Jake's blessings. "Always be sure you mount
from the left," he warned, for somehow in all the
fussing, Molly had turned around and was facing the
opposite direction.
Dutifully, Alexa turned Molly and swung into the
saddle as she had seen David do. She was now
confronted with one small problem. Her feet dangled
at the side of the horse nowhere near the stirrups.
Alexa hooked her knee over the saddle horn and
gathered her skirts out of his way, while Jake replaced
each stirrup until it was the right length. Alexa went
walking happily off across the meadow and along a
trail into the trees.
Then, she bounced painfully in the saddle. Once on
the trail, Molly broke into a trot and Alexa jounced
helplessly, and couldn't get Molly to travel at any
other gait. Finally, the stitch in her side became so
severe, she could hardly breathe. "Molly, whoa!"
Molly kept on trotting, heedless of Alexa's command.
"Stop, girl," Alexa begged and pulled back hard on
the reins. Molly stopped suddenly. If it hadn't been
for the high pommel, Alexa would have sailed right
over Molly's head. Alexa slipped her feet from the
stirrups and slid to the ground. She pressed her side in
an attempt to cure the stitch and breathe normally
again.
"Well, Miss Spence, you certainly present an
arresting sight. One not seen every day out here in the
woods.'

61

She recognized Martin Taylor's voice, but she couldn't see him. "Martin Taylor, where are you? And what do you mean spying on a lady in distress?"

"The lady rode into my territory, although I am forced to qualify the term 'lady.' Never saw a lady riding as you just were." He walked toward her from out of the woods, leading his horse.

Alexa stood, still clutching her side. "I refuse to ride sidesaddle. That is one tenet of being a lady I intend to flaunt. However, I find I don't have as much control as I thought I would."

"Molly's trotting give you a stitch in your side?" he asked, eyeing her hand.

She nodded.

"Bend over," he commanded.

She did but apparently not far enough to suit him for she felt his hand in the middle of her back and then her nose nearly hit the ground as he shoved her roughly. She felt her hat roll off into the dirt. "Ugh!" she gasped breathlessly. Even against her determined struggle to straighten up, his superior weight kept her pinned in a most uncomfortable and undignified position. "Let me up!" she sputtered, her words muffled by her skirt.

"I will in a minute," he answered casually and continued to hold her down.

"Martin Taylor, you let me up this minute!" And she fought against his hand.

As suddenly as he had pushed her down, he released her. Unexpectedly set free from the pressure, she staggered as she stood upright. He reached for her hat and dusted it off. "Strange hat for a lady. Don't see them wearing Stetsons too often," he commented as he handed it to her. "Stitch gone?"

Amazingly enough, it was. "Yes." Then grudgingly, she added, "Thanks."

"What in tarnation made you choose Molly? She's stubborn about staying at a trot, and a killer at that as you learned."

"Ignorance," Alexa replied. But she was wondering why David had chosen Molly for her. If Molly's gait was a well known trot, then David had to know. Of course, he hadn't expected Alexa to take off on her own, either, and Molly had been gentle around the barn yard.

"Come on. If you're determined to learn to ride, and it appears you are, let's go get a decent horse and start you off right."

"If 'right' is to ride round and round a corral, forget it. I've started out to see my ranch, and I intend to accomplish that goal, Mr. Taylor."

"Miss Spence, I asked you earlier to call me Martin. Now, I'm telling you I won't answer to 'Mr. Taylor', so swallow your proper manners or our communication will rapidly cease."

"Of course, Mr. Taylor," she teased. "Please call me Alexa . . . Martin. I'd hate to think our communication might cease."

"I'll ride that plug you're on," he offered, "but we'll have to switch saddles. I don't relish sitting in that straight jacket.

"Not good?"

"Not good. Don't the front of your thighs and hip bones feel sore from bouncing against that high flat pommel."

She felt. They did. Then she blushed. He had spoken frankly in terms not used in mixed company and not excused himself or seemed the slightest bit remorseful. "Martin, you are no gentleman." She hoped her voice was cold enough to give him frost bite.

He finished the final cinch knot on his saddle now resting on Molly. "Alexa, don't up and pull you parlor manners on me. You can't have it both ways. If you want to be treated like a delicate hothouse flower then you have to abide by the rules . . . sidesaddle, parasol, freckle bleaching cream, proper clothing . . .

63

the lot. You can't suddenly toss away convention and then call it back when it suits you.''

She wanted to throw something at him. The beast! His remarks were made the more maddening because he was right. Worse, she found him most disconcerting because he had the courage to put her in her place. Gentlemen never upbraided a lady or engaged her in argument. She hadn't encountered such honesty in an unrelated male and didn't quite know how to deal with it.

He ignored her obvious dilemma, bent over, and made a cradle of his gloved hands. ''Here, put your foot in my hands and I'll boost you onto my horse.''

She stepped up, grabbed the saddle horn, and struggled up onto a horse that dwarfed Molly. She couldn't get her balance, and began to slip sideways. Martin reached up and gave her leg the needed push to set her straight in the saddle. The urge to rail at him rose in her, but she bit her tongue. He hadn't seemed to take any more notice of his actions than if she had been a boy.

Alexa watched him swing onto Molly and Molly started off at her usual body-wracking trot. Martin jerked her to a stop. ''It's time, horse, you learned some manners. Now, you walk or I'll make your life miserable.''

''Think she understands you?'' Alexa asked.

''I think she's going to test me.''

And Molly didn't disappoint him. She returned to that devastating trot, but this time Martin laid into her with spurs. Molly leaped into a gallop, and they disappeared down the trail in a cloud of dust, while Alexa followed at a pleasant comfortable walk on Martin's horse.

She had begun wondering if Molly and Martin were ever coming back when a lathered defeated Molly walked slowly around a bend in the trail. ''I've wanted to have a go at this little beast for a long time, but she was always Clyde's favorite. He spoiled her rotten. Got so he couldn't ride her though, and yet he wouldn't let anyone teach her some manners."

"Looks as if she's learned a lesson today," Alexa observed.

"That remains to be seen. How she acts when you get on her will be the test."

"By the way, what's your horse's name?"

"Doesn't have a name," Martin said.

"Doesn't have a name! Why not?"

"I don't give animals names."

Alexa couldn't comprehend. She named everything, including the mouse that continued to evade the trap in the buttery. "Why not?"

"You name something, means its special. Nothing special about an animal. They just die on you, and then you have to get another."

She couldn't see his face, and his back gave her no clue to the emotions running through him. It was clear, though, from the harsh tones of his voice that he had been deeply hurt by the death of a pet and had never gotten over it.

"Martin, I need to rest a few minutes. Could we stop?"

"Probably a good idea. There's a small stream off the trail a few steps This little beast would probably be grateful for a drink."

She followed him through the trees until they arrived at a willow-lined stream. Dismounting, she walked to the water's edge and looked into the shallows where the stream ran as transparent as glass. Along the bottom, many colored stones formed a unique mosaic shadowed by swimming fish. She followed the creek to deeper places where the water, a translucent jade green, flowed slowly before it churned frothy white over miniature craggy rapids. Resting in pools at the foot of a short falls, it turned into subdued indigo blue.

"This is a beautiful spot," she breathed softly.

"This whole place is beautiful," he answered.

"Then why are you so set on destroying it?" she asked, remembering Mrs. Hornbeck's comment.

"I'm not destroying it. I'm not cutting timber anywhere near here."

Alexa would continue this conversation another time. But right now she had stopped for a different reason. Sitting on a fallen log, she watched Martin water the horses. He turned them to graze, then came to sit beside her.

"What kind of pet did you have that died?" she asked softly.

He looked at her. His eyes narrowed and his mouth tightened, showing his displeasure at her abrupt question. "None of your business."

"I know it isn't, but your voice when you spoke of your pet showed how deeply you had cared. Can't you share your sorrow?" Would he answer? She hoped so; it was clear that he still carried grief over a loss she guessed was many years old. A childhood grief that continued to cast a pall over his life even today.

CHAPTER 6

MARTIN REMOVED HIS GLOVES and laid them on the log. Reaching out, he plucked a stem of new growth from a nearby choke cherry bush and began shredding each leaf with intense deliberation. Alexa stared at the destruction, stared at the knife-like fingernail as it sliced open the veins until all the leaves lay in shapeless ruins.

Finally, she broke the silence. "Was it a dog?" she asked gently.

He nodded and again the silence hung heavy between them.

She wondered if she dared ask her next question for it was the one that had brought them to this moment. She decided she had better and get his reaction over with. "What was his name?"

Another long silence. "Tramp," Martin answered at last, his voice barely a whisper as though it had been a very long time since he had said the name.

"How did you get him?"

He plucked another branch and began again the methodical destruction of its leaves. Much later he spoke. "My father was a railroad engineer. The dog was hurt in the train yard and nearly starved to death because he couldn't get food. One day, he followed my father home from work. I was playing in front of the house when they came up the street, a gray short-haired dog limping along behind, and my father trying to get him to go back." Martin stopped and it seemed he wasn't going to continue.

"What happened next?"

"I asked him about the dog. He said that the mutt had attached himself to the train crew, but after he was hurt he was real ugly and boney. Nobody wanted him. My father didn't want him either, but Tramp and I took to each other right off."

Alexa watched and waited as Martin began slowly pacing back and forth through the grass. It was a long time before he spoke again. He seemed to have forgotten her entirely. His pacing created a well-defined path and still he walked.

At last, he returned to the log, took off his hat, and laid it on the grass as he sat down beside her. He ran long, slender fingers through the mop of untamed hair . . . the fingers and hands of a gentleman, not an unmannered logger. Leaning forward, he propped his elbows along his thighs. The hands dropped limply from the wrists and hung, unmoving in mid-air. His deep, sometimes overloud growl was gone when he began to speak, replaced by a quiet and cultivated, satin-smooth bass. "I had a passel of brothers and sisters, and I was kinda lost in the middle somewhere. My mother wasn't very well, and she had a hard time handling all of us. With my father away from home so much, she did what had to be done. Unless you were sick or in trouble, you weren't noticed much. We weren't allowed out of the yard unless it was to run an errand, and nobody was permitted to come play. Ma said she had enough of her own; she didn't need to tend other people's kids. Tramp became my best friend."

Alexa felt a knot of tears rise in her throat. She could picture a lonesome little boy curled up with his dog and she wanted to touch him, let him know someone cared, but she refrained lest he misunderstand.

"Did he sleep with you?"

A quick bitter laugh punctuated his answer. "There wasn't room. We slept three and four to a bed as it was. Sure no place to put a dog, too. I used to get up on summer nights, though, and go lie with Tramp on the back porch." A shy smile at the memory changed the severity of his face. The love for that dog still radiated from Martin like heat from a stove.

"How long did you have him?" Alexa asked.

"Six years."

"What happened?"

Briefly, Martin turned stricken eyes to her, the pupils large and dark. Then he bowed his head so she could see nothing but the profile of his face. In the long interval that followed, she became conscious of cheerful bird calls and the soft happy-sounding splash of the water as it ran past...incongruous sounds. The chomping of the horses as they ate grew uncommonly loud in the deathly hush that fell between them.

A very long time passed before he spoke again. She had difficulty recognizing the small broken voice as he choked, "When I was thirteen someone poisoned him."

"Oh, no, why?"

Martin shook his head slowly back and forth. "I don't know," he answered in a whisper, separating and accenting each word. "I tried and tried to figure it out . . . tried to remember if I'd done something to someone so they'd want to get even. Tried to remember if Tramp had been doing things he shouldn't. I just couldn't make any sense of it . . . then or now." He almost looked like that puzzled young boy trying to understand how such a calamity could occur.

Alexa felt the hurt deep inside him. Knew somehow it had been the pivot point of his life when he had ceased to trust anyone or share his private feelings. "What did your parents do?"

He faced her and she looked into deep pools of grief openly revealed in his eyes. "Nothing." The word hung in the air between them, cold and unforgiving.

So this was the bottom of the pit . . . the reason he withdrew from emotions of tenderness, lived the transitory existence of a baudy logger, allowed no permanent relationships. She had known him for very little time, but she had already felt his barbed wire warnings to stay clear of his private territory..

When she recovered her voice, she asked softly, "Why not?"

"Ma was having another baby and Pa was on a run. When he got home and I told him about Tramp, he said 'Good. Glad to be rid of that mangy beast. He was an embarrassment to the family. Get you a good dog, now.' And he did. He brought me home a pedigreed Irish Setter from my aunt's kennel." The empty tone in Martin's voice told her all she needed to know about his relationship with the new dog.

Silent tears spilled down Alexa's face. "Tell me the rest of Tramp's story, please," she said brokenly.

He started to speak, cleared his throat, and tried again. Still nothing came out. He stood up, his back to her, head bowed, and shoulders hunched forward. His thumbs were tucked in his front pockets, something she hadn't noticed him do before. She watched him dig a hole with the toe of his boot. And still he didn't say anything. Was this the thirteen-year-old Martin she was seeing? The forlorn, heartbroken boy reliving agonizing moments alone again?

She couldn't stand his solitary suffering any longer. He'd suffered through Tramp's death by himself the first time. She wasn't going to let him re-live the memory alone even if it meant breaking all the rules in Aunt Cassy's book.

Alexa took off her hat and rose from the log to stand in front of him. Wrapping her arms around his waist, she laid her head against his chest and hugged him to her. "It's all right to cry, Martin. It doesn't make you less a man. It makes you more of a human being." She raised her tear-stained face to his and watched his face knot in emotional anguish. A deep, wrenching sob ripped itself loose from his heart where it had been imprisoned all these years. It brought with it all the lonely hurting and emotional neglect from his childhood . . . the lack of time for affection, the isolation amid numbers of brothers and sisters, the limited understanding of his need for love, and finally the tortured death of the thing he loved most.

Once the dam was broken, Martin crushed her against him and continued to sob harsh cleansing tears. She could feel his hands working, kneading her back until the emotional storm spent itself. At last, he let her go and groped in his pocket for a handkerchief. She found his hand and pulled him down until they sat beside each other on the ground with their backs resting against the log. When he had returned the handkerchief to the pants pocket, she reached over and took his hand again.

"Did you watch Tramp die?"

He nodded. "It was a warm fall night, and I heard him whine underneath the open bedroom window. He hadn't acted that way before so I knew something was wrong. I dressed and tiptoed downstairs."

Alexa could see the muscles working in Martin's jaws. He placed his other hand on top of hers and clasped it close to him.

"When I got to him, his whole body was trembling and he was crying in little yips. He couldn't walk, so I picked him up and carried him over to a vacant lot where his cries of pain wouldn't disturb anyone. Then I sat with him. I didn't know what else to do. He'd drag himself along the ground on his belly trying to ease the pain, then he'd stop and shudder all over. Finally, he grew so weak he just lay with his head in my lap, and I prayed, while we both cried."

Alexa felt his warm tears drop on her hand. She took her handkerchief and gently wiped his cheeks.

"When Tramp had gone, I sat a long time petting him. I couldn't believe my only real friend was dead. Finally, I dug a grave and buried him where he'd died, there in the vacant lot under a big oak tree. I prayed over his grave, and then sat with him until morning."

Shaking again with sobs, Martin took Alexa in his arms as he wept away the last of the too-long harbored grief. Eventually, washed clean of this burden, his breathing returned to normal. He unclasped her and fell back against the log. Seeking and finding her hand, he laced his fingers through hers, closed his eyes, and rested his head on the log. She laid her head on his shoulder, and they quietly sat as the sun passed its zenith and turned the morning to afternoon.

At last, he stirred and looked down at Alexa. "You're very young. Where did you get all that old wisdom?" His eyes, now a soft misty gray, warmed her with their glow. In their depths lay a new peace.

She smiled up at him. "Comes from being a woman."

"Not from any woman I've ever known."

"Have you ever given one a chance to know you?"

"None ever wanted to."

"Sure about that?"

"Very sure."

She had a nearly overwhelming urge to throw her arms around him and hug him, show him how much she cared. But she restrained herself lest he misread the meaning of so rash an act. Besides, she had broken enough rules of decorum for one day.

In an attempt to return to the easy comraderie they had enjoyed earlier, she grabbed at the first thing that crossed her mind. "Do you suppose we'd feel better if we washed our faces in the stream?" she suggested, her voice bright and vigorous.

Without a word, he stood, and pulled her to her feet. Walking to his saddle, he opened one of the bags lashed to the side and took out a towel. "That water runs right off a snow bank. It's going to freeze your freckles," he warned, and flashed her a wide smile that spread creases across his face like pebble-tossed circles over the surface of still water.

"Any chance the freezing would make them drop off?"

"None. Besides I like them. Makes you look less like the perfect doll who arrived in our little valley, and more like a real person." He hung the towel around his neck and knelt beside a quiet pool created where the water ran slow. He reached up a hand to Alexa, and accepting his offer of support, she knelt beside him.

She hadn't taken his warning about the water temperature seriously. However, it took only a few well-placed handfuls to numb both her hands and face and she came up dripping. He met her with the towel and tenderly patted her face and hands dry. Turning, he laid the towel over the log in the sun. "Not smart to pack a wet towel."

Then, he enfolded her in his arms and she clasped her hands around his back. It seemed so natural to stand with him like this—one not leaning on the other, but meeting squarely and equally. She stood, aware of his vitality, and yet he seemed also to recognize and respect her strengths.

At last, she broke the silence between them. "I feel a great desire to pray and give thanks. Will you join me?"

Wordless, they turned and knelt, bowed their heads, and rested their folded hands on the log. "Thank you, Lord, for the peace that has been

73

restored to Martin. Thank you, Lord, for this beautiful world and this perfect spot in it. Thank you for the friendship that Martin and I enjoy. Amen." Alexa sensed that Martin, too, wished to pray and so they continued to kneel.

He cleared his throat, then reached for her hand. With hands joined together, he began, "Lord, I haven't been on my knees as often as I should, but I'd like to change that . . . beginning right now. Thank you for sending Alexa, for I know you did, to cleanse my heart and make it whole again. Thank you for giving me another chance to make something of my life. Amen."

Then they stood and walked together in peace and tranquility through the meadow, letting the serenity of God fill their souls.

At last, Martin broke the silence. " I've told you a great deal about my life. I know scarcely anything about yours."

She smiled into his dappled gray eyes. "I was thinking how similar our childhoods were. I was orphaned at four and went to live with Aunt Cassy who was no relation at all. Her husband was a salesman and away much of the time. She had only boys and was happy to take me. She had always wanted a little girl and I became the pride of her life. I constantly tried to do her bidding for fear she would send me away if I didn't."

He interrupted. "You mean she threatened you."

"She never even hinted at such a thing. I built the whole thing in my mind because I thought I was completely alone in the world. I didn't know about my Uncle Clyde until just a few years ago when he finally tracked me down. Since he left me all this, I'm finally beginning to learn about the real me buried underneath all the layers of right-doing. I fear I may discover a very rebellious soul if today is an example."

He laughed. "You think the world will stop spinning because you refuse to ride sidesaddle and wear a poke bonnet? Well, it won't. And you won't be any less a lady. You're very modestly clad and that Stetson looks far more like a rancher than a bonnet. I, for one, approve heartily"

"And I'm grateful for your support. But this isn't getting me a different horse and a riding lesson. Or do you think Molly has learned her lesson and will be good?"

"She may have learned her lesson from me, but you don't have what it takes yet to convince her. Give yourself a little time, then you can show that mule who's boss. Just promise to let me know, though, the day you decide on the lesson."

"I will." Alexa suddenly felt so full of life she couldn't stand to walk, and so she raced off toward the grazing horses as fast as she could run. Martin, in his heavy boots, came pounding after her, caught up, and ran along side until they arrived at the horses.

Her hair, fallen from its pins, streamed down her back as she leaned against a tree gasping for breath. "I look like a wanton woman and I don't have enough pins left to repair the damage," she said, running fingers through the untamed locks.

"Braid it. You still have a few pins. They'll hold the braids." Martin helped locate the few pins that hadn't fallen out completely as the two of them ran. "Here, hold these," he ordered.

She held out her palm, and he dropped his supply of pins into it.

"Turn around." He spoke softly as he took her by the shoulders and pivoted her until her back was to him.

"What are you doing?"

"Braiding your hair." His voice, smooth and casual, warmed her.

She hadn't had her hair braided since she was a

75

young child. Aunt Cassy said braids were common so Alexa had endured endless nights with her hair rolled up in rags to make curls and then painful hours combing the curls into a proper hairdo.

"This isn't going to be a first-rate job since we don't have a comb or a brush, but at least your hair will be up." He worked silently. She could feel him part the hair with his fingers and work the three strands into a single braid that fell to the middle of her back. "You have beautiful hair, thick and sweet-smelling," he said as he finished pinning the braid around her head. He held her away from him and studied the results. "I'm not crazy about that style. I like the braid just hanging down your back, better."

"Very well, since you're the one who has to look at me, let it hang."

He took out the pins and let the rope of russet hair fall down her back. He reached for her hat and set it carefully on her head. Raising a crooked index finger, he tilted her chin until their eyes met and she stood looking into deep, unfathomable pools of light gray mist. She watched as he slowly bent his face over her. Then, she closed her eyes as she felt his lips move on hers, gentle, sweet-tasting. Felt the slight tickle of his beard on the sensitive skin around her mouth. Felt his breath warm on her cheek. Felt his hand on her cheek as he released her lips and held her from him. She embraced his hand, brought it to her lips, and kissed it. Looking into his eyes she saw tears brimming the edges and felt a rising lump in her throat.

Deciding they had both had enough high emotion for one day, she grasped at any topic that would serve to lighten the mood. "Where did you learn to braid hair?"

He seemed greatly relieved not to be plunged into tears again. "When you had as many little sisters as I did, you learned in a hurry. Keep my skills sharp braiding horses tails."

She moved away and toward the feeding animals. "Speaking of horses, we still haven't solved the problem of a name for your horse."

"How about Alexa in honor of the lady who wanted him to have one?" Martin's eyes danced as he waited for her rebuttal to his ridiculous suggestion.

She determined to surprise him. "That's a very lovely thought, Martin, and I am deeply appreciative of your thoughtfulness. However, I don't think a 'he' would like a girl's name. If you're determined to honor me, how about Alexander? You could call him Alex for short." There, that should hold Martin for a minute or two, she thought smuggly and continued to eye him with her most innocent look.

"You really think so?" Martin didn't sound too enthusiastic over the name.

"Oh, absolutely. That's a fine name for a splendid horse. Think of the strength of Alexander the Great. It's really captured in your horse."

"Weeelll, all right," he said reluctantly. "If you insist."

"Martin, I don't insist," she objected. "That would be conceited on my part, insisting you name your horse after me. I was only attempting to accede to your wishes. Please feel free to change his name. My feelings won't be hurt a bit. Not even a little bit."

"I may be an insensitive male, but I know that to be a bald-faced lie. You'd be mad as a dunked cat, so Alex it is and Alex it shall remain."

"Actually, as I look at him, I'm not sure he's a fine enough horse to carry the name Alex. Alexander was an emperor, and I think your horse is only worth a king's name. How does King strike you?"

"You'd settle for King and not be mad?"

"Certainly. There's nothing worse than an animal with a name he can't live up to. I feel much better about the name King."

"So do I," Martin said emphatically.

"It's decided then. Come on, King, start getting used to your name," she said as she found a rock and led him to it. Martin stayed near as she climbed up the rock, and slid easily onto King's back.

Molly's memory wasn't too long, and she tried to trot with Martin again. However, he took her on one more gallop down the trail, and when she returned she walked, chastened and proper, behind Alexa and King.

Long shadows slanted across the fenced meadow as Alexa and Martin rode side-by-side. "I'm afraid it's a little late to try to teach me to ride. What do you think?" she asked.

He examined her face carefully. "I don't think you're too old to learn to ride. People older than you do it all the time."

She looked at his poker face and broke into a laugh. "You know what I mean."

He grinned. "I don't want to agree with you because I don't want a special day to end, but unfortunately, you're right. Got a day full of plans for tomorrow?"

"Nothing that can't wait."

"Good. I'll get the crew going and be over. I planned to scout timber this week. You can go with me."

He didn't leave her weak, trembling, giddy the way David did, but she enjoyed being with Martin. "I'd like that. Shall I have Emmie prepare a lunch?"

"Only as long as it's packed with delicacies, and tasty little surprises to whet the jaded appetite." They arrived at the barn, and he helped her down from King and began to change saddles.

"Don't want much, do you?"

"You obviously haven't tasted the cuisine of a logging camp or you wouldn't ask." He tightened the girth around King's belly and grasping the saddle horn, pulled and pushed the saddle to see how it held.

Satisfied, he dropped the stirrup into place and patted King's rump.

"I haven't been invited."

He looked surprised. "You mean you'd come?"

"Is there a reason I shouldn't?"

"No. It's just so few ladies find a lumber camp with its rowdy men socially acceptable. But then . . . I keep forgetting you're no lady."

She folded her arms across her chest and stamped her black leather booted foot. "Martin Taylor!"

He laughed, low and easy as he wrapped his arms around her rigid shoulders. "I love it when you get your dander up. Your eyes turn to glittering ice crystals and your jaw sets like granite. You're one dandy woman, Alexa Spence. Real and honest as buttermilk."

She smiled at him, but kept her arms folded. "You make it terribly difficult to be angry."

"I try," he answered, breezily. Looking at the lowering sun, he said, "Get on King, and I'll take you to the house."

Alexa looked at him. "Ride double?"

He settled easily into the saddle and kicked his foot out of the stirrup. "Stand on the stump and I'll help you swing up behind me."

She did as he directed and found it wasn't as hard as it looked. Once on the horse's back and seated on the skirt of the saddle, she grabbed the back of the saddle seat to hold on to. Martin sat back firmly in the saddle and pinned her fingers tight. She felt the blood rush into her face. Worse, she didn't know what to do. What was he thinking, for he surely could feel her hands? What would she think if she moved them? She saw his shoulders begin to shake as he cleared his throat.

"Maybe you could hold on better if you put your hands around my waist."

He leaned forward enough to release her fingers and

after he had settled back, she slid her arms around him. She tried very hard to keep some distance between them, but he was so large and her arms so short, it was impossible. She ended up leaning firmly against him, her cheek against his back.

"That's better," was all he said.

She wondered if this would become a great laugh among the loggers back at the camp. Then she knew he wouldn't share it, anymore than he would the rest of the things that had passed between them this day— this very special day in which they had both moved a bit closer to accepting their pasts.

CHAPTER 7

ALEXA ROSE EARLY AND RUSHED to look out the window. The sky was still a creamy blue along the rim of the mountains as the not yet risen sun diluted an unmarred sky. Martin hadn't said what time he would come for her and she wanted to be ready. This wasn't a day to miss a minute of. *Thank you, God, for another perfect day,* she prayed. *And thank you for the friendship of Martin Taylor. I've never met anyone like him. He doesn't make me all shivery like David does, but he's wonderful to be with and makes me feel I can grow and learn to be myself. Please help him, Lord, to accept himself as the fine person he is. And help me to know how to help Emmie. She's keeping deep secrets and hurts she isn't sharing. Amen.*

After her morning Bible reading and quiet time, Alexa dressed and went into the kitchen where Emmie was busy making breakfast. "Good morning. Anything I can do to help?" she asked.

Emmie gave her a casual glance that turned into a disapproving glare. "You going to wear that heathen costume this morning?" she complained.

"This morning and the rest of the day. And as soon as I can get to town, I'm going to buy some more material and make others. I'll probably wear this or another costume like it most of the time this whole summer," Alexa shot back, keeping her voice even but determined.

"It don't bother you none what the neighbors'll think?"

"Emmie, I don't intend to prance into town dressed like this or go out calling. This skirt is for my own comfort when riding here on the ranch, nothing more."

Emmie's answering "Hummph" let Alexa know she hadn't convinced Emmie of a thing. It didn't matter, though. She liked the feel of the skirt and she planned to wear it.

"Sit down and eat," Emmie ordered and placed a platter of ham and eggs on the table. "The men'll be here in a minute for theirs."

"Good. I need to talk with them," Alexa said as she helped herself to fried eggs fresh from Jake's chickens.

As if they had heard Emmie, the two hands stomped their boots free of dust on the porch and came in through the kitchen. They stopped short when they saw Alexa sitting at the breakfast table. It apparently still bothered them to eat with her.

"Come on and sit down," Alexa invited. "I need some information and advice from you gentlemen. This morning seemed a good time to get it before you're gone and busy."

Bill and Jake hung their hats on the coat rack in the corner and smoothed their hair as they walked to the table. Jake didn't have any problem, for he had only a salt and pepper fringe around a scrubbed bald head. Bill's was another matter, however. He had a fine head of wiry brown hair that refused to be tamed under anything less than his hat.

They pulled up chairs at the far end of the table, leaving a considerable distance between themselves and Alexa. She felt like a reigning potentate from her place at the head of the table, but it was useless to ask them to move closer. They had shut up like clams, and she would not get a word out of either of them.

"How are things with the cattle?" she asked Bill.

"A real good crop of spring calves now I got 'em rounded up and moved where I could count 'em. Need to get 'em branded before they go on the public range, though.

"What do you need to do that?"

"A couple more hands. Jake can tend the fire. Get 'em in. Won't take more'n two, maybe three days." Bill continued to eat, not letting the conversation interfere with his meal.

Apparently the two had talked this over earlier for Jake nodded his agreement.

"You'll need a cook for the bunkhouse, then," she said.

"Cookin' ain't a full-time job for a crew that size. Get three hands. One can cook and work, too" Bill said.

"Very well. Will you see to it?"

"Beggin' your pardon, ma'am, but I already have."

Alexa leaned forward, her forearms resting on the table. "Bill, I don't intend faulting you for your actions. You know what needs doing and I don't. In the future, though, I feel we need to talk each day about the ranch. You can teach me what running a ranch takes. I want to know."

Bill's face turned red. Alexa couldn't tell if it was from her mild reprimand over his taking actions not discussed with her, or if he didn't think a woman had any place in the man's world of ranching. She didn't much care. This was her ranch and she was going to learn about it, from the finances that the banker in town had explained to her, down to the smallest detail of the working day.

"When do you plan to cut the meadow hay?" she asked, changing the subject.

"Middle of July. Looks like a good crop this year." There seemed to be a new respect in Bill's voice. "We'll need extra help then, too."

"Can you keep the men you hire for branding busy until then? Seems a shame to find some good men and then have to hunt for more in a month."

"Got a lot of fence needs fencing. 'Specially over in the woods between us and the loggin' outfit."

"Mr. Taylor assured me he had taken care of that section. Has he not done as he said?"

"It's not that he ain't done anything. Loggers don't fix fences. They just prop 'em up."

"You're saying it's not a permanent repair job."

"Yes'm."

"Very well, then. Let's keep the branding crew if you can find enough for them to do. Now, what time of day is most convenient for you to inform me of the day's accomplishments and what work will need to be done in the future?"

Bill's whole posture altered during this exchange with Alexa. He sat straighter in his chair and gave her his full attention. His voice lost its slightly patronizing edge, and he spoke as employee to employer. "Evenin's when we get through supper, if that's agreeable with you."

"Fine." Alexa turned to Jake. "Are you able to milk a cow?"

He looked startled, then brought up his hands and flexed the thick, calloused fingers. "I could probably get the milk out."

"You don't have arthritis in your hands?"

"No, ma'am. Just ma'knees and most days its not too bad. Gets worse with the cold and damp."

"Would you object to the added chore of milking a cow? I am used to fresh milk and dairy products. Emmie knows how to make cheese and I understand

84

berry season isn't too far away. Cream would turn them into a great treat."

"When you point out all the virtues, I'd be a sorry man to refuse. Gotta tell you, though, been trying for years to sell Clyde on getting a cow. He always felt that was beneath a rancher. Warn't no dairy herd gonna eat up his meadow, he'd say."

My goodness, Alexa thought, *Jake hadn't spoken that many words total to her since she came.* "If he felt that way, how do you happen to have chickens. Doesn't seem he'd have wanted them around either."

Jake's face creased with a little smile accompanied by a cracked chuckle. "I bought me a couple little hens and kept 'em real quiet while Clyde enjoyed fresh eggs for breakfast. By the time he found the hens, he was hooked. Had chickens ever since."

Alexa and Bill laughed aloud and Jake looked proud of himself. "You're a sneaky fellow. Bill, we'd better watch out for him," Alexa said.

Bill gave Jake a fond look. "That man can have anything I have if he gets me thick fresh cream for my coffee."

"And I'll be eternally thankful if I can have some fresh cold milk and butter."

"I'll find us a cow, new freshened. Today if I can."

"Today would be good, because I'll have that branding crew hired and ready to work by Friday," Bill reminded him.

Alexa, scarcely able to contain her delight at the change in the men's attitude toward her, pushed back her chair, indicating they were free to leave. "I don't believe we'll need to talk this evening, do you?" she said to Bill as the men stood.

"Not unless something unexpected comes up. I'll come to you anytime, in that case."

"Thank you, both, very much. I'll alert Emmie to be prepared to take care of the milk, Jake, and tomorrow I'll stock the bunkhouse with food."

As Alexa stacked the dishes and cleaned off the table, she could hear Emmie in the kitchen preparing the basket lunch. She had not known how to take Martin's statement concerning logging camp food, but she quoted his comments about delicacies to Emmie. She apparently knew more than Alexa for she started planning immediately how to produce tasty delights to tease Martin's palate.

Emmie set the picnic basket in the buttery to stay cool and went on about her work. Alexa spent the time waiting for Martin by sewing straps to her hat, so she could slip it off her head and still keep track of it. She had no intention of wearing it semi-permanently attached as did the men, only doffing it briefly in the presence of a lady and removing it the last thing before their heads touched the pillow at night.

It was shortly before ten when Martin rode up and tied his horse to the new hitching post. Alexa debated if she should wait until he knocked, but decided that was for beaux coming to call. Martin certainly didn't fit in that category so she ran out to meet him.

"Good morning," she called as he finished tying King.

"'Morning. See King's had his last nibble of your hollihocks," Martin said as he patted the hitching post.

"I hope so. He made a real meal the last time he was here." She pointed to a section of well-cropped flowers struggling with new growth.

Martin gave the plants a cursory glance as he walked up the steps to join her. "Ready?"

"As soon as I get my hat and gloves, and the lunch basket."

"Lunch basket! You mean 'basket' as in . . . big basket?" He made a shape in the air with his hands approximately the size of the one Emmie had packed.

"Yes," she said, puzzled at his emphasis.

"Have you thought how you're going to transport it? Pack mule, maybe?"

She hadn't thought and Emmie obviously hadn't either. She looked at him, speechless.

"Then, may I suggest we find you a horse, grab a couple of quick sandwiches for the saddle bags, and save the basket until we get back. Maybe take it down by the creek for our supper?" He cocked his head and waited for her decision.

She smiled and nodded. "Sounds like a most diplomatic solution. However, let's prepare the food and take it to the barn with us."

"Fine with me," he said and opened the door for her to enter the house.

Emmie was out in the garden so Alexa prepared cold sliced beef sandwiches and some oatmeal and raisin cookies, wrapped them in paper and tied the packages with string. Martin lounged against the corner of one of the cupboards, watching her and munching on cookies while he waited.

"You look right at home in the kitchen," he commented.

"I've spent a lot of time in one, but thanks to Emmie or someone like her, I don't plan to in the future." Alexa spoke most emphatically, not leaving any doubt as to her new role.

"Well, then Rancher Spence, let's be on our way."

They went out the kitchen door and walked along the porch to where King stood, patiently waiting. Martin packed their noon meal in his saddle bag, unfastened the reins, and swung into the saddle. Riding King to the foot of the steps where Alexa waited, he stretched out his hand. "Ready?" he asked, his eyes dancing as he looked at her.

She knew what he was thinking and couldn't help blushing. All she did was nod, though. The blush was all the recognition he was going to get of the saddle seat incident last night. She placed her foot in the stirrup and she could feel the strength in his hand and arm as he swept her up behind him. This time he didn't let go of her hand so quickly, and she adjusted her balance before wrapping her arms around his waist.

He turned his head and squinted over his shoulder at her. "Settled?"

"Settled."

She looked down and noticed he gave King the signal to start with a slight pressure of his legs. The horse moved off at the comfortable walk she had enjoyed yesterday. She could have relaxed her grip around Martin and been perfectly safe, but there was a feeling of strength and confidence she gained from the close contact.

Again she watched him signal King with his legs and the horse stopped almost instantly. Martin brought his right leg out of the stirrup, over the front of the saddle, and slid to the ground. He raised his arms to take her from the horse and she beheld his loving face. The soft, gentle look she saw there surprised her. The suspicious narrowing of his eyes and slightly cynical twist to the mouth were gone, replaced by wide-open frankness framed by thick black eyelashes.

"Martin Taylor, it's not fair for a man to have such beautiful long eyelashes. I know women who would kill for lashes like those," she said as she leaned over and placed her hands on his shoulders. His only answer was to smile, wide and relaxed, and she felt his hands close around her waist as he lifted her from King's back.

Her feet securely on the ground, Alexa started to step away, but he continued his grip on her waist. She tipped her face up and met dancing gray eyes. He looked her face over thoroughly. "I'm relieved to see I have no worry in your presence. Your lashes are at least as long as mine. They don't look it, though, because they are lighter auburn at the tips." He took her chin in his hand and moved her head from side to side. "Don't seem to have grown any new freckles since yesterday."

"How could you possibly tell? My face is one continuous freckle."

"I know, but I can tell. Did you have so many when you arrived? I don't seem to remember them."

"By using all manner of creams and a bit of powder, I fooled nearly everyone into believing I had a flawless complexion. It was a lot of work and sacrifice to keep up the masquerade. I'm not willing any more. He who doesn't like my freckles, doesn't like me."

He laughed and hugged her to himself. "I like all of you very much."

They stepped apart and after procurring a halter and some oats, went to select Alexa a horse. They found Jake in the field where the horses were grazing, saddling his horse.

"'Morning, Jake," Martin said. "I've been keeping my eye out for you. You know this stock better than anyone. Which would be a good horse for Miss Alexa?"

Jake returned Martin's greeting with a black glare, completely unlike the warm cooperation he had shown around David. She wondered why and made a mental note to ask him about it when they were alone.

Jake turned to her. "Didn't like Molly, huh?"

"She was wonderful in the corral and around the barn yard. On the trail, it was a different story."

"She needs a strong hand to show her who's boss. Then, she'll be a good horse again," Jake answered.

Alexa thought it wise not to tell him about Martin's already having given Molly her first lessons. "I want a horse with a smooth gait, and one who will mind," she said.

"Got plenty here with a good gait, but ain't no horse gonna mind 'til they know you're boss," Jake informed her.

Rather like a couple of hands I know, Alexa thought. "That's the lesson I hope to learn today," was all she said.

"Well, then. That red roan gelding over there is as good a horse as there is. A might frisky. Ain't been rode this spring. Get him wore down, and he'll be fine."

While she and Jake talked, Martin snared the horse and brought him to her. "Horse got a name?" he asked Jake.

Alexa's heart leaped at the question. *Thank you, Lord, for bringing Martin so far from his hurtful past, so quickly.*

"I call him Red," Jake answered brusquely before he mounted his horse. Turning to Alexa, he said, "I'm off to see about a cow."

She wished him good luck, and he rode off toward town.

She started to take the oat bucket from Martin, but he handed her the halter rope instead. "He's your horse. Better start right now to let him know that. Jake was right when he said the best horse can be rotten if he finds out he's the boss and not you."

Martin handed her the halter rope and walked beside her as she led Red along. He made no further mention of Jake, but was sure he had noticed Jake's cool treatment. Apparently he didn't plan to make any more of it. David's hostility toward Martin, and now Jake's, continued to puzzle her and she fretted over it as they walked back to the barn. What was he doing that would make two such different men react in such a similar way.

When they arrived at the barn, Martin checked Red's feet. "Jake does a good shoeing job," he said, then disappeared into the barn to choose a saddle and bring it out. "This is a twenty-five pound saddle, but can't find one any lighter that's fit to ride. And, the seat's higher in the back than most. It'll give you good support."

"I'm much more interested in the saddle horn. I want something to grip if things start to get out of hand," she said, eyeing the leather-wrapped flat-topped knob.

"Got a good horn," he said, grinning at her.

Red was a good-sized horse so she led him over to the stump. Martin said nothing as Alexa took the saddle blanket from him and laid it over Red's back and smoothed out the wrinkles. She hefted the saddle. For being a fourth of her weight, it wasn't as bad as she had expected. It was bulky and awkward to handle, but she grabbed it, front and back. Stepping up on the stump, she gave it a swing and plumped it down squarely in the middle of Red's back.

"Not bad," Martin commented.

"What do you mean, 'not bad'? That was perfect," Alexa announced, pleased with herself for having succeeded on the first try. She set about tightening the double cinches while Martin watched every move she made. She finished the final knot and gave Red a slap on the rump as she had seen Jake do.

Martin squinted at her from under the wide brim of his hat. "Where'd you learn to saddle a horse?"

His voice held an astonishment that pleased Alexa no end. "I could lie and tell you I've been doing it for years, or say that Jake taught me yesterday."

"He did a good job teaching you."

"On the contrary," she retorted as she slipped the bit into Red's mouth. "I did a great job of learning."

"A little success went right to your head, I see," he commented dryly, and double checked the tightness of her saddle.

She laughed, slightly embarrassed. "I received so little praise from Aunt Cassy, no matter how hard I tried to accomplish something, that I took to praising myself silently. Then I didn't feel so bad at not achieving to her expectations. My little pat on the back slipped out. You weren't supposed to hear it."

He put his arm around her shoulder and hugged her to him. "We both had it kinda rough, didn't we?"

"We did, but look at the character it developed."

"Did you say . . . characters?"

They both laughed, leaned a moment together as another strand was added to the bond between them, then they separated to mount their horses.

"I'll set your stirrup length after you get on," he said.

The stirrups were so long, she had a little trouble swinging into the saddle. Then she hooked her left leg around the horn while he re-laced the stirrup. Shortening stirrups was a tedious job and when it was finished, the saddle would become hers by virtue of the stirrup length.

At last, Martin was satisfied. "Stand in 'em," he ordered.

"You mean, literally?"

"I do."

She put the stirrups on the balls of her feet and stood. She cleared the saddle seat by about three inches.

"You need to ride with your feet like they are now. Also, if we move faster than a walk you can do what's called posting. You stand and move with the gait of the horse," he instructed.

"You don't ride that way," she objected.

"I've also been riding for years."

"Did you start by riding that way?"

"No," he confessed.

"Then, I don't intend to either," she announced and sat back on the seat.

"You are one stubborn woman, Alexa Spence." But admiration rang in his voice, and she took his remark as a compliment. "I know you don't want to ride around the corral today, but Red's been roaming all spring. It's always wise to test your horse before you get too far from home. Check first to see if he'll rein from the neck."

She laid the rein against his neck and he turned his head the opposite way.

"Good. Now, get him started."

She remembered the way Martin signaled King, and tightened her knees against Red's side. He moved into a brisk walk. She reined his neck and he turned back. Pressing her knees into his sides, he stopped. She reached down and patted his neck. "You are going to be a fine horse."

Martin rode up beside her and showed her how to hold the reins. She slipped the reins between her fingers as he demonstrated, and started off at a brisk trot. She was bouncing all over the place again, and she reined Red to a stop.

"That, my dear, is why you post when you can't sit the saddle," he said quietly.

"You're sitting your saddle and you're not posting. What are you doing differently?" she demanded to know.

"I'm not trotting my horse, for one thing. I don't care a lot about riding that gait. If you don't either, move him into a canter. It's a bit faster and a lot smoother. Then, sit back firm in the saddle and relax. Get the feel of your horse and go with it."

They started again and she moved Red quickly into the canter. Martin was right. This was a lovely gait and she concentrated on doing as he had instructed. She pushed firmly into the saddle and tried to go with the horse. Soon, she had the feel of him and urged him into a gallop. It was stimulating to feel Red's powerful rippling muscles propelling her forward at such a rate. The wind rushed against her face and through her hair as she flew along. She felt transported to another place and time. A place where nothing could suppress her great spirit and it rose, free at last, to fill all space and time in the enchanted land. Riding horseback was the grandest thing she had ever done.

CHAPTER 8

"You bin hunched over them ledgers all morning. It's time you took a stretch," Emmie ordered, as she entered Alexa's bedroom and set a small plate of cookies and a glass of milk on the rolltop desk next to her. "You're gonna be so stiff from your ride yesterday, you won't move normal for a week."

"You're too late. I didn't know I had so many different muscles in my body, and everyone of them objecting to their treatment," Alexa said, bracing her hands on top of the desk and pushing herself to a standing position.

Emmie sniffed and retreated to the doorway. "I don't wonder, galloping around like a wild schoolboy. You'll get no sympathy from me."

Alexa gritted her teeth and turned to walk toward Emmie. She bit back the moan that threatened to escape as the abused and over-worked muscles screamed their distress at the treatment they'd received. "How long am I going to be like this?" she asked when she could speak.

"A good long time if you don't get some exercise," Emmie said.

Alexa took a step and gasped at the amount of pain it caused. "Exercise! I can hardly move."

Emmie shrugged. "Up to you. You're the boss. Got plenty of people to wait on you until you recover." She moved toward the bed with its tall handcarved, oak headboard. "Want me to turn your covers down?"

Alexa eyed the bed with longing. She knew Emmie was right. If she crawled between the covers of the inviting feather bed, she would probably turn into a stick of wood and never walk again, much less get on a horse. "What sort of exercise do you recommend?"

"While it will pain you greatly at first, the best kind is getting back on that horse." Emmie stood unbending, her arms folded across her body, allowing no pity for Alexa to escape. "Might try the sidesaddle this time," she needled.

That did it. "Never!" Alexa stormed. "I'll ride my western saddle until I die or it kills me. At the moment either option seems imminent and can't occur too soon." Her storm ended in a pitiful whimper.

Emmie dropped her arms and peered closely into Alexa's face. "Face looks a mite pale and pinched. Hurt that bad?"

Alexa drew a deep, rugged breath. "Hurts worse," she said as she hobbled slowly toward the door, groaning inwardly with each step.

In the next moment, Emmie's arm descended around Alexa's shoulder and she mopped the perspiration beading on Alexa's upper lip and forehead as she continued the tortuous way down the hall.

"I'll make you some catnip tea. Help the pain a bit, but the only real cure is to get back on your horse."

At the thought of hauling herself on top of Red, Alexa could hardly keep back the tears. In fact, the thought of walking to the barn and then out to catch him in the pasture was enough to make her whole body scream.

Alexa eased into a chair and watched Emmie dip water from the bucket standing near the sink into a small tin copper-bottomed tea kettle and set it on the stove. "Was your day yesterday worth this?" she asked as she prepared the herbs in a cup.

For the first time this morning, Alexa smiled. "Yes, Emmie, it most definitely was. We rode through the big timber at the back of my place. I've never seen trees like that. Cedars a thousand years old, hemlock, and Douglas fir. And acres of white pine. The ground underneath was covered with different types of ferns growing thick and high." She paused in reflection before continuing. "There was an undisturbed solitude that made one feel holy." Nodding slowly, she concluded, "Yes, it truly was worth today's misery."

"Glad it makes your pain bearable. Bin a shame to suffer for nothing." Emmie set the teacup in front of her. "Let it steep awhile longer 'fore you drink it."

"I didn't tell you, but Martin said you can come cook for his crew any time. In fact, he might even try to hire you away from me."

Emmie, standing at the stove, looked back over her shoulder disapprovingly at Alexa. "I may be desperate someday, but not that desperate. Cooking for a bawdy logging crew is more'n even I can stomach."

"Are they that bad?" Alexa tried to imagine Martin, strong and determined when the occasion called for it, but gentle and tender underneath, behaving as she had heard loggers did—then drinking and womanizing his money away after a long day's work.

"Worse!" and she refused to discuss the subject further.

Alexa drank her tea and, deciding to take Emmie's advice, put on her hat and gloves and hobbled to the barn. The walk, slow and pain-wracked, took a great deal of determination. By the time she caught Red and saddled him, she wondered if Emmie wasn't right and she had lost any good sense she had ever had.

Standing on the stump, she slipped her foot in the stirrup and started to swing her right leg over the horse. The pain that shot through her brought tears and a cry she couldn't contain. As she sat astride Red trying to regain a bit of composure, Jake came hurrying out of the barn.

"You all right, Ma'am?" he asked, worry creasing his forehead above a hawklike nose and faded blue eyes.

"I'm not, but there's nothing you can do about it," she said, her voice still trembling slightly from the effect of the stabbing pains.

A smile of understanding crossed Jake's face replacing the tense concern. "Overdid the riding a mite yesterday?"

"You're welcome to call it 'a mite'. I'd refer to it as greatly overdone. Emmie, however, tells me this is the best way to undo the damage." Alexa shifted her position in the saddle in an attempt to relieve the throbbing ache.

"She's right. Ride awhile, then get off and walk. Take you about a week to work all the stiffness out."

"A week! Are you serious?"

"Won't hurt like it does now. Even be better by this afternoon if you'll do what I say. You'll feel less and less sore each day. Be stiff when you get out of bed in the morning, for a spell, but a few hours in the saddle'll ease it right away. But here I stand ajawin', takin' up yer ridin' time."

He whacked Red across the rump and Alexa trotted out of the barnyard. She immediately slowed Red to a walk, regained her breath, and rode off toward the woods.

Alexa found Emmie bent nearly double with her head inside a cupboard when she returned late in the afternoon. Emmie straightened quickly at the sounds of Alexa opening the door and crossed to her immediately. "Land, girl, I didn't mean you was to

97

put in another full day on the back of that horse," she said as Alexa limped through the kitchen door. "You ain't even had a bit to eat since breakfast."

"I'm not hungry," Alexa said.

"I got some water hot in the bath. A good soak should relax you, then some food and a nap. Make you feel a heap better." All the while she talked, Emmie led Alexa across the hall to the bathroom.

While Alexa removed her clothes, Emmie prepared the bath. "You get in and heat it up gradual. Make it as hot as you can stand."

After Emmie left, Alexa hung her white muslin robe on the back of the door and stepped into the warm water. She poured in hot water until she felt sure she would come out boiled, and lay back to soak. She must have dozed off, for the timid knock on the door startled her.

"You still in there?" Emmie said softly.

"Yes, Emmie, but I'm getting out right now."

"There's a cowhand here from Mr. Hornbeck's ranch. He's got a letter for you."

Alexa's heart took a great leap. David! "I'll be decent in a minute," she answered and, ignoring the still stiff muscles, vigorously toweled herself dry. Wrapping up in the robe, she opened the door slightly.

Emmie handed Alexa the letter through the crack. "He's waiting for an answer," Emmie said.

"Thank you. I'll hurry." Alexa tore open the heavy cream colored envelope and removed the letter. She read the well-formed masculine script.

Dear Alexa,

If it is agreeable, I would very much like to come calling this evening about eight. I find I am unable to wait to see you until Mother comes to visit on Tuesday.

Your obedient servant,

David Hornbeck

Alexa rushed to her roll-top desk near the front door of the bedroom, praying all the while that her hand would stop shaking enough to answer his request properly. She found some suitable white linen paper trimmed with a small gold border and quickly assured David that she would be delighted to have him call this evening. Folding it, she slipped the note into a matching envelope and sealed it.

Alexa opened the door enough to hand Emmie the letter.

Dashing back to the bathroom, she knelt beside the tub and poured water through her hair to wet it.

"Child, what are you doing in there?" Emmie called through the door.

"Washing my hair." Keeping her eyes squeezed shut against the dripping water, Alexa fumbled for the towel.

"Washing your hair! With that stock you have, it'll never be dry by midnight, much less before Mister David comes." Emmie sounded thoroughly vexed.

Alexa wrapped her head in a towel, turban-style, and rushed across the hall into the kitchen where Emmie had just finished setting out a meal. "You didn't have to prepare something special for me. I could have waited until supper," Alexa objected.

"I suppose you could have, but you need a nap and time to dress proper for Mr. David. And now, time to dry and curl your hair." Emmie gave Alexa a pinch-mouthed look of disapproval. "Wait for supper and you'll be rushed." Emmie set the bowl of stew in front of Alexa as she sat at the small work table in the kitchen.

Alexa stared up at Emmie. "How did you know what was in the letter?"

Emmie jammed her hands into her apron pockets and rocked back slightly on her heels, a smug look spread all over her face. "It don't take a lot to guess. Way that young fella looks at you is hint enough.

Knew he'd never be able to go 'til Tuesday without seein' ya. And if he hadn't come here, I'm guessing you'd a figured a way to go there."

"Emmie!" Alexa protested, shock at the suggestion vibrating through her voice. "I would never do such a thing."

"We won't know, will we? Since Mr. Hornbeck's so obliging and saved you the trouble of cooking up a scheme."

Before Alexa could raise further objections, Emmie disappeared through the door. It pained Alexa to admit it, but Emmie was right. She had been thinking about David all afternoon and wondering if she was going to be able to go until Tuesday without seeing him.

Her stew finished, she walked to her bedroom, noting as she went how much less stiff and sore she was. Thank goodness for people like Emmie and Jake. Emmie had the bed turned down and Alexa longed to slide between the cool white sheets. But she had to dry her hair first.

Alexa went out on the porch where the sun and warm breeze would dry her hair quickly. Then she braided the rust-colored tresses loosely in single rope down her back, which reminded her of Martin's gentle touch. Through a drowsy fog, she tried to imagine David Hornbeck braiding a woman's hair, but she couldn't conjure up a picture of him performing such a service. Sometime during this musing, she sank into a renewing sleep and dreamed that David read her poetry while Martin braided her hair.

A soft tapping on her door wakened Alexa. "Yes," she answered, her voice filled with sleep.

"Time to wake up if you don't want to hurry in your preparations for Mister David," Emmie said.

"Thanks, Emmie." Alexa rolled over slowly and found as she moved, the tightness in her muscles was much improved.

Throwing back the covers to let the bed air, she stood and did some slow stretching moves. It was truly amazing how well she felt. She crossed the royal blue, flowered carpet to the large wardrobe standing against the bathroom. Opening it, she removed several dresses, but decided they were too formal. She didn't want to appear too eager so she chose a heliotrope, chambray shirtwaist with large bishop sleeves and a double ruffle down the front and back. The heat of the day seemed to be lingering, so she decided on a black poplin skirt with four inch knife pleats around the bottom. The three rows of white braid trimmed the pleats.

Over her white muslin drawers and chemise, she placed a proper corset. Just as she prepared to call Emmie, a knock sounded at the door. "You need me to help you lace your corset?"

"Come in. I would swear you have a gift. I was just going to call you," Alexa said.

"I'm glad to see you're going to look like a lady again," was Emmie's only comment as she tightened the corset laces.

"Oh, Emmie, that hurts! Please don't lace me so tight."

However, Emmie ignored Alexa's complaints and continued to cinch her tightly into the steel ribbed, satin covered undergarment. "You been running loose too long. You'll forget how a lady dresses," Emmie scolded. "Where's your corset cover and underskirt?"

Alexa nodded toward the oak dresser. "Middle drawer."

Emmie chose a set and helped Alexa slip them on, tying and buttoning them. "You do have dainty garments," she said wistfully as she eyed the luxurious lace trimmings at the bottom of the skirt and around the neck of the corset cover.

"With your first pay, you should buy some trim and cambric and we'll make you some," Alexa suggested.

"That would be nice. Luke'd like that a lot."

"And how will Luke know what kind of underthings you're wearing?"

Emmie looked a bit flustered and her face turned a bright pink. "I write him," she confessed. "He wants to know everything about me, he says. Wants me to tell him little personal things. Says it don't make jail so hard if I do."

Alexa slipped into a pair of black low-cut shoes and then put on her shirtwaist and skirt. She stood admiring herself in the mirror.

"Heliotrope brings out the color of your eyes," Emmie remarked. "Now, if you'll set down, I'll twist up your hair." Armed with brush, comb, and hair pins, she soon had Alexa's hair combed into bangs in the front while the rest was curled and pinned securely high on her head. Emmie stepped back to admire her work. "You look like a real lady. Now mind your manners and you'll fool Mister David completely," she said dryly.

Alexa fastened her timepiece with its elaborately engraved gold case around her neck and inspected the time. It was ten minutes to eight. She checked the turned down collar of her shirtwaist and ran her hand up the back of her head. Everything seemed to be in order. Looking in the mirror, she gave her cheeks a quick pinch to bring up a bit more color. Dabbing a few drops of perfume on her wrists and handkerchief, she mentally declared herself ready to receive Mr. David Hornbeck.

CHAPTER 9

ALEXA STEPPED FROM THE BEDROOM and crossed the hall to the parlor. Emmie had lit the lamps, and their soft light gave the room a serene glow until it reached the chandelier. There it drew life from the multi-faceted crystals and sparkled and danced about the room like a flirtatious debutante. Alexa busied herself fluffing the pillows on the couch and re-arranging them in an attempt to ease her nervousness. The other times she and David had spent alone had been informal, but this was different. It was a formal call, and she knew he expected her to act the part. Lost in her thoughts and fears, she jumped as the clock struck eight. With hands grown cold under the tension, she flipped open the cover on her timepiece. The two clocks agreed. She wanted desperately to lift the curtain and peer out, but manners forbade. If David should be arriving and see her, he could easily conclude she awaited his arrival with great eagerness. While she did, it would be gauche for her to give such a broad hint.

Looking about for something to occupy herself

while she waited, she noticed a thin book lying on a lamp table. Picking up the leather-bound volume of Elizabeth Barrett Browning's poetry, Alexa perched on a small, maroon velvet chair facing the door. Taking great care, she spread her skirts and placed her feet flat on the floor with the heel of one foot nestled in the arch of the other. Icy fingers opened the book cover and turned the pages. Her eyes briefly scanned the pages until she came to Sonnet 43. Here it seemed was what she had unconsciously been searching out. "How do I love thee? Let me count the ways . . ." Although attempting to read, her eyes refused to focus further on the words. David's face replaced the print, and she became lost in the remembrance of his kiss and the imprint of his lips in the palm of her hand.

The knock on the front door startled her. She was so adrift in her memories, she had even failed to hear the hoofbeats of his horse. Careful to return the volume to its place, she stood, smoothing the gored skirt over firm hips. Reassured that everything was in order, she proceeded to the front door, taking the small quick steps society proclaimed most ladylike.

Before opening the door, she took a deep breath to calm herself. If thoughts of David could turn her into a witless ninny, she didn't dare think what actually seeing him might do. She let her hand run one last check on her hair. Why was she stalling? Was she afraid he wasn't so wonderful as she remembered? Could that be it? Would she rather have her memories than face the real man? *Alexa, open that door before he turns around and leaves.*

Straightening her shoulders and lifting her chin, Alexa grabbed the doorknob and jerked open the door. Leaning casually against the frame, David stood grinning at her. "I began to wonder if you'd received my letter. Thought maybe my cowhand had returned with a forgery."

His voice flowed over her like warm honey and she felt her knees grow watery with the realness of him. She needn't have worried about his looks. He was even more handsome than she remembered. She found everything about him appealing — from the dark brown hat sitting low over his eyes, to the bronze-tanned skin pulled taut across his high cheek bones, his flawless mustache, and the full, softly smiling, lips.

Beaming him a smile of welcome because she felt unable to trust her voice, she stepped back into the hall and gestured for him to enter. The effects of the languid movement of his arm as he removed his hat, the effortless flow of his body as he pushed away from his position against the door jamb and stepped into the hallway, left her straining for breath. His eyes never left her, but moved unhurriedly over her face, stopped at each feature as though memorizing its quality and placement, lingered on her mouth and grew misty at the memories.

Emmie had laced her corset impossibly tight. Alexa decided this was the cause of her breathing trouble.

"I'm pleased you were free to receive me this evening," he said at last, his voice, a smooth cultivated baritone without a trace of western twang.

"I'm delighted that you were free to come," she answered in a voice breathless with anticipation.

His cerulian eyes narrowed slightly and he ran a finger around the celuloid turn-down collar. "I wasn't free," he said, his eyes leaving her face and traveling slowly, taking time to absorb each detail of her throat, the ruffled shirtwaist, the tiny waist corseted to an enviable eighteen inches. "I couldn't stand not seeing you until Tuesday."

His words, spoken soft and intimate against her cheek as he took her hand and tucked it into the bend of her arm, scrambled her senses badly and only by using the greatest determination was she able to force herself to respond in a way resembling proper behavior.

"Tuesday is a long way off," she agreed as they strolled into the parlor.

Sitting on the couch, he took her hand from his arm and held it in his firm grasp, thus making sure they sat close together. She could feel him next to her, feel the hard muscles of his arm flex through his wool tweed suit jacket as her arm lay against his. He laid his hat on the couch and turned to look at her.

Running a finger over her face, he said, "I hope you'll forgive me, but I don't seem to remember so many freckles. They make the blue of your eyes much more intense. I like them."

"That's very kind of you to say. The sun here seems just the right strength to grow a splendid crop."

"I've also noticed your tendency to go about in the sun bare-headed."

"An open act of defiance, I'm sorry to say. Aunt Cassy insisted I wear a poke bonnet at all times. I grew tired of viewing the world from such a narrow perspective."

He laughed. "I approve of your defiance in that regard. I shall encourage you to other such acts."

This seemed a good opportunity to feel him out about her horseback riding. "Would you support my riding a western saddle rather than the sidesaddle you so thoughtfully provided?"

"Perhaps I should have added, within reason."

"I take it you don't feel riding astride is ladylike?"

"Not only is it not ladylike, it could be downright dangerous."

"Dangerous? How so?"

He tensed and his face turned dark red under the tan. "It's not a topic one usually discusses on the first formal call," he said.

Alexa felt terribly slow-witted, but she couldn't for the life of her interpret his line of thinking. "Perhaps I should ask Emmie?"

He sighed audibly. "Yes, I think that would be an excellent idea. I'm sure she can elucidate my meaning."

She felt the tension drain from him and he relaxed against her again. "Tell me about yourself," she urged wanting desperately to change the subject. "You obviously aren't from the west originally. How do you happen to be here in Idaho?"

He toyed with her fingers, rubbing the backs of them with his thumb while he thought. "I'm not trying to avoid your question. It's just, I don't know where to start."

"Have you thought about the beginning?"

"That far back?"

"It obviously had a great effect on your being here this evening," she reminded him.

He looked at her and chuckled. "I can't argue with that. All right," he launched. "I was born in Boston, attended prep schools, and graduated from Harvard."

Harvard! That makes him more of a mystery than he already is, and explains his thinking about sidesaddles. She felt herself grow pale at the ramifications of his disclosure. He had been raised in a home of proper manners and would recognize even a minute slip. And she had acted casually about proprieties, feeling that no one in Idaho would know the difference. What a mistake that was! At least, her instincts about his mother had been right. She most definitely hadn't let the frontier contaminate propriety, and Alexa knew she would expect to be received with all due respect on Tuesday. She had waited until she was sure she would be.

"How long have you lived out here?"

"Ten years full time. Summers before that."

"Summers?"

"Mother had always wanted to visit the west, so when I was eleven she arranged a tour. We came by Pullman to San Francisco with many stops along the way. Then we took the train up the coast to Seattle. Through mutual friends, Mother met Robert Hornbeck, banker and gentleman rancher. He persuaded her to return east along the northern route and pay a visit to a real cattle ranch . . . his. That brought us here. Robert Hornbeck and I got along so well, he asked if I could stay the rest of the summer. Robert wrote me regularly during the school year. In the spring when the rest of the boys went off to summer camps, I came to northern Idaho."

"So the Rathrum Plain became your second home."

"My only home. I lived for summers, the love of a good man, and the stability I found here. My natural father died the year before I graduated from college. Mother, after the proper mourning period, came west with me.

"Obviously she and Mr. Hornbeck fell in love and married."

"Yes. I'd never seen Mother so happy." David stopped talking and stared at the floor.

Alexa wanted to ask why, but he seemed drawn into his own world and she felt her question would intrude. She waited quietly, hoping he wouldn't change the subject.

He looked at her, studied her with different eyes. She felt he scrutinized her in a way nobody ever had before. What was he expecting to find in her? She had no idea, so she steadily returned his gaze and waited.

Finally, he continued. "My father was a man obsessed with power and position. He was a self-made shipping magnate, and although he possessed great wealth, he had no social background. That made him unacceptable in Boston society. My mother was young, beautiful, with all the right relatives, but financially strapped. Mother never has said, but I concluded early on that it was a marriage of convenience. His money for her social connections. I

108

always thought I was the result of the only union they ever had." He gulped and cast a shocked look at Alexa. "My apologies. You must be horrified," he gasped. "I got lost in my story and it just slipped out." His face went red then white as he agonized over his social gaffe.

She laughed softly. "I'm an Illinois farm girl, not a Boston debutante. Aunt Cassy trained me in manners, but she couldn't do much about the farm environment, so I don't shock readily." She hoped her comments would restore his calm. She wanted to hear the rest of the story. She was sure she would never hear this version from his mother.

"My father thought with Mother's connections, he would be accepted into Boston society, and he was. They were received at all the right places. He built a huge mansion and entertained all the right people in return. They spent summers in Cape Cod, autumns on the coast of France, and were in Boston for 'the season.' I spent those years in boarding schools." A bitter note crept into his voice.

The lonely little rich boy, Alexa thought. *How sad.* "It's hard for me to conceive your choosing to live here, and burying all your college training. It's almost as if those years were wasted."

"I use my business background at the bank. I enjoyed the life here tremendously until Dad Hornbeck died. I belonged to a family for the first time in my memory. Robert Hornbeck treated me like a son. I legally took his name because I loved him so much. I don't know who has suffered most over his death, Mother or me."

"Was his death sudden?"

"A heart attack at the bank. He was gone before Mother and I could even get to his side. That was two years ago. I'm only beginning to feel normal again and able to think about doing something with my life. My biggest concern is Mother. She entertains exquisitely, has a whole host of good works she's active with, and manages an impeccably smooth house. However, she has never had any head for business nor any desire to learn. She loved it here in the west, but I can't leave her to run the ranch." His shoulders dropped forward into a slump of despair.

"Isn't there someone you could trust to manage the ranch business?"

"No one now. Mother and your Uncle Clyde got along famously. I don't know if marriage had been discussed, but he had her design and oversee the building of this house down to the towels in the bath, and stocking the kitchen with the proper utensils. It was a splendid diversion for her after Dad died. The house was finished just a few weeks before Clyde died. In fact, it was the day before the big open house Mother had been planning for weeks."

"Your mother must be a very strong woman to survive such shattering blows and still go on so vigorously."

"Boston breeding, my dear. One does not show one's emotions in public no matter how badly one hurts inside. And she is hurting for I know she greatly misses Clyde and is terribly concerned with what to do about our ranch."

"Are you willing to stay and run it?"

There was an abnormally long pause and Alexa couldn't imagine why. Was he actually making up his mind about what to do? Perhaps he didn't want to give her a direct answer and didn't know how to tactfully skirt the issue. On second thought, that wasn't likely. Not with the training he had had. He would never be at a loss for the proper phrase or way to express himself.

"I'm not sure. I need a change. There isn't enough challenge to our ranch. I'd like to obtain more ground and do some experimenting with breeding. Doc Ward, our valley horse doctor, is very interested in trying his hand. I've taken some home study courses in veterinary medicine and I find it fascinating."

"That sounds like a most exciting thing to do. Why do you hesitate?"

"Our land doesn't grow adequate feed and our water supply is erratic. Not an ideal situation under which to pursue experiments in animal husbandry."

"Under those conditions, I can understand your reluctance to begin such an ambitious project." Alexa remembered his remarks earlier about her desirable land and water and now she realized what was bothering her. Were his attentions directed at her because he liked her or because he wanted her ranch? She didn't want to think it was the latter, but having had little in her life, she understood and recognized avarice when she saw it. It was time to change the subject. If it was the ranch he wanted and not her, she wasn't up to facing that fact right now.

Suddenly he moved from her and slid to the edge of the couch. Reaching for the book of poems she had been reading earlier, he read the title, then opened the cover and leafed the pages. "I've always envied Elizabeth and Robert Browning—their love and their ability to express it in immortal fashion."

"I, too, find that their poetry expresses the deep feelings of my heart as I shall never be able to. Which of hers is your favorite?"

"While I do find Sonnet 43 most moving, I have never loved with such depth and find it difficult to fully comprehend. Sonnet 26 captures both my experiences and dreams."

"Would you read it?" Alexa asked, remembering her earlier vision of his reading poetry to her. She hadn't dared hope it might be from Elizabeth Barrett Browning's *Sonnets from the Portugese* even though she had made the collection easily accessible.

He cleared his throat and moved to sit so he might see her well as he read.

"I lived with visions for my company
Instead of men and women, years ago,
And found them gentle mates, nor thought to know
A sweeter music than they played to me.
But soon their trailing purple was not free
Of this world's dust, their lures did silent grow,
And I myself grew faint and blind below
Their vanished eyes. Then Thou didst come to be,
Their songs, their splendors (better, yet the same,
As river water hallowed into fonts),
Met in thee, and from out thee overcame
My soul with satisfaction of all wants:
Because God's gifts put man's best dreams to
shame."

He raised his eyes to her and she saw in them a
forlorn, rejected young man sitting alone, trying to
find solace and understanding for his condition.
"You must have been terribly unhappy being left
alone so much," she said softly.
"I didn't know how miserable I was then. Most of
the boys in the dormitory were in exactly the same
situation so it seemed natural. Only after Mother and I
moved here did I realize how pitifully devoid of love
my earlier years had been. Mother feels terribly guilty
over her neglect, but her husband demanded that she
be with him and I can only imagine the tactics he used
to assure that his wishes were fulfilled."
"Hasn't your mother ever confided in you?"
"She never talks about him or their life together.
When she refers to that time, it's always about a
place, an event, or other people. I doubt I shall ever
know what she went through." He gently shut the
book and laid it back on the table. "Perhaps it's just
as well, since I can do nothing to change those years
for her or myself. The less known or remembered
about them the better."
All he was telling her came as a great shock to

Alexa. She had somehow thought if one were rich, life held no problems that couldn't be easily resolved. She thought one resided in a perfectly happy and carefree world. And here was David revealing to her that his childhood was even more barren than Martin's. The two men's revelations caused her to see that she herself had been reared in near-ideal circumstances.

He reached for her hand again. "Dear Alexa, you've been such a patient listener as I've burdened you with my unhappy past. I do wish to apologize. That was not my intent when I asked to call this evening."

"Unless people are willing to share the good and the bad, there can never be an honest relationship. I feel you have not shared these feelings with many people. Thank you for trusting me with them."

"You're very easy to talk with. You have a special quality of nurturing that makes one being in your presence feel safe and secure. Your Uncle Clyde had that same quality. I spent a great deal of time with him. He, more than any other, helped me reconcile my bitterness and accept my past as part of my present. Now, I have to learn to take what he taught me and move into my future."

"Have you tried prayer? I find I can talk with the Lord and I know exactly what I'm to do."

"I'm working on it. God has only come into my life in the last few years, and I still forget to turn to him on occasion."

There was a humility about David she hadn't sensed before. He really was trying to find his way. Silently, she vowed to pray diligently for him.

The chiming clock cut through the silence enfolding them. She felt him start at the sound. "I didn't realize it had grown so late. Here it is, ten o'clock and I haven't stopped talking about myself long enough to learn anything about you."

"How fortunate. Now you have an excuse to call again," she said, smiling.

"I don't need an excuse. I find I think about you most of the time, and finally the longing to see you grows until I can contain it no longer. I have to take the cattle out to the range and shall be away until Monday afternoon. I knew I had to see you before I left."

"I'm glad you did."

He slid his arm around her shoulders, and pulled her gently toward him. "I've waited a very long time for you to come into my life, but perhaps I wasn't ready until now to recognize an angel when God sent one to me."

Alexa could only blush at such extravagant praise. But she thoroughly enjoyed hearing it. Tilting her chin so their eyes met, he bent his head and kissed her. This time it wasn't the gentle, parting kiss she had expected. There simmered in his taking of her lips the deep longing of a man for a woman, the promise of an ecstasy she could only imagine. She slid her arms around his neck as he embraced her, drawing them together so closely she could feel the beating of his heart even through her shirtwaist. She withdrew her lips reluctantly and felt the throbbing of his heart in his throat. She felt his rapid pulse, strong with his desire for her.

She began to like all this too much. She felt control of her emotions slipping away. Moving back from him, she cradled the side of his face in her hand. "I fear for your safety if you tarry with me longer. The moon will soon be down and you will have no light with which to see."

"I know. I must go and yet I can hardly bring myself to leave you, knowing it will be Tuesday before I can see you again."

This time, however, she turned her cheek so that his kiss fell there. She had only herself to rely on for control and she wasn't sure how much will-power she would have if he kissed her a second time as passionately.

He accepted the rebuff, picked up his hat, and placing his arm around her shoulders, they made their way to the door.

"Goodnight, David. Have a safe trip to the mountains and I shall pray for you."

"Knowing you are thinking about me will keep me safe until Tuesday. But it won't do a thing to ease the longing for you," he said and took her hand. Again he left her with the imprint of his kiss tingling in her palm and on the inside of her wrist. Then, quite unexpectedly, he bent and claimed her mouth once more . . . gently, tenderly, lovingly. This kiss left her more helpless than the one earlier.

He placed his hat securely on his head and bounded down the steps and onto his horse. She stood watching as he rode away, the sound of the hoofbeats distinct in the still night air. She stood listening and watching until he became a misty shadow and the hoofbeats dulled to tiny muffled drums.

She put out the lamps and undressed in the dark. The beams of moonlight through the window gave her sufficient light to make her way to bed. Her mind was full of David and all that he had told her and she was a long time going to sleep.

Finally, as she began to doze off, she heard the kitchen door open and close. Alexa recognized Emmie's step. The step creaked as she crept up the stairs. Alexa remembered hearing the clock strike eleven. What on earth was Emmie doing outside at this hour?

CHAPTER 10

AS ALEXA WALKED DOWN THE HALL TO BREAKFAST, she could hear Emmie humming contentedly in the kitchen. No telling how long the housekeeper had been up, but she usually never slept past five-thirty. That meant she'd had about five hours of sleep. Yet, as Alexa stood watching unnoticed in the kitchen doorway she observed that Emmie had never looked better. Freshly washed and curled up on her head in an imitation of Alexa's style, Emmie's normally mousy brown hair shone a soft fawn color, and her new calico dress rustled with starch as she moved briskly between sink and stove.

She set a pot full of water on the stove and turned to survey Alexa. "See you finally decided to start the day," she said in a flinty voice, but her face made a lie of her stern reprimand. The tired sag that caused her face to look older than her years was gone, and her eyes sparkled with a light not previously there.

There's only one thing brings out all this in a woman, Alexa thought. *A man.* She wondered if Emmie and Bill were attracted to each other. *But what about Emmie's husband, Luke?* Calloused as it seemed, if things were as bad as Emmie had indicated she would be a widow before long.

"You're mighty quiet this morning," Emmie commented when Alexa failed to respond. "Didn't things go well with Mister David?"

"Oh, yes, Emmie," Alexa assured her. She sat at the work table and watched Emmie dish up a bowl of hot cereal. "Things went just fine. He's going to take their cattle to summer range and will be gone until Monday," she said, making it sound as though he planned to be away several months.

"Poor boy, could not he leave you for three days without showin' up here?"

Alexa giggled. Put that way, it seemed quite ridiculous. "Apparently not," was all Alexa chose to say. Emmie wasn't going to bait her into revealing anything about last night. Knowledge of David's life was too new, and Alexa wanted time to savor the details and the emotions they aroused in her. She needed to sort those things meant for her only, from those she could share.

Alexa reached for the cream pitcher. "It's certainly a treat to have fresh cream for one's cereal," she said, changing the subject. "Is Jake content having the extra duty of milking the cow?"

Emmie sniffed. "I reckon. Calls her 'Pansy' Brushes her and talks to her like a lover. I think he's workin' with half a deck, but Bill says it's good for the old man to have things to care for."

It delighted Alexa to have Emmie growing so crusty and independent. Little remained of the unkempt defeated soul who'd crawled out of the attic wardrobe. In fact, Emmie would be almost pretty were it not for that missing front tooth. Perhaps there was a dentist in Spokane experienced with false teeth. She must ask Jane Hornbeck on Tuesday.

Alexa looked up to see Emmie, arms akimbo,

117

standing in the middle of the kitchen floor staring at her. "You sure you're all right?" Emmie's voice had a definite edge of concern.

"I truly am. Why do you ask?"

"'Cause you keep driftin' off somewhere's while we're talkin'. Rather, I'm talkin', but you ain't listenin' or talkin' worth nothin'."

"I am listening. I've heard everything you've said."

"Then you're havin' trouble digestin' my talk 'cause there be some unnaturally long pauses between answers."

Alexa puzzled a minute over Emmie's accusation, then laughed. "Emmie Dugan, I am not going to tell you what went on last night between David and me. Rest assured, however, nothing unseemly occurred. He and his mother will be here Tuesday afternoon to pay a formal call, and I will receive them most properly and in good conscience."

"Hummph," Emmie snorted. "It still ain't proper to entertain a suitor without a chaperone. Temptation's gonna overtake you, girl. You mark my words." Thunder clouds of disapproval hung over Emmie's face and rolled through her voice.

Alexa sighed. *Shades of Aunt Cassy. Why was love so hard to live with sometimes?* "Emmie, I promise not to entertain suitors again in the house without a chaperone — though I didn't realize until late last night that the house was empty."

Emmie's face remained passive and she ignored Alexa's sharp reminder. "I should think so," she replied brusquely, but the softening of her features let Alexa know that Emmie was relieved at having extracted the promise. "Now, it's time you were off on your horse."

Alexa carried her bowl and glass to the sink and added them to the dishpan. "I do need to spend some time on the books, but I'm still stiff and sore, though nothing compared to yesterday."

"All your sufferin' be a waste if you don't finish workin' out the cramps. Turn right back to yesterday's worst, the next time you ride. Want that again?"

"Never! I'm going, I'm going. Don't wait any meals for me. I have no idea when I'll be back."

"Any idea where you're goin'?"

"I may go east today. Yesterday, I covered a lot of the land to the north and some on the west. I'd like to see the problem with the fences between Mr. Taylor's land and mine."

"You're ridin' skirt's fresh ironed on the back of a chair in the sitting room."

Surprise flooded through Alexa at Emmie's grudging acceptance of the unapproved riding style, and she threw her arms about Emmie to bestow an extravagant hug. "I do appreciate you, Emmie, and all you do for me. Thanks."

Emmie kept her head tucked, but blushed her pleasure. "Get on with you, girl. If you insist on that heathen skirt, can't have it lookin' like a cat's bed."

Alexa hurried and changed. When she reached the barn, she could see Jake in one of the corrals. She walked to where he was piling more wood on a hot fire. Metal handles protruded from the fire, and Alexa recognized branding irons.

"How's the branding going?" she asked.

"A trifle slow. One of the new hands had a powerful thirst he tried to quench in one sittin'. Bill had to fire him so we're working one man short. We'll be fine, though. Goin' riding?"

"Yes, Emmie says I must or I'll never get over being sore." Alexa looked out into the pasture and sighed. "I love riding, but I do dislike having to walk a mile each time to get to Red."

"Whistle for him."

"I can't whistle. I've always been told it's unladylike."

119

"I guess it is, but sure saves steps when you need a horse in a hurry."

The idea intrigued her. "Can you teach me?"

"I can try. Whistle has to be loud or the horse won't hear."

"How loud?"

Jake demonstrated. It was shrill and piercing and Alexa clapped her hands over her ears. She watched as the horses raised their heads, and Red looked toward Alexa and Jake. Then Jake whistled again, and Red wheeled and trotted toward the barn.

"Oh, Jake, I am impressed. Is Red the only horse trained to come when you whistle?"

"Only one trained to that whistle."

Red arrived, blowing and snorting, and began nuzzling Jake. "Excuse me, Miss Alexa, gotta get some oats. Red expects a treat for obeyin'."

Alexa watched as Red followed Jake to the outbuilding where the oats were stored. While they were gone, she looked at her two little fingers. Some of Aunt Cassy's boys could whistle the way Jake just had, but they used the thumb and first finger on one hand. When she was about eleven, she'd practiced secretly for hours in an attempt to make that wonderful piercing sound, but the skill had eluded her.

Jake had whistled by placing the tip of the little finger of each hand in his mouth. Putting her fingers in her mouth the way she thought Jake did and blowing out the quick hard breath she'd seen Jake use, she produced a fine wind sound. She adjusted her tongue and tried again. Nothing. She was having no more success than when she'd tried years earlier. There was a definite purpose in learning now, though, and she vowed that with Jake's instruction, this time she would master it.

Jake returned with Red trailing him. He watched her futile attempts for a few minutes, then passed on by, leaving her to practice while he saddled Red for her.

When Jake returned, Alexa looked at him and sighed. "I think I'm missing some of the fine points of whistling."

Jake hobbled his way over to stand next to her. "Let me see how you're a doin' it?" He peered carefully at her as she demonstrated. "You ain't lickin' the tips afore you stick 'em in your mouth." He gave his fingers a quick swipe with his tongue before placing them in his mouth. "Now, curl your tongue up and put your fingers on top to hold it curled."

She did as he'd instructed, but nearly choked when she looked to see him bent over squinting intently into her mouth.

"Dad gum! That's the way. Now blow."

Alexa did, but her whistle sounded like wind whistling down the chimney. She looked at him and sighed again.

"Now, don't you go gettin' discouraged. You got the fundamentals right. Takes a lotta practice. You just keep at it and one day you'll surprise yourself and old Red, too."

"I'll keep working on it. Thanks for saddling Red for me."

Alexa swung into the saddle and rode out along the trail to the east. She quickly left the meadow and entered a stand of lodge pole pine reaching high over her head. She knew nothing about judging distances so couldn't even guess at their height. She must ask Martin when she saw him again. Alders, willows, mountain maple, and choke cherries provided dense cover and food for the abundant game Martin said lived in the forest. She rode into a small meadow with a creek flowing through.

As she neared a gurgling stream, she could smell the perfumed fragrances from the blooming plants along its banks. She dismounted and stood at the edge of one of the side pools. The scene reminded her of the Twenty-third psalm as she sat near the still water mirroring the sky and deep green shrubs. Looking down along the creek, she thrilled at stately cottonwoods forming a canopy of cathedral-like arches over the ever widening stream.

The sounds along the stream were far from churchlike, though. The air was filled with the strident chatter of darting flickers and the clear sustained warble of handsome goldfinches. Ducks, the white bars of their wings beating out a primitive rhythm, sped above the sparkling water and lifted into the sky, quacking their delight. Alexa heard small, red-shafted birds she couldn't name add their drum-like tattoo to the cacophony as they hollowed out homes in the cottonwoods. She did recognize swallows as they emerged from their mud nests along the underside of the bank to swoop and dive for their breakfast of insects, plentiful in shrubs and trees.

Reluctant to leave the absorbing scene, she nevertheless had set out to make herself familiar with the east fence. She again mounted Red and turned him back along the trail.

Alexa rode through small groups of trees and then into lush meadows. A small trickle of water ran through every one. Was this what David had been referring to? Even she could see this was great cattle country.

This time when she rode into the trees, they didn't break into a meadow but became more and more dense, larger in diameter. Before she had ridden very long, she and Red were brought up short by a gated fence. *So this is the boundary.* She slid off Red and tied him to the branches of a fallen log. As she walked along the fence, she soon saw what Bill had been saying about loggers and fence repair. All along the boundary, the broken fence posts had been propped up with tree limbs. It didn't bespeak excellence, most definitely. But why were the fences in such condition?

She examined the broken posts. The wood wasn't rotted. What had caused the posts to snap like matchsticks? She must ask Martin about this. If this was normal each spring, then she needed a different type of fencing.

Returning to where Red nipped at the tops of tender grasses and low shrubs, she decided to ride on through the gate. This had to be Martin's property she entered, and he wouldn't mind her exploring a bit.

Deeper into the woods, the type of trees changed. Now they grew so tall that nothing but their deep green tips met in communion with the sun. They permitted only gauzy remnants of day to seep through to the forest floor. Alexa rejoiced as occasional silver-white threads of sunlight escaped the barrier of thick branches to tack golden buttons of light to the forest floor. The dank, musty smell of eternally damp rotting vegetation lay heavy, and she felt an enchantment grow slowly inside her as she rode deeper into the muted silence. A silence, nourished through lack of expression, grew until it evolved into a living force. Even the thud of the horse's hooves became deadened, the life of their sound absorbed to feed the force.

Suddenly, Red's ears pricked forward and then she heard the sound, too. The distant screech and whine of a saw violated the spell and directed her to the right at a fork in the trail. She hadn't considered until this moment that she might not be welcome. However, having come this far and never having seen a lumber camp, curiosity drove her on.

She rode to the edge of the clearing and reined Red to a stop. Across the clearing, steam and smoke rose from the shed of the small sawmill backed up against a steep slope. The strident squeal of the saw echoed eerie and harsh against the denuded mountain covered with stumps, proof of the logging already completed. A short distance away stood the camp buildings built of roughhewn lumber—a cookhouse, bunkhouse, a rude shelter for the horses and oxen, a pigsty and chicken coop, a smokehouse, a cabin separate from the rest, and a few outhouses. The enormous surrounding forest contrasted to make the buildings seem as toys set out for play. Alexa felt herself begin to shrink and her comprehensions grow unclear in this Gulliver-type world. She wondered how the men who worked here kept their perspective.

Timidly, she urged Red forward, praying all the while that Martin was somewhere close and might see her. She would feel terribly foolish asking for him. At the thought, she started to turn Red about and leave before anyone noticed her. In the lull of the saw, however, she heard a voice call her name. She watched men's heads swivel in her direction as Martin came bounding out of the sawmill toward her.

He took out his handkerchief and wiped his hands and face as he approached. She saw his shirt, sweatstained, with traces of sawdust still clinging to his shoulders. Gone was the Stetson and, in its place, a wide-brimmed hat well sprinkled with sawdust. He took it off and slapped it against his leg as he walked, dislodging the wood chips.

"Alexa, good to see you. I honestly didn't think you'd come for dinner, but I'm happy I was wrong." He reached up, clasped his hands around her waist and swung her to the ground.

"I didn't start out with that notion. I wanted to see the fence between our spreads for myself. Now that I have, I must say I'm not much impressed with your fence repair. A child could knock over those posts propping up the fence."

"Ah, but there's a large difference. A child is smart enough to know that. The cattle aren't."

"I examined the posts and there seems to be nothing wrong with them. Why are great distances of sound poles snapped off?"

"Snow lays on the fence and the weight breaks them."

Alexa considered his information. "Then it would seem we need a different type of fence. Isn't there something that could withstand the deep snow?"

"A notched log one would."

"Then why hasn't one been built. Uncle Clyde certainly had the money."

"Money wasn't his problem. It's mine," Martin admitted reluctantly. "Any idea how much fencing you're talking about?"

"Probably not," she was forced to concede.

"Miles."

"Oh," she said, and dropped the conversation as they grew close to a group of men. One stepped out and walked toward her, his body corded with sinewy muscles from years of hard labor, the lines of his face deep-creased from the elements.

"Flint's our camp boss," Martin said, introducing the two. "Miss Spence is Clyde's niece. Been out surveying her place and got a bit off the track."

"How do." He looked both embarrassed and pleased. "Mighty happy to have you in camp, ma'am. Mighty happy." And to prove his point, a big grin locked his mouth open.

Martin's curt nod sent the man back to his duties. Then Martin led her to the cookshack. "Better let Slim know there'll be a guest for dinner," he said. He pushed open the door and ushered her inside.

Alexa didn't know what she expected to find, but it wasn't this. The aroma of cake filled the room and she could hear meat sizzling on the big stoves. Two long tales stood spread with red and white striped oil cloth, while a tin plate and cup turned upside down marked each place. Wondering what one ate with, she lifted a plate and there lay the utensils covered against the ever-present flies. Unpainted backless benches lined the tables. Two men and a young boy were busy in the

125

kitchen part of the room. Martin introduced the three but took special pains to let her know the importance of Slim, the head cook.

Slim weighed three hundred pounds if he weighed an ounce, and Alexa had a hard time accepting a name that seemed to poke fun at a person's weakness or disability. She would have liked to know his real name, but now wasn't the time to delve into it. "I do hope I'm not an inconvenience," she apologized.

"Ma'am, you're as welcome as sunshine and clear weather anytime you want to drop by. Gets lonesome out here with nothing to look at but them bearded, ugly-faced loggers. Can't take time off to get to town when cutting weather's good. And when the weather's bad, it's so rotten even us desperate ones don't make the trek often." He turned to Martin. "You and the lady want to eat in your cabin."

"I think that might be best," Martin agreed. "I'll take her out to where they're cutting, let her see a big one go down. Be back in about an hour." He took her arm and guided her outside.

They hiked to an area where the men were working. Alexa watched, learning the rhythm of the crew as the big-muscled men moved in choreographed precision, each man knowing his job, yet each dependent on the other.

"Those are the fallers," Martin explained as he pointed to two men working together, cutting notches up a tree, then shoving springboards in to make a place to stand, removing them, and repeating the process until they were about fifteen feet above the ground. "They're getting up the tree away from the swollen pitch-filled base of the Douglas fir. The tree's about eight feet in diameter where they're going to start cutting. Watch, they're ready now for the first cut."

Alexa watched in awe as the two men swung their long, narrow double-bladed axes in synchronized rhythm, one on each side of the emerging cut, one swinging right-handed, one left. It seemed impossible that two toy-sized figures chopping away at the mammoth tree could bring it down.

"The tree is about two-hundred-twenty-five feet tall." Martin's voice held a tinge of reverence. The open wedge on the side of the tree grew ever wider as the fallers worked with their steady rhythm. They stopped and poured something from a can over their axes.

"They're pouring oil on their axes to thin the pitch that builds up," Martin told her. "Most of the crew use old whiskey bottles to do the job. Reminds them of the pleasure they had emptying them when they were new."

"I'd heard loggers were hard drinkers."

Martin chuckled. "Ma'am, you ain't heard the half of it." He pointed to the ground crew working beneath the tree. "These men aren't as showy as the fallers, but without them, we'd never get these monsters out of here. The swampers clear the underbush so we can get to the other trees, the hooktenders determine the 'ride' or natural resting position of each log. They 'snipe' or chop the front end of the resting log round and smooth so it won't catch on the skidroad going down the mountain."

"Did I see the skidroad?" Alexa asked, trying to recall what he was talking about.

"No. It's made of skids—foot-thick timbers at least twelve feet long, laid like railroad ties and half buried in the ground." They walked over to a wide path through the trees and Martin explained what she was seeing. "The skids are spaced at seven-and-a-half-foot intervals so that the logs, all longer then sixteen feet, will always rest across two of them. A scallop is cut out of the top surface of each skid to cradle the passing logs."

"What are those men doing?" she asked, pointing

to men working alone, each around his own fallen tree.

"Those are the buckers. They cut the fallen trees into manageable lengths for the hooktenders who drive metal spikes into the logs. Next, they fasten chains which run forward through these—metal 'dogs' to the lead log and are hooked to the yokes of the oxen."

A large, burly man wearing a floppy hat, galluses over a bright red and black plaid shirt, and heavy caulked boots waved at Martin and then proceeded to bellow, "Hump, you, Buck! Move!" Then he cracked a whip in the air and Alexa watched eight pairs of huge oxen strain to move the string of about a dozen chained-together logs, each about five feet thick.

"Each log weighs about five tons," Martin said. "Those Durham oxen are some of my most valuable assets, and Bull babies them like they were family."

All the while Martin had been instructing her in the fine points of logging, Alexa couldn't keep her eyes from straying back to the aerial dance of the fallers. Martin followed her glance. "That tree won't come down today, but if you don't mind walking a bit farther into the woods, I can show you one that will."

"Oh, yes. I do want to see the final reward for all that effort and assure myself that it is possible for midgets to accomplish such a mighty task. Really makes one a believer in the David and Goliath story, doesn't it?"

"I hadn't thought of it, but you're right."

She felt him suddenly grab her arm. She had been gawking so at her surroundings, she had nearly tripped over a large tree root growing across the trail. "Thanks. Guess I'd better watch where I'm walking."

"It's hard to keep your eyes on the ground when there's so much beauty above your head."

At last they arrived where a giant fir was nearly

ready to go down. Martin pointed to a slender stake driven in the ground. "That's the guide mark for where the tree should fall."

Alexa watched as two fallers, using only their axes and one springboard each, made cuts in the base of the tree up as far as they could reach, thrust the board in, and hauled themselves up. Then, after making another cut high above their heads, they drove their axes deep into the trunk and stood on them while they pulled out the boards and wedged them into the higher cuts and swung up to them.

"That's incredible the way they're climbing up that tree," Alexa gasped.

Martin chuckled. "They're putting on a bit of a show for you. Word came up the hill you'd be here to watch the fall."

At last the two men were in position opposite the undercut, about twenty feet above the ground. "They'll make the backcut now. That takes away the last support from the tree." Even Martin spoke in hushed tones as a ritualistic silence settled over the men. As many times as they had seen this, Alexa felt the anticipation of those who watched. Each man eyed the tree and checked his position to be sure he was out of harm's way.

The only sound in the deep woods was the ringing of the fallers' axes. It was as though the forest and all who dwelt there united into one force hanging suspended, breathless, out of respect for the last moments of life of a giant, centuries old.

Time stopped, began again in slow motion, and Alexa felt drawn into the vortex of the unfolding drama. The cry, "Timber!" cut the measured silence just before the anguished groan of the tree, a cracked, whining roar, rent the air. Goliath crashed and the earth shuddered with the impact.

She saw and heard it all and would have screamed had not Martin seen it coming and clamped his hand over her mouth, damming up the release of the emotions aroused at the marauding band who dared desecrate God's handiwork. Alexa saw the fallers fling their axes through the air. She watched the axes slowly spin their way to the ground, watched the fallers leap and fall, endlessly in the time alteration. Floating debris wavered through the air, through the moment of absolute silence, consecrating the spot. A final benediction beat upon the heart, demanding remembrance of this irreplaceable tree, growing here while Vikings walked the land on the east coast. The felled titan sighed its last settling noises, and the men broke into whoops of joy.

Martin took his hand away and Alexa didn't make a sound. She sagged against him, burying her face in his chest and trembling against him. She tried to say what filled her, but choking sobs came out instead.

He patted her back and held her head close to him with his other hand. "I'm sorry, Alexa. I couldn't let you scream. You'd have startled the men, and they might have missed their spot. For safety's sake, they throw their axes first and then jump clear just before the tree goes down. I should have warned you, though. I just didn't think. I've seen this so many times."

She pushed away from him and turned to see the two fallers receiving congratulations and jokes from the ground crew but looking anxiously her way. She managed a thin smile and a small wave. They seemed satisfied and each gave her a clumsy bow.

Her attention was again drawn to the fallen tree. She looked for the stake but saw the tree lay directly in the path, burying the stake. The fallers had been extremely accurate. She tipped her head back to see the gaping hole left in the green roof of the forest. Blue sky shown through and a shaft of sun found the opening and pierced the dimness, spotlighting the stump, the ugly remnant left as a testimony to the glory that had once stood there. The air still carried the turbulence and scent of upheaval, the scent of dust, decaying matter, the odor of death.

She had witnessed a murder, heard the groan of the victim, helpless under the tiny but deadly axes. She had seen the final death throes.

Alexa turned back to Martin, churning inside, knowing her mouth trembled with still unshed tears. A vision of death still raged inside her, the final swaying, the frozen instant of motionlessness, the falling . . . all etched indelibly onto her mind.

"I know the wood is needed for so many things and there are so many trees, but it's like watching a fragment of eternity die, never to be duplicated or replaced."

Martin took her face in his hands and looked deep into her eyes. "I know," he said, his voice a choked whisper. "I felt it the first time with agonizing clarity. I'm still not free of it."

She stared into the gun-metal gray of his eyes and marveled at the complexity of him. The man who could mourn the death of an ancient forest while engineering its extinction. She understood now the feeling in the valley against Martin and his men. The people who had seen these trees, felt their power, also mourned their deaths and helpless to punish their killers, hated them the more.

"How can you continue to destroy the forest?" Alexa asked.

Martin's face closed, his eyes turned opaque, and he shrugged. "It's a living." Abruptly he turned and left to talk with one of the men.

She stood alone. The feeling of desolation crept through her, leaving her cold and fraught with frustration.

CHAPTER II

JANE HORNBECK AND DAVID CAME TO CALL on Tuesday. Alexa poured tea from the carefully polished tea service and Emmie served lemon tarts with whipped cream. Everyone was very proper and mannerly, and Alexa, instead of enjoying the afternoon she had looked forward to for so long, found it boring. Jane Hornbeck couldn't help letting her longing to be mistress of the beautiful house show and Alexa felt sorry for her. It would be hard to build and furnish your dream house and then watch someone else inherit it.

David hovered over his mother like a moth around a flame, anticipating her every wish. His attentions seemed overdone and left Alexa wondering why he found such solicitude necessary. The Hornbecks stayed the required time and then left promptly with the promise to come by at seven-thirty on Saturday evening to take her to the social.

"It's Thursday, Miss Alexa. Don't you think it's time to start thinking about decorating your box?" Emmie reminded her.

"Yes. What size box do you want, Emmie? Long as I'm getting mine, might as well find one for you, too."

"Don't believe I'll be going." Then something else occurred to her. "Are Bill and Jake planning to attend?"

"I think Jake is, but I can't say about Bill." Emmie left abruptly for the garden without further discussion.

When Alexa heard Emmie return from harvesting the garden, she came into the kitchen and asked, "Emmie, do you have any idea where I might find some paint?"

"Attic's only place I can suggest." Emmie set a kettle on the stove and gave her full attention to Alexa. "What you doing with two boxes?" Suspicion brought back the wariness to her eyes.

"Fixing you a box. You have to go, Emmie, and so do Jake and Bill. I'll not have it said I wouldn't give the Bar S Ranch help time off for the box social."

"Heard this was a free country," Emmie said, sullen and uncooperative. "Thought we could do as we wanted."

"Not when it looks bad for the ranch, you can't. This social is to raise money. You're not going to make it look like I don't pay you enough to furnish a proper box, or I'm such a slave driver you can't get time away to go to the party. Either way, a lie is born. If you don't want to stay for the dancing, that's fine, but you all *have* to go to the social."

"I'm no good with this sort of thing," Emmie said. "If you insist I have a box, you're gonna have to do the decorating."

"I love decorating boxes. I won't mind doing yours. When was the last time you went to a social?" Alexa asked.

"Never have been," Emmie said in a low voice.

"You've never been to a box social!" This confession was nearly impossible for Alexa to comprehend. "Never, in your whole life? What have you done for fun?"

"Never had time for fun. As young'uns, we lived too far in the hills to come out for such nonsense. Didn't have no money for doodads to decorate a box with or fancy food to put in it."

"A couple times after I got big and left home. I ain't real good, though. Got two left feet." Emmie acted nervous as talk of the dance proceeded, twisting her hands in her apron and shifting her weight from one foot to the other. Then her face brightened. "I ain't got a proper dress to wear. Wouldn't do me being seen without corsets and a decent dress."

Alexa looked up at her. "Emmie Dugan, you're not going to get out of going on such flimsy grounds. I'll take you to town for corsets, and I have plenty of time to make you a dress or a skirt and shirtwaist, whichever you'd feel more comfortable wearing. Emmie, you are going to that social, like it or not. It'll be a lot more fun if you decided to like it."

Deep worry lines altered Emmie's face and she looked absolutely miserable. "Don't guess you're giving me much choice."

"Do you want a shirtwaist and skirt, or a dress?" Alexa asked. We may have fabric here that would do."

"I'm thinking the skirt outfit would be more serviceable."

"So do I."

By the time they were ready to leave for town, the worry lines in Emmie's face had subsided, to be replaced by a happy glow. After they were seated in the buggy and clattering down the road, Emmie confided to Alexa, "I ain't never had a new corset. Not in my whole life. Always had a good enough figure for my work and when I needed to, I had a second-hand one I'd get on."

Emmie's confession touched Alexa although it was hard for her to conceive of any woman reaching maturity without having several corsets for different occasions. "What kind of work were you in?" Alexa asked innocently.

When Emmie didn't answer, Alexa turned to see an angry blush creep up Emmie's neck and she looked extremely uncomfortable. "Only kind I knew to do, with no education and living in roaring mining towns. Actually, that's how I met Luke. Found we both wanted to change our ways so we lit out together. Stopped in Cheyenne on our way up here and tied the knot. We was honeymooning when he got dragged off to jail."

Alexa reached over and placed her hand over Emmie's ungloved knotted fingers moving nervously in her lap. "I didn't mean to pry, but I thank you for sharing something of your past with me. The Lord will forgive you your sins if you have a sincere heart. All you have to do is ask."

Emmie sat with bowed head. She didn't speak again until they neared town. "I'd like to believe what you've told me is true."

"It is, Emmie. All any of us has to do is repent of our sins, take the Lord Jesus Christ as our Savior, and try to sin no more."

"I'd sure like to get washed clean and get Luke to do the same."

"There must be an itinerant preacher who comes through here. I shall ask at the social. I don't know what you can do about Luke, though. I suppose they have a preacher for the prisoners. I can find out about that too, if you'd like."

Emmie smiled and nodded. Alexa beamed with joy. She hadn't expected this trip to yield such rich rewards.

They located a lady's apparel shop, small but elegantly stocked, and Emmie was fitted with a fine steel-ribbed, sateen-covered corset. It was remarkable how much better she looked even in the unstylish calico. "I declare, Emmie Dugan, you'll be the belle of the social when we get you a proper outfit made," Alexa bubbled.

Emmie again reddened under the unaccustomed praise. "Ain't no one gonna compete with you," she said softly.

Alexa stopped at the large drygoods store and purchased the few items she needed. The two women arrived home early enough that Alexa had time to cut out Emmie's skirt before supper.

"You won't get your ridin' in today," Emmie observed as they finished the dishes.

"As soon as I hang up this dishtowel and have my talk with Bill, I intend to take a short ride.

Bill, Jake, and the other two hands were lazing on the log bench set against the bunkhouse when she broke out of the trees and approached them. Bill stood and walked to meet her. Together they strolled toward the barn and discussed the ranching activities as they went.

"There's one other thing I've failed to mention," Alexa said. "Saturday night, the school board's holding a box social and square dance. Since the other men don't belong permanently to the valley, I wouldn't be upset if they stayed away, but I'd appreciate it if you and Jake made plans to attend."

Bill took off his hat and scratched his head. "Hhmmph," He cleared his throat. "I already give the boys permission to go into town. They been working real steady and have a need to blow off a little steam. That leaves the place alone if I was to go, too. Don't think that's wise. With everybody gone, Indians'll take it as an invitation to help themselves. I do believe it'd be good business to lock the house up tight, but leave a fire banked so it shows smoke. I'll stay and make my presence known both up here and around the house."

Alexa stood gaping at him. "Indians! I haven't seen a single one in all my travels."

"But they've seen you. Reservation's not far away. They have free access to your land. They ride across the place all the time, but don't you try the same privilege with theirs," Bill warned.

"Well, under the circumstances, I suppose it would be wise to leave someone here," she conceded.

"You can bet the rest of the ranches will," he said, returning his hat to his head and looking tremendously relieved.

Bill left her and sauntered back to join the crew. Alexa, dashing to the edge of the pasture, licked her thumb and first finger, placed them against her teeth, and blew. Martin had demonstrated this method when she had showed him Jake's style. This seemed more comfortable than the two little fingers and took only one hand. She practiced religiously each day, but she was still unable to produce more than a loud windy sound. She refused to give up, though. If Jake and Martin could do it, so could she.

Carefully, she moistened the fingers and reset her position. Arching her tongue just so, she blew again producing a fine blast. Red left his grazing and came trotting up to the barnyard. "That's a good horse," she crooned as she fed him oats.

Red soon stood saddled and ready. The muscles in her left leg had strengthened greatly. By grabbing the saddle horn and jumping a few times on her right foot, she could pull herself into the saddle.

Sitting firmly in the saddle, and pushing back solidly against the cantle, she fell into the rhythm of the horse and found herself riding with him instead of meeting him somewhere in the middle of his stride and slapping against the saddle seat. It was such times that kept her coming back again and again.

The light prevailing wind from the north began cooling the Plain and Alexa slipped into her cloak. She never tired of watching night come. It brought a peaceful hush over the busy sounds of the day. She stopped to watch some deer and a large elk feeding on the willows and other shrubs growing in the marsh. She sat, entranced by the does with their young, until she heard slow, soft hoofbeats coming toward her. Her heart leaped into her throat. Indians? And here she was, a good distance from home. Alone. Red felt her panic and he started to shake his head, prance sideways, and refuse to respond to the reins on his neck. She pulled the bit tight in his mouth and bowed his neck to keep him from bolting.

While she was thus occupied, a horseman rode into view. "What's the matter with Red?" Martin called.

Alexa breathed a sigh of relief. When Martin was closer, she said, "I thought you were Indians and Red reacted to my fear."

"Who's been scaring you about the Indians?"

"Bill said they could see me but I couldn't see them, and they rode over my ranch all the time."

"He's right about that, but there's no need to be afraid. They won't hurt you." King fell into step beside Red and they continued slowly down the road. "What brings you out of the woods this evening?" Alexa asked.

"Exactly that. The woods. I start feeling real hemmed in some nights."

Alexa didn't know why she suddenly felt so elated. After all, he was nothing more than a friend and a casual one at that. "You planning to go to the social and dance Saturday night?" she asked.

"I hadn't given it much thought. Probably not, now that you call it to my attention."

"I think that's a mistake. It doesn't seem you're very well liked in the valley as it is. Might help people's opinion of you if you came and spent some money on a good cause."

"I don't think anything I might do would change public opinion of me or my men. As a whole our reputation is even more tarnished than the miners' and that's saying a lot."

"And I think you're wrong. If you were to present yourself looking like a gentleman, beard and hair trimmed, wearing a proper suit of clothes, you just might be surprised at your reception. You're quite handsome . . . or could be. The young things would no doubt swoon all over you."

"And what about you?"

"I'm a bit old for swooning, but I would save a dance for you." She lowered her head and batted her eyes extravagantly at him.

He chuckled. "With such bait coming from underneath that cowboy hat, how can I refuse?"

Martin escorted her back to the ranch and helped unsaddle Red. Somehow, Alexa didn't want Martin to ride away. "Won't you come down to the house for a piece of Emmie's blueberry pie?"

"You have more than one way to tempt a man, haven't you? You could become downright dangerous if something isn't done to control you."

"Any suggestions?" she teased back.

"Yes, but I'd prefer not having an audience while I demonstrate."

Looking over at the bunkhouse, she waved at the men still lounging against the side. She could feel their eyes on her as Martin led her along the path into the trees and out of their sight.

"There, that's better," he said, stopping in the trail and pulling her to him.

Startled, she looked up into his shadowed eyes, then realized his intent. A small shiver of anticipation ran through her. Their previous kisses had been those of compassion and caring. This time promised to be different. As he bent over her, she closed her eyes and raised her lips to meet his. They met gently at first, then she wound her arms about his neck and the kiss turned more intense. She felt a rush of liquid fire pouring through her veins and a low groan escaped from him as he attempted to draw her even tighter to him.

Little warning signals went off in her head and she knew she must put an end to this or they would both be lost. Slowly she removed her arms and placed her fingers on his cheeks. She drew herself away, breaking the kiss. Not willing to let her escape entirely, he enfolded her to him and held her tightly against his chest. She could feel the wild beating of his heart and knew it matched her own.

Now what was she going to do? She had thought no one but David could bring about such a response in her. And yet here she stood, content in the circle of Martin's embrace, moved emotionally by his kiss as she had been by no other. *Alexa, you're a wanton woman with no morals whatsoever. It would serve you right if neither man had any more to do with you.*

Preparations for the box social and square dance occupied every minute of the rest of the week. Coupled with her determination to ride every day, Alexa was left with little time for anything else. She refused to allow any thought of Martin to form, and speculation on how David would handle three passengers in the buggy with Mrs. Hornbeck as chaperone. She had the horrible feeling she would be expected to ride alone in the second seat while his mother sat in front beside him.

As Saturday grew closer, the vision of this awkward arrangement crossed her mind more often, but she managed to dispel it quickly.

CHAPTER 12

SATURDAY MORNING DAWNED in another cloudless sky. It hadn't rained a drop since Alexa arrived. Hadn't even seriously clouded up.

She rushed to the sewing machine to finish Emmie's skirt.

"Land child, you're sewing with a hot needle and galloping thread!" Emmie exclaimed as she stepped into the sewing alcove.

"I am, but I only have to stitch one more row of wide lace to trim the bottom and your skirt will be finished," Alexa answered. "How are you coming in the kitchen?"

"Jake's making the supreme sacrifice and parting with two of his prize roosters so we can have fried chicken. Said he would bring 'em down soon as he gets 'em plucked."

Alexa continued to pump the treadle vigorously while they visited.

"I ain't wearin' a corset. Wouldn't fit worth nothin'. I know it'll be just fine," she said.

Feet scraping on the back porch alerted Emmie that

Jake had arrived with the chickens. She hurried away, leaving Alexa to her final stitching.

After pressing the skirt, Alexa carried it upstairs and placed it on Emmie's bed next to the blouse and new undergarments Emmie had already laid out. *These are probably the nicest clothes she's ever had. She's trying not to show it, but I think she's really excited about tonight.* Alexa couldn't help singing as she tripped happily down the stairs.

Tying on an apron, Alexa presented herself in the kitchen. "What can I do to help?"

"You can stay out of the way," Emmie answered curtly.

Taken aback, Alexa crossed to the sink where Emmie scrubbed the chickens with much more vigor than they seemed to warrant. "Emmie?" Alexa peered into Emmie's face.

Emmie turned away, but not before Alexa saw the tears glistening on her cheeks. "Emmie, tell me this instant what's troubling you," Alexa demanded. But her words seemed to fall on deaf ears.

"Emmie! I must know why you're crying."

"You know, Miss Alexa. You're the cause." Emmie brushed Alexa aside and carried the pan full of chicken to the work table.

The accusation caught Alexa completely by surprise and left her dumbfounded. "Whatever are you saying? I wouldn't knowingly do anything to cause you grief."

Emmie faced Alexa, hands on her hips. "Jake says Bill's not going. Says he has to stay and look after things."

Righteous indignation poured through Alexa. How dare Bill make it sound as if she was forcing him to remain behind. "That was Bill's decision. I practically threatened to dismiss him if he didn't attend the social, but he insisted it was necessary to have someone here in case the Indians decided to annex us into their reservation."

Emmie looked at the floor. "That the truth?"

"It most certainly is. Ask Bill.

Alexa watched as the floured chicken pieces sizzled in the hot grease and slowly turned a tempting golden brown. Mulling the problem over in her mind, Alexa guessed Emmie had been counting on Bill to buy her box. She knew no one else she would feel comfortable with. And then Alexa smiled. There was one other person Emmie knew, and he promised he would be there "if nothin' broke or come untwisted". All Alexa had to do was make sure Jake knew which box was Emmie's. It solved another dilemma. She and Emmie would ride together in the back seat of the Hornbeck's buggy.

The rest of the day sped by and almost before Alexa knew it, it was time to bathe and dress.

While Alexa fixed her hair, she kept an ear tuned to the familiar creak of the third step from the bottom that would let her know when Emmie arrived in the downstairs hall. Much as Alexa enjoyed wearing her own finery, she could hardly wait to see Emmie in hers. The creaky signal came just as Alexa placed the last comb in her upswept curls. She dashed into the hall. There stood an unrecognizable Emmie.

Alexa couldn't contain a gasp of surprise. "Emmie! You look absolutely beautiful."

Emmie smiled without revealing any teeth and so kept the striking image intact. "Don't look too bad, do I?"

"Bad! You have a marvelous figure.

"'Course, having an exclusive dressmaker helps. Designs originals for me," Emmie said and sashayed down the hall to the kitchen.

Alexa's laughter pealed through the house. She was delighted that Emmie's good humor had returned. She had prayed all day for this. *Thank you, Lord, for hearing and answering my prayers.*

The wagon yard was full when they arrived, but David drove their buggy inside.

David assisted his mother from the buggy, as Alexa and Emmie quickly jumped out to help Jake place their supper boxes with the other baskets and boxes already assembled.

David drove the buggy away and Mrs. Hornbeck nodded pleasantly toward a group of women seated on benches under the trees. They were talking and fanning with equal speed, but everything halted as Jane Hornbeck, with Alexa in tow and Emmie following respectfully behind, sailed into their midst.

"Girls, I want you to meet Clyde's niece, Alexa, and her housekeeper, Emmie."

Names began dropping at a rapid rate and Alexa could not keep track.

"And this beautiful lady is our school teacher, Miss Helen Bearnson," Jane Hornbeck said, her manner growing formal and aloof despite the warm words.

Helen truly was beautiful. Tall, stately of bearing, soft blond hair and a winsome face. The fiber of strength in her character made itself felt even among the adults. She was a lady from the dotting of her 'i's' to the color of her ribbons. *Can't imagine a child ever trying to test her,* Alexa thought. And, Mrs. Hornbeck's accent on the word 'Miss' hadn't escaped her.

"I've heard how lovely you are," Helen said to Alexa. "The reports were not exaggerated. Welcome to our valley."

"Thank you. I've loved every minute so far." Alexa liked her immediately, but grew confused at the messages Jane Hornbeck sent. Did she or didn't she approve of the teacher? Or in his mother's eyes, was there no woman good enough for David Hornbeck? Had Alexa's coming interrupted a budding romance between David and Helen or was David considered the catch of the valley with every eligible girl setting her cap for him? Helen didn't look the type to chase a man. Alexa determined to watch the evening's proceedings very closely.

Her help was needed at one of the booths and Helen Bearson excused herself. Mrs. Hornbeck stopped to chat with friends, and Alexa and Emmie were at last free to wander about.

Wires were strung between the trees, and old sheets and blankets were pinned up to form small booths. Inside each odd shaped booth, a game, contest, or entertainment run by Helen's students enticed the citizenry to part with pennies or nickels. There was a ring-toss and pin-the-tail-on-the-donkey. A long line of little children stood in front of the fish pond. At the camera booth, the children allowed a father to operate the camera, but they took the money and posed the patrons.

"Want to knock over some pins with a baseball?" Alexa asked Emmie.

"Not me. Never could throw straight."

Alexa paid her nickel for three balls. Taking careful aim, she grasped the ball and let it fly. Pins sailed in all directions.

"Bet Aunt Cassy never caught you playing second base," Martin's voice said from behind her, a soft chuckle breaking up the sentence.

Without looking at him, Alexa laughed. She didn't tell him she had practiced pitching on the sly for years. "Can't be a lady all the time." She claimed her prize, a crocheted pot holder, then turned around. When she saw Martin, her mouth dropped open. Here stood a perfectly groomed gentleman in an expensive well-cut gray pinstripe suit. He hadn't forsaken the Stetson, but it was a soft gray to match the suit and his eyes. And he wore fine black leather boots, highly shined.

"I don't believe I've had the pleasure," she said softly.

Martin doffed his hat with a fine flourish. "David Hornbeck isn't the only dandy in the country."

Alexa ignored the remark. "I'm glad you decided to come."

145

"So am I. It was worth it to see you splatter those pins. And now would you introduce me to this lovely lady?" Martin turned his full attention to Emmie. "May I present Mr. Martin Taylor . . . Mrs. Emmie Dugan." "I'd never have recognized you, Emmie. You look like a picture from *Godey's*."

"And how would you know that?" Alexa asked. Now it was Martin's turn to laugh. "One of the boys in camp has a subscription. Keeps us right up to date on the latest in women's wear . . . from the skin out."

Unable to contain a full laugh, Emmie spread her fan across her mouth. But Alexa, having memorized each monthly issue for years, pictured Martin's inferences precisely and blushed uncontrollably. She could only think to retreat until she could collect herself. He might be dressed like a gentleman, but he sadly lacked refinement.

"Oh, Alexa," Helen Bearson called, her voice cutting through Alexa's churning thoughts. "I think Doc Ward's about to begin the auction. If you're free, would you mind helping serve coffee?"

"I'd be most happy to," Alexa answered, grateful for something to keep her busy.

"Doc Ward's our local veterinarian," Helen explained, not realizing Alexa knew. "He says he's going to run for the senate this fall, but I don't think he has much chance of being elected. If he wins, the folks in these parts will be without a horse doctor, and they'll never let that happen."

Alexa and Helen began setting the cups in their saucers and checking the sugar and creamers. "If he has no chance of winning, why is he going to run?" Alexa asked. He didn't sound awfully bright.

"He's been trying to get Jane Hornbeck to notice him since Robert passed on, but she's only had eyes for your uncle. Came as a terrible shock when he died so suddenly. I surmise Doc thinks if he does something terribly respectable and a bit exciting like getting elected to congress and can offer her Washington D.C., she might give him a tumble."

"I don't think Doc Ward has a chance as long as she has David to do her bidding. If David decided to leave the valley or take himself a wife, I suspect Mother would jump into the first open arms extended her way."

"Unfortunately, I doubt that David will consider marriage until he is sure Mother is well-taken of. Turns into a stand-off," Helen said, and a look of longing crossed her face as her eyes sought out David across the school yard.

During a lull in the bidding, Alexa turned to set out more cups and saucers. Several men passed slowly behind her visiting as they walked. She couldn't help overhearing their conversation. "Heard the facts right from the sheriff's deputy. Says the fellow got clean away on 'em as they was taking him from Coeur d'Alene to Boise City."

"I say we ought to do somethin'. Ain't safe having a murdering train robber running loose. Just might all wake up dead one morning. Kilt in our sleep, helpless as new babes."

"What kinda something you got in mind?"

"Well, I'm toting my gun. Leastways, I'll have some protection."

"Looking at the size o' that hunk a metal, what you'll have is a rupture."

The men all laughed and the subject changed. Apparently they weren't unduly concerned about Luke's escaping up into the valley. Alexa knew better, though. That explained Emmie's immediate and long disappearances each evening after supper. She knew where Luke was and obviously visited him as frequently as possible. She hadn't been upset that Bill couldn't come to the social. Emmie had planned to spend this evening with Luke, and Alexa had spoiled the plans by nearly forcing Emmie to come to the social. *Probably going to make up a fancy box and have Luke to the house for a private party.* Deep in thought, Alexa turned around in time to see Emmie's box go up for auction.

The oooh's and aaah's of appreciation caused Emmie to beam with pleasure. "What am I bid for this beautiful box?" Doc Ward boomed in his best senatorial voice.

Jake leaped to his feet. "Fifty cents!"

"Must be something special about this box for the gentleman to open the bid so high."

There is, Alexa thought. *His chickens.*

"Seventy-five cents," an unknown bidder countered.

"One dollar," Jake shouted at him.

"One twenty-five."

"One fifty."

Some people came for coffee and Alexa lost track of the bidding. By the time she could return to it, Jake's face had turned beet-red and he was mopping sweat with a large handkerchief. The silence thickened as Jake counted and re-counted his money. Then she saw a hand slip him a bill.

"Ten dollars and fifty cents!" Jake shouted triumphantly.

A number of over-sized people had formed a phalanx in front of Alexa and she couldn't see who was bidding against Jake.

"Ten seventy-five," came the muffled reply, so soft Alexa could scarcely hear it.

Jake stood defeated and more woe-begone than anyone she had seen in ages as Doc Ward intoned, "Going once, going twice, going three times. Gone! Pay the clerk, Mr. Taylor, and claim your girl."

Martin Taylor! Martin had bought Emmie's box! Alexa's hand shook as she poured the next few cups of coffee. Things weren't turning out as she had planned at all.

"David, my boy," Doc Ward called. "Come, run this auction. I want to bid on the next basket coming down the aisle."

Alexa stopped pouring coffee and watched Jane Hornbeck's basket being set on the auction table. Doc Ward moved into the audience and opened the bidding. His rancher friends had a great time bidding against him even though they were all married. Their wives encouraged the bidding until Doc let it be known he was near the end of his bankroll.

"Sold to Doc Ward. Will the owner please claim her basket?" David pronounced, somehow managing to keep a straight face.

David jumped off the auctioneer's stump and went to stand with a group of rough-looking men. They must be single to look that unkempt, Alexa concluded.

"Oh, there goes mine," Helen whispered, and she strained forward.

The bidding for Helen's basket was vigorous and soon ran into the teens. There was much laughter and shouted comments, especially from the group around David, as the bidding climbed higher. Finally, when it appeared a particularly tough looking man from the group was going to buy Helen's box, David entered the bidding, and it took a turn from friendly to nearly open warfare. The man glared fiercely at David, then dropped to his knees and emptied his pockets spreading out all his bills and change on the ground. "Someone loan me some money. I'm good for it," he bellowed. Several of his companions responded and the bidding continued. Helen kept a passive face, but Alexa noticed she held the coffee pitcher with a white-knuckled hand.

When the men could raise no more money, David won the bidding and Helen's basket. Now it was

Alexa's turn to pour coffee with a clenched hand. Martin and David had made their purchases. Who would buy her box?

She was so deep into her misery she didn't realize it was her box up for bids until Jake again leaped to his feet. "Five dollars!"

Several men bid against Jake, but he was relentless and finally, Doc Ward pronounced him the winner for thirteen dollars and fifty-seven cents. Jake turned and gave Alexa a delighted smile before he shuffled down the aisle to pay the clerk and claim his prize.

He came to stand in front of her. "I came here promising my tonsils fried chicken and I dad-blamed ain't about to disappoint 'em."

"I can't think of anyone I'd rather eat with," Alexa said, hoping the Lord would forgive her the white lie.

"Looks like the folks is saving us a spot," Jake said and pointed to David and Helen who were motioning them over. Jake almost pranced as he carried Alexa's box toward the table where Martin and Emmie were already seated next to David and Helen. Doc Ward came to join the group proudly escorting Jane Hornbeck. Alexa fervently wished she was anywhere else, but there seemed no graceful way out. She sat as inconspicuously as possible at the far end of the table, making sure Jake sat next to Mrs. Hornbeck. David and Helen moved down and David, across the table from Alexa, gave her a gentle, wistful smile.

Helen looked at David with warm and grateful eyes. "Thank you for rescuing me,' she said as she dished up their supper.

"I wouldn't allow him to buy your basket. He had been drinking heavily, and I couldn't persuade him not to bid for it. Seems those fellows heard about our beautiful school marm and came up from Coeur d'Alene to pay you a call."

Alexa grew misty-eyed at David's gallantry. He hadn't rejected her, after all. And she was sitting across from him which was nearly as good as sitting next to him.

"David," Doc boomed. "I heard the state of Idaho is working on an exhibit for the World's Columbian Exposition to be held in Chicago next year. A friend told me they needed someone to be in charge of it. Right away, I thought of you. Said to bring you next time I came down to Boise City. I'm going next week. Interested?"

David glanced sideways at his mother. "W—W— why, yes," he stammered. "I'd like to hear what they're planning."

Mrs. Hornbeck looked aghast. "What are you saying, David? How can you think of leaving with all there is to do on our ranch? And what will Alexa do without you to help her?"

Doc answered for David. "Nothing needs doing right now, Jane, that won't wait 'til we're back. Boy needs to get out of here and down to the city. Been cooped up here for months without a break. We'll only be gone a week at most."

Martin, grinning like a cheshire cat, said, "And I'll be glad to look in frequently on Alexa during David's absence. Make sure everything's running smooth at the ranch. Check on your place too, if you like."

Doc looked enormously proud of himself. "See, Jane. Everything's all worked out and settled."

Jane Hornbeck didn't look pleased with the solutions offered, though. Not pleased at all.

CHAPTER 13

PILED-UP GREEN-BLACK THUNDERCLOUDS swept southeast across the mountain tops. From inside the clouds, intermittent blue-white flashes escaped, piercing the September afternoon sky. Thunder, long in arriving, echoed through the house, surrounding meadows and forest. Rain fell in spits and sputters.

"Just enough to spot the windows. Won't even wet down the dust, much less the grass and trees," Emmie grumped as she stood in the open back door, folding the last of the laundry she and Alexa had just rescued from the clothesline.

Alexa with Tiger in her lap, attempted to relax in the porch rocker. It was warm . . . unseasonably warm, and she unbuttoned the top buttons of her dress and laid back the collar. No breeze moved the heavy oppressive air as she looked out across the small, ripe, brown meadow and into the forest beyond. There had been no measurable rain in the valley since June and the land lay bone-dry and baked. Among the trees, a resinous odor hung above a carpet of dead pine-needles, and the branch tips, their moisture evaporated, looked more gray than green.

"If we don't get some rain and soon, we're bound to burn this whole forest down," Emmie observed in a voice tinged with desperation. "Maybe even the house and barns."

"I've heard this is the worst dry spell they've ever had. Even worse than last year."

"Bill says if you put two years like these last two back-to-back, folks are gonna go broke." Emmie stood wringing her hands in the newly washed dishtowel she had folded and obviously forgotten about.

"I know the only good cut of hay we got was in July, and we're luckier than most. Both Bill and David say we can't get through the winter with the hay we have unless we sell most of the cattle. Means we won't have much stock to breed with for next year if we do that."

"Also means you won't get much money for your beef 'cause everyone else is in the same fix and selling right and left," Emmie reminded Alexa.

"I know," Alexa said with a deep sigh. This wasn't the way she had planned for things to go and even though it wasn't her fault, she still felt responsible for the state of the ranch affairs. She had only been saved from the impending ruin many of the other ranchers faced by the dedicated work of Jake and Bill, and the wise and loving advice given by David. She did miss David. He had spent much of the summer in Boise City working with the Idaho exhibit for the Columbian Exposition. Even made a couple of trips to Chicago over the matter. He had written faithfully, though, and she had a small stack of letters tied with a blue satin ribbon tucked carefully in her bureau drawer. These she read and reread each evening.

"When's Mister David expected back?" Emmie asked as though reading Alexa's mind.

"This weekend, I hope. He promised me he'd return in time to attend the social a week from

Wednesday to help Doc Ward's campaign for congress." Alexa doubted Doc Ward would win. Just as Helen had predicted, although the people liked him a great deal, he was getting only lip service as support from them. With the stock breeding that was going on, the ranchers kept Doc busy. He was too good a veterinarian for them to send him away deliberately. And Mrs. Hornbeck relied more and more on him for advice regarding her ranch since David's time and attention centered on the exhibit.

"They still gonna have that dinner, even if nobody plans on voting for Doc?"

"Most definitely. Haven't had a real social since the box social in June. With the drought, people feel a need to get together and share their misery. I know I do."

Alexa felt rather than saw the raging violence building inside the cloud as it changed in shape and size. It was grown enough now to block out the sun. The air cooled and the great cloud mass bulged ever higher into the sky. She watched it move slowly, steadily out over the forest toward Martin's mill.

Thinking of Martin, she reminded herself that she must ride over soon and let him know of the social. Things hadn't been going well for him, and he hadn't been to see her much lately. His logging operation ran on too slim a budget and major equipment failures, accidents, and labor problems took more and more of his time and attention.

The tension in the cloud broke. A jagged streak of white-hot lightning cracked between cloud and earth. A flash half-blinded her. The nearly instant thunder-clap indicated how close the strike had been and jarred through her and rattled the windows and dishes in the house. Now the cloud seemed no longer able to control the electrical charges, and they arced, flashed, and struck with abandon.

Emmie and Alexa watched the forward edge of the

massive cloud approach the slope of the mountain where Martin's crew worked. It seemed to pause a fraction of a second before loosing a bolt of lightning. Alexa saw the flash squarely and directly, and its serpentine image remained clearly on her retina as she blinked her eyes. Even in the interval between the strike and the accompanying thunder, the cloud seemed to have grown less theatening. It continued on its path across the mountains to thè east, but with diluted menace.

"All passion spent," Alexa quoted softly aloud.

"You say something?" Emmie asked.

"No . . . no." Alexa stood, dumping Tiger unceremoniously onto the porch floor, and started for the barn. Maybe in her restless mood, a ride on Red would calm her.

Martin looked up at the darkening afternoon sky from the ridge he was riding along, a ridge well-covered by a fine forest of Douglas fir. The dark, nearly black bark absorbed the limited light and added to the mysterious aura of the deep timberland. From an open space, he paused to watch the ominous cloud. Its leading edge approached him, growing more menacing by the minute. Since he was only part-way up the slope, he wasn't concerned, knowing that lightning always strikes the tallest object. He dismounted King and stood, leaning against the trunk of an unpretentious fir to wait out the storm. Across the narrow steep canyon from him, he spotted a white pine, remarkably vigorous and healthy. Although the tallest tree in its immediate vicinity, it was much farther from the cloud than the trees on the ridge crest. The vigorous looking growth of that tree was no accident. Its roots undoubtedly tapped some underground water source. If the tree was higher on the ridge, its sharp growing-tip would offer an excellent attraction for lightning.

Then suddenly, a blue-white flash a few millionths of a second long poured between cloud and earth through the tree. A terrifying force spiraled up the sap channel just under the bark. Along this narrow channel the intense heat vaporized not only the sap, but the wood itself. The pressure build-up exploded. A long spiral weal rose from tip to root. Pieces of bark blew out and hurtled through the air. Deafening sounds of rending and explosion split the air and rolled as reverberating thunder through the canyon.

Martin sank against his backrest and gripped King's reins. The air filled with left-over electricity crackled around them. Martin felt his hair stand up and King reared, pawing the charged air. "Whoa, boy. Whoa," he crooned to the startled horse. Momentarily blinded by the brilliant bolt, Martin didn't dare move. King, although quivering from the shock, responded to Martin's voice and stood quiet. He continued to show his agitation, nonetheless, through his heavy breathing and short shrill whickerings.

When Martin could see again, he carefully scanned the tree. It appeared that little had changed by its ordeal. The most noticeable was its tip, lopped over like a wilting plant, and a faint tar-like odor that hung in the still air. A slight charred smell from the intense heat drifted toward him, but plentiful sap must have oozed in quickly and kept the wood from burning.

He sat, watching the tree for signs of smoke. He'd make the effort to cross the steep canyon if there seemed a need. The tinder-dry forest could ignite from even a tiny spark. He kept his vigil for a couple of hours, but even through binoculars, he could see no sign of smoke. It was growing late, and he would be caught in the forest at dark if he didn't start back. Even with the full moon for a candle, traveling at night was still dangerous. The country was cut with ravines whose sheer edges were camouflaged by trees and berry bushes, and the shadows made them still more deceptive.

"Come on, King. Let's get out of here. We'll come back up the other side tomorrow and make sure there's no fire alive in the tree."

Martin slept poorly that night as though anticipating the day to come. It began early with burned bacon and coffee that tasted like it had been brewed in the heel of an old boot. It was becoming increasingly obvious that Slim needed a weekend in town away from the cook shack.

Soon after breakfast, the wide leather belt that drove the saw slipped off its shaft. Turned into a deadly weapon, it narrowly missed the crew and flew spinning out of control until it slammed into a huge fir and collapsed in a tortured heap at the foot. The mill was then shut down for the remainder of the day while repairs were made.

Up the mountain where the crews were cutting, a new faller missed his spot when he jumped clear and broke his leg. By the time Martin got back from taking him to the doctor in town, it was too late to ride up and check on the lightning strike. He did walk to the top of the hill in back of the camp where he could look into the canyon beyond, but he could see no smoke. *Been more'n twenty-four hours. Most likely no damage has been done, or it would have been smoking by now.* The picture of the exploding bark nagged him though, and his hair again stood on end at the memory of the feeling of the charged air after the strike. *Guess I won't feel right 'til I make sure there's no live sparks. First thing in the morning, I'll ride up there.*

The evening after the storm found Alexa, at sunset, feeling the heat of another abnormally warm September day ebb away. The hot breeze died down, and the autumn haze shrank earthward, leaving her world cool and calm and clear. Unconsciously she raised her eyes to the ridge where the lightning had struck yesterday. She couldn't believe such a strike hadn't

157

produced instant smoke, but there was no hint of where the violent bolt had hit.

"Well, Tiger, looks like we escaped a fire again. Wish we'd get rain or snow and put an end to this everlasting worry."

The light faded into early evening and Alexa, with Tiger in her arms, retreated from the chill into the warmth of the sitting room made cozy by a small crackling fire in the heating stove. Bill would soon be down from the bunkhouse for their evening discussion of ranch affairs, and Alexa needed to finish her ledgers.

David grew very aware of the smoke-filled valley as he rode in. Thank heaven, the smoke was from a big fire in Oregon that he had heard about. He had worried all week about the lightning storm that had passed over Idaho five days earlier. It caused numerous fires, but the Rathdrum area had apparently been spared. Nevertheless, he looked to his beloved mountains just in case. But the smoke, acrid to the nose, was too thick to see through.

Urging his horse into a cantor, he returned his thoughts to Boise City and Idaho's Exposition exhibit. Taking a shortcut in his haste to be home, he prepared to walk his horse through the small stream that ran across the corner of the Hornbeck ranch. His thoughts were jerked into the present when he discovered a pitiful trickle of water running through the gravelly bottom where a clear, flowing stream usually flowed. He hadn't been in the valley for nearly three weeks and the lack of moisture had obviously grown acute in his absence. He couldn't remember when this creek didn't flow and he had heard no stories of its drying up in the past. Anxious now, he prodded his horse into a faster gait and hurried to the ranch.

Martin couldn't sleep. Heavy smoke from the coast fires made him so nervous that the past three nights he had wakened in a cold sweat from nightmares of blazing forests. He got out of bed and looked out the window. He decided it was near enough to daylight to stay up and ride out to take a look into the canyon where he would see the strike. He hadn't been able to get up there since the storm six days ago. Perhaps seeing the spot would ease his mind and permit him to get some rest.

He crested one ridge just as the sun crested the other, but what he saw stopped his heart. The fire had eaten away from the base of the lightning-stricken tree and found a downed log about sixty or seventy feet long that it was consuming lazily. A pine cone had apparently caught fire and then rolled down the canyon spreading sparks as it went, for there was a strip of fire about thirty feet long downhill. The fire had only destroyed a clump of brush. No big trees were in its path. If he could get a crew up here fast, they could build a line around the fire and contain it swiftly with no damage to the forest. He wheeled King about and rode as quickly as the rough terrain would allow, back to camp for his men.

Despite their varied clothing, the loggers looked like a band of primitive warriors marching to battle, their double-bitted axes, shovels, and cross-saws carried over their shoulders like weapons for hand-to-hand combat. They strung out single-file along the narrow trail as Martin, as their chieftan, led the way. With two miles to travel, Martin set a brisk pace.

"There she is!" Martin yelled as he halted to re-evaluate the situation since he had left. The men crowded around him and looked into the canyon where a faint trace of smoke surrounded a denser column.

"Come on!" Martin thundered and plunged diagonally down the steep hillside through trees and brush in the shortest distance to the fire. He halted the men about twenty feet from where the smoke rose along the upper side of the log. Here they paused to catch their breath.

"We'll make a fire-line and let it burn itself out. A foot or two wide, free of duff will be enough. Flint, take your crew and get rid of any low-hanging branches, brush, or sapplings that could go up along the line."

The men set to work with a great show of spirit accompanied by the usual lengthy string of curses that punctuated their speech. Martin left them and scouted the fire.

When he returned, five of the men were chopping up the big log that lay across their intended fire line. Seeing a third of his crew so occupied while most of the fire burned uncontrolled, Martin cursed them roundly and sent them to the upper end of the fire.

The autumn sun struck fiercely against the slope where they worked. The breeze fell off and an oven-like mid-morning calm lay in the canyon. The scraping and shoveling caused a fine dust to rise and it hung in the air, irritating throats and nostrils. The men grew tired. Their hands and faces, sooty and dusty, were streaked where sweat-beads rolled continuously down.

Martin stopped sawing limbs, assessed the crew's position, and realized they were making fine progress. At the rate they were going, the line should be closed in another hour. As though aware they were close to victory, the men sucked water from their canteens, grabbed quick bites from Slim's thick roast beef sandwiches, and continued their tasks, taking no real breaks.

Something changed and Martin looked about. The breeze came first as a little puff and then a long sigh as if a giant had been holding his breath. The smaller branches swayed gently. Wicks of flame wavered and spiraled, then leaned backward and stayed that way. For a moment, it seemed as if the wind might aid the warriors, blowing the flames back into the burn. The fresh breeze moved the stagnant air, cooled their faces and gave them smoke-free air to breathe. Then they remembered the other side of the fire. Instantly, what had been the front of the fire became its rear. Instead of advancing down-canyon where the crew worked, it shifted and took off up-canyon.

The speed with which it advanced wasn't great, but it moved much more rapidly than a tired crew could build a fire-line.

"She's outsmarted us!" Flint shouted.

Martin, sick at heart, stopped to weigh his alternatives. Either he could fall back well up-canyon and try to build a line across the front of the fire, or he could keep the crew where they were and try to narrow the front and gradually squeeze it off. He looked at the tired men and chose the safer strategy.

"We'll stay here and flank her, men. We'll catch her!" he said, with prayer in his heart. "This wind'll die down pretty soon." And if it didn't, he stood to lose all his forest and with that, the men, their jobs. They were all fighting for their lives against an enemy that knew no compassion or remorse, and fought to the death.

"Come on!" he yelled. "Let's get to work. We'll catch her on the up-side!" And with one Paul Bunyon-like ax-stroke, he cut clean through the butt of a young tree standing too close to the line.

Leaving the men working with renewed vigor, Martin again hiked to higher ground where he could see the scope of the fire. His practiced eye measured the distance. It had burned an area somewhat more than a quarter of a mile long. There was still a chance of controlling it, if he could get some fresh men to take over while his loggers ate and rested.

Surely someone in the valley had seen the smoke by

now and was coming with reinforcements. Martin looked at his pocket watch. The time since they had arrived had sped by and it was already after twelve o'clock. The sun didn't seem as hot as usual for noon. Looking skyward, he watched a thin white gauze of high clouds coming from the west dim the sun a trifle. Did this mean a chance of rain? If the clouds deepened and continued to cool the sun, the fire could cease to burn as hot this afternoon. Perhaps the Lord had heard his desperate prayer after all.

David couldn't sleep and rose early. Today he had to decide what to do with their cattle. It was down to how many cows they could keep and feed since their range was dried up and water scarce.

The house was still quiet when he finished dressing. From habit, as soon as he stepped outside, he surveyed the sky. A wind during the night had cleared the smoke from the valley, and he could see the last stars clearly in the pre-dawn sky. However, when he turned to the east his heart stopped. There, in the faint light, from the mountain behind Alexa's ranch rose a tall thin plume of smoke.

He decided too many days had passed for the fire to be have been caused by the storm. "Darn some careless logger!" David swore and broke into a run toward the bunkhouse. "May his soul rot for starting that fire!" He didn't need this sort of interruption to his plans. He had come home for one specific reason and when that was accomplished, he would be returning to Boise City and then on to Chicago.

Abruptly roused, the hands dressed quickly, all the while roundly cursing the fire and the party who had set it.

"Shall I ride for help?" someone asked.

"No need," David replied. "Soon as folks wake and spot it, they'll do just as we are. There'll be plenty of help in no time. Be sure to take all our cross-

162

cut saws, axes, and shovels," David reminded them. "Don't forget to fill your canteens. Don't count on the usual water supplies." Taking the cook aside, David instructed him to prepare lunches while the men wrangled their horses.

The dew had burned off by the time they were ready to leave, but the amount of smoke rising seemed to remain constant. Maybe he and his men were going to be in time to keep the fire from running away after all.

The terrain was rough and cut by canyons. This slowed their progress, making it late afternoon before David and his men arrived at the fire. The trail broke clear of the trees at the top of the ridge and they could look down on the fire-line.

Even believing the loggers had started the fire and angry as he was at them, David felt sorry for Martin's crew as they stood, dog-tired, grimy, and sweaty, leaning on their shovels watching the back-fires spring to life and go roaring toward the main fire. The flames were sucked along by the draft that the main fire pulled in toward itself.

David saw the head-on clash of the two fires as they piled together like two large waves ripping into each other. A clump of underbrush suddenly disappeared in white-yellow flames. Close by, a ninety-foot fir tree, its resins vaporized by the heat, exploded into a flame that towered at least a hundred feet upward. It issued a long-drawn hiss that stopped just short of a roar. For a few seconds the dying tree stood out, its needles a white-hot torch of flaming gas. The tips of its branches burned red for a moment, then the tree cooled and stood, reduced to a darkened silhouette of naked branches against the fire-lit sky.

David gave a shout to Martin who waved and came running to meet the fresh crew. "Pull your men out for a rest and we'll take over," David said. "I'm sure there'll be more help along soon."

Martin nodded and spread the word quickly through his crew. As the loggers fell back to rest, the warm dry breeze that had been blowing much of the day turned cool and damp. They tried to make themselves comfortable by building a fire in the burned area. Grown accustomed to the heat of the forest fire, now they were cold despite the campfire. And having eaten the last of their sandwiches long ago, they added hunger to the growing list of miseries.

Joining them, Martin said, "Feels like rain. What do your joints say, Cliff?"

"Say you're right," the old man answered as he sat near the fire rubbing his knees.

Martin tipped his head back and felt the first tiny drops splatter across his face. Breathing a silent prayer of thanksgiving, he lay down on the ground in the sooty ashes to sleep. He was nearly out when he heard an unmistakable 'crink-crunk-squinch' that signaled the coming of a pack train.

The little sprinkle of rain in the night hadn't amounted to anything. Growing increasingly anxious this morning, Alexa kept leaving her ledgers to look out the window at the column of smoke. It stayed much the same until mid-morning, then suddenly it changed shades of gray and increased noticeably in volume.

Seeking Emmie in the kitchen, Alexa found her stoically peeling potatoes. "Isn't there something we can do?" she wailed at Emmie, and reached for a potato to peel. "It's going to burn up our forest and here we sit, doing nothing."

"Nothing!" Emmie gestured with her hand toward the oven where she had roasts and hams baking. Pies cooled on all the tables and windowsills. And now she was making a large batch of potato salad.

"Who's going to eat all this food?" Alexa asked. "Are the fire fighters going to come back here? That is, if there is anyone up there."

"There's men up there, all right. Don't think an experienced lumber man like Martin's gonna let his forest go up in flames without a fight, do you?"

Alexa's reply was interrupted by the sound of a wagon coming up to the house. She rushed out the back door in time to welcome Jane Hornbeck as she pulled her buckboard to a halt next to the porch. This wasn't the fashionable lady Alexa knew. Rather, she was dressed in calico, a full matching apron, a poke bonnet, and drove the team with considerable expertise. Alexa's mouth fell open and she stood staring.

Mrs. Hornbeck climbed briskly from the wagon and hurried up the back steps. "Come, girl. Don't stand there gawking. We've got work to do. Your ranch is closest to the fire so it'll serve as a base camp. We'll load the food and blankets from here and take them to the men." When she walked into the kitchen, she paused and gaped. "I didn't think you'd have anything done. I owe you an apology."

"I've only been helping. Emmie gets the credit for knowing what to do," Alexa said, feeling young and useless.

Mrs. Hornbeck whipped off her bonnet, rolled up her sleeves, and began rinsing the newly peeled potatoes. "No matter who did it. It's done and that's what's important. Rest of the women should be coming right along with their things. Potato salad'll taste good to the men, Emmie." She turned to Alexa. "Is Jake around?"

"I think so."

"Go fetch him and bring him down here," Jane Hornbeck ordered. All the soft lady-like manners were gone and in their place a hard-working knowledgeable ranch woman.

As she ran to the barn, thankful to be free of the kitchen, Alexa wondered if David had ever seen his mother like this. If he had, he surely wouldn't fuss and worry over her like he did.

When the corrals came into view, she was surprised to see mules barricaded inside and packing boxes stacked against the barn. Jake was busy stringing harnesses over the fence. "What are you doing with all those mules?" she asked.

"Neighbors brought 'em over. Gonna make a packstring to take supplies into the fire fighters."

"You're not planning to make such a trip, I hope. I need you here a lot worse than they need you there."

Jake looked uncomfortable. "Nope. Me'n Bill had that out this morning. He says the same as you, so he's taking the train. But he don't know the lay of the land like I do. What if he gets lost?" Jake obviously wasn't giving up without one last try.

"I imagine with all the cattle herding Bill's done this summer, he knows the country enough not to get lost. Mrs. Hornbeck's here and wants you down at the house," Alexa said.

Jake's look turned sour. "I thought I was through dancing for that bossy old woman. You tell her I got things to do at the barn."

"I will not. I imagine what she wants is equally as important as what you have to do here."

"What she wants is to tell me how to put a packtrain together as if I didn't know after forty years of 'doin'it," Jake retorted. But he dropped the harness he was holding and joined Alexa in the walk back to the house.

The yard in front of the house was full of wagons when they arrived.

Jake recognized the two old men lounging near the front steps and hobbled over to them.

Alexa started in the kitchen door, but the room was so full of women packing boxes and crates with food, she felt in the way. Jane Hornbeck spotted her, though, and came quickly through the crowd.

"Did you get Jake?"

Alexa nodded and pointed. Mrs. Hornbeck bustled

down the porch to where the men were visiting. "You men! Take my wagon load down to the barn and start filling the pack boxes. Move now, and don't dawdle. We've hungry, tired men up on that fire. It's up to us to get them supplies." Coming back to where Alexa stood, she said, "You start driving these other wagons up to the barn and help put the supplies in the boxes. Bring back the first empty wagon, and we'll be ready to load the food you have here." She paused to look at the jeweled watch pinned to her dress. "Should have that train on its way by three o'clock."

Alexa, at last feeling useful, untied the horses of the closest wagon and climbed in. Much as the cause of the excitement distressed her, she found herself being drawn into the action surrounding her and relishing the diversion. She wondered briefly if Martin and David felt the same stimulation.

CHAPTER 14

THE FIRE HAD RAGED ITS DESTRUCTION for three days now, and an overwhelming sense of defeat and fear hovered over the gathering of the faithful in the little wooden building being used as a temporary church. The itinerant preacher in his long prayer added a simple petition "for those loved ones who are struggling to save our livelihood and our forest, and who may be, this day, in danger." He had hardly finished and announced his text when one of Jake's elderly friends slipped quietly up the aisle and whispered to the organist, his employer.

Her neighbors bent close to hear and then a wave of whispers spread outward. People leaned across pews to get the message. No one was listening to the sermon, and the preacher, a sensible man and curious as the rest, stopped talking and motioned to the organist to come up and tell him the news. Then he cleared his throat.

"Apparently the battle to control the fire has been lost and word has been brought to us that it rages out of control and some of our men are thought to be trapped."

Gasps of dismay issued from those to whom this was news. The rest sat in stricken silence. Alexa felt her heart race, stop, and then beat an irregular pattern that made breathing difficult. Were any of the men David and Martin? *Oh, Lord, please don't let it be them.* Then, embarrassed at her selfishness, prayed, *Forgive me, Lord, for thinking only of myself. Please let all who have labored so long and diligently be safe.*

The preacher, a wise man, said, "Let us join in singing 'Praise God from whom all blessings flow,' after which, considering the circumstances, I shall pronounce the benediction and dismiss you to go to your homes. There I hope you can find comfort and peace in communion with the Lord until we are brought happier news."

When the people stepped outside, they were horrified to see that the column of gray smoke had grown to huge proportions during the short time they had been there. Alexa and Emmie wasted no time in visiting but hurried straight to their buggy.

"Alexa," Jane Hornbeck called. "Won't you come stay with me? A number of the ladies who's husbands are at the fire are coming over."

"Thanks for asking, but my land's burning and I feel a need to be there." She was sure Mrs. Hornbeck didn't understand that when Alexa looked at the fire destroying Martin's timber and her ranch, she felt personally violated and powerless to fight back. She needed solitude in which to face the knowledge that Martin and David might be dead. She didn't want to turn her agony into a public death watch complete with weeping and the wringing of hands. All she wanted was to saddle Red and ride alone to a high ridge from which to watch her ruin. Then she remembered Emmie. "Would you like to join the women?"

"No." In a voice thick with tears, Emmie asked. "Did you know Bill went to the fire this morning. He took another train of food in and medical supplies. Took Doc Ward with him."

"Bill! Oh, Emmie, I am sorry."

Emmie only shrugged and continued knotting and unknotting her handkerchief. Alexa sat a moment wondering if she should tell Jane Hornbeck about Doc Ward. Then she decided Mrs. Hornbeck had enough to bear knowing David might be trapped. She didn't need to hear of Doc's whereabouts as well.

Alexa and Emmie drove home in silence, their eyes glued to the towering plume of smoke in front of them. Once home, she changed into her riding clothes, grabbed Uncle Clyde's binoculars, and ran to the barn, stopping only long enough to give Red a whistle. He responded immediately and by the time she arrived, she stood at the barn door, nickering and blowing. "Good boy," she said and gave him the expected lump of sugar. Carrying lumps of sugar was infinitely easier than packing around oats to serve as Red's reward.

Entering the barn on her way to get her saddle and bridle, she stopped short. There sat Jake on a saw horse, shoulders hunched forward and head bowed, watching the chickens. "Jake?" she called softly.

Without looking at her, he asked, "Where you going Miss Alexa?"

"If my trees are going to burn, I'm want to be there to see them."

"Need to get up high for that," he said in a tired voice. "Best take Molly. She's more sure-footed than Red, and she won't shy if you get too close to the fire."

"What about that bone-wracking trot?"

"I think you're in the mood to take that out of her today," he said and raised his head for the first time to look at Alexa through sad eyes.

"You're right about that," Alexa said grimly and grabbed the tack.

170

"I'll whistle her in for you," Jake offered and with obvious effort and pain made his way outside. "Sure do wish I was going with you. Mighty hard having to sit and wait while others is taking the action."

"I don't think there's much action. From the looks of the smoke, things are completely out of control. You've served well by taking care of the pack-trains, Jake. Couldn't have fed and bedded all those men without you." She put her arm around his shoulder and hugged him.

All the while Alexa saddled Molly, she talked to her, warning Molly of the consequences if she tried her famous trot. Alexa swung into the saddle and signalled her to start. Off she went, not having given any heed to Alexa's words. Alexa raked Molly with the rowels of her spurs and the stunned horse leaped into a full gallop. Alexa pulled Molly up after a short distance. She didn't want the horse winded and tired to begin the strenuous trip. "Now, are you ready to behave and walk like a lady?" Alexa demanded.

Again when Alexa gave Molly the signal to go, the horse started into the trot, but Alexa pulled back firmly on the reins and Molly settled at once into a rhythmic walk. "Good girl," Alexa said and patted the little mare's neck. "We're going to get along fine."

Alexa rode the familiar trail to the deserted logging camp and then followed the now well-worn path made by the pack-trains into the hills. The trail led up and up, lurching and twisting through the forested mountains. Tall fir trees overhung the path dimming the light until she broke free of boughs on the ridge crest. Here she stopped to let Molly blow a bit and watch the smoke, varied shades of gray full of whorls and convolutions filling the sky above her. The sun, high overhead, shone as a red disk through the dense smoke. Although Alexa still cast a shadow, the light had changed to an ominous yellow. Bits of feathery ash settled over her, and her nostrils felt parched from the smoke and hot dry wind that blew toward her.

She hadn't brought a canteen and realized she had been foolish. She had heard how the water sources had dried up. Still, she hoped she might find a spring this high up so she kept looking as she rode along. At last, off the trail through the trees, she could see a clearing. Dismounting, Alexa walked through the underbrush to a lovely little glade set like an emerald at the foot of a cliff. She stepped into a tiny enchanted world. A small, crystal-clear stream fed from springs in the cliff, dropped in gentle falls over glistening rocks from pool to shimmering pool. The rocks above the pools were covered with deep cushion moss kept always green by the dainty spray from the miniature waterfalls. Farther back from the stream, where the air was still moist, ferns grew, delicate and lush. The air was filled with delightful perfumed scents of colorful wildflowers. Out of the carpet of ferns and meadow grass, red-brown fluted trunks of red cedars rose, and high overhead, the lacy canopy of branches let the sunlight penetrate through in long rays.

The glade was cool and the air, quiet. Alexa took off her hat, and stepping carefully among the ferns so as not to break any fronds, crossed the opening and knelt by the stream. The water was so clear that the tiny sprigs of algae in it seemed to be suspended in space. Small rainbow trout darted away when she leaned over to drink.

Her thirst satisfied, she stood and gazed about. Alexa prayed Martin and David had found a safe spot, and refused to think harm had come to any of the crews. As she breathed deeply from air not yet contaminated, she gave thanks for these few minutes of peace before she watered Molly, swung into the saddle, and started on.

By late afternoon, Alexa reached high spot along the ridge, where she could look full on the fire.

Through the smoke she could barely make out the far ridges, blackened and fire-swept. Below her in the canyon, the whole forest blazed. As she watched, a gust of wind struck, sending the fire forward. It engulfed a clump of young trees and she saw the flames shoot up. Heat, driven by the wind, beat against her face as it swept up-slope. And then the fire advanced into a stand of regal Douglas firs.

She remembered her grief at man's slaying of one of the beauties. But she had been able to partially accept the destruction when Martin explained the uses man made of the fine lumber. This wanton destruction filled her with rage, and her heart grew sick over the useless burning.

Alexa dismounted and settled down to watch. As the fire entered the thicker forest, it began to show a difference. Instead of the steady consuming creep, now it acted like a furnace, the tremendous heat drying out the needles, and then igniting a large section of the magnificent tree tops. With a deep roar—*like a freight train passing in the night,* Alexa thought—flames and dark smoke rose hundreds of feet, carrying blazing twigs, needles, and strips of bark up with it.

Having established a crown-fire, the dry canyon wind sent the fire toward Alexa at a steady rate. One tree after another disappeared with a deep hiss into a towering column of flame. For about a half a minute the hiss deepened into a roar. The burning boughs tossed as though blown by a hard wind. Then as the tree burned out, the roar faded.

But the heat had already dried the neighboring trees and they immediately towered in flaming ruin. As the crown-fire moved up the ridge, the great pines and fires burned like stalks of wheat in a field fire, only these flames leaped up hundreds of feet.

Alexa wet her lips parched by the heat, but they grew drier still, and cracked. She looked up to see a great rush of air wildly toss the high branches growing over her head. The tree-tops bent nearly double as powerful air currents clashed in a gigantic swirl. They tore bits of bark, needles, and rotten wood, swirled the litter upward and hurled it away. Dense smoke suddenly engulfed her and obscured her view. A strip of burning bark fell a short distance from her and the forest, dry as well-kept gun powder, flared instantly.

She started toward the spot fire. It was so small, she felt confident she could stamp it out, but at Molly's shrill neigh, Alexa turned. Burning debris was falling all around and igniting the duff. Flames flared into bushes and low branches and raced across the carpet of dry needles. Suddenly, smoke and fire sprang up all around her.

Alexa ran to where Molly, tied to a branch, trembled and shied from the fire. "Come, girl. Stay calm and we'll get out of here." Grabbing Molly's reins, Alexa ran back down the trail until a piece of burning branch fell on Molly's rump. She let out a terrified neigh, lunged free of Alexa, and plunged down the smoke-filled path out of sight.

Thick smoke blew out along the ground, flat before the wind. Alexa coughed and choked with it, and her eyes watered and stung. The air, furnace-hot, seared her lungs and throat. Smoke shut out the sun and she could only keep her direction by feeling the downhill slope.

The parching wind sucked the last memory of moisture from the fir forest and the pall of smoke hung, an impenetrable curtain. She lost the trail and began fighting her way through the brush and dense timber. Her run became a shuffle as she bent to catch the slightly cleaner air near the ground. All worry about Martin's and David's safety fled. She began praying harder than at anytime in her life for her own survival.

Then, directly ahead through the smoke, she saw

the glowing red-hot branches of a bush. Sparks from behind came sailing past letting her know it was useless going back. Left with no alternative, she went on through the blinding smoke toward the glowing branches. The bush was scarcely burning along its windward side. She looked about. Fire was everywhere. Here was the only way out. She threw her hands over her head, drew a deep breath, and dashed past the bush and the line of fire. Safely through, she slapped frantically at the burning spots on her clothes and wiggled her feet, uncomfortably warm in the hot shoes.

She seemed to be in a small clearing covered with meadow grass and ferns. Keeping low to the ground, she explored her tiny fire-guarded prison. The smoke was so dense she nearly stepped in the stream. "Oh!" she exclaimed as she realized she was in the little glade she had explored earlier. "Thank you, Lord," she breathed aloud.

Several deer, trying to out-run the fire, bounded through the clearing, startling her. Alexa pushed aside the charred wind-strewn debris covering the water and drank her fill. Then she took off her shoes and waded into the deepest of the pools and lay down. Her heart pounded with terror as the forest around her erupted with a roar into a crowning fire. A brown bear lumbered past, oblivious to her presence.

She kept her head low against the water where the air was cooler. However, she continued to cough from the thick smoke and pant from the effort. The pool was too shallow to cover her so she turned from side to side to keep her clothes wet and extinguish any undetected sparks.

A hideous screaming hiss rose from the forest floor and swept over the little glade. Her world turned a flaming yellow-orange as the fire rose over the small sanctuary. A searing blast of heat accompanied the fire. She snatched a quick breath, held it, and thrust her head under the water. When her lungs felt near to bursting, she surfaced and shivered as the inferno raced on.

Earlier, Alexa had observed islands of forest untouched except for the withering heat. By some miracle, it had left another such little island of forest, her tiny glade.

Alexa lay trembling from the shock of having escaped. Her teeth chattered and when she tried to stand, her knees refused to hold her. Crawling out onto the bank, she sat among the heat-shriveled ferns and wept.

At last she cried, wondering if Molly had escaped. How many of the men fighting the fire had experienced what she had just gone through, only not been so forunate? She sat for a very long time staring at the ruin around her. What had been beautiful, productive, full of life, now was a place of desolation, ugliness, and death. Martin's forest stood burned and useless, and her's would soon be left the same way.

The wind cleared the air, blowing the smoke before the fire. She could look up through the standing black skeletons of once mighty trees and see gray cloud-patched sky. With its dunking, her watch failed to run—she could only guess the time. Late afternoon she decided. It was much too late to try walking back to the logging camp so she prepared to spend the night. Unfortunately, there was little to prepare. No delicate boughs were left to soften the ground. The best she could do was clear the sooty duff from under a once glorious cedar and curl into the untidy burrow.

Using a short flat stick, she began scratching away layers of long dead needles. The crude tool turned her work into an arduous chore. Her arms grew tired and she was forced to rest often.

The unexpected cracking sounds of branches and twigs caused her to pause and look up. There, standing at the edge of the clearing, was David, his

176

face black with soot and smoke, and smeared on his cheeks where he had wiped it.

"David!" She scarcely recognized the rough scratchy croak issuing from her heat-seared throat. Leaping up, she ran to him and they fell into each other's arms. She looked into his blood-shot eyes, which shone out of the blackness of his face with a strange glare. One shirt sleeve was gone and dried blood crusted over a long ugly gash. Holes were burned in his shirt and his hat was gone. He limped as he walked with her to the stream's edge.

Still without speaking, he dropped to his knees and drank thirstily from the ash-covered water. His thirst finally satisfied, Alexa helped him remove his scarred boots and he plunged blistered feet into the cool water. He tried to talk but no sound would come forth. She lip-read, "Martin's trapped." Learning that, she curled into David's arms and sobbed. Mutely they shared the horror each had survived.

It was late afternoon when Martin set the first back-fire to take advantage of the switch in the wind direction. Two loggers jumped in and took care of a point of fire that jumped the hastily cleared fire line. As they came running out, their shirts steaming, Martin lit the next stretch of back-fire and on the other side of the line, David did the same. Between the two back-fires, the danger was great. Constantly checking behind himself to make sure no men were left, Martin continued to thrust his blazing torch into dead leaves and fallen branches.

With a few miracles, they might even hold the fire tonight. A billowing curl of smoke circled him, and he coughed and shut his eyes. Sparks lit on his shirt sleeve and he slapped them out. As he stepped away from the heat of the last back-fire, a long warning whoop came from behind him.

Martin swung around. "Run, men!" he shouted.

Flinging his torch into the bushes, he joined them in flight. "Where's David?" he asked of no one in particular.

The fleeing men either didn't hear him or didn't know, for they kept running without answering. Martin turned and looked frantically through the rising smoke and flames. "David!" he shouted repeatedly. At last, receiving no answer and finding the heat rapidly growing unbearable, he also ran.

It was hot and smoky and Martin was soon panting hard. The fire spread across the fire-line. It erupted out of control and quickly spread of its own accord. Martin was trapped.

He stopped, blowing hard. He had been in too many tight places in his life to panic. Upon closer examination, things didn't look too bad ahead. He wrapped his bandana over his nose and mouth, pulled his felt hat low, took a deep breath, and dashed along the line into the fire.

The first few leaps were bad. Flames grasped at him and searing hot smoke swirled around him. Just as he wondered if he was going to survive, he came out into an open space. He fell down and rubbed his smoking clothes with dirt. Then he was up and dashing through another bad spot ahead.

The next hole turned out better than he had hoped. He was in brush and away from the thick-growing trees, but as he ran up the steep canyon, blood pounded hard in his ears from the effort and strain. His legs felt like they had lead bolts attached. His chest tightened against the smoke-thickened air as he struggled upward. He climbed another hundred feet before his heart began pounding so violently he had to stop for breath. Looking to the right, he saw a point of fire running almost even with him.

He plunged ahead once more. Just when he felt he could go no farther, he came to a cleared place . . . a deer trail perhaps . . . and now he followed the

switch-backs up the steep canyonside. Swirling, suffo-
cating smoke impeded his progress, forcing him to
bend low to the ground for air. He grew so weary it
took all his determination to keep forging ahead. At
last, his throat and lungs burned unbearably from the
smoke and coughing, he was forced to rest.

Leaning against a snag, he attempted to catch his
breath and ease the pain. Over the crackling hiss of
the fire, he thought he heard the terror-stricken
neighing of a horse. He listened intently. There it was
again! Just off the trail above him. Quickly scrambling
around the rocks, Martin dived into a thick clump of
young trees. Beyond, he could see flames licking at
the outer edges of the fine timber and rearing frantically in the middle was Molly, her reins hopelessly
snared by the underbrush.

While he freed the horse, his thoughts raced. What
was Molly doing here wearing the saddle Alexa
always used? *Oh, dear Lord, please don't let Alexa be
out in this,* he prayed. But his mind wouldn't be stilled
and he knew she had come to watch her trees burn.
First David and now Alexa. These thoughts sickened
him so, he leaned against the trembling Molly and
silent tears slid down sooty cheeks and dripped
unnoticed onto his shirt front.

"Oh, Alexa," he moaned. "Lord, help me to find
her. Speak to me and lead me," he prayed softly.

"Come, Molly." He led the over-wrought horse up
the final twists and turns to the top of the ridge. Once
there, Martin found everything aflame in front of him.
"We're going to have to wait it out, Molly. Can't go
through that wall of fire." He sank down against a tree
trunk, bowed his head to block the sight of the raging
insatiable monster that refused to be stopped, and
tried not to think of Alexa's whereabouts. Words from
Jeremiah came to him . . . "I will kindle a fire in the
forest and it shall devour all things round about it." It
gave him no comfort at all, but a consoling passage
would not come to mind.

179

Finally, the ground grew cool enough to walk on. Leading Molly, Martin, numb with grief and exhaustion, stumbled uncertainly along the trail that would eventually lead to the logging camp.

Tearing a strip of cloth from the tail of her shirtwaist, Alexa washed David's arm. "The cut is at least clean. In the morning when we get back to the ranch, we'll tend it properly."

David still lay, eyes closed. "Thank you, Alexa," he whispered.

"You're welcome," she answered softly. After making him as comfortable as possible, she asked, "What did you mean to say about Martin?"

David shuddered. "I think he was trapped by the back-fire we were setting. I heard him shouting, but I couldn't get across the line to help him."

Alexa lapsed into silence, trying to absorb the horror. Gradually, muted hoof beats entered the silence. "Molly!" Alexa leaped to her feet and ran back up the trail toward the sound. To her amazement, there coming toward her through the fading light were Martin and Molly.

"Martin!" Alexa cried. "Oh, Martin. We thought you'd been trapped in the fire. And you've found Molly." She threw her arms around him.

But he pushed her from him. "And you, my foolish girl . . . what are you even doing up here? I didn't think you'd behave so irresponsibly."

She looked quickly into his face to see tears seep over the rims of his eyes and down his cheeks, taking the sting from his words.

"I'm sorry. I had no idea how deadly a fire could be."

They entered the glade together and joined David. The two men recounted how they had escaped the fire.

"Isn't there anything that can stop it?" Alexa asked.

Martin sank down beside David. "Nothing man can do. We're left with prayer. When the Lord decides enough is enough, he'll put it out."

"Then, it seems we ought to pray," Alexa said. The two men rose to their knees and Alexa knelt between them. David prayed first, then Alexa added her plea, and Martin concluded their petitions. They remained kneeling in silence, too weary and heartsick to move.

The cool breeze drove them to the cliff where they found shelter under an overhanging rock. They huddled together, miserable in the cold and dirt, and finally fell into an exhausted sleep.

Sometime in the early morning Alexa stirred against the protective grip of Martin and David. She was damp and cold. Becoming increasingly alert, she now recognized a familiar plop-plop-plop. Rain! Quiet, unhurried, sure, like a spoken promise from God that life and her world would go on.

CHAPTER 15

ALEXA STOOD IN FRONT OF THE LONG MIRROR, carefully examining her appearance. Even after three days and numerous scrubbings, she thought she could still see soot in the pores of her face and neck. *I'm going to be marked for life*, she decided mournfully.

She deliberately concentrated on the insignificant because she wasn't able to cope with the loss of her cattle herd just yet. Bill reported to her this morning that they had gotten through the one small section of the fence not yet re-built and onto Martin's land. The entire herd had been wiped out and with it, her only source of income.

A firm knock at the front door interrupted her dismal thoughts, and glad for another excuse to postpone facing her ruinous problems, she ran quickly to answer it.

She flung open the large door to find David, dressed in his finest clothes, nervously shaping and re-shaping his hat. "Why, David!" she gasped, nearly speechless with surprise.

"I do wish to apologize for calling at such an early hour and without warning," he stammered.

What on earth can he want that would cause him such anxiety?

"May I come in?" he asked shyly.

"Y—y—yes, of course," Alexa managed, and stepped into the hallway to let him pass. "Will you join me in the parlor?" she asked, her poise restored. "Thank you," he murmured and followed her into the shade-darkened room.

Before joining David on the couch, Alexa quickly raised the shades and let the cloud-filtered light in.

"I know I have put you at a disadvantage, coming this way, but I have much to say to you and little time left before I must return to Boise City."

"What news do you bring from the capital?"

"Not a great deal that affects this area. The problems with the Coeur d'Alene miners are at last resolved and they are back at work. I also learned that the true train robbers have been caught which means Emmie's husband really didn't commit the crimes he was accused of."

David imparted the information casually, catching Alexa completely off-guard. She wanted to run to the kitchen at once and tell Emmie the good news, but etiquette prevented such a spontaneous reaction. Instead, Alexa said calmly, "The plans for the exhibit are coming well, I take it."

"Very well. I leave for Chicago next week where we will be choosing the lot on which to build the Idaho House. The design is completed and many of my suggestions have been incorporated."

Excitement radiated from him and she became caught up in his enthusiasm. "Tell me about it."

"Twenty thousand dollars have been appropriated for our exhibit. A most generous amount with which to work. Our theme is "Idaho—The Switzerland of America," and we are going to construct our house in the Swiss style, entirely of logs set on a basaltic rock and lava foundation. All the building materials are to be shipped to Chicago from Idaho. The main reception room will represent a hunter's cabin with a rock fireplace. I suggested we have the andirons made from two immense bear traps.''

"It sounds so captivating. How I'd love to see it.''

"You would?''

"Of course I would. It's going to be the most exciting event of my lifetime . It's hard to even imagine anything so grand.''

David took her hand between his two cold ones. "Then, Alexa, my dearest heart, marry me, and you shall see it for our honeymoon.''

Alexa sat stunned. Her brain whirled and she felt slightly giddy. She had dreamed of, but never really expected, his proposal. And now . . . "What about your mother?'' was all she could think of to say.

"Mother's fine. She and Doc Ward are going to announce their own marriage plans immediately after the election. He'll take splendid care of her and the ranch. I'm free to leave this beautiful, but confining little valley and seek the challenges and adventure I crave. And I most desperately want you by my side, love.''

And still Alexa hesitated. What was the matter with her? "Th—th— this is so sudden,'' she said lamely.

"Of necessity it is, and I apologize. But I learned only last week that I was being sent to Chicago. It seemed such a splendid trip for a honeymoon, I hurried home to ask you to marry me.''

"How long would we stay there?''

"Since I'm to over-see the building and decorating of the house, I would suspect we would be there most of next year. After that, who knows?'' He smiled that slow, dazzling smile that always flustered her thoroughly.

"David, may I have a couple of days to ponder it? With the fire and all, I just can't seem to think straight, and you're asking me not only to marry you,

184

but to give up the ranch and leave Rathdrum. These are two very large decisions that I must sort out."

"Mother would happily buy your ranch. She's been looking to expand her holdings for a long time. You have no problem there. I can understand your need to dwell a bit on such matters, but I am working against a dead-line. Do you have any idea when may I expect an answer?"

"Tomorrow," she said firmly. "I will let you know tomorrow."

At the door, Alexa found herself in David's arms. He studied her face intently. "I do love you, my Alexa. I will be a good husband," he said before he bent and kissed her tenderly.

David's proposal bothered her terribly, but she didn't feel able to examine its uprooting effects on her life just yet. She stood on the porch and watched until she could no longer see him, then dashed to the kitchen to tell Emmie the news about the train robbers. Emmie's reaction wasn't what Alexa had expected.

"Don't take no stock in hearsay," Emmie said in a stiff voice.

"But Emmie, David heard it in Boise City. He wouldn't tell an untruth about something so important."

"Won't believe a word until I have proof it's true." Emmie, her mouth set in a stubborn line, continued about the business of preparing dinner.

"What constitutes proof to you?" Alexa asked, frustrated with Emmie's behavior.

"Word from the Sheriff in Boise City."

"Very well, get your cloak and bonnet. We're going to town to the telegraph office." Alexa, grateful for something that required action instead of thinking, slipped into her gray, wool cloak and rushed out the door on her way to hitch up the buggy.

The Rathdrum telegraph office was a busy place this

morning. In fact, there were so many horses and pack animals tied to the hitching post, Alexa stopped down the street and she and Emmie had to walk back. Emmie was so anxious, she fairly flew along the street. Alexa gave up trying to stay with her, and slowed her pace to a saunter, eyeing the horses as she walked past.

Suddenly, she stopped. There stood King with a pack-horse tied to his saddle. Martin was leaving! And without saying goodbye. Alexa's heart dropped into her shoes. She hadn't realized how much she had grown to depend on him until now, and the thought that he would just ride away without a word left her paralyzed. She still hadn't recovered from her shock when he strode out of the telegraph office. His head bent while he read a piece of paper, he failed to see her and nearly knocked her down in his haste.

He grabbed wildly to save them both from a public tumble. "Alexa!" he gasped. "I'm sorry."

"Sorry isn't good enough. What do you mean riding away without saying so much as a by-your-leave? How dare you, Martin Taylor!" she fumed.

Martin took her arm and escorted her around the corner of the main street. "Alexa, I know I should have come by, but I couldn't face saying goodbye. I . . . just couldn't," he ended feebly.

Alexa looked carefully into his eyes and saw a gentleness, a tender caring he couldn't hide. "Martin, all my cattle are destroyed and Mrs. Hornbeck wants to buy the ranch. I don't know what to do." She felt his arms slip around her and he enfolded her to him. Resting against him, she drew strength from his giving spirit. "How is it? You always make things seem better," she whispered.

They remained thus, looking at each other, their eyes speaking a private language they both understood. They stayed that way until the giving became mutual, saying no word, yet both become more and

186

more aware of the deep bond that had grown between them over the past months.

"Let's get away from here," Martin said in a husky whisper. Taking her arm, he guided her back onto the main street to get the horses.

As they passed the telegraph office, Emmie came flying out waving her telegram. "It's true! It's true! My Luke's a free man," she said through streaming tears.

Alexa embraced the happy woman. "Emmie, that's wonderful news. You must go to him at once."

Martin handed Emmie the reins. "Here, Emmie. Take the buggy. I'll see Alexa gets home."

Martin and Alexa walked slowly to the edge of town where a clear stream flowed. She sat on the bank and he sat down near her. "Seems we've sat like this before," he said softly.

They stayed all afternoon, talking, listening to the silvery bell-sounds of the river, watching eagles soar high overhead. Then, they hardly talked at all. There wasn't much to say. There was too much to say. Her pride wouldn't ask him to stay and since he had lost everything, his pride wouldn't let him.

The sun sank low and it grew chilly. "We'd better get you home before you freeze," he said.

Her arms firmly around his waist and her cheek pressed tightly against the firm muscles of his shoulder, they rode double back to the ranch. Emmie, her face aglow, greeted them as they entered the kitchen. Bill was lounging comfortably against the wall, watching Emmie prepare supper.

Emmie broke into a wide grin. "Like you both to meet my husband, Luke," she said proudly and crossed the kitchen to stand with him.

Alexa looked from one to the other, too stunned to speak. "Bill, you're Luke?" Laughter filled the room, and Alexa and Martin joined in hugging the happy couple.

"Martin, at least say you'll stay for supper and spend the night," Alexa urged. "You can sleep in the bunkhouse. Plenty of room there with Bill moving down here 'til we can get a house built."

Luke and Emmie looked delighted at the suggestion. "Just fixin' to spread the table. Got plenty," Emmie said.

They ate a simple, filling meal. During supper, the men talked of the prospects for Alexa's ranch.

"Without cattle and that good fence nearly finished, you could take up horse breeding. You got good stock in the valley to mix with. Could turn a fair profit, I'm thinking," Martin said.

"Ever thought of settling down and trying it yourself?" Luke asked Martin.

"Guess not. When the traveling life gets in the blood, you get used to looking for the crest of the next hill," Martin said, staring into the flames of the kerosene lantern on the table.

"Ever find it?" Luke asked. "Ever find what you was searching for?"

Alexa slipped away from the table and walked quickly down the hall and into the dark parlor. She heard Martin's steps and fought back the tears, trying to wipe them away. As he reached her, she turned to face him, feeling foolish and childish and embarrassed all at once. He came and took her by the shoulders. Tears insisted this time and Alexa couldn't hold them back. He pulled her to him, her forehead against his chest. She wrapped her arms tight around his body and felt his arms holding her securely to him. They stood entwined for a long time before Martin spoke.

"I've tried to put you out of my mind, night after night. Tried to tell myself we had nothing in common, that I didn't want to be tied to one piece of land. But I don't seem to lie well, even to myself."

She gave a little laugh and looked up into his face.

He took a deep breath and she could feel the rise of

his chest. "I do love you, Alexa . . . with all my heart. I have nothing to offer you but a burned-out lumber operation. And love enough to last several lifetimes."

"And I love you. We've got your land and my ranch. We're strong and full of dreams. With God's help, we'll build something wonderful here— together."

He touched her lips with his fingers and caressed her cheek, then bent over her, taking her lips in a warm loving kiss full of the promises of the good things to come.